Copyrig   MW01243456

ISBN-13: 9781234567890
ISBN-10: 1477123456

Cover design by: Art Painter
Library of Congress Control Number: 2018675309
Printed in the United States of America

Wormhole Moon

An Alien Civilization's Alliance with Earth

By John Williams

Table of Contents

CHAPTER ONE
The Landing

The road is paved yet bumpy. The cab ride back to the airport is not quite as smooth as the ride through the streets of Cebu City, in the Philippines. Captain Arial Tumang is on his way back to the United States as he concludes his vacation break from his starship, the USS Colin Powell. Once he arrives, he will spend the last precious couple of days at home with his family, then board a space transport to the orbiting Space Command and Control Center (SCCC). His ship has been in the space dock for the last thirty days for repairs and new upgrades. From there, he will inspect his ship and crew, and prepare for another mission.

He is a skilled, capable captain, strongly admired and revered by his crew. He takes a special interest in learning all their names and a little something extra about each one. As he and his wife drive to the airport, he sees the little airfield out the window where he learned to fly as a young boy. He remembers that he was barely tall enough to reach the foot pedals. Flying that rickety little airplane was the experience that hooked him into the world of aviation for life. He is very proud and grateful to his mom and dad for working so hard to provide his education and the special opportunities he had during his youth. It was the sacrifices they made that started him on his career path in aviation.

Although very proud of his country and heritage, he does not make a big deal of being from the Philippines. In fact, he barely mentions it. His demeanor is that of a man who has mastered leadership with great confidence, poise and humility. He never thought in a lifetime that he would be doing what he is doing now. He has it all: a beautiful wife, and family who love him and are very proud of him. He's earned the respect of his peers in the space community. Captain Tumang feels that he is blessed among men, and for all these things he is truly grateful.

* * *

Deep space looks ominous. It is marvelous on the eyes but completely unforgiving and especially intolerable to mistakes. No one knows this better than U.S. astronaut and ship's captain, Commander Steve Wilory (retired). He's flying with astronaut and co-pilot Major Deon Striker in the deep space cruiser (DSC) Relentless during a routine mission.

Captain Wilory, a Naval Academy Honor Graduate, who hails from Bergen Field, New Jersey, started at the tender age of eighteen when he entered the Navy. His former rank would be equivalent to a full-bird colonel (retired) in the other armed forces. Now aged fifty-two, he has had a successful thirty-four-year career in the Navy. Wilory is married with three girls, all now grown, the youngest just about to enter college. He's a straight shooter, but not ignorant to protocol and the way things work. A team player, he is always focused on the mission at hand. He has the skill set to lead large organizations extremely well, but has turned down such opportunities in order to stay in the action. He has been a squadron commander of an aircraft carrier and worked as a staff officer for the Navy.

After retiring from the Navy, he jumped at the opportunity to work for NASA as a test pilot. He then moved on to testing various ships in space. He finally settled in the job of flying deep space cruisers. He flies ten days a month, giving him time at home with his family to enjoy the semi-retired life. He has too many hobbies, but two he is very passionate about: his restoration of his 1971 Corvette Stingray, and the study of famous statesmen. He has always dreamed of being a statesman someday. He has read a plethora of books on history, and even more autobiographies. He's been preparing for more than half of his life.

* * *

Major Deon Striker is from North Platte, Nebraska. He entered Penn State on a lacrosse scholarship and studied engineering. He is also an honors graduate. He always had a very high aptitude for mechanics and making things with his hands. His father was an engineer, and he picked up the trait from building things with his dad.

He developed a love for aviation and entered the Air Force as a pilot, exemplifying excellence in all his classes and training. He was so capable, he was asked to become a flight instructor in flight school, and he did so for a couple of years. Once his tour as an instructor was up, he elected to fly fighters in a tactical air wing. The combination of his flight record and engineering education got him paired as assistant with a visiting team from the Defense Advance Research Projects Agency (DARPA). The team quickly noticed his sharp skills as an engineer paired with his flying ability and he was invited and assigned by the Air Force as a Fellow to work on some of their projects.

His work on the design of the deep space cruiser opened the door for him to obtain a flying position on the Deep Space Data Collection Project (DSDC). At thirty-one years of age, he is probably the youngest major with a line number for lieutenant colonel in the Air Force, and certainly the youngest pilot on the Deep Space Cruiser Program. He will likely stay in this program for the remainder of his career. Although his success sometimes tends to go to his head, Steve Wilory, his captain and friend, keeps him straight.

Their ship, the Relentless, is equipped with digital sensors, cameras and banks of super-computers that record, measure and store celestial data. This information provides valuable navigational information for future space missions. The Relentless is about the length of a Boeing 757-200, at approximately a hundred and fifty-five feet long. The fuselage of the ship is thirty feet wide by twenty feet tall and the total width is about fifty feet at the engine nacelles at the aft of the ship. It houses a few creature comforts for the crew such as sleeping quarters, a galley and of course a rest room.

This is their 32nd mission in Sector 12. They have been flying together for two and a half years, and have shared time together both professionally and personally. Deon has been a guest at Steve's home on numerous occasions, including Steve's daughter's graduations, birthdays, holidays and even a weekend or two. Steve helped Deon through his difficult divorce, getting him out of trouble and offering moral support. Particularly, toward the end of Deon's divorce, the local bartender would call Steve, to keep Deon from driving home drunk. Although their age difference is more than twenty years, they are as good friends as any friends could be.

As they fly through space, they are talking about things back home to pass the time.

"So, Deon," says Captain Wilory, "how's things going with that girl you're dating—now what's her name again?"

"Ilene."

"Yeah, that's right—Ilene."

"We're doing great. She's an incredible girl—she's smart, funny, very considerate, compassionate and patient. I don't know, she just might be the one, seriously. She's already talking about me meeting her parents."

"Seems like the next step towards a committed relationship. How does she feel about your flying and being away from home so much? I recall that it didn't fare well with the first relationship, and I'm sure it's hard on a new one. It takes a unique kind of person to be married to a deep space pilot, ya know," says Steve.

"Well, you're right about that," Deon replies, "but she says she knows what she's getting herself into and that she thinks she'll be able to handle it. I don't plan on doing this forever. I want to settle down someday."

"Well, that's good to hear. There's nothing like having a good woman—better yet, a great wife. How does she handle money?"

"Well, she likes brand-name merchandise—you know Coach, Burberry and the like, and she spends money pretty quickly. I'm working with her, but it seems it's going to be a long road before she gets it. For now, I don't see it as being a deal breaker, though."

"Hey, don't give up," Steve says. "It took quite some time before my wife and I came to terms with money, but we got there in the end. If she's as good as you say, give her time. The most important thing is that you trust her, and you both communicate, especially during the tough times. As long as she's willing to be honest, you two will be all right."

The navigation alert rings out.

"Waypoint," says Steve.

"Got it," Deon replies. "We're turning right, three degrees in five, four, three, two, one, turn right, heading zero-eight-zero."

"Turning right, heading zero-eight-zero. New heading now, zero-eight-zero," says Captain Wilory.

"Confirmed."

"Maintaining current heading and speed. Next waypoint in one-two-zero minutes," says Steve.

"Roger."

The ship settles easily on its new course, flying as straight and smooth as before. The Relentless has proven extremely reliable, given the numerous hours it has previously flown, and the two-man crew has grown accustomed to its reliability—often joking that "it's got backup systems for the backup systems."

"Once we clear that moon, we'll capture the new data and then head back on our way home," says Steve.

"By the way, how's your 'Vette coming? Are you going to paint it battleship gray or navy white?"

"I see you've got jokes," Steve laughs. Actually, I was going

9

to give it a coat of cherry red and shoot it with three coats of clear. It will give it that wet-look all the time. I am having issues with the tranny, though. Looks like I'm going to have to pull it again."

"If you need a hand let me know. It shouldn't take long."

"Thanks. I may have to take you up on that—that is if a 'high-speed' Air Force guy like yourself doesn't mind helping out an ole 'brown shoe' like me."

"You're right, but I'll make an exception this time. You want some coffee?" "Sure, I'll have a cup."

Major Striker goes back to the ship's galley and pours two cups of coffee then returns to the flight deck carrying sugars, stirrers, and both coffees.

"Thanks. Hey, careful with that!"

"I got it… I think." Deon puts his coffee and assorted items on his crew tray next to his seat. He begins to fasten his seat harness when the unthinkable happens: one of the buckles hooks the cup of coffee and spills the coffee onto the floor. "Oh, shit!"

"What happened?"

"Damn it! I spilled my coffee!" He grabs the spilled cup with lightning reflexes, saving about half a cup, but it's too late; the remaining spilled coffee runs along a seam in the flight deck floor and down onto an avionics rack below. A loud "pop" is heard.

"What was that?" Steve asks.

"I heard it too. I'm going down to take a look."

"Okay," says Steve. He puts on his helmet. It is space command procedure that a pilot has to go on oxygen if the other has to leave the cockpit for any reason.

Major Striker goes below and views the travel of the spilled coffee. He sees that it has simply pooled in one area on the avionics rack, and tries to soak it up using the remaining napkins he'd brought with the coffees. As he soaks up the liquid, he is unaware there is a screw missing on the avionics rack drip pan. Without realizing it, he inadvertently pushes the coffee further onto the avionics racks below. The worst happens: a short circuit flashes in one of the avionics units and smoke starts billowing out of it.

Captain Wilory yells from the flight deck, "Deon, I need you up here now!"

"We got smoke in the avionics bay!"

"Put it out and get up here quickly! We're losing altitude, and we're heading for this little moon! Its gravitational pull is sucking us in!"

Major Striker grabs a fire extinguisher off the wall and quickly puts the fire out. He heads upstairs to assist the captain, strapping himself in his seat and donning his helmet.

"I can't get the right maneuvering thrusters to fire," the captain says. This is not good."

"We're already committed to orbit," says Striker.

"Looks like we're going to be making a landing. Surface landing checklist," commands the captain.

"Roger. Surface landing checklist."

"Reverse thrusters!"

The major parrots the command in military fashion, "Reverse thrusters!" and selects the buttons that will fire them.

The ship begins shuddering like a twenty-five-hundred-pound steer that refuses to submit.

"We're coming in too fast!" yells Captain Wilory. "Full reverse thrusters!" he commands again.

"Roger. Full reverse thrusters," replies Striker, selecting the thrusters.

The ship reluctantly obeys and slowly follows directional commands.

"There she goes," says the captain, "over there."

"Got it," replies Major Striker.

"Give me RAD ALT," [radar altimeter] says the captain.

The ship slowly begins to descend toward the surface of the moon, and a massive dust cloud engulfs the ship.

"Forty, thirty, twenty-five, twenty feet, ten, five..." says Major Striker.

There is an expected yet distinct thump as the ship touches down on the unknown moon for the first time.

"Landing check," says the captain.

"Roger. Landing Check," replies Major Striker and begins to read the items in sequential order until completed. There is an eerie silence and a sense of fearful relief. They have landed.

Captain Wilory says, "I'll call it in."

"I'll check on the fire," replies the major.

* * *

The headquarters of Space Command is housed in a state-of-the-art Space Command and Control Center (SCCC) that orbits the Earth. After years of seeing and tracking numerous unidentified objects in our solar system, it was decided that it may be prudent to be prepared to meet celestial enemies in space rather than trying to defend ourselves from invasion on Earth. That said, the primary world governments decided to launch the World Space Defense Initiative. That Initiative started with the Space Command and Control Center. It is home to nearly fifteen thousand people, ten heavy cruisers, fifteen space destroyers, three squadrons of space fighters and a mixture of thirty other ships consisting of deep space cruisers like the Relentless, auxiliary cargo ships and other utility vessels.

The Space Command and Control Center is funded and manned by governments from nearly every country of the world. These include the United States, the United Kingdom, Canada, Germany, France, Italy, Russia, China and Japan, all of which led the way in the funding of the project. Experts from space programs in all of these countries, as well as Israel, Sweden, Saudi Arabia, Jordan, and the United Arab Emirates, provided professional expertise in the form of scientists, pilots, engineers, technicians, operations specialists, etc., who also assist and help man the station on a temporary basis.

The language of the SCCC is English, the language of aviation. Although there are many different nationalities in the center, one of the key conditions for an opportunity to work there is a requirement to adhere to the "English Only" policy at all times. Political correctness has no place here.

There is a very proactive leadership structure at the SCCC; it is structured after the NASA mission control model, with a section focused on tactical missions based on the U.S. Air Force model. Long-range sensors and analysis, flight, movement control and communications are all housed in one room. The communication center monitors transmissions from Earth, Earth's moon, deep space probes from all over the galaxy, and spaceship traffic.

Chief Technician Carla Kelly is a communications specialist on duty serving on temporary assignment from Britain's Royal Air Force. She receives a long-range transmission from the Relentless.

"Roger, Relentless. I read you four-by-five. Over," says Chief Kelly.

"We have experienced an electrical fire on the ship, and we have landed on a little moon at the following coordinates —transmitting coordinate data now," replies Wilory.

"Roger, captain. We received the coordinates. Stand by, sir," replies the chief.

Flight Director Commander Gerald Powell (FIDO) listens in on the communication and waves over the director of the SCCC, Mr. Willard Pickett.

"What've we got, Carla?" asks the flight director.

"Captain Wilory says he's landed on a moon in Sector 12 due to an electrical fire on the Relentless.

Mr. Pickett hears the conversation as he approaches the communications desk.

"Is that Captain Steve Wilory's voice I hear?" asks Pickett.

"Yes, sir," says Chief Kelly.

Mr. Pickett looks at Commander Powell and says, "Geri, he's a good guy. He and my son flew F-35s together in the Middle East conflict. Let's get him the help he needs as soon as we can."

"Yes, sir," replies Commander Powell. Powell gets on the

radio with Captain Wilory. "Hello, Steve? This is Flight Director Powell. Where did the electrical fire originate? Over."

"The fire started in the avionics bay just below the flight deck floor, sir. Over."

Director Powell yells over to the Electrical, Environmental & Consumables Manager (EECOM) for the SCCC. "EECOM! What do you have over there?"

"FIDO—I got nothing!" the manager replies. "No data yet!"

The director immediately replies to Captain Wilory. "We read you, and we're sending a support and rescue team, but we cannot get there for at least five days. I want you to hunker down and watch your six until we arrive. Over."

"Roger, Command," Wilory answers. "Hunker down, ETA (Estimated Time of Arrival) five days. Hey, would you mind informing our families we're going to be late?"

"Will do, captain," Powell replies. I will take care of it personally. You two be safe out there. We're going to do everything we can to get out there as soon as possible and bring you back home."

"Thank you, sir. We appreciate it. Wilory out," replies the captain.

Captain Wilory is not worried about the provisions needed to stay on the moon for five days; all cruisers are equipped with food replicators and supplies that could feed a two-man crew for nearly ninety days. What he is concerned about is what he and his fellow crewmember are going to do for the next five days.

* * *

It has been three days now since the Relentless crew landed on the foreign moon. Major Striker has assessed the condition of the fire-damaged area and the exterior of the ship. The damage is not too severe, but a few parts are now needed in order to operate the ship safely. He also took pictures of the damage, the exterior of the ship and the surface of the foreign moon and sent them all to the SCCC. It seems one of the thruster control modules was the second fire that caused the failure of the thrusters on the right side of the ship. They could have lost directional control altogether, so were actually lucky to be alive. Steve Wilory's piloting had saved the day.

There is a little more gravity than expected for such a small moon and the view of the sky is breathtaking. There is no atmosphere on the moon, so life support is essential. Now that all the work is done, they have a two-day wait.

They are grateful for their iPads, which they usually bring along with them, to help pass the time. They've watched movies and played more "Run Robber Run" and "Zombie Gunship" than they would care to admit. Now they're seriously bored, and Deon is ready for a little adventure.

"Hey, Steve, how about a little outing today?"

"What did you have in mind?"

"I noticed a mountain range on the way in—and as you know, I'm a novice climber. I was thinking, maybe we could do a little moon climbing today."

"Moon climbing, huh? Well, I'm not much of a climber, but I do know you're not supposed climb by yourself, so I guess I'm in."

"Woo hoo!" Deon yells. "I'll get some gear. I know we have rope, and I think I can jury-rig some devices that may work."

The alien moon has a four times faster rotation than that of our own moon but slower than the rate of our planet Earth. This means that one day on the alien moon is the equivalent to three Earth days.

Major Striker and Captain Wilory don their spacesuits and helmets and head out the hatch door. They take with them the climbing gear, food and supplies for their trip and assorted gear for the unexpected. They have identified a small mountain range ahead, so they head in that direction. The terrain is much like desert terrain on Earth. The mountain range is further than expected, and they reach the bottom of the mountains after walking about one and a half hours.

They stop to rest. After having some food and water, they begin exploring the mountain. Suddenly, Deon sees what looks like the mouth of a cave. The opening is very wide, and they proceed with caution as they enter it. There is nothing unusual about it at first—and then they see it. About forty feet from the entrance is a very large hole that looks as if it is engineered. It appears to be nearly one hundred feet across and the walls seem to have a slight rippled pattern that looks as if it continues all the way down.

"Wow, what could have done this?" says Deon. "The machinery with the capability to do this on Earth would not even fit in here. We have to check this out. Give me a light stick."

Deon activates the light and throws it in the hole. They see the light reflect off the walls as it falls, and suddenly it disappears—nothing. Major Striker approaches the edge of the hole and peers in.

"Hold your horses, buddy," says Colonel Striker. "We are the only two people here—if something happens, no one is going to know where we are."

"You're right."

"Hey, how about this? What do you say we record the coordinates of this cave so we can leave a message for the SCCC? That's just in case some alien beast swallows us whole. Worst-case scenario, they'll know where to look for our sorry carcasses!" A sly smile spreads over Deon's face.

"That sounds like a prudent idea. Besides, there are no such things as aliens."

They input the coordinates in their data recorder in relation to the position of the ship. "Okay. I think we should head back to the ship," says Steve.

"One second—I want to see what the composition of the cavern walls is." Deon pulls out a hammer and begins to smash at the wall. "This material is very hard. I can't say I've ever seen anything like it. I may need to improve what I had in mind for our climbing devices—don't want to take any chances."

"That's sounds like a good idea. Wherever that hole ends, we want to be able to get out. Let's go," says Steve.

They make their way back to the ship, have a bite to eat then bed down for the night. Deon reflects on the new design for the climbing devices, which he plans to fabricate tomorrow. Steve is thinking of his family back home. He says a quiet prayer then falls asleep.

The next morning, Deon gets up very early. He tries not to make too much noise as he gathers the materials for the climbing devices he is going to make. One of his favorite courses in college was metallurgy; he had been excited to learn, at an extensive level, what his dad had tried to teach him as a little boy as they tinkered around the old garage. He missed those times. Working on projects like this always reminded him of those precious times he had had with his dad. Unfortunately, Deon's father died two years ago from cancer. He grabs the plasma cutter and the material he needs to work on for the day and opens the hatch. He will need to cut this material outside.

Steve stirs a bit when the hatch opens, but decides to carry on sleeping. He knows Deon will be all over this thing until he completes it. That is one of the qualities Steve really likes about Deon: he's a finisher. Steve recalls a time when NASA was designing the deep space cruisers. Deon and Steve were among the few pilots selected to assist the engineers in the design process. While all the other engineers would work nine-to-five, Deon assigned himself an engineering workstation, and he would come in early, stay late and even work some weekends. He came up with great designs that genuinely surprised some of the other NASA staff engineers. He simply would not rest until the job was done and did so with great excellence.

The result of all this hard work was a great ship and a handsome offer to become an NASA Fellow working full-time as an NASA engineer. He declined and was given the option to become one of the youngest deep space pilots in the program. Most of the crews selected were high-time astronaut shuttle pilot types, like Steve, yet Deon was selected having no shuttle time at all. The senior staff recognized his engineering skills and his pursuit of excellence, despite his being just a junior officer. As a result, he and Captain Wilory had been given the opportunity to fly the very first mission in their ship, the Relentless.

Deon finishes cutting the metal and comes inside. He stows the gear and begins working the metal by hand, filing, sanding and polishing.

Steve awakes as the hatch door opens again. He walks out of the crew quarters, his hair sticking up. "Hey, do you want some breakfast?"

"Sure!" Deon replies.

"You know, you don't have to polish that; it's going to be hammered into the rock anyway."

"I know—it's just something I like to do. My dad used to say, 'Anything worth doing is worth doing well,' right?"

"Right!" Steve replies. "I'll get breakfast started."

* * *

Back at the SCCC, the crew of the Crash Recovery & Rescue Ship (CRRS) Colin Powell are preparing for their next mission: the recovery of the Relentless. The group, consisting of highly skilled engineers, technicians, and medical staff, counts about a hundred and thirty people in all—professional men, women, fathers, mothers, sons, daughters, husbands and wives.

Captain Tumang walks through the halls of his ship on his way to the bridge. The crewmembers grown to admire and respect their captain; each one greets him as he passes them in the hall. He's been a mentor to some and a source of strength to others during their missions in space. His professionalism provides a sense of safety and confidence amongst the crew.

"Welcome back, captain."

"Welcome back, sir."

"Captain."

"Hey, skipper!"

"Hello... Carry on," he replies.

His communications officer passes and greets him with an enthusiastic, "Hi, Captain! How was your trip home?"

"Lieutenant Frie. How are you? It was very enjoyable—had a great time. How's Mikey?"

"He's doing great in school but a little terror at home. He misses his mommy."

"Tell him I said hello. See you on the bridge."

"Will do, sir!" Sally says.

The crew of the Colin Powell has just completed their week of drills and trials on all systems. All equipment has been tested and is deemed mission-ready. They are excited to see what this next mission holds in store.

Little do they know it will be a lot more than they expect.

* * *

The Relentless crew has finished breakfast—freeze-dried eggs, frozen sausage and orange juice—and is preparing to return to the cave.

"Before we leave," says Steve, "I'm going to transmit a message to Command, giving them the coordinates of where we're going."

"Roger. Sounds good," says Deon.

They are going to carry less gear this time because they know what to expect—or so they think.

They take less time to get to the cave, and immediately prepare to rappel down the wall. Deon, as the more experienced climber, gives a safety brief. Steve listens attentively, and they get their gear on. Steve throws one more light stick into the great hole. Again, the light reflects off the caramel-purple ribbed wall as it falls below then disappears completely.

"Hey, I brought the wave gun," says Deon. "Let's see if we can get a better measurement on this hole." He first points the gun at the wall of the cave. Thirty-two point three six. The gun works. He then points the gun down the hole but gets an error reading—it must be beyond the range of the gun.

"Are you certain you want to do this?" Steve asks. "I don't doubt your skills as an engineer; I'm confident the devices that you fabricated will work—but we should be able to see the light fall all the way to the bottom, and we can't. It seems we may not have enough rope to reach the bottom."

"I get it, Steve. If nothing else, I just want to try to get another sample at a lower depth of the wall."

"Okay, Captain Kirk. Let's boldly go where no man's gone before."

They drive one stake each into the ground and tie off to it. The devices seem to hold pretty well. Deon's engineering skills are excellent. They turn on their headlamps and start down the wall. As they rappel down, it is obvious that Deon is a pro—although he's always very modest about it; his movements are smooth yet deliberate. Steve's, on the other hand, are awkward and a little jerky.

"Slow and steady, Steve."

"I'm trying, captain," Steve says, faking a Scottish accent.

When they reach the ends of their ropes, Deon stops and begins hammering in another device. Once finished, he ties himself off with the new rope and passes the hammer to Steve, who begins hammering in his device. Steve ties himself off, and they begin to rappel again. The second time Steve pushes off, he feels his device give way a little.

"Hold on, Steve. Are you sure you hammered that in all the way?"

"Sure—same as you."

"I didn't like the way that looked. Maybe you should get onto my line."

Just as Deon finishes speaking, a tremor starts to shake the small moon and the device breaks loose from the wall. Steve frantically grabs hold of Deon's leg. The device grazes his helmet as it falls into the abyss.

"Steve, give me your hand!"

"I'm trying!"

Deon is now holding on to the shoulder of Steve's suit with one hand and the rope with the other. Steve has a death grip on Deon's leg. Although the gravity on the little moon is not as much as that on Earth, it is still taking its toll. Deon is strong and fit, but even he is getting tired holding on to a two-hundred-and-twenty-pound man.

"Steve, I can't hold you much longer," Deon yells. "See if you can lower yourself onto the rope!"

Steve begins slowly lowering himself onto the rope. The device top-side is becoming increasingly unstable, as it is gradually being pulled out of the wall, unable to sustain the weight of both men. Deon tries to get to the previous rope tied to the ground, topside, but he is one-handed until Steve makes it to the rope.

Then it happens. The device, now holding both men, sings out, twanging like a tuning fork as the extra weight yanks it out of the wall. It happens as if in slow motion. The resistance on the rope has gone, and the two men begin falling until they eventually reach a velocity of around thirty-two feet per second.

Both men yell as they fall, their lives flashing before them, knowing that they may not see their families, friends, or their next day again as their velocity steadily increases. Hearts pounding, sweat pouring from their faces, their legs and arms flail about like two wounded pigeons as they keep falling and falling... and... falling... And suddenly there is a blinding flash of colorful, brilliant light.

In an instant, they have the sensation of not falling anymore; instead, they now feel as if they are being pulled in an upward motion. The sensation is scary yet comforting, as they intuitively know that they may survive this. The view changes; it is as if they are in a tunnel of swirling lights of color and plasma trails, almost like the ones Steve remembers seeing coming off the space shuttle's nose as it re-entered Earth's atmosphere.

They come to an abrupt yet gentle halt, with a sensation of being immersed in a fluid-like substance. It feels like water, but it is different somehow. Their survival instincts kick in, and they throw off their gear and begin to swim toward the light of the surface. The sunlight is coming through the water-like substance pretty clearly so they know that they are likely not very deep. The effort and speed at which they are moving through the water is astonishingly easy and fast. They swim to what seems like a sand bar, stand and walk about thirty yards to the shore.

They look around as they walk. There are no clouds to speak of; the sky has an orange hue to it that is subdued rather than overpowering. There are distant islands in view of the shore. It almost looks like the U.S. Caribbean with a galactic twist. The colors of everything are vibrant. In a strange way, it could almost seem like a perfect day. There are two suns and several moons in clear view.

Although what they are seeing is magnificent, they are still trying to wrap their minds around their fall. They are also both very aware that their current location is far from Earth or any ship or receiver they could get a transmission to.

Where is this place? they are both thinking.

They remove their helmets as they approach the shore, they flop down on the glistening sand for a rest. As they sit, to their surprise the sand chimes—calming audible tones fill the air around them. Awestruck, they touch the sand with their hands, asking almost in unison, "Where are we?"

CHAPTER TWO
The Discovery of Planet Meritor

After receiving flight clearance from the communications officer, Captain Tumang gives the order to the helmsman to maneuver the Crash Recovery & Rescue Ship (CRRS) Colin Powell from the space dock. Work crews, officers and everyone in between salute the moving ship as it exits the space dock. The crew is ready, and there is a feeling of excitement and curiosity. They are unsure of what to expect on the alien moon, but are confident in themselves and in the experience of their captain.

Captain Ariel Tumang began his career after graduating from the University of the Philippines, Cebu College in 2038. He then joined the Philippine Air Force flying fighter jets and eventually became a squadron commander. He fell in love with the United States while participating in a United States Air Force Officer's Exchange Program. He finished his tour in the military and received an engineering job with NASA, with the endorsement of a few key U.S. connections.

The Space Command and Control Center was formed during his employment at NASA, and he saw an opportunity to be a part of it. He applied and became one of the first Space Command Academy graduates. He then went on to command ships of all sizes over the years, and finally got an opportunity to command his first galaxy-class spaceship just last year, the CRRS Colin Powell.

He and his crew are bringing pretty much everything but the kitchen sink to the scene, to ensure the recovery effort of the Relentless is successful. Their ship is equipped with all the expertise and tooling they need to first rescue a downed ship, and then repair up to at least a quarter of it if necessary. If a ship were damaged more than that, it would be scuttled and destroyed. Due to the size of the Colin Powell, it cannot make a surface landing; the team will have to shuttle to the moon once they arrive after the five-day trip.

Also on board is Major Todd McNeal, Space Command Maintenance Officer, "B" Squadron. He's been in the shadow of Major Deon Striker's limelight for years. They both started together in the Air Force, and he was there when DARPA recruited Striker on to bigger and better things. He's followed Major Striker's career from a distance ever since. Although he would never admit it, he's a little jealous of Striker's success. Major McNeal is a talented engineer; however, he possesses an unsavory attitude. He's the type who will put people down in order to make himself look good. He mistreats those whom he thinks are the "little people" and he has proven to be a self-seeking, opportunistic leader—with the results in when he comes close to promotions or unique opportunities, people find out his motives and pass him over. He was just recently promoted from captain to major after applying to Space Command several times. He eventually got into an available "major" slot and seized a chance to join the Space Command, assigned to a spacecraft maintenance squadron.

In preparation for the repair and recovery of the Relentless, McNeal has accessed the ship's records from the Colin Powell through a communication interface installed on all ships. He is particularly interested in the ship's communication logs.

So, my old buddy Deon Striker found a cavern containing what seems to be an engineered hole, did he? Well, I'll have to check that out for myself! I will have to figure out how to get away from the ship for three hours or so. It's not going to be easy, but I'll look for an open door of opportunity, he says to himself.

* * *

Back on the newly discovered alien planet, Captain Wilory and Major Striker just sit for a while and take in all the scenery. The waves of the substance that looks like water were remarkably slower-moving than Earth water. Even more interesting is the fact that their soaked spacesuits are now completely dry. They decide that food and water would be a good idea at this point—they have been through quite an ordeal. They remove the food rations from their leg pockets and begin to eat.

Steve stands up and starts to walk along the beach. The sand is like the finest white sand on Earth, with the addition of what looks like tiny diamond crystals mixed in. The harmonic tones continue to emanate from the shimmering sand with each step he takes; when he scoops the sand up in his hands and lets it run through his fingers, a symphony of soothing melodies ring out as the sand hits the beach.

The colors of what looks like beach grass are vibrant, and the smell is sweet, almost intoxicating, like a combination of almonds and maple syrup.

Deon gets up too, sprinting for twenty yards then coming back. He's amused by the music he's making as he runs along the sand. He starts to dance. Steve, returning from his stroll, is amused, shaking his head. "You always seem to find a way to have a good time!"

"Hey, watch this!" Deon says as he executes a perfect back flip. As he lands, the sand sings out in harmony, and he raises his hands in triumph as if he is a world-class gymnast.

Suddenly, a deafening clap of sound fills the air, startling the two astronauts. The smell of ozone is all around them, almost to the point of being suffocating—there's an alien ship about forty feet in the air, just a hundred feet down the beach!

The ship is completely silent. Grayish-black in color, it is acutely angled in form, probably to avoid detection. The hull of the ship is covered in what look like intricately carved designs and symbols. It begins to scan the astronauts with a light beam. They can feel the heat from the beam on their bodies as the ship approaches and descends very slowly.

Landing gear extends from the bottom of the ship and it sets down, a hatch on the side opening slowly. There is a pause and four very large humanoid figures emerge. They are wearing a sort of crystalline armor that appears to bend light as a means of camouflage. They carry what looks like a ring of light in one of their hands that measures approximately four feet in diameter, obviously some sort of weapon. The sentries take up position in front of the ship. It is clear that their technology is more advanced than Earth technology. Two more ships suddenly appear on either side of the astronauts.

A tall alien emerges from the ship. He is dressed in elaborate headgear and robe-type attire, an elegant, crystalline mask covering half of its face, leaving just its mouth exposed. The alien appears to be a person of authority.

"Stay where you are," he says. His mouth does not move —apparently, the alien is a telepath. The astronauts think to themselves, "They speak English?"

"No. You hear your own language," the alien replies.

* * *

The alien's name is Balan-Gaal, chief of security for the planet. He was one of the few original settlers on Meritor and one of the architects responsible for the design of the wormhole moon. His personality is formal and methodical in nature. To date, he does not jest, quip or joke in any way. He is completely focused on his role and responsibilities and is very proactive when carrying them out. He duplicates himself in his personal guards and staff, leading and mentoring them well. He has the innate ability to hear everything going on around him, even during a full conversation. Formerly the assistant to the chief of security of their original home planet, he basically ran the entire security force for the former chief, personally selecting and training the elite guards that protect the Planet's Brajeh and family. [Brajeh is the Meritor equivalent to an earthly king.]

When their archenemies, the Khorathians and Chemdi-Shakahr, attacked and destroyed their planet, they killed the chief of security. Balan-Gaal, who also performed as the chief's personal bodyguard, took on five Chemdi-Shakahr at once to protect the former chief, killing them all before being transported to the new planet. That was no small feat for a force of one. The mask he currently wears covers the injury he sustained to his face in that fight. It is said that he still personally carries the shame of his assumed failure to save his chief, mentor and friend ever since.

Balan-Gaal was sent by the Brajeh as one of the key members of the forward team to administrate the population and security of their new planet, Meritor. Enemies who are even only slightly familiar with him do not underestimate him.

* * *

Steve looks over at Deon and quips, "So, Mr. Science—there's no such thing as aliens?"

The tall alien looks at and slowly nods to the sentries. Two of them throw rings of light toward the astronauts with amazing speed—the motion comparable to the devastating serve of world-class tennis player Roger Federer. As the rings instantly approach, the lights and colors they emit are spectacular and nearly blinding. The rings strike the astronauts squarely in their chests, and they fall unconsciously to the ground, as if dead.

The sentries carefully recover the fallen astronauts and their helmets and carry them onto the ship. The two ships providing cover rise and rotate a hundred and eighty degrees. The central ship rises and joins them. The ships fly away silently in tight formation and at amazing speed toward the city. There, the astronauts will be interrogated as spies.

* * *

The astronauts wake simultaneously. They are lying on a floor and each has a slight headache. Looking around, they see that they appear to be in a cell of some sort but without walls. Their spacesuits have been removed and they are now wearing some sort of white, microfiber shorts and a shirt-type garment. The clothes are very comfortable—in fact they have never felt anything like it before. In the very center of the white floor lies a large round silver symbol.

Steve gets up and walks to the edge of the cell. "Holy crap! We must be three hundred feet or more in the air!"

Deon walks over to see for himself. "Wow!"

"Don't fall off!" says Steve

They can see the ground below, teaming with aliens going about their business.

"Hey! You there!" Deon yells.

The aliens look up, ignore them and returning to their activities.

"What the hell... he ignored me!"

"Hey, Deon, keep a cool head. We're in their environment, remember? So far we're not guests—we're prisoners. For all we know, they think we're spies, and our next moments may not be pleasant, so don't provoke them. Heck, we don't even know whom we're dealing with. My advice to you is take off the uniform and the attitude for the time being and just play along. Maybe we'll live through this."

"Sorry, Steve. This is a little stressful—and I'm starving."

"I get it. I'm stressed and hungry too. Use your survival training, remember?"

"Yeah, yeah, you're right. Heck, that was years ago. You're right, though; we have got to survive."

As they finish speaking, their attention is drawn by a light gradually starting to glow from the symbol on the floor. As it gets brighter, a figure suddenly appears in what looks like a cylindrical elevator of light. The alien has feminine features and, to Deon's delight, is somewhat curvy. Her face closely resembles that of a human female. The only difference is that her eyes are nearly three times larger. She has icy-blue-colored short hair and her waist is dramatically smaller than her curvy hips. Her arms are defined and her legs look very strong. She is wearing an attractive white and light-blue outfit that fits smartly over her broad shoulders and is drawn in around her waist by a tight-fitting belt. She has no weapons. She motions to the astronauts to advance. Steve and Deon look at each other and approach.

Major Striker thinks to himself, They only sent one?

As they enter the cylinder of light, the alien follows in behind them and turns to face the door. Steve and Deon are standing behind and on each side of the alien. The major begins to ogle the alien, forming the words to Steve, "She's hot!"

Steve sees the look on Deon's face and discreetly shakes his head, "no."

Deon has his hands one over the other in front of him, raising one hand as if to reach out to touch the alien. He's already got that little-boy "I'm about to do something stupid" look on his face.

Again, Steve discreetly shakes his head and forms the word "no." Deon persists, each time his hand getting a little closer to the alien. Steve forms the words "no, don't" this time. But Deon can't resist—his boyish curiosity getting the better of him. He cautiously reaches out to touch the alien. Then, in what seems like a millisecond, the alien grabs Deon's arm without even turning around. Suddenly, Deon's feet are where his head had been, and his face is on the floor! It is as if the alien had been able to see him, despite being faced toward the elevator door. The alien then turns and leans in toward Deon, raising one of her four fingers in front of Deon's now flattened face. She wags it from side to side.

"Sorry about that," Deon says, speaking with only one half of his mouth, the other side being crushed into the floor.

Watching this incident unfold, Steve is amazed at how incredibly strong the alien appears to be for her size; he would say she has the strength of four humans. He considers at first not helping his friend, for fear of getting the same treatment, but decides to risk it anyway and reaches out to grab Deon's arm to help him stand back up. The female alien doesn't retaliate.

Steve says in a quiet voice, "Nice work, hero. Are you okay? This is my best guess, but I think that was a lesson learned. Don't you?"

"Yeah—no shit," Deon says with a half smile.

Steve continues, "You never friggin' listen to me. I must say though, I've never seen anybody turned upside down so quickly in my life. Very impressive."

"Something tells me I'm never going to live this one down."

"Believe it," Steve says, snickering faintly and nodding his head.

The elevator stops and the alien motions for them to follow. They do so, and are led down a well-lit corridor—which strikes Steve as odd, as there are no lights in view to speak of. Deon is still a little shaken, limping a bit and rubbing his face, but alert.

They turn right and walk into a large room in which five aliens are seated at a long white table. The one seated in the middle is one they both recognize from earlier.

"Enter!" He says, his mouth moving this time. The sentry positions herself about four feet behind the astronauts.

"I am Chief Security Officer Balan-Gaal of planet Meritor. You have entered our sovereign world uninvited. How did you know the secret to enter our world and why have you come? Are you spies?"

"My name is Captain Steven Wilory, of planet Earth, Space Command Captain of the deep space cruiser Relentless. This is my First Officer, United States Air Force Major Deon Striker. We are not spies, Security Officer Balan-Gaal. We are explorers who landed on your moon to await assistance from our space station for our disabled ship. We were only exploring your moon when we fell into the great hole in the cave. We decided to explore your planet, since our rescue team is not due to arrive for at least three days."

Balan-Gaal looks down at his console and then slowly

looks to the left and right as if silently communicating something to the four other aliens. He pauses, as if for effect, then
looks back at the astronauts. "You are telling the truth," he
says. How did you find the secret to entering our world? Many
have attempted to enter and were not successful. Tell us!"
Balan-Gaal demands.

"We were attempting to climb down to get a sample of
the rock wall," Steve replies. "There was a tremor and our
climbing gear failed, and we fell. We had no idea that it was a
portal to another planet."

Again, Balan-Gaal looks down at his console, then slowly
to the left and right as if communicating with the other aliens.
He looks back at the astronauts. "Again, your words are true,"
he says.

"Excuse me," says Steve. "You say that my words are true
—how do you know whether or not I am telling you the
truth?"

A scowl comes over the security officer's face and his eyes
squint a bit. He replies.

"As of this moment, I am the one asking the questions!"

"I understand," Steve replies.

Balan-Gaal goes on to ask them a variety of questions. He
even asks them about their partners, by name—at which Deon
grows quite agitated and receives a thump from the sentry for
his tone and behavior. When the astronauts will not answer
specific tactical or military strategy questions, it is Balan-
Gaal's turn to get annoyed. He continues, "When your rescue
team arrives, will the nature of their presence be strictly rescue or exploration also?"

"Their presence here will simply be a rescue mission,"
Steve answers. "Our team will bring all of the necessary resources to repair and recover the ship. I cannot give you an
exact idea as to how long it will take. We sincerely had no in-

tention of landing on your moon."

After about an hour or so, Balan-Gaal asks each of the astronauts some final questions: "Captain Wilory, what is a 1971 Corvette?"

Steve looks slowly at Deon, who returns his friend's stare. "It's... it's a car... an automobile," says Steve. "A mode of surface transportation on our planet."

Balan-Gaal nods as if he already knew what it was, although it was very clear he hadn't the slightest idea. He then looks at Major Striker with another distinct scowl and asks the Major a question. "Major Striker, What is a Chinese straight sword?"

Again, the astronauts exchange glances. Deon answers, "The Chinese straight sword or Jian is an ancient weapon formerly used by a race of people on our planet called the Chinese."

Balan-Gaal pauses, scowls again and continues. "Deadly, is it?"

"In the right hands, very," says Deon.

"You must show me this weapon."

"Sure. Uh... anytime," Deon says, again glancing over at Steve.

Steve is very puzzled but does not say anything at this time.

The four aliens seem surprised at the last request of their Planet Chief of Security. Balan-Gaal looks to the left and right again, and all five aliens stand and exit the room in single file in perfectly equal distance from each other. The sentry then returns the astronauts to their cell. They ask if they can have some food, to which the sentry replies by blinking twice. She then turns and leaves them in their cell without walls, Not saying a word or having any facial expression.

"Damn! What the heck was that last bit about?" says Steve. "And how did he know about my Corvette? Heck—he even knew it was a 71! Geez, that's creepy. And you... what about all of that Chinese straight sword business?"

"Well I never told you, but I've been doing a little extra-curricular homework," says Deon. "Although I love climbing and cycling, they are not really challenging me like they did before, so I took up something else that did. I have been learning to use the Jian."

"What for? Isn't that a little impractical for bar fights?" asks Steve, laughing.

Deon shares the laughter and continues, "Jokes... I see you've got jokes. Seriously, I played Lacrosse for nearly four years in college, and I liked to wield the shaft and get a little physical sometimes. In my ignorance, I thought taking up the Jian would be a natural transition. In fact, it's completely different. However, I found after I trained with it for a while, I actually started to like it and got pretty good at it. It's a deep workout requiring strength, agility and form. I have never been in better shape."

"Well, if that's what kept you from dropping me into the abyss when I nearly fell to my death, I'm grateful."

"Don't mention it, buddy. You've saved me numerous times and in more ways than one." Deon gives Steve a manly slap on the shoulder. Steve returns the gesture.

Just then, the floor lights up once again, and another alien appears in the light elevator. She walks out with great poise and confidence. Dressed strikingly in a flowing garb of an assortment of colors, with an elegantly sculpted silver headpiece adorning her head, she does not resemble the aliens they have encountered so far. Her demeanor is unlike that of the others, too—very confident, her disposition almost suggesting she owns the place. She walks out of the light elevator and approaches them.

Holding her hands open wide, she says, "Welcome to Meritor. I am Aioli. I have been assigned to you as your guide and protocol officer. It is my pleasure to accompany and serve you for the remainder of your stay."

Steve and Deon feel as if they have been rescued. They look at each other with great relief and expectation.

"Thank you, Aioli. My name is Captain Steve Wilory—you can call me Steve."

Major Striker nods his head and says, "Deon. We have a number of questions we would like to ask you—like, for instance, how long is our stay going to be?"

"I know you are concerned," Aioli says, "and I'm sure you have many more questions. Let's begin by getting you into some proper clothing. After that, we will enjoy a delicious meal and discuss all of your questions one at a time. Is that acceptable?"

"Yes, absolutely. Please lead the way. But one more question: you said you were assigned to us. Who assigned you?" asks Steve.

"You are now considered to be our guests. You have nothing to fear. I will answer that question and many more. Let's proceed, shall we?"

They enter a room decorated with myriad flowing fabrics hanging from the ceiling and walls. The attendants are busy with their work, making garments of all types. They seem to discuss it telepathically. One of the attendants rushes over to Aioli and shows her the clothing prepared for us.

The Meritorians are evidently a very efficient race and have used the scanned data of the astronauts' body measurements to make clothing for them. Every garment fits perfectly. Their clothing is not as colorful as Aioli's; instead, it is in natural tones, very stylish indeed. Steve's ensemble includes a vest. Deon's does not. It is uncanny how their styles intuitively fit their personalities. Meritor technology appears to be incredibly advanced.

They enter a room in which there is a table set for three, beautifully adorned with a tablecloth of many colors, fabrics and textures, and a sash running down the center of the table. Their utensils are similar to their usual Earth ones, but ergonomically designed for alien hands with four fingers. The vessels used for drinking look almost like champagne glasses but made of some other material. The food arrives shortly, and

Aioli looks at the two men and smiles, as if it is the best meal to be served on the entire planet. It looks rather bland and unpromising to them—very little color and shaped into strips about one inch wide.

"These are some of the most liked recipes on our planet," Aioli says. We modified the food to duplicate an Earth diet, to better suit your physiology."

"What would happen if you had not modified the food?" asks Major Striker.

"It would likely make you violently sick and may even mortally harm you. The nutrient requirements for our bodies would be toxic for yours, Aioli replies. Changing the subject, she continues, "We want to give you a gift to better serve you while you are visiting our planet. This device is called a Zehrea. This is a communication device and data interface that you wear on your clothing. It contains your dietary needs and other useful information about you wherever you go on the planet." She gently attaches these devices to their clothing.

"Can this track us as well?" asks Steve.

"Yes, it can. We can also communicate to you from anywhere on Meritor and within range of another Zehrea, communication node or Meritor ship. It is advisable for your safety and your own protection."

They start to eat—and are more than pleasantly surprised; the flavors explode in their mouths. The food is unlike anything they have tasted before—truly delicious.

Aioli starts the question-and-answer session. "So, Steve, Deon, what questions do you have? I will endeavor to answer them to the best of my ability."

"How is it that you can speak our language and do so extremely well?" Steve asks.

"Our data-gathering system is very thorough. It captures many types of data—even that which I believe you would call mnemonic data."

"You mean you have access to our memories?" asks Deon.

"Yes."

"Wow, I'm a little embarrassed. In fact, I'm feeling very exposed," says Deon.

"We do not judge subjects or the contents of their memories one way or another," Aioli replies. "We simply mine the data we need to enable us to effectively communicate in your language and assess other attributes. This saves time and needless destructive methods of interrogation that usually result in severe trauma to the subject or even death. The Chemdi-Shakahr is known for using such techniques."

"So you can speak our language now. Yet I don't see the connection between the data scans and your learning our language flawlessly," says Steve.

"Most Meritorians have what you would call telepathic and empathic ability. Some may have one or the other of these abilities. Those of us in Protocol are required to have both telepathic and empathic ability. This is needful in order for us to use the data we collect from our scans. It is then processed and used in a way applicable only to those who need it to accomplish a specific purpose—in this case, the ability to learn how to speak your language."

"I'm very uncomfortable with this," says Steve. This means you know all of our tactical secrets and intelligence?"

"Yes and no. We scan and mine your brainwaves and convert mnemonic data into data we can understand. We do not understand all that we collect. Learning from willing specimens helps us to put the pieces together. Although intelligence is important, it is not our uppermost priority; learning to understand a previously unknown language is our primary goal. We find that effective communication can avoid misunderstandings that lead to serious conflicts and even war. This is how our people have avoided war for what you on Earth would call eons."

"Ah, so this is how Balan-Gaal knew my wife's name," says Steve.

"Exactly."

"So if I understand you correctly," Deon says, "even though you can mine our memories, you are not sure of the meaning of all of the data you collect."

"That's right. Again, we see the pieces of what you humans would call a puzzle. We then use the sudden changes in your body chemistry, even to the cellular level, to determine whether or not you are telling the truth. So, if you had lied to the chief security officer, he would have known immediately because the body's chemistry changes drastically in most species when they are lying. The exception to this is that sometimes, under extreme duress, subjects may have false memories or may even fabricate them. In such a state, the mind cannot tell the difference between the truth or a lie —thus, neither can our technology."

"So your technology, as excellent as it is, has limitations?" asks Deon.

"All technology has limitations, Major."

"How far are we from our planet?" asks Steve.

"We estimate the distance to be the equivalent of five of your light years away. We have come to this conclusion because we have been tracking your ship movements for about three of your Earth years," replies Aioli.

"So you must have known that we landed on your moon," says Steve.

"We did. We have sensors on the moon. We did not expect you to find the secret to entering our world through what we call a Vitalius Bridge."

Deon repeats her words, "Vitalius Bridge?"

"Our ancestor, Neolan Vitalius, a famous Meritorian scientist in space navigation, astrometrics and physics, discovered the first one in space many of your Earth centuries ago. The phenomenon is like a fold in space that allows a ship to travel many light years from one part of space to another in a fraction of the usual time. We now call this phenomenon a Vitalius Bridge. I believe the equivalent Earth term would be Wormhole. We later discovered how to find them and make them stable enough to use as a means of traveling from one galaxy to another."

"Your superior asked us how we found the secret to coming here. We still don't know what that secret is," says Steve.

"Allow me to explain. We had to design a way to transport our people to our new planet without being detected by the Khorathians or the Chemdi-Shakahr. If they had known our plans, they would have destroyed the moon—or, worse, used it to enter our new planet and annex it as well. We also needed a way to conceal the Vitalius Bridge from a landed assault on the moon. So we devised the following plan: During the time we were at war with the Khorathians and the Chemdi-Shakahr, we used to supply an outpost one half of your light years away from that insignificant moon, and our flight path took us right past it. As we flew through that sector, our enemies never suspected our freighters nor scanned them at all; they focused all of their attention on our warships until the very end of our war campaign.

Our conclusion was to select the moon as the entrance to our new home enabling us to beam our people down, just above the hole as we passed the moon. The design of the Vitalius Bridge means that it opens only when an object of a certain size and weight falls into it, at a specific velocity. Our logic was that no sentient species would willingly jump to their death to investigate the possibility of a secret entrance, and that logic has served us well... at least until now."

"So did your enemies ever get suspicious?" asks Steve.

"Yes, they did, captain. The Chemdi-Shakahr noticed the activity was increasing in that area, so they began to dispatch more warships to investigate. We responded by attacking their ships in a nearby sector to draw them away from the flight path of the transports. We also had to fly more freighters as the Chemdi-Shakahr increased their attacks. We lost both freighters and warships in the process. Still, they never made the connection with the moon. What also assisted our efforts was the development of a transport beam that we now use on our ships, which cannot be detected by our enemy's sensor arrays. The average enemy crewmember would interpret our transport beam to be a small but simple space anomaly when activated."

"Wow. Brilliant. How long did the whole process take your people to accomplish?" Deon asks.

"It took the equivalent of two of your Earth years, captain."

"You seem to keep mentioning the two enemies, the Khorathians and Chemdi...?" asks Steve

"Chemdi-Shakahr, captain," replies Aioli.

"Can you give us an understanding of who they are and their relationship with each other?" asks Deon.

"Certainly. The Khorathians are a shrewd and cunning race. However, not all Khorathians are our enemies. Overall, they do not like to physically engage in war. Due to being too few in number, they use subversion, sabotage and internal conflict to conquer their enemies. They are very patient and are willing to wait as long as it takes to achieve their goals. However, on rare occasions when they do engage in battle, they are a formidable foe and extremely accurate with their use of all weapons.

"To date, we do not know the exact location of their home world, but we do know that the Khorathians and Chemdi live closely together. The Chemdi-Shakahr are the front-line warriors for the Khorathians. They like to fight. They are obedient unto death, often executing their orders without finesse, and destroying everything in their path. The Khorathians realized that to be efficient in their conquest of worlds, they would need ground warriors to secure the planets they chose to occupy. To this end, they use the Chemdi-Shakahr. The Khorathians conquered the Chemdi by destroying their ability to produce their own unique food supply. They negotiated a truce on the condition that the Chemdi will do the fighting for the Khorathians in exchange for their survival."

"Ah—extortion. Why can't the Chemdi produce their own food?" asks Deon.

"The Chemdi-Shakahr has a unique food source that has a correlation to their planet. Khorathians destroyed their planet's ability to produce food and now exclusively produces the food they need. Chemdi warriors have the ability to replicate food similar to that of their home world but at the cost of shortening their life span as a result. Therefore it is not suitable for the population. The Chemdi-Shakahr are very attached to their world for religious reasons, and their Elders will not consider moving to another planet. To date, they remain hopelessly dependent on the Khorathians for their survival and in return, they are their war machine."

"You said not all Khorathians are your enemies—what did you mean by that exactly?" asks Steve.

"Well, major, in the early beginnings of the war on our original home world, a number of Khorathians broke rank within their government and secretly approached us in an effort to talk peace. They were high officials in the Khorathian regime and wanted our assistance to help them organize a coup to overthrow their government. Ever since their home was destroyed, they have remained here in exile. In their gratitude, they have sworn to protect and advise our Brajeh and support our government. No one truly knows how old they are, but they are full of wisdom and unmatched in combat strategy and skills. We have yet to actually see their fighting skills but are told they are virtually unrivaled and completely deadly with whatever weapon they use. If they were caught or captured by their people, they would certainly be tortured and executed."

"Wouldn't the Brajeh be afraid that they would turn on him or become spies?" asks Deon.

"Khorathians are especially known for doing exactly what they say," Aioli continues. Once they commit, it is the same as if it has already been completed. This attribute is an important part of their culture. They will complete a task even if it results in their own demise. It is because of this trait that it is nearly impossible to get them to commit to anything."

"What do Meritorians do for fun? Do you dance, sing, play sports?"

"Well, Deon, Please pardon me, but I must study these words first, and I will have an acceptable answer for you. I have only had a day to prepare. We do participate in many forms of recreation. As to which ones would be categorized in Earth terms as sports, I just do not know the translation yet. Again, I will have an answer for you next time. We have communicated for quite a while. Now I will show you to your living space and prepare your protocol training. You are not allowed outside the compound gates until you have completed your training."

"How long will it take?" asks Deon.

"Not long at all. This is also for your own safety—as Major Striker learned today."

"Me? Learned what?" says a slightly embarrassed Deon.

"Meritorians are what you would call in Earth terms very conservative," Aioli continues, "and their traditions date back to the equivalent of thousands of your Earth years. For example, Meritorians do not like to be touched unless they have touched you first. Then, from that point, it is permissible to physically touch them in an appropriate way. If you touch them without their permission, it is our law that they have the right to rebuff you in whatever manner seems fit to them. However, they are not permitted to maim, paralyze or kill you for such an offense. The path of cruelty is not our way. Most Meritorians choose to enforce this edict with the minimum amount of force, as necessary. Isn't that right, Major Striker?"

"I guess minimum is a relative term. If what I experienced was an example of minimum this morning, I would hate to see what moderate force looks like! It was as if she saw me without turning around. She manhandled me as if I were a toy," exclaims Deon.

"Well, for your information, she did see you. Scuffling with a Meritorian is unwise as our physiology tends us to be stronger and faster than that of humans," replies Aioli.

"What? What do you mean, she saw me?" Deon asks.

"Yes. All Meritorians are born with a third eye. The most important thing to remember about this is that it is forbidden to speak of it unless in the privacy of a close and intimate relationship, and usually within your private space. Our third eye can also be located in different places on our bodies. Well, gentlemen, we can cover more of your questions tomorrow. I'm sure you are very tired and ready to see your new living quarters."

"We aren't going to have to go back to our sky cell?" asks Captain Wilory.

"No, of course not. You have been thoroughly debriefed and the chief of security is satisfied. As I have said before, we consider you now as guests. Our treatment of you will be very courteous and hospitable. I will now escort you."

Aioli walks them outside to a waiting transport. Although from the exterior it appears not to have any windows in it, once they step inside, they have a panoramic view from all angles, even of the ground beneath them. The comfort of the seating is superb and the interior exquisitely elegant. The Meritorians definitely had a sense of style. The takeoff is so smooth it is practically imperceptible. As they leave the compound, it becomes clear that this is a secure area separated from the rest of the world. Obviously no one gets in or out without permission.

They can see a very tall building in the distance. It looks as if it is the centerpiece of the city and can be seen from miles around. As the vehicle makes its way towards the city, they see countless amazing sights whizzing past: waterfalls flowing upwards instead of falling; roads that at first seem to be dead ends, only to exit elsewhere. As they approach the city, they fly above a vast ocean that separates the two landmasses.

The city comes into view in the far distance.

The transport slows as it enters the ramp and glides into the water. The entry is a little bumpy at first then becomes smooth and steady as they move through the unique water-like substance. A stunning array of brightly colored sea creatures of all shapes and sizes swim among the jagged rock formations. The journey continues and they head towards a ring of light up ahead. This is the entrance to the city. The transport enters a tunnel and they exit the sea, finding themselves back on land again.

The main thoroughfare is teaming with activity—a bit like an alien version of New York and Las Vegas rolled into one. A variety of different species can be seen congregating together along the length of the street.

As they approach the great building, they see a crowd of aliens gathered in front, seemingly very excited. The entrance is magnificent; colorful foliage adorns the construction and doormen stand either side like soldiers. The transport stops and the doors glide silently open. Aioli exits and communicates with three other aliens who have approached the vehicle as if expecting their arrival. She motions to the astronauts to exit the transport and leads the way into the building.

As they enter, Aioli waves off the approaching hotel staff who are proffering drinks and alien hors d'oeuvres (some of which, Deon notes, are moving on the plates), and personally walks the astronauts through the entrance toward their new accommodations. As they cross through the enormous lobby, they find themselves in the midst of singers, musicians and dancers, all in the throes of performance. The music is unlike anything they have ever heard on Earth. The dancers leap high into the air as if flying, gracefully landing as if gravity has no effect here. Lights stream through the air, back and forth like luminescent liquid, changing color and movement in time with the music. Aliens are everywhere, all dressed in elegant, flowing robes and colorful attire. Some of them pause to look at the human astronauts as they walk by. Large alien birds with colorful translucent wings occasionally fly from one side of the great lobby to the other. It is quite a spectacle.

Very high walkways with no railings crisscross the lobby, leading to adjacent buildings. Aioli continues to walk confidently, as if leading a parade, and passes a bank of elevators of light before heading to a separate bank of two elevators that look as if they may be reserved for private use. The doors open and they all enter. As they arrive at their floor, they step out into what seems like an endless hallway with no doors.

Aioli walks about twenty feet and stops. There is no apparent entrance, just a wall. She waves her hand in front of the wall and an opening appears, revealing a stunning suite with spectacularly high ceilings. Some couches and two sets of tables and chairs sit in the center of the room, capable of seating a number of guests. What seems to be the restroom sits off to the right and the balcony offers exquisite views of the city.

Steve turns to Aioli. "Thank you. This is very nice. We are grateful."

"Yeah, thanks," says Deon.

"Don't thank me; I am not responsible. However, you will be meeting the one who is tomorrow night at a gathering in your honor: you both will meet our Brajeh. Please get plenty of rest because tomorrow I will be preparing you both for the event."

As she turns to exit, she adds, "Oh, these accommodations are designed to anticipate the needs and desires of the guests. Be careful of what you desire. Enjoy." She turns and leaves. The wall reappears.

"Wow, Steve—can you believe this place? This is like the best hotel on Earth, on steroids!"

"Well, high-speed, I don't know about you, but I'm tired and I'm going to turn in. We don't know what time Aioli is coming back, so you should get some rest too."

"Yeah, you're right. I'm going to sit up just for a little while, and I'll turn in right behind you."

Steve retires, and Deon steps out onto the balcony, taking in all the splendor of this new world he and Steve find themselves in. He thinks about how they have both walked into the history books forever and how, if they ever make it back, they will be set for life, with book deals, interviews—maybe even the Tonight Show. "What am I thinking?" he says to himself. "I have to stay focused and survive this first!" His thoughts then turn to home and what Ilene may be doing, how she may be worrying about him and when and if he will return.

* * *

Back at the alien moon, the CRRS Colin Powell approaches and enters an orbit around the moon. The ship's captain, Ariel Tumang, the first and only Philippine space captain in the Space Command fleet, has been trying to establish radio contact with the crew of the Relentless, to no avail. Teams are bustling to get prepared to shuttle down to the surface where they will assess the damage to the Relentless and begin repairs. Major McNeal will take the lead in shuttle number one. Each shuttle can hold about twenty people. The gear needed to repair the ship will take up considerable space, so shuttle one's crew will now consist of only ten. Since no radio contact has been made with the crew, Colonel Seoyeon Suh will follow the maintenance team in shuttle number two with a medical team.

Major McNeal calls over to the maintenance chief. "Hey, chief, do you have all that you need?"

"Yes, sir," Chief Stapp replies. "It's primarily an electrical problem. My guys are studied up, and they will know exactly what to do. If things go as expected, we should be in and out in a couple of days."

"Great, chief," says McNeal.

The major shouts to Colonel Seoyeon Suh, "Hey, Seoyeon —lookin' good!"

Colonel Seoyeon Suh is a five-foot-four South Korean beauty who also happens to be a medical doctor on loan from the South Korean Air Force. A certified trauma surgeon, she has been with Space Command for the last four years and has flown on many missions. She is your typical erudite but not arrogant or elitist in any way. She does not make a big deal of her obvious beauty. In fact, she always displays humility when doing her job or interacting with people. She is extremely capable and exudes great talent whenever exercising her profession.

"Yeah, yeah. How's that rash?" she replies.

"Thanks for the help on that—it's better. How about dinner again when we get back?" says the major.

"Sorry, Todd, I'm all booked up," she quips.

"What? Was it something I said?" replies the major.

"I don't know; maybe it was the constant raving about your career, or maybe how you complained that most women don't seem to understand you. Other than that, no, of course not."

"Did I do that? Hmm, I guess I did."

"Ah, yeah—gotta go," exclaims the colonel.

"Well, if you change your mind, call me!" says the major shyly.

The colonel runs off and meets with her team.

The major struts over to his team and yells, "Okay, guys—let's rock and roll!"

The crews board the shuttles and they dispatch from the ship. The flight crew is following the locator signal being transmitted by the Relentless. Although the signal is strong, there is still no reply from her crew.

"The signal is five by five, sir," the shuttle pilot says. "We should be on the surface in twenty minutes."

"Roger," replies McNeal.

The shuttles land and the crews approach the ship. Some of the crewmembers fan out and start the exterior inspection of the ship. The senior staff enter the ship and find what they were expecting: a missing crew.

"Chief, get the assessment going," says McNeal. I'm going to see if I can pull the crew logs."

"Roger, sir," Chief Stapp replies. "I will pull the maintenance records. You heard the major—you guys get started."

"Where's the crew?" asks Seoyeon.

"The crew went to explore a location on the moon it says here," McNeal answers. "I have the coordinates. Once we get the repairs assessed and going, I suggest we investigate."

"Good idea. How far is it?" asks the colonel.

"It can't be too far. According to our location, I say about forty-five minutes to an hour," replies McNeal.

"Okay, sir. I have assessed the data. I've got a game plan, and we're going to get started," says the chief.

"What happened?" asks McNeal.

"It looks like we had a failure of one of the thrust control modules. That is what caught fire. This would explain all the faults in these circuits right here. They're all common to this one wire bundle."

"I will call it in to the Colin Powell and tell the captain we're going to get started," says the major.

Major McNeal ends his conversation with Captain Tumang. "Be safe and don't take any unnecessary chances, major. It's my intent to get this job done and to bring my crew and the ship home safely."

"Yes, sir, captain," says McNeal. "McNeal out."

Chief Stapp and his team continue the repairs on the ship. The major and the medical team prepare to make their journey to find the crew of the Relentless. They exit the ship and head for the area that was last reported by the crew. The hike is not too difficult even with the some of the gear they're carrying. The direction is fairly easy to follow thanks to the tracks left by the Relentless crew. No one says a word. Although the view is stunningly beautiful to behold, there is an underlying sense of unease about what they will find at their destination.

The team arrives and cautiously enters the cave. After a moment of observation, they see the footprints of the missing astronauts and the devices fabricated by Major Striker stuck in the ground, the ropes still attached. There are also two bags containing water, food and other supplies. Major McNeal informs the captain of their findings and the captain dispatches another shuttle to the scene containing rescue personnel trained in climbing. The Colin Powell is equipped with the resources to handle almost any rescue and recovery scenario.

The rescue team shuttle arrives and sets down about thirty yards just outside the entrance of the cave. The lead orders lights, a sling and many other tools to assist in this rescue. This team is focused, and each member takes their job seriously and personally. They will find and rescue the crew—or die trying.

The lights are set up and the rescue sling brought in. Although very large, it is light, only requiring two men to carry it. It has four legs that they drive into the ground effortlessly with a machine resembling a large nail gun. No manual labor for these guys; a wench on the sling does all the work via a small remote. The cable diameter is tiny but extremely strong; three men will connect to it and have the ability to descend to a maximum depth of 6070 feet, just shy of one nautical mile or 1.6 kilometers. The rescue team has state-of-the-art communications, including helmet cams, head-up display (HUD) face shields that display infrared, night vision, and enhanced material identification data. Their suits have built-in knee and elbow pads and are made of a special microfiber enhanced with Kevlar.

The team lead monitors all vital signs and communications from back in the rescue shuttle. He sees and hears what each rescue team member says and does. "Okay, gentlemen, let's get this show on the road!" he barks. "I have your vitals, and you are all coming in loud and clear. We're going to see if our crew is at the bottom of this... hole... or whatever this is. They may be still alive, or barely. Either way we will recover them, so take it slow and easy. Johnny Gage, you have the remote; descend at your discretion."

"Roger. We're in and descending."

CHAPTER THREE

The Chemdi-Shakahr Arrive

The sun goes down on Meritor only for a short time; when one sun goes down, it's not long before the next comes up, so nighttime lasts only a few hours. This is not a problem, however, because a Meritor's day is equivalent to thirty-six Earth hours.

The astronauts are sleeping soundly when Aioli arrives and wakes them. She walks in, her bubbly personality and beautiful attire lighting up the room. "Good morning! Did I say that right?" She pokes her head into the astronauts' rooms. "Greetings, Earth visitors—it is time to start our day! We have reserved the Center for Wellbeing and Growth so you two can exercise, so let's get going! We have a full set of clothing for you at the facility so no need to look for attire."

What Aioli does not say is that many prearranged schedules have been canceled in order to accommodate their guests and make them feel welcome.

Captain Wilory sits up on the edge of the oval-shaped bed and runs his hands through his hair.

The sound of feet shuffling across the stone-like tile floor precede a scowling Major Striker. "Aioli!" Deon says. "Are you serious? We've only been asleep for a couple of hours!"

"Actually it's been nine hours and thirty-seven minutes in Earth time," Aioli says with a smile. "Your bodies have fully benefited from the sleep you have had. Any more would simply be a waste of valuable time," she adds as she walks around room removing the dark-tinted doorway coverings to the balcony with a simple wave of her four-fingered hand.

Deon and Steve prepare to go to the "alien gym." Aioli walks over to a part of the room they had noticed briefly upon their arrival but to which they had not paid much attention. She stops, turns and motions for them to join her, then links her arms through theirs. A section of the floor begins to light up in a similar fashion to that of the prison elevator. In an instant, they are in the Meritor Center for Wellbeing and Growth. The walls are an opaque color they have never seen before. Interestingly, there is nothing in the room—no weights, no machines, or indeed anything resembling gym equipment.

A Meritorian is present in the room. Both astronauts recognize him as one of the people who had been sat beside Balan-Gaal during their interrogation. He motions to the captain and major to come toward him.

Aioli says, "This is one of our security heads. He will show you Meritorian defensive and offensive basics."

The alien motions again for them to stand either side of him, about ten feet back, then slowly begins to demonstrate a series of physical body movements. It looks like a combination of martial arts, dance and calisthenics performed all at the same time. The astronauts follow the movements, finding it relatively easy at first, but after fifteen minutes it becomes increasingly difficult. It is at this point that Aioli leaves the room.

As the astronauts seem to be struggling with the combination of movements, the session is paused and wand-like sticks are introduced, using the same movements. These are Meritorian weapons known as Shleahs. Deon wonders to himself whether these short sticks would be effective in any tactical defensive or offensive situation.

Sweat is pouring off the astronauts now, after what seems like an eternity—although in fact only forty Earth minutes have passed.

"Okay, okay," Steve says. "I think I've had enough." He

bends over, both hands on his knees, panting loudly.

"Wow!" says Deon. "What a great workout. What do you call this?"

The alien displays it in Meritorian text on the walls of the work area but it means nothing to the two astronauts.

Aioli walks in as if on cue. "Captain Wilory, if you would like, I am here to show you to your quarters where you may get refreshed before your first meal."

"Thanks, but I'll wait for Deon."

"He may be a while as he is scheduled for a session with a special visitor."

"Wow," says Steve. "I would like to see that."

"I'm sorry, captain. The special visitor has requested a closed session. I am sure you understand."

"Well, of course... he won't be in any danger or anything?" Steve asks.

"No, of course not. All I can say is that the visitor arranged this directly after your interrogation."

"I see," says Steve. "Well, I'm sure I can wait for Deon in our quarters."

"Thank you for understanding," Aioli escorts Steve to his quarters.

Meanwhile, Deon thanks the Meritor security head, who leaves the room. With the entrance of the room closed, it is difficult to see exactly where the opening is. Suddenly the opening appears again and in walks another familiar face. It is the sentry who had pushed Deon's face into the floor.

"Oh, no—not you again. You're not going to beat me up again are you?" Deon asks.

The alien puts her hands together and bows her head as if to display sincere humility. She motions to the two Shelahs on the floor then picks them up and humbly hands one to Deon. He takes it with all the humility he can muster. Suddenly, the wand in her hand transforms into what looks like a modified Syrian Sabre, only with two opposing blades, one over the other.

She sees the major's surprise and explains, "Just imagine what weapon you would like to use, and it will obey you."

Deon does so and his wand transforms into the Chinese long sword that he trains with at home. It even includes the nicks in the handle! Suddenly, she takes a fighting stance, holding her Shelah in front of her with two hands. Deon responds with his usual stance—left arm pointing two fingers forward and his Jian pointing forward over his head, his elbow at ninety degrees. His knees are bent, and he places a little more weight on his rear foot. As he looks at his foe, he becomes keenly aware that he is likely the first human in history to face a Meritorian with a Chinese Jian. He doesn't want an intergalactic mishap, so he figures that he'd best go easy on her.

The alien fakes a thrust move and executes a spinning maneuver in the opposite direction. Striker is a little surprised at the unorthodox style but is not unprepared and meets her sword with an unapologetic metallic clang. She seems somewhat surprised herself, even impressed. She pauses and smiles to herself, then continues to attack. Striker has been well trained and is highly disciplined with the sword; his skill has risen to the level where technique merges with art.

The two-edged weapon adversaries dance this potentially dangerous dance for the next thirty minutes, blades flashing, kicks soaring and grunts emanating. Striker is sweating profusely but the alien is calm and collected. Each admires the other's skill and prowess with the respective weapons. Before the next strike, the alien stands tall and raises her left hand to motion a pause in the sparring match. Deon returns to the "guard" position. The alien lowers her weapon and stretches out her hand.

"I am Miiya," she says. "Well done, Major Striker. Your skill is formidable."

The major now stands tall but is cautious to shake her hand due to the initial response he received from her the day before.

"It's okay to shake my hand," she says. "I have already touched you first; you are now welcome to touch me appropriately."

The major reaches out his hand and shakes hers, replying with fascination, "Wow, you are really good. Your form is a little unorthodox but very effective!"

"We have expert trainers who train all of the guards and sentries. We are trained to use just about any weapon. I, however, am privileged to receive special training so my skill is better than that of most of my peers."

"It sounds like you have been given a great opportunity."

"I have, and I am grateful."

"May I ask from whom have you received this training?"

"You may, but I cannot say," Miiya answers. "It's no matter —you have one more appointment for the morning."

"Hey, I'm beat. I've been at it all morning. I'd like to freshen up a bit and get something to eat if that's okay."

"I'm sure that is true, major, but your appointment will enter once I leave," she replies.

"Okay then. By the way, what's the big secret?"

"This appointment is very special. Few other people on the planet get the opportunity you are about to experience and many would be very envious if they knew. Enjoy!" she retorts with a slight smirk before whisking out of the door.

The door opens again immediately and in walk four very large, long-robed sentries. Their stride is long and deliberate. Their headgear is elaborate and tall with colorful plumes on the top. Their broad shoulder pads are adorned with exquisite designs, and their breastplates are the same crystalline material the astronauts saw the sentries wearing when they were first arrested, only these are carved with intricate designs as well. It is apparent that these are not just any sentries; these guys and gal look like real ultra-experts. They each have a walk that trumpets, "Sure, go ahead and try me—it'll be over before it begins!"

Immediately after the four sentries enter and take their

opposing positions in the room, another figure darkens the door. Deon sees the familiar alien and screams to himself... Oh, crap! It's Balan-Gaal.

* * *

The Chemdi-Shakahr have been cruising the galaxy and have dropped out of hyper speed. They are aboard the Chemdi-Shakahr battle cruiser, the Mok-Tar, a no-nonsense battle cruiser with great firepower. It has the usual sensor arrays, battle armor, cloaking arrays, modulating shields and high-energy laser cannons.

The Mok-Tar is a black, menacing-looking vessel designed primarily for reconnaissance—a battleship fit for any engagement. It has a long fuselage with blister-like sections all over the exterior of the ship. Six main engines, configured between the stern and on nacelles amidships, power it through space. Its main sensor arrays are located at the top and bottom. The main deck is not readily identifiable from the exterior because it is about one-third of the way within the interior of the ship.

It also carries the new and very deadly regenerative ray weapon. This weapon is designed to disassemble matter on the molecular level and regenerate it someplace else. It is a cruel and demoralizing weapon capable of ripping a ship apart into large chunks and regenerating entire sections in space for the remaining victimized crews to see, thereby leaving hundreds of casualties and necessary assets floating in space apart from the vessel. The Meritorians have outlawed the use of this type of weapon on their vessels and have made destroying Chemdi ships like this a priority when they find them.

The Mok-Tar's communication officer has picked up the metallic signature of a ship and reports it to the captain. It's the Colin Powell.

"Are you sure it is not a Meritorian ship?" the Mok-Tar captain says.

"Yes, captain," comes the reply. "It does not have the construction or the propulsion signature of a Meritorian ship."

"Set a new course," barks the captain. "It looks like we're about to meet another species. We go! All officers, prepare for attack!"

* * *

Back on Meritor, Balan-Gaal greets Major Striker. "Major Striker! Allow me to first thank you for meeting me during your workout. I trust you have found the skill of my sentries satisfactory? They are well trained and can use most any weapon, especially edged weapons."

"Chief security officer," Deon replies, "I am honored, sir, that you would take time from your busy schedule to meet with me. Yes, their skill is formidable."

"Please, you may dispense with my title; simply address me as Balan-Gaal. I personally train my senior security staff in the combative arts. They in turn train the other staff. I select the best to be my personal bodyguards. During your interrogation, I was very interested in the weapon we mined from your memories. As I said, I would like to see your Chinese long sword or Jian as you called it, and how it is used."

"Well sir, here it is." Deon imagines his long sword again and it reappears.

Suddenly, with lightning speed, all four sentries are wielding an array of weapons. One has a long spear; another a sword with what seems to be a two-foot-wide blade; one has a wicked-looking gun-type weapon, and the last sentry holds what looks like an electrified whip with crystalline maces on the ends. Two out of the four have shields.

Balan-Gaal raises his hand and they reluctantly stand down. "My apologies, major. As I said, they are the best at what they do. Let's begin, shall we?"

Balan-Gaal produces an elaborate serpentine blade in one hand and another weapon that looks like a futuristic trident in the other. He assumes a wide stance that is very intimidating. Deon adopts his usual stance and waits for the attack.

"Where are my manners?" says Balan-Gaal. "You are our guest—I will fight with only one of my weapons." He throws the trident to one of the sentries and the sentry catches it as if he had known it was coming. Balan-Gaal returns to his stance and begins swinging his blade in a horizontal figure-of-eight pattern while circling Deon.

Deon maintains his defensive posture and circles in the opposite direction. Balan-Gaal swings his sword toward Striker and it makes an alarming clang as it meets with the Chinese long sword. Deon fakes two attacks to Balan-Gaal's torso and exposes his back to Balan-Gaal—a clear mistake. Balan-Gaal takes the bait and attacks, only to see the point of Deon's blade peering under the major's right arm as it comes within about two inches of Balan-Gaal's breastplate. Balan-Gaal smiles at the fact that he has been so easily fooled by the deception.

Strike after strike, Balan-Gaal's attack is returned by the Chinese long sword. Deon strikes his opponent squarely in the chest with the palm of his hand, and with a spinning move, cuts the right sleeve of his garment. The guards are not pleased and attempt to approach the match. Balan-Gaal holds up one hand and assures them that this is appropriate in such a match. He and Deon continue. The major is holding his own, but it becomes obvious that Balan-Gaal is holding back a little as he sees the major is tiring. Suddenly, he stops the match. He has remembered that Meritorians are more than four times stronger than humans and have approximately ten times more stamina.

"Your skill is formidable and commands respect," Balan-Gaal says.

"My apologies for your sleeve sir," Deon replies.

"No apology necessary. That was my reward for being careless and underestimating your skill. May I see this Chinese long sword?"

Deon reverently hands the sword to the security chief. The Meritorian Shelahs remain in their current state if passed from one hand to another; they only assume their original shape if the user imagines it or sets it down.

"Ah, yes. It's fairly light, a sharp blade." Balan-Gaal whips the blade around in a professional fashion. He even mimics a move just performed by Major Striker.

Deon is clearly impressed. "My, you learn pretty fast, sir."

"If ever you get the opportunity to fight a Chemdi-Shakahr, the one thing you will learn is the art of adaptation means life. Failure to do so is death. They have four arms that are quick and hungry for death and destruction. You must think ahead and anticipate your enemy's every move. Perhaps we can discuss this further if we get a chance for another session. My time is up. Thank you, major. I have truly enjoyed your demonstration."

Balan-Gaal looks at the sentries, throws the sword to the one holding the trident and exits the room as quickly as he entered. Major Striker feels exhausted and exhilarated at the same time. He knows this moment is somehow significant.

The coming days ahead will reveal how true this is.

* * *

Back on the alien moon, the rescue team members have descended approximately twenty feet from the bottom of the hole. It is clear that the crew of the Relentless are not there. The team lead radios back to the Colin Powell. Captain Tumang orders the deployment of every available shuttlecraft to scan the moon for the crew. He also requests more ships from the SCCC, to help in the rescue effort. The investigation continues. At least ten more shuttlecraft exit the ship with four crew members on board.

The Colin Powell will continue its orbit as the shuttles search. They have started a search pattern that should cover the little moon in about two Earth days. Each shuttle will fly for about two hours and check in at thirty-minute intervals.

* * *

The Mok-Tar is closing in on the moon. The crew is prepared for an engagement. They are not worried, because, although the ship is designed primarily for recon, it is weaponized to destroy almost any vessel and has yet to be defeated.

The ship's long-range scanners have now picked up more than one ship. The Mok-Tar is cloaked and will travel undetected until the very last minute, as is the custom for Chemdi-Shakahr captains. The captain grows more curious about these contacts and has ordered maximum thrust, in order to arrive sooner. Khorathian Command has received the report and has dispatched another Chemdi-Shakahr cruiser to the area to assist. This ship is called the Talliel.

* * *

It has been about five Earth days, and ships from the Space Command & Control Center are now arriving: the Star Battleship (SBS) "Colossus", two Space Star Destroyers (SSD) "Sentinel" and "Titan", and one Star Tender (SST), the "Opulence".

SBS Colossus is equipped with specialized sensor arrays to detect signals on many spectrums, radio frequencies, light and anomalies in space, and the like. It is also equipped with high-energy lasers and rail cannons that use very large aluminum rounds, much like the classic battleships of WWII, only smaller and lighter. The rounds are fired at a hyper velocity that closes in on an enemy at a rate that is nearly impossible to defend.

The primary weapon, which is powered by the ship's engines, is its quantum pulse cannon. The quantum pulse cannon is a devastating weapon that fires pulses of high energy ten thousand times faster than the speed of light. The effect of the weapon at the site of impact is vaporization. The resulting effect of high vibration of materials furthest away from the site of impact is the fusing of dissimilar or unnatural matter together—glass and flesh, metal and plastic, etc.—rendering the repair of any ship impossible.

The Star Destroyers Sentinel and Titan have similar armament, less the quantum cannon of the Colossus. However, they additionally carry self-guided, fire-and-forget missiles that are smaller than those of the Colossus but more maneuverable. Each ship also carries a select number of self-guided space mines.

The shuttles from the Colin Powell are prepared to conduct their last day of the search of the small moon for Captain Steve Wilory and Major Deon Striker, the crew of the Relentless.

Captain James Avery of the ship Colossus offers to dispatch the remaining shuttles, fifteen in all, to undertake the last day of searching, to give the Colin Powell crews a rest. "XO, make sure to brief the crews not to fly for more than two hours. We have enough time to finish the job and I don't want any fatigued crews out there," the captain says.

"Roger, sir. The crews will dispatch in approximately two hours, sir," says the executive officer.

"Very well. Keep me abreast of their progress."

The ship's security chief yells out, "Captain, the ship's long-range sensors are picking up something on the port side, sir. Can't quite make it out, but there is definitely something there!"

"Is it moving?" asks the captain.

"Sir... I don't really know. If I had to guess, I'd say yes. Sir, there are now two contacts, same signature as the other, being picked up by ship's sensors and they are definitely moving!"

The captain barks out the order, "Red Alert! Attention all ships. Train all weapons to the current coordinates!"

The ships Sentinel and Titan snap their guns to the coordinates received from the Colossus. They are unaware as to exactly what they are looking for but they will soon find out.

Captain Tumang of the Colin Powell is also completing his orbit of the moon and is about to rendezvous with the other ships. He is on the back side of the moon and will see the other ships in about five minutes. He hears the communication from the Colossus and is very concerned as to why the three ships are training their weapons on the targeted coordinates. Either way, he orders his crew to do the same as they approach the other ships. As they come around the moon, he sees the three ships now in view. He orders the helmsman to slow the ship as they approach. They are now about ten miles from the group.

The Mok-Tar approaches and targets the ships in orbit around the moon. The Mok-Tar communication officer alerts his captain, "Captain, the Talliel has just joined our formation and is hailing us."

The Talliel is a space cruiser equipped with modulating shields, high-energy laser weapons and plasma-energy torpedoes.

The captain of the Talliel says to the Mok-Tar captain, "Hail, Mok-Tar. It is apparent that we have a new enemy."

"It is," replies the Mok-Tar captain. "We must find out more about this new foe. I will attack the larger ship. You destroy one of the two little ships and board the other. We must get the location of their home world and their capability," says the Mok-Tar captain.

The Talliel captain replies, "Command received and initiating."

"Weapons officer, target the engines of the larger ship and fire!" orders the Mok-Tar captain.

The cannons of the Mok-Tar are concealed within the ship's hull. Large bi-fold doors open on the top of the ship and two huge guns rise like deadly black panthers about to pounce on their prey. They track the Colossus's movement immediately and pinpoint the engine nacelles. Suddenly, there is a series of blinding lights and the boom of high-energy laser cannon blasts begins.

The Mok-Tar communications officer yells out "Captain, new contact! A ship has just appeared from around the moon!"

As the crew of the Colossus is analyzing the unseen target, they see from the bridge's viewer screen a series of blinding flashes of light coming from the direction of the targeted coordinates. The weapons officer of the Colossus exclaims, "What the hell is that! Captain incoming!"

"All ships, fire on contact!" commands Captain Avery. Suddenly a huge explosion rips through the rear of Colossus. The force of the explosion moves the position of the ship as it yaws to port. Crewmembers are thrown to the walls and debris flies through the ship, exiting through the new breach in the hull in the engineering section. The quantum cannon of the Colossus gets one shot off but it's a near miss on the Mok-Tar, now cloaked.

The Colossus has lost primary power, and four out of the six engines are burning in space. Star destroyers Sentinel and Titan both fire their high-energy cannons at the now cloaked Mok-Tar. All but one blast hits the Mok-Tar and the other hits the Talliel that is starboard in the two-ship formation. The shots from the Titan and Sentinel hit the shields of the Mok-Tar and Talliel, outlining their signature.

Captain Avery of the Colossus sees the outlined ships and orders the correction of the new firing coordinates. The destroyers are firing everything they have got at the targets. The rail cannons are blazing and the self-guided missiles have launched and have acquired their targets. The aluminum rounds from the destroyers are hindered by the Mok-Tar's shields but make their way through to the ship's hull, punching holes in the ship. Although the structural damage is minimal, the aluminum rounds damage vital ship's systems and kill Chemdi crewmembers as they go.

The Chemdi ship Talliel fires a volley of laser blasts at the Titan and completely destroys it with a direct hit. The blast is loud, unapologetic; the light it emits is blinding. The debris from the Titan hits the Sentinel, and gases from her hull are now venting into space. The Talliel suffers substantial damage from the weapons of the Sentinel and is now adrift at the moment in space.

The Earth ship Colossus has corrected its coordinates. It then targets and fires the quantum cannon at the Mok-Tar with the power generated from its remaining two engines. The quantum cannon strikes through the bottom of the ship at a raising diagonal angle until it exits through the rear. Scores of Mok-Tar crewmembers are vaporized and significant damage is done to the ship. Vital systems of the Mok-Tar are now fused together, never to be repaired again. The Mok-Tar loses its cloaking ability and is now plainly visible in space.

The captain of the Earth ship Sentinel can now see the very visible Mok-Tar and takes advantage of the opportunity. He is determined to revenge his sister ship destroyed by the Mok-Tar. He trains his ship's weapons at the enemy ship and fires everything he's got. Missiles, aluminum rounds and high-energy lasers blaze from the Sentinel, hitting the Mok-Tar with reckless abandon. The Mok-Tar fires the regenerative weapon at the Colossus. The weapon hits amidships just forward of the now destroyed engines on the Colossus. Suddenly a huge section is removed and reappears about two miles away.

Crewmembers are floating in space, their eyes now black and faces frozen. All that can be hoped is that they died from hypoxia so they will not have felt their body fluids boil from the effects of ebullism [the result of fluids boiling when pressure drops below 6.3kPa—kPa = Kilopascal, unit of pressure]. The debris from the Earth ship Sentinel is pouring into space: chairs, tables, liquids now frozen, forklifts and all sorts of personal items. The Colossus is completely disabled from the devastating blast of the regenerative weapon of the Mok-Tar. The Mok-Tar fires a last round of laser blasts at the Colossus and the remainder of the ship blows up in a spectacular explosion. All eleven hundred crewmembers are lost.

The Sentinel defiantly continues firing at the outline of the Chemdi ship Talliel, damaging its ability to remain cloaked and exposing the ship. Its shields are down. Unfortunately, the laser blasts of the Sentinel ignite its own venting gases and the Sentinel blows up in a fiery explosion.

The captain of the Chemdi ship Talliel sees the fate of the Colossus and Sentinel, which he had been ordered to board, and decides now to board the incoming Earth ship, Colin Powell. He sends four Chemdi-Shakahr via transport beam to the bridge of the Colin Powell.

* * *

Chemdi-Shakahr suddenly appear in the midst of the crew on the bridge of the Colin Powell. They seem to tower over the human crew. Long robes of black and purple adorned with hanging stoles of gold and silver cover these harbingers of death and destruction. Their hands are very large and their shoeless feet are webbed, capable of traversing practically any terrain. Their faces are covered with a guard from their helmets, which are adorned with extravagant designs. Their four eyes are red with fire, two in front and two slightly to the sides of their menacing faces. They are frighteningly ugly beasts.

The security officer is the first to react. He sees the beam starting to materialize in their midst and exclaims, "Captain—intruders! Security to the bridge!" His laser weapon is drawn in preparation to fire when the materialization process is finished. He gets off one shot directly in the chest of one of the four-armed Chemdi-Shakahr, who falls to the floor of the bridge. He finishes him off with two more blasts. Another Chemdi immediately swats the security chief across the bridge, as if he were an annoying fly. They kill everyone on the bridge except the captain.

The captain is indignant that his ship has been boarded by aliens and his crew killed. The leader of the Chemdi team pulls out a long blade then backhands the captain, who flies across the bridge onto the floor. The Chemdi slowly drives the blade through his shoulder, pinning him to the floor. The culture of the Chemdi-Shakahr has a healthy respect for captains, even enemy captains. This is likely why they did not kill Captain Tumang as they did the other bridge crewmembers.

A Chemdi crew member pulls out what looks like a crystal cube, which he holds up. It begins to emit an intense bluish light, and the ship's computers immediately appear to be responding to it. It is apparent that they are mining the ship's computer data with the device. The process does not take long. As the Chemdi puts the cube back in the bag, the bridge door opens. The security detail requested by the deceased security chief enters. Laser fire fills the bridge. One more Chemdi is down.

The lead Chemdi runs over to Captain Tumang, pulls the blade from his shoulder and throws it into one of the security officers. The Lead Chemdi speaks and the transport beam begins to materialize. The other Chemdi grabs a female security officer in an effort to take her. The transport beam is now growing stronger. Major McNeal has tagged along with the detail to assist and has entered the bridge as well.

The female security officer looks to McNeal. She would rather be killed by one of her own than taken prisoner. "Do it!! Do it now! Please?" she screams, tears rolling down her face. He takes aim and shoots her with his laser, center of mass. She dies and the Chemdi drops her to the floor.

The major is unaware of how fast the Chemdi are and before he knows it, he's been disarmed by the Chemdi-Shakahr and has been taken as a prisoner in her place. The Chemdi kills the final security officer and transfers to their ship with the ship's stolen data and their new human prisoner.

The captain of the Star Tender (SST) Opulence watches all this horror unfolding in space around him. He knows they are just a cargo ship with very little, if any, weapons, but in spite of this, he still orders the weapon's officer to fire their two laser cannons at the Talliel. The captain of the Chemdi ship sees the cargo ship is no match, and the Talliel does not disappoint. Only two laser blasts are fired back at the Opulence and she also explodes into a fiery blaze. The Colin Powell is the only Earth ship left.

The wounded Talliel uses positioning thrusters, comes about and takes aim at the Colin Powell then fires. The Talliel weapon's array is apparently experiencing targeting trouble rendered by the Earth ships. One shot misses and the other only grazes one of the Colin Powell's engine nacelles.

Captain Tumang wastes no time. He sets his meager cannons to auto-fire at the enemy ship and sets a course that intersects both ships. It will automate going to warp just before he collides into both. He makes an announcement. "Attention all hands. This is the captain. We have been boarded by a hostile alien race. They have taken data from our computers that can lead them to our planet. We are badly damaged. We have little time and we must destroy them before they can use that vital information.

"All available crews, board the escape pods and shuttles and egress the ship. I will meet up with you all on the alien moon. I'll try to hold them off for as long as I can. It's been an honor and pleasure serving with you all. Survive for each other and your families. May God bless us all. To the remaining crew, brace for impact!

"Engineering, this is the captain. If there is anyone there, I need you to hold the ship together for one more maneuver!"

"Aye, captain. I'm with you sir!" says the chief engineer.

The captain says a little prayer for his crew and their families. He knows he and the remaining crew are living the last few moments of their lives. The captain now cherishes his last moment. He looks around the bridge at the bodies of his crew. He recalls how the Chemdi slaughtered them like animals. He recalls the first time he met each one of them. He recalls the times he has met some of their families and friends. He savors the people they were and how they have faithfully served him as captain. He remembers his lovely wife and daughters and the little plane that he first flew.

The last shuttle has signaled that it is clear and away. He knows his last duty. All of his senses now feel heightened—everything is very sharp and clear. The smell of the electrical fires and burnt flesh from crewmembers' bodies as a result of the alien's laser blasts fills his nostrils. Captain Tumang sits regally in his captain's chair and engages the ship's star drive for the last time. As the ship begins to move, the Talliel fires another laser blast, narrowly missing the Colin Powell but hitting two of the escaping shuttles, killing all on board. The Colin Powell builds speed.

The captain of the Talliel is painfully aware of the fate that awaits his own ship. The captain and a few other crewmembers scurry for the captain's launch. The Colin Powell is now entering light speed and, at the fullness of its velocity, contacts the Chemdi cruiser Talliel with a stupendous crash. The result destroys both ships. The debris of the Colin Powell and Talliel is now travelling well over thirty thousand miles per hour and spews into the wounded Mok-Tar, peppering it with a wall of debris of all sizes from both of the destroyed ships. The mighty Mok-Tar finally suffers the fate that it has inflicted on many other ships before: it becomes a ragged explosive spectacle. None of her crew on board survive. The mighty Mok-Tar is reduced to a vanquished cloud of floating debris in space.

The remaining shuttles from the now destroyed Colin Powell rendezvous on the surface of the moon near the wormhole cave where they started their journey. They are emotionally compromised after seeing their Captain, crew and their ship destroyed. Some are staring at nothing, some openly weeping. They have only each other now and they do not know whether or not more enemy ships are on the way. They huddle together in the only shelter they have now. They radio in and wait.

CHAPTER FOUR

Earth is Angry And Plans A Response

Meritorian sentry Miiya returns to the workout area to escort Major Striker to the transporter pad.

Deon is truly exhausted as he returns the training wands to their holders. The door opens and in walks Miiya. "Hello, again, major. How was your workout?"

"Oh, it's you again. Coming to further insult my ego after I got my ass kicked?" Deon asks.

"Ass? What is ass?"

Deon pats his rear end with his hand.

"Ah... Bulot. Oh, no, major—in fact, I have come to congratulate you."

"Congratulate me? Heck, it was embarrassing! I felt like Balan-Gaal was holding back to keep from humiliating me further. It makes me want to put down my sword altogether."

Miiya walks over to the major, placing her face right up close to his. "You, Major Striker, are one of the only sparring partners he has ever...complimented. He does not give praise very easily and he never wastes words. Furthermore, he spars only with select people because he is a formidable foe and his enemies may have sent spies among us just waiting to kill him, if possible. He is a person of deep devotion to his Brajeh and his people. He does not have what you would call friends. However, those he chooses to associate with are very few. Besides, you cannot put down your sword for good because he has scheduled you for more training." She pats him gently on the shoulder.

"Great! That's just excellent!" Striker says sarcastically. He continues: "What a minute—you're a sentry. How do you know all of this stuff about him? I find it just... a little strange."

"You are very astute, major. Yes, it is unique but not so for me. You see, Balan-Gaal is my father."

You could have pushed Deon over with a feather. A million questions flood his mind. "Is this common in your culture?" he asks.

"What do you mean?" She replies.

"I mean the Chief of Security for the planet could select anyone to be a sentry. Why does he put his own daughter in harms way?"

Miiya senses the struggle within him to understand and simply smiles and explains.

"I was orphaned during the attack on our planet. His entire family was killed as well. He took pity on me and adopted me as his own daughter. It's not something we openly discuss, for security reasons, but I think it's important to let you know that I find you interesting. If you would permit, I would like to show you a special place on Meritor, in an effort to learn more about you and your culture and for you to perhaps learn more about me...if you like."

Deon is shocked. He had thought she did not like him, especially after the elevator incident. He is beside himself with wonder. Not only is he the first human to spar with a Meritorian—he's also the first to date one!

"Well, Miiya, I'm almost at a loss for words," he says.

"I don't understand. Did I offend you?" She asks.

"Let me put it this way; I am very happy and surprised that you would honor me by asking me to join you to see your special place. I would enjoy seeing it very much. I must first get back to freshen up a bit and see what Aioli has planned for Steve and me. We're supposed to meet your Brajeh."

"I understand. I will be in contact with you later, Major."

"Oh, and one thing—please call me Deon."

"Deon? Deon," Miiya practices the pronunciation. "Okay,

Deon then. Bye, Deon."

"Take care," he replies and disappears on the pad for his room.

* * *

The pads on the floor light up and Deon appears in the hotel. Steve looks up and sees his co-pilot and friend. "Hey! You've been gone for a while. It's good to see you—but, boy, you look tired," he says.

"Wow. What a day it's been. I don't know where to begin," says Deon.

"Well, let's start with your secret meeting with the secret visitor."

"Secret—my ass. It was Balan-Gaal!"

"Balan-Gaal? The big guy? What did he want with you?"

"Remember the question about the Chinese long sword? He was serious and he wanted me to demonstrate it."

"You're kidding!" exclaims Steve.

"Yeah. The guy's a galactic martial art bad-ass. He took me to school and started to hold back to keep from embarrassing me. It was the best and most challenging workout I've ever had."

"No shit? Are you sure you didn't school him just a little bit?"

"In my dreams maybe. I could tell that he was holding back. He could have really embarrassed me if he'd wanted to. Funny thing is, though, it seemed as if he was tutoring me... sort of, preparing me for something."

"Maybe. This whole experience is a tutoring session," replies Steve. "Not to change the subject, but are you hungry? Aioli is going to meet us here and give us more training on meeting their Brajeh. She's never been late before—I expect she'll be here shortly."

"Okay, I'll get cleaned up and be out in a few. It shouldn't take me long to get ready. If she arrives before then, you two can start without me."

Just as Deon disappears into his bedroom, the door lights

up and a very calming bell rings. "Enter!" he shouts, and in comes Aioli. He has never seen her face looking like this—very serious, sad even, as if whatever news she's about to share is not going to be good.

"Good morning, Captain Wilory," she says. "Major Striker, will you please join us?" She sits down at the table that is set for their breakfast.

Major Striker comes into the room in a pair of shorts. His hair is wet and he's drying off with a towel.

"We have received some very disturbing data from our moon. The sensors on our moon have detected your rescue team. Apparently they were looking for you. When they did not find you, your people sent for more ships. The Chemdi-Shakahr detected those ships and a battle ensued."

"Wait—you said ships; how many ships?" Steve asks.

"We detected a total of five. We also detected a total of two Chemdi ships. One of the ships we recognized as the notorious Mok-Tar. It carries their latest "Regenerative" weapon. It's very dangerous and few ships can withstand even a single blast from that weapon."

"So what happened?" Deon asks.

"It appears that the Chemdi-Shakahr was attempting to enter the moon's orbit during a routine patrol. When they saw your ships, a battle took place and the Chemdi-Shakahr destroyed your people. However, we also detected two secondary explosions of the Chemdi ships. Both Chemdi ships were destroyed, including the Mok-Tar. Destroying that ship is no small feat. There is also evidence that there are survivors on the moon. It appears that they escaped in little ships. However, they won't last very long, especially if the Chemdi return."

"We must first save those people on the moon," Steve replies. "Second, we must get a message to our world that we are okay so they do not send more ships. Had we been there, this might not have occurred. This is our fault!"

"Captain, that is a very inaccurate assumption," Aioli replies. "Had you been there, they might have killed you and Major Striker as well."

Deon, his voice full of dismay, asks, "Is there any way the Meritorians can help us get a message to the folks on the moon? Their only hope may be to come to Meritor the same way we did."

"This situation calls for decisions that are above my position. I will talk with Balan-Gaal, but for now we must complete your protocol training before you meet our Brajeh. I am sure there is already a plan being devised—as to what, I will find out soon. However, this still does not change the fact that you must finish your training. I feel great sorrow about your people."

Servants enter the room with food and they serve them with quiet perfection. The mood at the table is somber and tense at the same time.

Deon is especially disturbed. "We would not have attacked them first. It's not our way."

"Whatever the situation, it will all be recorded on the ship's data recorders," says Steve. "They continually send back all ship's data to the SCCC. It may take a while to get there, but you can be sure they will get it."

As they finish eating, Aioli begins teaching them the ways of the Meritorian Royal court, as in what to expect and what not to do. It is pretty easy because everything is done for them. The most important element to remember is to make no sudden moves and not to address the Brajeh or his court directly; always to liaise through the appointed emissary, in this case Aioli.

The door chime rings again. It's an emissary of the Brajeh. "The Brajeh has summoned the astronauts immediately!" he says.

Their clothing for the occasion has already been delivered to the room and Aioli instructs them to get dressed because they will be leaving immediately.

* * *

Communications Technician Chief Kelly is getting some very disturbing long-range traffic from the Colossus and the Sentinel. "Everyone, please be quiet! Commander Powell, our ships are under attack! It appears they arrived at the moon and came under attack almost immediately!"

The PROP engineer exclaims, "FLIGHT. I've got four engines down on the "Colossus!"

The DSP engineer also yells, "FLIGHT. I also see weapons fire from the Colossus, Sentinel and the Titan!"

"Do we have any data as to who attacked them?" asks the director.

"Yes, sir. Video feed from both ships is still loading. We should have it in a few minutes."

Flight Director Powell yells to Director Pickett, "Will! Get over here quick! Our ship's under attack!"

By now, some controllers and staff members are beginning to gather around Chief Kelly's communication station. The controllers for the Colossus, Titan, and Sentinel are glued to their screens. Just as Director Pickett arrives, the video feed is loaded and Chief Kelly begins to play it on her screen.

"Carla, would you play it on the big screen?" he asks, his voice laced with urgency and panic.

"Yes sir," Carla replies.

The Space Command and Control Center is cylindrical in its construction, designed to have a three-hundred-and-sixty-degree view. Just above the outside viewing windows sit very large view screens that follow the curvature of the station—not a second of this video feed will be missed. As the video begins to play, a shot is shown from the bridge of the Sentinel. It shows a clear view of the Colossus firing her quantum cannon at the outline of the Mok-Tar and missing the enemy ship. The Colossus's four engines can be seen burning in space.

The Star Destroyer Sentinel returns fire, hitting the outline of the Mok-Tar and also hitting the Talliel. The Mok-Tar fires its regenerative weapon at the Colossus, which uses its cannon one more time resulting in a direct hit to the Chemdi spaceship Mok-Tar. The Mok-Tar is now de-cloaked, its sinister aspect in full view. The eyes of all in the Space Command and Control Center watch aghast with unbelief at what they are seeing, mortified that an alien enemy is attacking their ships.

"Who in the hell is that and why are they attacking us?" yells the SCCC director.

The SCCC staff continues to watch the events unfold on screen. The Colossus gets destroyed in a spectacular explosion. Chief Kelly now switches to the Colin Powell's bridge video. The view from the video feed of the destroyed ship goes black, leaving a void on the huge display screens of the SCCC. They see the Titan destroyed and the Sentinel fire its last volley at the enemy ships. The Sentinel blows up in a fiery explosion. The Opulence is next. Again, the large screens go black.

Next, they witness the boarding of Colin Powell by the Chemdi-Shakahr, viewing their enemy for the first time. Evil, terrifying-looking beasts, they have four fiery red eyes and four arms, and a physique that appears formidably powerful, impenetrable. This perspective is challenged as two of them fall as the security teams blast multiple rounds of laser fire into their cloaked bodies.

Next they witness the device that mines the ship's computer and the exit of the Chemdi from the ship as one of their own people begs to be killed rather than taken prisoner. They also see the kidnapping of the major and hear the speech by the captain in his final heroic moments.

People are now openly weeping, tears streaming down their faces, even the director. The flight director is tearing up and Chief Kelly covers her face, her tears seeping through her fingers, her shoulders shuddering in her deep sorrow.

"Chief... chief!" yells the director. "I want that footage sent to my office immediately!" Get me the SECDEF! [Secretary of Defense] We have a new threat—not just to the United States but to Earth itself! Geri, put everyone on high alert— and we need to confab on whether or not to prepare ships to rescue the remaining people on that moon. If so, our new enemy may be in the area so we need to be armed to the teeth. Our new mission is to assess whether or not we can get in, save our remaining folks and get out.

"This enemy could also be headed our way! We need to know all we can about them. We need our best people to figure out our new enemy's weaponry and capability. It's obvious our weapons are effective, but they got the jump on us somehow and we're going to review everything to figure out how. They've killed our people, our friends. We're going to figure out their weaknesses. We're going to become experts on who and what this enemy is. Then we are going to respond— swiftly, decisively and with deliberate lethal force! Do I make myself clear?"

You could hear a pin drop in the room. People start wiping the tears from their faces. Their newfound determination can be seen on their faces as they turn their emotional pain and sorrow into focused thought, tenacity to learn about and defeat this new enemy.

"Okay, then," the director continues. Somebody make some coffee because it is going to be a long day and night! Let's go, people! There is no time to futz around. We've got a lot of work to do, so let's move it!"

* * *

The crew of the former Colin Powell has landed on the alien moon. Shuttles are positioned just outside the entrance of the wormhole cave where they had initially gathered to look for the Relentless crew. There are about seven shuttles in all, each containing enough rations to last a number of days. The crews are tired, scared and focused on survival.

Crewmembers are performing first-aid on the wounded, in constant fear of their new enemy coming back and attacking them. Nervous, they try to remember their Space Command training and to focus on the task at hand: survival, forcing themselves not to worry about something that has not happened yet. They quickly determine the ranking officer for the detail—the doctor, Colonel Seoyeon Suh. Although she is the highest-ranking officer, she is not command staff-qualified. Operational command now falls to Captain Daniel Lewis, supply officer.

* * *

Aioli and the astronauts travel in a transport vehicle to the residence of the Brajeh. They fly over the grounds at incredible speed, and still it seems to take about thirty minutes to get to the structure. The surrounding area looks about the size of Texas. The grounds are adorned with fountains, alien flora, and a building featuring stunning designs and tall stained-glass windows that faintly reveal some of the building's splendor inside.

As Deon and Steve exit the transport, Deon thinks to himself, "That's a little weird; we flew for what seemed like thousands of miles at high speed and did not see one ship to escort us or vet us out before we reached the structure."

As if on cue, six sizable, highly menacing-looking ships de-cloak above them, three on each side. "Ah..." says Deon, realizing they had in fact been escorted from the moment they had entered the property boundary.

Steve strolls around as if he has just pulled up in front of the Hilton Hotel. Deon silently marvels at how his friend looks so comfortable, as if he's already familiar with this environment.

Aioli and the Brajeh's palace guards escort the astronauts into the elaborate structure. Fountains abound and beautiful patterns cover the walls. The architectural design is unpretentious and elegant at the same time. Although it is obvious that you are in a state residence, it offers a charm that is missing in most Earth state buildings. Tall doors, stretching about fifty feet high, appear to protect the main palace court.

They take a right turn into a smaller hallway in which the ceilings are about twenty-foot high. A security detail stands on both sides of the hall. The emissary who had visited them at the hotel is standing in the middle of the hallway. He raises his hand to stop them, turns and opens wide the double doors, and, in a booming voice, announces their arrival with regal flare. For the first time since they arrive, Aioli positions herself behind them and the astronauts enter the court. It's magnificent!

* * *

Back at the Space Command and Control Center, the director sits behind the closed doors of his secure office pondering the events of the past few hours. His hairy little friend, Corky, a purebred Bichon Frisé, jumps into his chair to get a quick pat and rub on the head. Pets are not usually allowed on space stations; Mr. Pickett had obtained a special waiver for Corky because he made him available for limited experiments in the lab. A knock on the door breaks the silence and in walks Flight Director Geri Powell.

"Have a seat, Geri," says the director.

Just then, the White House operator's voice cuts through the atmosphere on speaker like a Wüsthof knife. "Director, please hold for the secretary of defense, sir."

Mr. Pickett puts down his dog and straightens up a bit. After a short moment, a voice comes through. "Director Pickett, this is Defense Secretary Roberts."

"Greetings, Mr. Secretary," says Pickett.

"First, please accept my apologies and condolences for the loss of your crews. They were all very fine men and women who defended our country and our world. It seems we're in a very serious situation. Now, if you would, please tell me what you know about this enemy."

"Mr. Secretary, they appear to have ships similar to ours but in many ways superior. They are using technology unfamiliar to us. We also know that our technology can hurt and destroy them. What is not shown on the video, sir, is that they also have the ability to cloak their vessels and approach nearly undetected."

"Nearly?" the secretary says.

"Yes, sir, nearly—the communications officer on the SBS

Colossus detected an anomaly in deep space and alerted the captain just before the attack. That was enough to give the captain the opportunity to train his weapons on the anomaly and gave the fleet a firing vector. Our team is in the process of analyzing how to increase our ability to detect these anomalies and target them sooner."

"The President and other world leaders are greatly distressed and are wondering whether we did anything to provoke this attack."

"Sir, as you have seen on the video feed, we were attacked first by a cloaked ship. To our knowledge, there was never any warning communicated to us by the aliens—or at least any warning in a language we understood."

"Well, I think we should consider staying on high alert and standing down on space ops so as not to lose any more people or ships."

"Sir, with all due respect," answers Pickett, "we have people down-range, stranded on an alien moon and their time is running out. They won't survive beyond their oxygen, sir."

"Pickett," said the SECDEF, "I get it. They're our people. But we can't risk another confrontation that will lead these beings to Earth!"

"Sir, it has not been fully substantiated that our enemy is not already on their way!"

"I understand. The President's orders are to stand down until further notice. That's an order, director. We'll be in touch. Oh... and by the way, I will be sending two of my representatives from Washington to join your team at the SCCC to observe and if necessary assist."

"Yes, sir."

"Out here," the secretary says.

Director Pickett lifts his weary head and looks at Geri Powell. "Geri... we can't just let our people die."

Powell pauses, his head down. Then suddenly he smiles, looks up and replies with enthusiasm and a look of mischief, "With all due respect, director, I have every intention of obeying our President's and the SECDEF's orders. However, if you'll excuse me, our crews are preparing for previously scheduled training missions and we have three days before they launch."

"We may not be able launch the two star destroyers or the repair ship. It will definitely draw too much attention."

"How about a small cargo ship that can carry all the stranded crews? It just may be a suicide mission, but it's all we've got."

Pickett looks at him with grave concern, nodding in agreement. You understand, worse case scenario, we could be tried for high treason. Best case, I could get fired. "If you get me fired, I'll be pissed!"

Geri laughs. "I hear federal prison is not so bad. Heck, I'll likely have a jail cell next to yours!"

They both walk at a fast pace down the hall to their teams who are waiting in the conference room. There is a large whiteboard at the front of the room with writing scribbled across it. The GNC [Guidance Navigation & Controls] system engineer is going through the analysis he has written on the board as the team listens intently.

The flight director is sitting in a chair just to the left of the end of the table. Mr. Pickett walks in front of the whiteboard and begins to address his team. Although he does not mention this openly, he is impressed at how, in such a small amount of time, the situation before the SCCC and the world has been summarized in very clear and defined categories on a damn whiteboard! Pickett says to himself, This is another example of the brilliant minds we have in our space program.

Seated around the table are the engineers and head controllers of the SCCC: communication (CAPCON), the flight directions officer (FIDO), guidance procedures officer (GPO), guidance navigation & controls (GNC) system engineer, data processing system (DPS) engineer, propulsion engineer (PROP), electrical, environmental & consumables manager (EECOM), maintenance controller (MC) and the weapons engineer (WEPS), and tactical (TAC).

Seated beside and standing behind each principal are his or her support engineers and managers. The fifty or so people in the room all have their ears finely tuned to the first part of the equation being presented. As professional engineers, their minds are poised to start the process of problem-solving and balancing the other side of the equation.

NASA, Houston and Cape Canaveral have dialed in. To join them on the call are key corporate principals and aerospace engineers from Honeywell, Bombardier, Northrop Grumman, Boeing, Lockheed-Martin, Rockwell-Collins, British Aerospace, General Electric, Saab and Israel Aircraft Industries. Support engineers from Mercedes, Apple, Oracle, Motorola, Microsoft and emQube join the fight. Bringing up the rear are design staff from Autodesk and even Disney Imagineers to complete the Earth research and development war chest. The Earth has answered the call to come together to defeat a common enemy.

As the various members are all dialed in to the inter-stellar video conference call, Director Pickett thanks the GNC engineer for his brief and he clears the front of the room.

Pickett addresses the team. "An alien enemy has engaged us a long way off from Earth. We suspect that they may be preparing to invade or even destroy our planet. We're going to err on the side of caution and assume that this is their purpose—and make sure we are prepared. We have information on some of their capabilities and are forming a game plan to prepare ourselves to repel and defeat this enemy. That said, I will need your help to create new and more effective ways to fight, communicate and serve our crews in space and beyond.

Nothing is off the table. We need this yesterday. We will communicate the needs as best we can and assign your companies specific tasks as they arise. We will ensure that the communication process is as robust as we can make it and that no obstacle will stand in the way of your success. Thank you for joining us today. Further CONFABS will be communicated to your respective section chiefs."

Mr. Pickett continues with the brief and shows the film footage. He tells them what the most pressing issues are and opens the floor to the companies that will likely handle the items. Intelligent questions are asked. Patents and intellectual property rights are not a factor in this setting. We're trying to save our planet. Project managers are assigned, tasks allocated and the tentative completion dates given. The meeting is a long one, stretching over nearly two hours.

As the others sign off, Mr. Pickett addresses the SCCC separately. "Now that we're done with that, let me address all of you here. Our mission is to come up with a game plan concerning this new enemy. We're going to do our very best to give them one. We need to feed the Earth teams the information on what we need. Section chiefs, bring your ideas to me to be vetted. I'll push the good stuff to COMO (SCCC Communications); COMO will push it to Earth. FLIGHT, I want you to get the teams going. Split them into smaller groups if necessary and get to work!

The room disperses like a tidal wave of people. In spite of the horribly overwhelming video they all have just seen, people start to pull themselves together again and get emotionally back on track to complete their respective missions.

Director Pickett draws a few key team members into his office—the key folks who can obtain the resources needed to rescue his stranded crew. They close the door behind them and turn towards the director.

"The reason I have asked you all in here is we have 'family business' to take care of. We have crews stuck on an alien moon. So before I go any further, you should all know that The President of The United States has ordered us to stand down and not rescue our crews. How I see it, we have a Space Command to run and I will not let that stop me from conducting the training missions needed to prepare my team for this new enemy. In short, I will basically be asking all of you to help me commit an act of high treason in an effort to save our people. If any of you object to this idea, please tell me now and it will not be held against you."

No one said a word, not one.

"We estimate that the survivors of the Colin Powell have about ten or eleven days of oxygen and rations left. It takes at least seven days at twenty-four-hour shifts to prepare our docked spaceships for the mission. I need us to squeeze that down to three days. We need to prepare a small but maneuverable cargo ship and arm it. We will then launch them on a training mission toward our moon and from there, they will head onward to rescue our teams. That's our first mission.

"The SECDEF of the United States is sending his representatives to the SCCC to assist us in the development of an action plan. When it comes to our first mission, all they need to know is that we're conducting a routine training mission. Is that clear?"

"Yes, sir!" they all reply.

"Let's go!" says Pickett.

* * *

Captain Wilory and Major Striker stare in awe at the Meritorian royal court spectacle. Subjects and elders line both sides of the hall, and aliens stand along either side of the Brajeh's court. Some appear to be female; others are standing with strange animals, seemingly pets. Aliens of all sizes and shapes watch the astronauts as they enter the great hall, which is extravagantly adorned in lush fabrics featuring alien designs— even the floor is covered with intricate patterns.

Palace guards are stationed about every ten feet on each side of the hall, along the aisle. At the very front of the hall sits the throne of the Brajeh and his rubenesque Meritorian Cojourn (Equivalent to an Earthly queen). Three beings robed in simple yet elegant garments stand on one side of the throne; four on the other. Although they are obviously bodyguards, they look a little frail to pose a threat to anyone. In spite of this, they have a majestic nature about them, with a presence almost as strong as that of the Brajeh himself. Their arms are slightly longer in relation to their bodies and they have small, slender heads. Alert and watchful, they constantly scan the room as if expecting something. It looks to the astronauts as if they have no weapons of any kind—highly unusual for body-guards.

Steve and Deon look at each other then proceed into the room. Aioli follows behind. As they approach, a very tall alien motions to them to approach the throne. The Brajeh appears very fit, full of life and spirit. The Cojourn is adorned as no one else in the room, and seems rather amused and genuinely fas-cinated upon seeing the Earth astronauts for the first time.

The Brajeh's emissary raises his hand to signal to the astronauts to stop about twenty feet from the throne. He then turns toward the throne and announces, "The Brajeh will now honor Captain Steve Wilory and Major Deon Striker with his presence!"

Almost immediately, a myriad of celebratory sounds ring through the air, and dancers move in time to the rhythm and percussion. Although this only lasts a few minutes, it seems like hours to Steve and Deon. The celebration suddenly stops as abruptly as it started.

The Brajeh looks at Aioli and speaks. Aioli translates. "Welcome. I am Brajeh of Meritor. You will excuse me if I look at you for a moment? You are the first humans I have met."

The Brajeh lunges from his throne and proceeds down the many stairs, almost as if he is floating. He stops about five feet away from the astronauts. The six beings on either side of the throne seem at first as if they are going to stay in place, but suddenly, in the blink of an eye, they are in front of the Brajeh. They moved so quickly it was as if they were a blur. Although their simultaneous movement startles the astronauts, it is evident that Aioli is not surprised at all.

The Brajeh looks intently at both astronauts until he has his fill. He smiles at each of them and returns to this throne. The six beings form a barrier between the Brajeh and the astronauts, turning their heads in vigilance. They wait until the Brajeh is seated before returning to their positions. The

Cojourn seems excited, remaining poised on her chaise during the whole process, as if sitting ringside at some national professional sports championship.

The Brajeh pauses for a moment as if the inspection was exhausting. Then he looks intently around the court and refocuses his gaze on the astronauts.

"I have been briefed on the circumstances by which you have arrived. I find it extraordinary. Although your technical trouble brought you to our moon, I am aware how you found our disguised Vitalius Bridge. You are the first to breach our portal. Unfortunately, your people's activity near your crash site has alerted our arch enemies, the Khorathians and the Chemdi-Shakahr of your presence. They are aware that your vessels are not from Meritor. Their discovering the existence of another race of people has opened a pathway to a collision course with them and your world. It is a course that your people are likely not prepared for.

The reason I invited you to my court is our people have been in search of a worthy ally to defeat the Khorathians and Chemdi-Shakahr. We are a formidable people, but after our last war, with the Khorathians and Chemdi, it resulted in the destruction of our former planet. Therefore, I have decided not to go to war again without an ally. We have lived here on Meritor for more than the equivalent of sixty of your Earth years. We always knew the day would come when we would engage with them again. I will meet with the high council and discuss our offer of an alliance with Earth. I will ask you to go and present our offer to your people. It is for certain that the Khorathians and Chemdi-Shakahr are planning to attack your planet. The time, captain, is at hand. In addition, I am also aware that your people are now stranded on our moon. At this time, we cannot assist you in their rescue."

Steve is about to speak but Aioli immediately raises her hand. He waits for her signal to him to reply. A chime rings after about a minute and Aioli slowly lowers her hand and nods at the captain.

He begins to speak, slowly and deliberately. "Mighty and powerful Brajeh, first let me thank you for your hospitality and the kindness you are showing my fellow crewmember, Major Striker, and I. We are grateful to you and your people. As you said, we were unaware of your portal; it was not our intention to come here by way of it. We ask your forgiveness for our ignorance; we are a curious people and it is in our nature to explore and to learn more about our surroundings. We apologize for any inconvenience or negative impact our actions may have caused to you and your world."

He pauses for effect and looks at Aioli. She conjures up a slight smile and a faint nod of approval. The captain continues. "As I look upon the wonders of your world and its magnificence, it is very obvious to me that you administrate and rule your world with great wisdom and prudence. Mighty Brajeh, the people of Earth, now on your moon, may be injured and dying. It takes five Earth days' travel for our ships to reach them. As an act and gesture of peace between our two worlds, which you are seeking an alliance, would it not be wise to offer assistance at a time such as this, Mighty Brajeh? Forgive me for asking such an indulgence so early in our association. However, as an Earth commander, it is my duty to do the best that I can for my people. Thank you, Mighty Brajeh, for your time and attention."

Steve then bows and remains in this stance for what seems like an eternity before standing upright again. Aioli seems very moved and pleased at his sincere and circumspect words. It appears that her training made this possible. No one in the great and high hall speaks. It is protocol in any king's court to be silent when a question is asked of the king until he answers or addresses, that which was posed to him in his throne room. The citizens present in the King's court also seem very moved by the captain's powerful words. The Cojourn is enamored by Captain Wilory's uninhibited bow before the king and court; she looks at him, with her hands clasped over her chest, as a child would look at a new Christmas puppy.

"I have heard your sincere request, Commander Wilory of Earth," replies the Brajeh. "I will consider it with great thought and patience. You are welcome to continue to enjoy our hospitality as you wait for my reply. Thank you for your presence today."

The Brajeh and Cojourn rise along with their entourage and immediately depart. The Cojourn affectionately holds the hand of the Brajeh as they disappear into the corridor of the palace.

Aioli looks at Captain Wilory and Major Striker with an "it's time to go now" look. The escort begins walking at a hurried pace and they follow, heading back to the waiting transport. As the transport rises and starts its journey back to their hotel, they talk about what has just transpired.

"Geez, Steve!" says Deon. "Where the heck did all that come from? I know Aioli was working with you, but when I heard you speaking, I felt like I didn't even know you! The statesmanship and the ease at which those incredible words flowed off of your golden tongue... and that never-ending bow! Wow! Where did you learn to do that? Man, I was impressed!"

"Captain Wilory, I've been a protocol officer for a long time," Aioli cuts in, "and I have never seen anyone foreign to his court make such a profound impression on the Brajeh or the Cojourn as you did. In fact, they usually say as few words as possible. You seem to have made them very communicative today."

"Well, thank you," Steve replies. "Obviously you know more about him than I do, but I felt that he hardly showed any emotion at all!"

"Exactly! Usually, the Brajeh displays more bravado, as you Earthlings say, when he meets with a guest for the first time. Not so with you, captain. You obviously made a distinct impression on him. Again, I am truly impressed."

"And for God's sake, who were those beings that moved

like ghosts?" asks Deon.

"Like what? I am not familiar with that Earth term."

"I'm sorry. Those seven beings moved very quickly. Who or what are they?"

"I was waiting for you to ask me about them," says Aioli. I waited to discuss them with you until you had seen them for yourself. Those beings were... Khorathians."

Deon and Steve stand open-mouthed in awe, wonder—and complete confusion.

"Did I hear you correctly?" asks Steve. "You mean the aliens responsible for the destruction of your people, our people and the stranded crews on your moon are the very ones guarding your Brajeh?"

"No. They are not responsible. Yes, they are of the same race. What I am about to tell you must be kept under strict confidence—it is information that even most Meritorians do not know.

"Just before our former planet was destroyed, a delegation of Khorathians contacted us to talk of peace and the possibility of our assistance to help them carry out a coup against their regime. It was one of the most guarded secrets of the war at that time. They secretly took a special ship to meet with us on Meritor. They were careful, so as to not be detected. The meetings began, but to our horror the Khorathians received a coded message that there was a spy among them and their plans were discovered. They killed the spy but, unfortunately, the damage was already done.

"Those who had helped them and their families were immediately executed and their friends killed. There is still a standing assassination order against them by their leaders on Khorath. The Khorathians who remained here knew that if the Khorathian leaders somehow found the location of Meritor and sent assassins to kill our Brajeh, the only ones who would have a chance to stop them would be other Khorathians. In return for their asylum here on Meritor, they offered their services to the King, as his personal bodyguards.

"To date, since our people at large have never seen a Khor-athian, they do not know who they are. Just a minute few in our government know that the Brajeh's personal bodyguards are from Khorath."

"Wow, that's incredible," says Deon. "They look so frail and easy to overpower."

"Do not look upon their appearance as weak. They are calculating, highly intelligent, and relentless. They strategize three to four steps ahead of most warriors. Movement in our world is as if it is in slow motion to them. Again, they have their own weapons and are extremely accurate with them. And as if all of this was not enough, they can easily adapt and be just as accurate with any weapon they use—edged weap-ons, plasma whips, phased weapons and especially warships. They are not many, but of all the races to go against in battle, they are the most feared across many galaxies."

"I can see now why they are the best choice, even over your mighty warriors here on Meritor," says Steve. "By the way, I noticed Balan-Gaal was not present."

"Very observant, captain. Although he is chief of security of the planet, he is fully confident in the ability of our Khora-thian bodyguards. Remember, they are very slow to commit, but when they do, it is steadfast, and they never fail in keeping a commitment they have made. This core attribute is deeply woven into their culture."

"Hey, while we're on our way to the hotel, maybe we could stop by a local establishment and try some of the Meri-torian beverages!" says Deon, changing the subject.

"Or maybe we could have a beverage of your choice brought to your accommodations," Aioli suggests.

"Well, the restaurant would be nice as it will also give us a chance to observe some of the locals," says Steve.

Aioli frowns. "That, captain, is exactly what I am con-cerned about. However, I think I know just the place. Driver, make the next left," she adds in Meritorian.

They pull over in front of a bustling entrance. Aliens of all types can be seen heading inside.

Deon raises his right hand and says in excited "home boy" vernacular, "Ah... now this is what I'm talking about, son!"

Steve high-fives his buddy.

Aioli looks a little perplexed but is nevertheless amused by the gesture. "I would like to try!" She holds up her four-fingered hand. Steve and Deon slap her hand at the same time. She is amused.

Steve is excited at the prospect of getting to mingle with the locals, but puts on his "I'm not impressed yet" face as they all walk into the restaurant together. The crowd, for the most part, does not seem to notice the first-time Earth visitors. They make their way to a table along the wall and are invited by a staff member to be seated. Steve and Deon look around as if their heads are on a swivel. They know they will have great stories to tell for a lifetime.

* * *

The SCCC crews have been working around the clock to prepare the cargo vessel. The space cargo ship (SCS) Lloyd Newton is being prepped for immediate launch. The hand-picked crew is in the briefing room getting ready to complete their preflight inspection and to board the craft. Maintenance is completing the weapons test before the final approval for flight.

The ship is small enough so as not to draw attention yet can surface-land on the moon. It is also large enough to accommodate the remaining crews. The flight director visits with the crew personally and wishes them a safe passage before they launch. They run through their checklist then launch. The ship is a little more sluggish than usual due to the extra weight of the new weapons. They head for Earth's moon as if they're making a standard cargo run to Moon Base Alpha.

As they get to the opposite side of the moon, out of view of the SCCC, they begin their journey toward the stranded crews. Estimated time of arrival: five Earth days.

* * *

Steve, Deon and Aioli are now seated and enjoying their drinks. There is an amazing light display— even the glasses they are drinking from light up and change color in tune with the room—and a variety of entertainment is going on throughout. But perhaps the most intriguing feature is the wall known as the "true to life" that spans the entire length of the establishment. It displays all that is going on in their world—almost like a transparent news channel with a combination of random spying all at the same time.

"Aioli, is there any way you can influence the Brajeh's decision to save our people?" asks Steve. "You must have some influence—or if not you, perhaps your superiors?"

"Steve, I assure you, if I could I would. This goes above my position and circle of influence. It is also possible that they have information that they are not willing to disclose, at least at this time. The Brajeh is a reasonable and excellent leader. He listened to you and I believe he will take what you said under great consideration. After all, it is his desire to form an alliance with your people."

Just as she has finished speaking, a seemingly irate and impolite Meritorian approaches. He starts speaking to Aioli in their native language and it is obvious that he is furious. Aioli tries to de-escalate the situation, but the more she speaks, the angrier he gets. Suddenly he grabs her arm in an attempt to force her to stand up. Deon, who is sitting directly across from Aioli, immediately kicks the back of the Meritorian's knee, simultaneously striking him in the throat with a "ridge hand" maneuver. The alien is surprised by the attack and falls to the floor.

Aioli yells, "Deon! No!"

The Meritorian recovers with lightning speed and grabs Deon by his clothing, literally tossing him into the air as if he is a bag of yesterday's trash. Meritorians all around them look alarmed and start to clear the area. Deon lands on the floor with a loud crash, wiping out a set of seats. The Meritorian starts to walk menacingly toward him to finish the job. As he reaches down towards Deon, there is suddenly a whirl of beautiful fabric, and the alien is kicked in the air himself. When he lands, the new aggressor is standing over him, speaking a few words close up to his face. The Meritorian grimaces, gets up and runs away.

As the rescuer turns to help Deon from the floor, he recognizes the face of the female Meritorian: it is Miiya, the daughter of Balan-Gaal.

Aioli rushes over to Deon, extremely agitated. "Deon, that was very unwise. You could have been killed! Remember, Meritorians are at least four times stronger than humans. What were you thinking!"

"That's damn right, high-speed!" Steve chimes in. "What the hell did you think you could achieve?!"

"Aw, you know me... I don't like ladies being disrespected —and more than that, Aioli's our friend. No one treats a lady friend of mine that way! Thanks, Miiya, for the assistance. I was just about ready to get it on and finish him off."

Miiya replies with a grin, "I saw your exceptional strength and skill come to bear as you were flying through the air, Major." She helps him up, taking one of his hands, as Steve takes the other.

"Major, I am truly flattered," Aioli replies, with a distinct twinkle in her alien eye. "No one has attempted to protect me like that before—especially someone from another planet. But I feel this is my fault. I should not have brought you here. I'm supposed to help you. It is inappropriate for a protocol officer to put their charge in harm's way. Next time, please just let me handle it."

"I saw the whole thing. I'll report it and inform your office," Miiya says to Aioli.

"Thank you," Aioli replies.

"And you, Major, need to get ready for your next training session which starts one templect from now," Miiya adds.

"What?" Steve exclaims. "I didn't know anything about a training session—and what the hell's a templect?"

"A templect can be compared to your Earth hours but it is measured in a hundred of our units," replies Aioli.

"I see. What is this appointment about, and who is it with?" Deon says pithily.

"Balan-Gaal enjoyed his time with you so much," replies Miiya, "that he has requested your presence once more! This is such an honor for you!" She is almost dancing with excitement.

Steve pats Deon on the shoulder and says, "I've got to admit, I'm feeling a little left out. Anyway, I'll chill out and wait for you at the hotel, buddy. By the way, maybe its me but I can't help but notice that only you could conjure up two ass-whippings in a couple of days on a foreign planet!"

"Yeah well, lucky for him Miiya showed up because he was about to get himself an Indiana beat-down!" Deon laughs as he heads off towards the waiting transport outside.

＊

The engineers of Space Command have been working around the clock analyzing the recordings of the space battle. They are examining the weaponry, tactics, hardware, software—everything—and coming up with viable solutions to some of the problems they feel they face with Earth's new enemy. Since the quantum cannon had proven so effective against the enemy vessel, all ships are in the process of being retrofitted with quantum weapons, even cargo vessels. Manufacturers of the radar and ship sensor array systems are designing new and upgraded systems to enhance the ship's capability to give captains earlier warning of this new enemy. This will hopefully result in a faster response time.

The video of the attack highlighted the fact that the physical strength of the aliens was alarming. It was suggested by the military medical and physical training community that not only did our troops need improved body armor, but strength enhancement as well. This request has been on the drawing boards for years and today a solution will be devised. Manufacturers are teaming up with unlikely companies to develop solutions; for example, well-known aerospace and sportswear manufacturers are designing and developing a strength-enhancing prosthetic suit for the Department of Defense (DoD). This will give troops greater protection and power against the aliens. Some of the companies involved are Patagonia, Adidas, Nike, Puma, Under Armor, Northrop Grumman, Lockheed Martin and BAE. All teams are working with a great sense of urgency and corporate benevolence. All know the enemy is coming. They just don't know when.

*　*　*

The crew of the Space Cargo Ship (SCS) Lloyd Newton is moving steadily through space. No contact has been made with any alien vessel. So far, so good. Rescue teams are reviewing their procedures and checking all the equipment. They are also going over the possible scenarios they might encounter once they reach the survivors on the alien moon. They are forty-eight hours into their journey and are looking forward to reaching their fellow team members, friends and families on the alien moon.

The two staff members from the Pentagon, as mentioned by the SECDEF, have arrived on the SCCC. They begin their work by first meeting with Director Pickett.

As they walk into the office, Corky makes himself known. One of the gentlemen comments, "Hey, look—they even have a little hairball on the station!"

Corky barks twice in disapproval.

"That 'hairball' is my Bichon, Corky," Director Pickett scowls. "He's the best dog in the world."

"Yes, sir. Of course, sir. No insult intended, sir," the aide replies, now verbally checked by both Corky and the director.

"Let's get to work, gentlemen. Close the door, please. We will go over the video here in my office. No need to share it with the team again. For most of us, seeing it once was enough," says Pickett.

They review the space battle between the Chemdi-Shakahr and Earth Space Command together. The aides are

clearly moved by what they see. Although obviously fascin-
ated by the environment they are now working in, they do not
allow this to distract them from their mission to report any
findings that would raise questions they can report back to
their superiors.

Director Pickett, ever in command, is not flustered by
their presence and continues business as usual. He ensures
they are kept busy with tours and briefings, to keep them
steered away from the controllers monitoring the Lloyd Newton.

CHAPTER FIVE

Assistance Is On The Way

Steve and Deon arrive at their quarters. Deon starts to prepare for his appointment with Balan-Gaal. Steve has not been involved in this process and is feeling a little left out; although he is not a martial arts expert like Deon, he is keen to at least come along and observe, so he asks his friend for an invitation. "You know, Deon, I've never really seen you do your long sword thing—I'd certainly like to observe if you don't mind."

Deon looks at his friend and assures him, "No problem, buddy. I get the sense you've been feeling left out since our first physical session. I'll make sure this time you get a chance to observe me 'getting my butt kicked' as you say, okay?"

A smile spreads across Steve's face. "Thanks. To be honest, even though I know I can't do all that fancy stuff you do, I still enjoy watching you do it so well."

Deon smiles and gives him a punch in the arm. His friend returns the man-love gesture.

They both walk to the light transporters and instantly arrive in the Athletic Center. Miiya is waiting and Deon requests that his crewmember be granted permission to observe today. She nods in agreement and they enter the room. Once again Balan-Gaal's menacing bodyguards are present—not looking quite as on edge this time, though; in fact they seem almost relaxed. Balan-Gaal seems genuinely glad to see Deon, yet a little perplexed to see Steve.

"Ah, major. It is good that you are here," says Balan-Gaal.

"Thank you. It is good to see you as well. My Captain has asked if he may observe—I hope you don't mind."

"Not at all, not at all. My training sessions are usually private but it is obvious that he is not a security risk. I welcome his presence. Thank you for joining us, Captain," replies Balan-Gaal, then continues, "As I reflected upon our last session, I realized that, due to your human physiology, your endurance is not as long as my own. My apologies for that oversight before we sparred. I have provided a gift for you, to assist in this regard. We call it an Alocae-Cha. It will give you faster movement and much greater strength. It also assists us in the virtual-training environment. All of our warriors wear these. I had one made to your specifications."

It was a body enhancement suit. It looked as if it was too flimsy to do anything, resembling a badly made piece of women's lingerie—basically a harness made of wider than standard lanyard strands. Miiya walks over to assist Deon in putting it on. To his surprise, it attaches itself as if it knows exactly where to go on his body. Remnants of light emit from it as it adheres to his limbs.

"Let's take it slow," says Balan-Gaal. You are wearing the Alocae-Cha for the first time. The first time is critical for it must initialize itself to your body first. During that process, if you overdo it, it can overexert your body and cause serious injury. Our warm-up will give it all the time it needs."

As Deon warms up using the movements he first learned when they arrived, Steve joins in. Balan-Gaal and Deon are pleased. They warm up for about thirty Earth minutes, then Balan-Gaal begins Deon's training.

"Today, I will show you some techniques that will be of benefit to you if you cross weapons with the Chemdi-Shakahr. Many of my own people do not know what I am about to show you. I show this to a select few whose skills I know will be enhanced. Those few will be called on to fight the Chemdi if they are needed. These techniques were learned during an actual fight with the Chemdi and proved very effective. You are the first of your species with this training."

Steve is thoroughly impressed that Deon's skills are deemed so formidable that another alien race is willing to share even their most secret techniques with him.

Little did they both know, this knowledge would prove invaluable in their near future.

"I am honored and deeply in your debt," replies Deon.

"I hope you'll never have to use what I am about to teach you, but if you do, it may save your life."

Deon grabs the Shelah and it becomes his long sword. Balan-Gaal produces his own weapon and they begin to spar. It is obvious Deon is a little apprehensive and self-conscious at first in his new suit. Balan-Gaal begins to push him, forcing him to get him to trust it and even use it to its fullest capacity.

"Major, you are faster than that! Stop holding back! I'm going to really challenge you—starting now!" Balan-Gaal shouts. He then starts to whirl his weapons like some crazed assassin.

Deon's eyes light up and he begins to match every swing of Balan-Gaal's blade with his own. It is a deadly ballet that would have killed any advanced swordsmen by now—the type of swordplay reserved only for real experts. This went on for almost forty minutes. Deon did not seem the least bit tired.

"I am really digging this Alocae-Cha," Deon says. He starts warming up for the next round of sparring but Balan-Gaal stops the match.

"Stop!" yells Balan-Gaal. "You are ready." He pauses. Even his security team seemed intrigued. "The Chemdi-Shakahr has four powerful arms. They also have an articulated spine that enables them to pivot almost three hundred thirty degrees. This means they are equally dangerous to those behind them as to those in front. The only chance of defeating them is to anticipate their every move. They telegraph the movement of their arms by slightly raising their shoulders first. Observe the simulation."

Miiya calls up the simulation of a Chemdi-Shakahr. This training session was going to be one for the books. The alien creature looks absolutely real and menacing, with its four eyes of fire and very wide stance—if nothing else, the Chemdi-Shakahr have an incredibly intimidating presence. It sends chills down Steve's as he looks at it. As Balan-Gaal interacts with the simulation, he is right; they do telegraph when they are going to use each arm. He also points out that, because they are so large and wide, it is very difficult for them to attack when an opponent is close in. This is why Balan-Gaal uses two blades, one to engage the Chemdi, the other to strike a deadly blow once in close.

At this point, Balan-Gaal gives him key instruction: "Major, the Chemdi, although ruthless warriors, have a code they live by and do not assuage in its regard: they will fight you with the same weapon—meaning that if you have an edged weapon, they will fight you with the same. It is an insult and dishonor for them to kill you with an advantage."

"Yes, sir," Deon replies.

"Then let's continue."

For the next hour, Balan-Gaal teaches Deon how to use his Chinese long sword partnered with a shorter one. He first tries a Trident like the one Balan-Gaal uses but it is rather awkward for him to handle, so he selects the Japanese twelve-inch Tanto knife. The simulation is not an easy ride; it is as fierce as the real thing. When the beast strikes Deon, the major's suit emits a sensation of pain to prove it. He struggles with the beast, but Balan-Gaal is a patient teacher. Deon gets frustrated at one point. To prove that the techniques work, Balan-Gaal gives each one of his bodyguards a shot at the beast, which they more than dominate and slew in less than ten seconds.

He even has his captain take on two Chemdi, which he does with poise and great success. Balan-Gaal walks over to Deon and brings his face right up close. "By now, you have heard that I have fought and defeated five Chemdi at once. This is true. Do you think I beat them with my sword and Trident, as you say, only? No, Major. I beat them with a vision that their immediate and imminent death would be their only outcome. I saw their fate in my mind before it became a reality. To succeed, you must... do the same. Again!" he yells before turning to Miiya and saying something in Meritorian that Deon cannot understand.

This is just as well, though, because before Deon realizes what is going on, three virtual Chemdi-Shakahr are approaching him. Deon's eyes open wide and he struggles a bit. Then it happens. It is as if he has a fire deep in his belly which then extends to every part of his being. The major strikes a mortal blow to one and he dies immediately. The second takes a little longer but finally dies too. The third has two blades that he seamlessly switches from one of the four hands to the other. He is very good, accurate and fast. Deon is not only better, though; he is focused and is fighting as if no longer needing to think about the mechanics. It is an astonishing deadly dance that ends in the defeat of the Chemdi simulation.

Balan-Gaal then ends the session. He is pleased about the major's performance. The bodyguards do not speak, but the looks on their faces say it all. Deon thanks Balan-Gaal again and shows the sign of respect to his guards, which they heartily return. He even gives a hearty back-slap to the one who had taken on the two Chemdi. Miiya chats with Deon for a little while then catches up with Steve at the light transports. As Steve and Deon head to their quarters, Deon tells his friend that he feels a bit dissatisfied with his performance and feels he could have done better.

Steve gives Deon a reality check. "Hey, buddy—you do realize where you are at, in this whole thing, don't you? First off, if you did not have the ability to do what you already do, they wouldn't have even taken the time with you. You are a human being from Earth! You're freakin' fighting a four-armed alien beast nearly twice your size, four times or more your weight and you killed three of them! Heck, Balan-Gaal's best man only killed two! C'mon, son! Give yourself a little credit!

You are literally doing the impossible. I know you are putting a lot of energy into this but remember this: you're still an outstanding pilot with a great future. You arc not a Jedi knight—and certainly no one expects you to be!"

"Steve, I appreciate your encouragement, I do. I also feel deep inside that there is a reason I've been given this gift of knowledge that I did not ask for. Besides, you know me—I can't do anything halfway. It's a hundred percent or not at all. I appreciate your words, buddy, I do. I'm going to change, eat and get some rest. It's been a long day. By the way, you were awesome today in the Brajeh's court—and honestly, maybe you're the one who's missed their first calling!"

They smiled in a way that only true friends can. Each retreated to their bedrooms and settled in for the evening. Tomorrow would surely hold another adventure in store.

*　*　*

Director Pickett walks down the hallway, the two aides from the Pentagon following close behind and calling out to him—like two pups nipping at the heels of a mailman.

"Director... Director Pickett... sir, can we have a moment of your time please?"

"Gentlemen, as you can see, I'm very busy. Can it wait?" Pickett replies.

"No, sir—actually it's quite urgent. We were looking over your flight logs and we've noticed that one of your cargo ships with a mission to Moon Base Alpha has not returned. Can you explain this, sir?"

"Yes, yes. We have a daily shuttle to the moon and it's not uncommon for the crew to stay a while—get a little bite to eat, chat with the ladies, you understand. Give them a few hours and they should be back. Nothing to be concerned about, gentlemen. So if you will excuse me..."

The flight director walks up and interjects, "Sir, I have those specs on the ship modifications that you asked for. Would you like to go over them now?"

"Yes, Geri. Let's take a look. I've been waiting for those.

Excuse me, gentlemen," says the director, quickly disappearing into his office, Powell close behind. As they get settled in, the director looks at his flight director. "Thanks for running interference for me, Geri. Those guys from the Pentagon are getting to be a real pain in my…"

Geri interrupts. "Hold on, Will—Corky's present."

The dog barks on cue. Pickett smiles. He's happy that his flight director is one of the few people on the station who doesn't give him grief over his dog. In fact, he enjoys how Geri seems to actually play along. Besides, he figures everyone who does give him grief or makes a snide or cute remark is likely upset they can't have their own dogs on the station too. He gets it.

"Besides, our crew should be reaching the alien moon in a number of days. Is there anything we need to be doing as a team? I honestly can't think of anything else we might have missed," says Powell.

"No. In fact, we have done all we can. If we send any more ships, even out to meet them on their return, it will raise too many questions. Besides, don't forget what we're all doing here is an act of treason."

"Don't remind me. There are any number of things that can go wrong. I just keep praying that they don't. By the way, we have three more ships retrofitted with quantum cannons. We have about twenty more ships to go."

"Just keep at it and don't forget to keep an eye on our crews. They're working over and above what they are usually accustomed to. There will be injuries and maybe even some accidents. I don't want to lose anyone, Geri. We need all hands on this one."

"I got it, skipper. I'll stay on it," Powell replies.

* * *

Colonel Suh has completed the surgery on the crewmember, successfully removing a metal shard from her leg. She has sedated her so she may rest. Two crewmembers have died from their injuries and have been placed outside the shuttle for recovery when the rescue ship arrives. It's been a long four days for the seven shuttle crews and they are getting a little edgy. The post-traumatic stress due to their recent experience in battle, the loss of their captain, shipmates and ship, seems to be settling in. This is the first time that many of the crewmembers have ever experienced real combat.

In shuttle three, a female crewmember starts to cry uncontrollably and is comforted by another female crewmember. Captain Lewis has requested that during Colonel Suh's rounds to the shuttles, she discuss the effects of post-traumatic stress with all crews. They only have one more day until the rescue ship arrives. The mood of the crews is somber, hopeful and sad. Some are still mourning their loss. Others are focused on surviving for their families' sakes. This has been an incredible experience for all and one that will bind them together for the rest of their lives.

* * *

The Space Cargo Ship (SCS) Lloyd Newton continues on her course to the alien moon. They have approximately twenty-four Earth hours before they arrive. They are as prepared as they will ever be. The captain has ordered all crews to stand down from drills and training so they may rest—he wants them all to be refreshed for their mission.

Steve and Deon are sitting on their balcony talking about what they would like to eat and going over the day's events. They know that this is an experience of a lifetime and will be told over and over to family and friends if they survive this. Suddenly the door chime sounds. Steve gets up to answer. He has learned a little more about their quarters—for example, he just needs to wave his hand across the door in order to literally see right through it!

"Ah, hey, lover boy—this must be for you."

"Why? Who is it?" Deon replies.

"I said lover boy, so you had better hope it's not a male. It's your alien lady friend and she's NOT dressed for physical training, brother! Hey, I thought your girl was the one! What's her name again?"

Deon leaps from the balcony chair and hurries to the door to see what Steve is seeing. As he approaches, he says, "Very funny—and it's Ilene. Wow... for an alien, she's really hot."

"I'm going to stay in this evening. You go and have a fabulous time. Don't forget, we're waiting to hear from the Brajeh. If he comes back with a positive answer, I'm going to want to go immediately so don't get lost—and stay out of trouble, Luke. Okay?"

"Roger, Master Yoda," Deon replies, snapping a British salute.

"Well don't just stand there—open the damn door!" Steve snaps.

Deon opens the door and Miiya walks in with a very elegant swagger. She greets both men. Steve and Miiya then disappear back onto the balcony, slightly out of view, but still within earshot.

Miiya says very sweetly, "Your performance today was outstanding. The bodyguards are still talking about it. For a human, you have done a pretty good job of impressing them —and, trust me, of all the security team members that serve, they are very hard to impress.

"Well, your father is a very good teacher," Deon replies. "By the way, what brings you here?"

"I was wondering if you and the captain would like to get something to eat? You must both be famished after that workout."

"Well, he said that he is going to stay in for the evening so he'll probably order in."

"Well, perhaps you would like to get something then," Miiya says. "Besides, I believe you said that you would join me in seeing my special place?"

"You know, I did—and I always keep my word. Okay, dinner and the special place. Let me change and then we are off."

"We are off?"

"No, no—it's an Earth expression. I meant to say then we

will leave."

She smiles. "Oh... very well."

Deon and Miiya exit the hotel. Waiting outside is what looks like a motorcycle without wheels. She boards and Deon joins her. Restraints automatically secure both riders. The machine lifts and begins to fly silently low across the ground at remarkable speed. There is no wind force due to the force field around the vehicle.

"Hey, this is really cool," exclaims Deon. "There's no wind."

"I turned on the protection to make you more comfortable. I will remove it."

Before Deon can get any words out, the wind fills his cheeks and they flap like the cheeks of a Boxer dog sticking his head out of a car window at fifty miles per hour. He tries to speak but to no avail. Finally, he pats Miiya on the back to get her attention and she cloaks the vehicle again with the force field.

"I'm sorry—did you say something?"

"Yes—I actually liked the protection. I'd like to talk on the way."

"So why did you not tell me? Funny Deon," she giggles.

She flies through the city, which is vibrating and pulsating with life and wonder. Meritorians are definitely a lively bunch; they appear to love life and they celebrate it. This becomes increasingly apparent as they continue their journey through city. Before long, they exit the city and enter the countryside. It is unlike anything Deon has seen before— all around them is a type of forest, but truly unique, with an abundance of delicate flora and fauna. The rock formations seem to be embedded with what looks like jewels and pearlescent stones. Miiya veers off into a beautiful meadow and lands the craft. She grabs Deon by the hand and heads up a small hill then down to a beautiful little clearing that has obviously been used before. It is breathtaking. Waterfalls cascade in the distance and a stream flows in front of them. The water, however, is completely silent.

Deon walks to the stream and scoops up the alien water. "What is this called?"

"Reeya."

"Reeya? Reeya. On Earth, we call something similar to this water."

"Otter?" Miiya says.

Deon chuckles and repeats, "No—w-a-t-e-r." He says it slowly this time, with more defined pronunciation.

"Water," she repeats perfectly. Miiya smiles as if she has won a prize, then quickly begins preparing for their late-evening dinner. The suns of Meritor are exchanging places, the bright sun going down and the muted sun rising.

Deon looks at Miiya. This is a different side to her—she seems almost giddy. Deon is a little embarrassed that she is focusing her attention completely on him now. Sure, he's dated other girls—in fact, he remembers that he is in a committed relationship, and if Ilene were here, she would likely be very hurt and even angry.

"This is my special place," Miiya says. I come here to rest my spirit and get away from the rigors of being a security officer. I like the way it calms me and makes me remember what my life could have been like had it not been for the goodness of my father."

"He seems like a very interesting Meritorian," Deon says.

"He is. In many ways he is mysterious as well. I think sometimes that he has not joined again because of me."

"That may not be correct. He may have simply loved his Cojourn so much that he chooses not to join again. That often happens on Earth as well. I also recall Aioli was saying that your father's family was killed. Perhaps he is still mourning their loss. It could be any number of reasons. I would not immediately assume that his not being joined again has something to do with you."

Miiya smiles as if relieved. Then she cocks her head slightly to the side and slowly approaches Deon for a warm embrace. She hugs him more than what is usually acceptable in a new relationship. "You are a very interesting Earth man as well."

"So… hmm… what made you become a security officer?" Deon asks, feeling a little overwhelmed.

"When my father took me in, I hated him at first. My parents were killed by the Meritorian guard during a rescue attempt from the Chemdi. I was lost and afraid as a young Meritorian female. He was hard on me and very demanding. He made me do many things I did not want to do and for a very long time. As I grew, I developed what you would call… disc… ipline?

"Yes, that's right"

"Many of the things he taught me became part of me and I loved him for it. He showed me how to not be afraid anymore. He earned my respect. He is a person who is highly respected and is second to no one in combat on the planet, yet he is still gentle enough, with me, to make me proud that I am his daughter. I have grown to admire these and many other things about him. So it was only natural to want to be like him. So, Major Striker of Earth, you are very capable and a highly intelligent astronaut. Is there someone on Earth that is joined to you?" Miiya asks.

"Please, call me Deon—and yes, I am in a relationship, but I am not joined yet. We call that married on Earth."

"On Meritor, we are available until joined, right up until the very moment."

"Wow, that must make for a very interesting wedding," Deon chuckles.

"Wedding?"

"Yes—that is the name of the Earth ceremony when we are joined."

"We call that Dlem," Miiya says.

Once she has finished setting the blanket with the food, she sits and signals to Deon to join her. As they eat, they talk about Earth, Meritor and the similarities and differences.

As they both finish eating, they reach for a drink at the same time and their eyes meet. They both feel a little embarrassed, but a mutual intrigue is growing.

Deon asks another question to squash the awkward moment. "So, besides coming here and going to the restaurant you saved me at, what else do you do for fun?"

Just as he finishes asking the question, his Zehrea sounds off. "Major Striker!" Deon looks shocked. An image of Aioli is projected in the air before them. "Major Striker."

"Striker here," he replies.

"Your presence is needed at your quarters. The Brajeh has come to his decision!"

"I'm on my way! Thank you. Striker out!"

Miiya and Striker start to pack their picnic. Miiya heads to the craft to load everything back in. As she turns to climb aboard, Deon puts his hands around her. Her cheeks blush a beautiful blue and he startles her with a short kiss.

"That is very strange to me, Deon. Are you not happy for our time together?"

"No, no—of course I am. This is an Earth custom when we are grateful and like the other person we are with. It is called a kiss. Okay, what do Meritorians do when they feel this way toward each other and they wish to show it?"

"We do this..." She takes the back of her hand and begins to gently rub it on the back of his neck."

"May I try?" Deon asks.

She seems even more shy now than before. She nods sheepishly.

Deon is intuitively careful and gentle as he returns the gesture. She closes her eyes in utter pleasure, seeming to grow weak at the knees—so much so that she gently takes his hand away. "This is Poaghh," she says, now visibly flustered. "We have to get you back. The Brajeh awaits."

Deon replies with muted laughter, "By the way, what is this called?" he asks, pointing at the craft.

"Dlong-dlong."

She hops on the craft as if she is an Earth motorcycle cop about to go after a speeder. Deon jumps on the back and they head off to the complex to hear the Brajeh's answer.

* * *

Captain Lewis and Colonel Suh awake in the shuttle. They eat a light breakfast then prepare to exit the shuttle. They notice that the air in the shuttle is growing increasingly stale. The filters are working fine, but many of them have not showered for the last two days so it is par for the course. The females were especially unhappy about the hygiene side of things. That said, the captain had ordered, as he had done two days earlier, for all the males to exit the shuttles for a time to give the ladies a chance to freshen up. He did not want a female mutiny on his hands.

Despite the smell, all the crewmembers are grateful they have survived up to day five. Captain Lewis and Col. Suh had reassured everyone that today was the day they would be rescued. They are happy and wait in eager anticipation of clean showers, real food and the comfort of being on a larger vessel as they head home.

They will need some rest, but they will not be released until they have each had a physical evaluation by the flight surgeon. That will also include a post-traumatic stress disorder assessment and, if needed, counseling. The bodies lying outside the shuttles are a stark reminder of their terrifying ordeal. There will be more challenges with this enemy in the future.

The Space Cargo Ship (SCS) Lloyd Newton is now only hours away from the moon. The rescue teams are eager to get started. You can feel the electricity in the air. The captain has given the order to sound the "red alert." All guns are manned and all systems are go. The Lloyd Newton is fitted with a prototype array that has been modified since Space Command's initial contact with the Chemdi-Shakahr, to give the captain more advanced notice, resulting in a better reaction time. No contacts have been detected so far. They are almost there. He will not transmit signals of any kind until they are in visual range of the moon. This will help them from being tracked long-distance in case the enemy is still on the station.

***

Deon and Miiya enter the astronaut's quarters where Aioli and a number of Meritorian security and staff are waiting.

"Boy, am I glad to see you," Steve says upon seeing his friend. "We're on our way home!"

"What's the decision?"

"The Brajeh wants to assist your crews on the moon," Aioli says. "He is prepared to send three Meritorian battle vessels to provide cover. You will both rendezvous with your people. The problem is we don't know how close they are yet so we have to move quickly. However, the Brajeh has requested to speak with you before you leave for your journey."

"Hey, do we really have time for that?" Deon asks.

Steve looks at him, with an annoyed look on his face. "Aioli, what is the plan if we miss the rescue team? Deon and I still must get back to our planet and debrief with our people."

"I have been given limited information, commander. We will hear the remainder of the plan when we meet with the Brajeh. For now, we have prepared and readied the space attire you arrived in. My team will assist you to get them on. We don't have any more time."

The astronauts are dressed quickly by the efficient Meritorian staff, then whisked away in the waiting transport. They arrive at the Meritorian military facility where the Meritorian ships were already launching into space. The place is chock-full with security due to the Brajeh's presence. They are escorted into what looks like a miniature replica of the Brajeh's throne room. The Cojourn is not present. The Brajeh is sitting on his throne and is clearly a little more aggressive in his movements and tone.

Aioli steps forward and addresses the Brajeh. The chime is rung and Aioli begins. "Mighty Brajeh, we have come at once at your request. We ask you to now honor us with your wisdom, direction and wise counsel."

The Brajeh replies, "The board senses, as do I, that the Khorathians are up to their old methods. As it may take time for your people to weigh and consider our invitation to an alliance, we wish to give them as much time as our mutual enemy will allow. All that you have witnessed and will tell them may not convince them of our reality. We will therefore send an advisor and trusted emissary to assist you in this regard, as a last resort. There is no more time—you must leave now. Whatever questions or direction you need, our emissary will provide. The hearts and spirit of Meritor be with you."

The Brajeh rises, as does his entourage, and he quickly departs. Aioli, Steve and Deon look at each other in amazement —they are just as uninformed as they were before they arrived.

Suddenly, a Meritorian officer approaches. "This way, commander," he says, leading the way to the entranceway of a waiting ship. As they approach, they all recognize the guards waiting outside the doorway. Suddenly out of the ship comes Balan-Gaal!

He bellows, "Captain! Major! Your time has finally come. We hope you enjoyed your stay. When you return, you'll not have to go through that ordeal again!"

Steve replies, "Balan-Gaal, I appreciate that—and we have enjoyed our stay."

Balan-Gaal approaches Deon as he exits the awaiting ship and says. "Major Striker!" He then hands him and Steve an elegant-looking bag covered in designs and markings unlike anything they have ever seen on Earth.

"For you—gifts. We have never given one of these to any other alien species. You two are the first. It is your Alocae-Chas. You may need them." He then proceeds to give them what look like the Shelahs from the Security Center, but the material these are made of is crystalline in nature.

"These are personal gifts from me," Balan-Gaal continues. It has been a pleasure meeting you both."

Both men thank him. Balan-Gaal pulls Deon to the side for a moment. "Major, your skill will take you far. Do not forget what you have learned here. I also look forward to... how do you say... workout... with you again."

Deon smiles a huge grin. Just as he is about to reply, Balan-Gaal walks slowly over to the major, kind of like a president would to his press secretary, and says in a voice barely above a whisper, "Oh... and... one last thing..."

There is a pregnant pause that seems so long it could have accommodated the reading of the Declaration of Independence. He continues, "Miiya has spoken very highly of you... Safe return."

Utterly flabbergasted at the fact that Balan-Gaal seems genuinely okay with him dating his daughter, Deon replies, "Thank you for the gracious gifts. I will use them with great pride in honor of you and the Meritorian people."

Miiya has been there since they left the hotel. She also pulls Deon aside to have a short word with him. She looks at him is if studying every detail and feature of his face, her demeanor pensive. "Deon, I have enjoyed meeting you and our time together at my special place. I would like very much to see you again. Will you return?"

"Miiya, I enjoyed our time too. I cannot tell you what the future holds, but if at all possible, I will certainly try. Take care and be safe."

Miiya hugs the major in the presence of all and sneaks him a kiss on the cheek. Deon is overjoyed, despite feeling a little embarrassed.

The emissary the Brajeh mentioned has showed up—and to their surprise, he is a Khorathian. He glides onto the ship without fanfare or introduction and takes his seat.

Once all the members are aboard the ship, security begins to depart from the dock hallway. The ship requires a single pilot, yet there are two. It thrusts away from the docks and pitches up into the Meritorian sky with impressive speed. As both pilots are pushed back into their seats, Deon thinks to himself, "The Relentless is nothing like this!"

* * *

The aides from the Pentagon are clearly suspicious and are following their hunch like a dog with a fresh bone.

Director Pickett is sitting in his office when there is a knock at the door. "Come in!" he says.

The aides enter, obviously annoyed. They know that the director is hiding something but they dare not accuse him directly. "Sir, forgive us for the interruption, but we are having a hard time finding that ship. Your records show that it never landed on the moon. Can you explain this, sir?"

Pickett replies, "You know, gentlemen, there is a lot going on right now. We're retrofitting twenty ships for an imminent attack. We have skeleton crews working around the clock. We're essentially preparing for war. We trying to prepare for whatever the President or SECDEF will direct us to do next. Essentially, we have a lot on our plates.

"To be candid, I don't like your insinuation that I am not aware of my operations or that we're so incompetent that we routinely lose ships! We understand that you are here to observe and report your findings. Let me remind you that you are also guests here. You may continue observing as you were, or you are welcome to do so from inside your quarters, if you get my meaning. I am not concerned, and my people will find the ship. However, a sole cargo ship does not make or break the operation. In fact, you should be more interested in the retrofits of the battle cruisers. These are the first we are installing. You would do well to gather valuable information to communicate to your superiors when they have to repeat the process on Earth. Do we understand each other?"

"Yes, sir. We apologize, sir. We certainly didn't mean to...."

Just as they are about to reply, the flight director, who was listening outside the door, enters with additional information.

"Excuse me, Will?" says Geri Powell.

Pickett replies, "C'mon in, Geri. What you got?"

"Thank you, sir. We located the ship. I forgot that I authorized the flight crew additional flight time for training purposes. We have a number of crewmembers who needed more flight hours for their upgrade training. We are training as many as we can on an accelerated program in preparation for war. They should be back in a few days.

"Great! Well, gentlemen—there you have it. Is there anything else?" asks Pickett.

"No, no, sir. That makes perfect sense. We're going to visit the maintenance area now and look at the retrofit process, as you suggested. Thank you for your time." The aides scuttle out of the room looking a little like dogs with their tails between their legs.

Pickett waits for them to clear the room before saying, "Great input, Geri. How did you know?"

"I overheard the conversation as I was about to enter your office."

"Good catch. Have we heard anything more from our team?"

"In fact we did, sir. They are less than an hour away and all teams are prepared. They have not encountered any enemy activity thus far. However, we do have one problem, sir: we won't be able to recover all the shuttles—there are simply too many including the ones already aboard the ship."

"We should stay long enough to salvage whatever parts we can and scuttle the remaining shuttles," Pickett replies.

"Roger, sir. I'll send the message," says Powell.

* * *

As the Lloyd Newton approaches the thirty-minutes-out mark, the captain tells the COMO officer to initiate the homing beacon. This will initiate a secure signal that only Earth ships are able to detect and decipher, meaning that any Earth ships in the vicinity will see and hear it. This includes all of the shuttles now on the moon. The communication panel in all shuttles will sound an alert for a few seconds when a Space

Command ship is approaching, even if the main aircraft power is turned off.

"Beep! Beep! Beep!"

The ensign is first to hear it. "Did you hear that?" he asks.

"Yeah, I did! They're here!" the yeoman cries, "We're saved!"

"That must mean they're at least thirty minutes away!" the ensign yells.

Tears of joy and sadness flow simultaneously aboard every shuttle, accompanied by crying, hugging and high-fives all round. Even Captain Lewis and Doctor Suh share a moment. It is a joyous occasion. Captain Lewis instructs the pilots to bring the shuttles to full electrical power and to prepare for departure. He dispatches details to police the bodies outside the shuttles in order to speed up the extraction process. Medical teams will take care of the dead when they arrive.

* * *

As the Meritorian ship makes its way to their moon, the Brajeh's emissary remains silent. Of course, Steve isn't going to stand for that, and in his uniquely friendly way, he reaches out his hand and strikes up a conversation. "I don't know if you speak my language so here goes. My name is Steve Wilory and this is my co-pilot Major Deon Striker. How shall we address you?'

The emissary hesitantly reaches out his hand as well, not quite knowing what to do with it. Steve solves his quandary and saves him from his embarrassment by grabbing his hand and shaking it firmly.

"We have collected enough language data from you and your major while you have been on Meritor. I have studied the language files and have learned your language. You may call me emissary."

"That's great—so we can communicate," Steve says.

"I have a question," Deon interjects. "You said they collected the data while we were on the planet. Exactly how did they do that?"

"Well, major, you did not think your Zehrea was simple a communication device, did you? It collects all data about you —your body temperature, changes in your chemistry, voice, even brain activity. Once they have enough of a profile, they can tell whether you are afraid, or authentic, even if you are about to commit a crime against the Meritor inhabitants."

Deon sits silently, an astonished look on his face, as if he has been forcibly undressed. "Boy, I feel violated! So my conversation with Miiya at her special place, conversations between Steve and I—everything?"

"Yes, of course. Because you are foreigners here, I'm sure they had to further confirm that you were not spies. There is no reason to be embarrassed, major. I expect the same—or even worse—treatment when I arrive at your Earth."

"So are you one of the Brajeh's bodyguards?" asks Steve. "Is that why you came with us?"

"I would not say that. I am chief of all of the Khorathians that remain on Meritor. I am the oldest and most experienced of the group. I am the equivalent of three hundred forty-two of your Earth years old. I was once chief strategist on Khorath— you might say on Earth an expert in plans, strategies, tactics, and operations. Many of the battle procedures and methods used by the Chemdi-Shakahr were authored by me."

"I see now why the Brajeh selected you—who better to send, especially during a time when war is at hand," Deon says.

"We are honored to serve with you," says Steve, "and I am confident that we will reach an agreement for an alliance. So what is our plan, emissary?"

"In this matter I have sown much thought. Without the knowledge of those I will be dealing with and the level of fear to make an alliance with an unknown race, I think it is best to keep it very simple. By that, I mean war is coming at any moment. The Chemdi will not expect Meritor to fight as well so we have the advantage of surprise. Once the enemy is convinced that their efforts to wage a battle with Earth are not going to be easy, they will slow their attacks—but they will certainly never quit. Convincing your people of this is the first goal."

"If we miss the rescue ship, how will we get to Earth?" asks Deon.

"This is a possibility. We will simply take you to your Earth and start our mission."

"It almost seems too much to achieve in such a short time," says Steve. "Our people can be hard to convince. However, the attack on our ships and lost crew may have been all the convincing they will need in order for them to listen to the Brajeh's proposal of an alliance."

"Let's hope you are right, captain. With your people's help, it is quite possible to defeat the Khorathians and the Chemdi."

* * *

Back on the Space Command and Control Center, Chief Kelly is receiving communications traffic on a secure signal from the (SCS) Lloyd Newton. "Go ahead, sir. We read you loud and clear."

"Yes, Ma'am. This is Captain Beavers of the (SCS) Lloyd Newton. We have arrived at our destination and we're beginning our approach to make a surface landing. We will commence rescue operations immediately after we land. We want to get in and out ASAP (As soon as possible). We have received a message from the director and will proceed as instructed."

"Roger, sir. Please keep us posted. Space Command out." Due to the sensitivity of the mission and all communications surrounding it, Chief Kelly writes a small note and will hand-carry the message to the SCCC director personally.

Captain Beavers and crew have successfully completed their surface landing of the (SCS) Lloyd Newton. He receives the OIC (officer in charge) of the surface detail, Captain Lewis, and welcomes him aboard. They discuss the immediate needs: to get the injured to the sick bay and to quickly begin to take on the remaining survivors.

Captain Beavers informs Captain Lewis that not all the shuttles will be recovered and at least three will have to be scuttled. He graciously gives Captain Lewis first choice as to which ones they will be. Once these have been decided, the crews immediately dispatch to remove all serviceable parts in the time they have—two hours. Captain Beavers does not know the status of their enemy and he wants to do as instructed without being detected.

The Relentless is still on the ground, its condition unknown. Captain Beavers instructs his pilots to take a look at it, to establish whether it can be recovered as well.

* * *

The planet Rhakmeh is the home world of the Chemdi-Shakahr. The captain of the now-destroyed Mok-Tar has escaped with a few survivors and returned to Rhakmeh in the captain's launch. Upon arrival they are met by other Chemdi, who turn over the alien prisoner, Major Todd McNeal. From there, they will escort him over to Intelligence for screening and interrogation. As he walks through countless halls and doors, he finally reaches his destination. The room is dank and cold, with barely enough light to see his hand in front of his face. He is stripped of his clothing and secured on a slightly upright oversized table. What looks like surgical instruments are laid out on tables to the side of him. McNeal is in the worst possible position anyone could be in. Even if he runs, where can he go? There seems to be a lot of commotion going on behind him. Four more Chemdi enter the room and two more roll in a rather large machine. They begin hooking wires and cuffs to his body.

His eyes wide and his breathing becoming increasingly erratic, he yells, "What are you doing? What is this?"

His words fall on deaf ears. They pause for a moment, look at each other, then continue with no sign of remorse or concern. They affix a helmet-like apparatus to his head and turn on the power. He screams as tiny needles penetrate his skull to contact with the brain. Blood is now dripping down his face. He is still alive, but there is no relief for the pain. He urinates and finally passes out.

The apparatus is the Chemdi method of mining mnemonic data from their prisoners. Having found in the past, that days of senseless torture generally prove ineffective, today they prefer this method, which enables them to obtain more data than expected. They can also see and record whatever data they want, like on a movie screen.

The Chemdi revive him—as the subject sees their own images, other thoughts are triggered, thus revealing more information. The pain is grueling for the major. He starts to see the Relentless and images of the ship's cockpit. He recalls the coordinates of the cave and now sees himself looking down the hole in the cave. His memories are all over the place, but each one reveals a little more information about the crews, the ship, and humans in general. Even his most private thoughts are revealed for all to see. McNeal is embarrassed as these even include time spent with one of the female crewmembers on board the Colin Powell.

It seems like an eternity, but finally they appear to have all the information they need, and remove the device. One of the Chemdi applies a ray to his skull; the pain immediately evaporates. A Chemdi soldier carries the major, who is too weak to walk, to the holding cell. They leave him a bowl of something that looks like oatmeal soup with crawling organisms in it and exit. McNeal does not know how long he is going to be there. He remembers his Air Force survival training; he sniffs the food, tastes a little bit, then eats it all to give himself the best chance of surviving for another day.

* * *

The Meritorian ship is quite fast and they should be at the Meritorian moon in about one hour. The ship's hull has multiphased shields that constantly modulate, fooling other ships' sensors into interpreting it as a hole in space—a very fast-moving hole. That said, the Meritorians have little reason to be concerned about being detected by the Chemdi-Shakahr or anyone else.

"Emissary," says Steve, "I noticed the great starships leaving Meritor as we were leaving—where were they going?"

"Ah, captain, you do your people well by being so astute," says the emissary. "I look forward to meeting more like you. We do not discuss such matters with outsiders, but seeing how we are working together by order of the Brajeh, I see no security threat. I will tell you. As a cultural tradition amongst our people, we like to practice "Frala"—I believe in your world you would say: "Being proactive." Khorathians and Meritorians, now more than ever before, do not wait for outcomes; we make them. Thus, in anticipation that the Meritorian alliance with Earth will be ratified, Meritor is positioning its ships in your solar system not far from your planet Earth, to await the Chemdi attack."

"Wow," says Deon. "You guys aren't kidding around!"

"Kidding?"

"No, no, emissary," explains Steve. "He is saying the Meritor people are serious about their commitment to Earth even before there is an official agreement. I too am impressed."

"What you must understand," the emissary continues, "is that the enemy Khorathian leadership has done all of this before. They will not be surprised or impressed by your ships and weaponry. If they are defeated, they will only return at a more opportune time. During that period, they will simply gather as much data about your people and planet as they can, to determine what they can exploit. They have time on their side so their main strategy is patience. They will only seek to cause you to use and expend your resources, to wear you down until they determine the best time to strike again."

They continue their journey through space. They have approximately thirty more minutes to go before—hopefully —contacting the rescue team on the Meritor moon.

* * *

The pilots from the Lloyd Newton access the condition of the Relentless. The maintenance records indicate that the repairs have been successfully completed and all that remains to do is a test flight. The Lloyd Newton has a second crew on board that will bring the Relentless back to base. The vessel's configuration is fairly standard and designed for ease of use, enabling it to be flown by any qualified SCCC pilot.

The technicians have finished removing the last salvageable parts from the shuttles to be scuttled and are now setting the last remaining charges. Their time estimate is accurate and the captain of the Lloyd Newton is pleased. The technicians begin to run toward the ship then enter and secure the hatch. The captain gives the order to lift off and the helmsman lifts the ship slowly, increases his ascent until they feel their bodies being firmly pushed down in their seats.

The new "Relentless" crew lifts off as well and starts their ascent into space. The ships are about five thousand feet from the moon's surface and out of range of the blast radius. The shuttles blow up with a spectacular light show. Dust and debris are thrown miles high into space. Nothing will be left behind to reverse-engineer. The captain gives the order to the communications officer to inform the SCCC that he is now a two-ship formation; he has the survivors and is on the way home. The mission is nearly complete.

CHAPTER SIX

Meritor Emissary Confabs With Earth

Director Pickett sits in his office, his furry companion on his lap. He is looking over the progress of the retrofits to all of the ships and the numbers are looking good. Even so, he is still not satisfied; he feels like there is a piece missing to this whole puzzle. The Space Command and Control Center was designed and built for such a time as this—the first roadblock for enemies from space. He is unsettled because he knows little about the enemy except that their technology is more advanced than ours: he does not know how many ships they have, or their exact capabilities. He needs more information! "It's like fighting a bigger, faster, and stronger opponent in the dark," he says to himself, "and he's the one with the night vision goggles!"

Flight Director Geri Powell looks round the director's door. "Boss?"

"Come in, Geri! I appreciate you showing me the respect to knock, but just come on in damn it! If I had two beautiful brunettes on my desk, I would've locked the door!" he laughs.

With a big smile, his eyebrows raised, Geri replies, "Yeah, sure—that'll be the day. Then I'll have to ask, 'Who are you and what have you done with my director's body?'"

They both share a good laugh. Geri continues, "Boss, we have good and bad news. The Lloyd Newton is on its way back with the survivors and the remains of the dead. The Relentless is flying in formation with them. I have cordoned off a special maintenance bay to provide privacy for the Lloyd Newton.

The Relentless will go to her usual dock. That said, maybe you can call a meeting with the pointy heads from the Pentagon to distract them while we receive the ships?"

"Sounds like a great idea. I'll set it up. How much time will you need?"

"Oh, at least two hours."

"I want the bodies prepped and stored in the morgue for now. It's a shame I have to do this. I know it must be difficult for the families, but until the President lifts that damn order and we can come up with a way to explain how we got them, this is the best we can do," says Pickett.

"Roger, sir. Ah... the bad news is we still have no contact from the original "Relentless" crew. It's not looking good, Will," Geri says before exiting the office.

* * *

The Meritor ship is slowing, to approach the Meritor moon. The astronauts are excited to see it again—but as they approach, it is very clear that they are too late. The hulls of the shuttles are now nothing but black ash and rubble on the moon floor. There are footprints leading to the landing area where the rescue ship landed. Furthermore, the Relentless is gone!

"Well, that's just fine and dandy!" says Steve.

"Hey!" yells Deon. "They took our bus! I know one thing; if somebody stole my iPad, I'm going to be pissed!"

"This sucks," says Steve. "Well, one thing is for certain; according to SCCC policy, the aircraft has to be secured and inventoried. They will mark and retain everything that was on board, especially personal items. We should be able to reclaim our belongings later."

"Well gentlemen," says the emissary, "looks like we are all going to be traveling to your planet together. Pilot, proceed."

The ship's pilot sets the coordinates and heads for Earth. It will not take them five Earth days to reach Earth, like the Earth ships; they will arrive in about one and a half hours. They will literally beat the rescue team to the SCCC. Once they arrive, you can be sure, there is going to be a whole lot of explaining to do!

* * *

The Chemdi have forwarded the data collected from the brain of Major McNeal for analysis and comment. The Khorathian High Council has reviewed it and asked that the Chemdi investigate the wormhole moon to see if they can enter it as well. Based on the data extracted from the major, they think it's worth a try. If they can successfully send two Chemdi through the wormhole and reach Meritor, they can send a signal to Rhakmeh and achieve a fix. They can also send more Chemdi and establish a stronghold on planet Meritor. They will send a ship to explore this possibility. There are risks but the Khorathians will not suffer the consequences—the Chemdi will—and if it is possible, they will complete the mission.

Back on Earth, the President has requested a special allocation of funds to meet the need to complete the retrofits of all the Earth ships in the maintenance docks on Earth. He wants to include in the same package monies to develop and build more spacecraft. The U.S. Congress is debating the justification for these funds. Although they have seen the classified video footage of the space battle and the destruction of four Earth ships, they are still on the fence about spending over a trillion dollars.

The passing of such a measure is pivotal because even though this is a global effort, The United States and her sister ally, Great Britain, always lead such initiatives first. In other words, if they fund it, the other countries will follow suit— basically, The U.S. and Britain foot the initial bill and the supporting countries pay them back with interest. So far, they are in deadlock and they do not have the votes to pass the bill. If they filibuster this, the ships will not be ready when the Chemdi attack. At this point in time, even if they had all that they needed, they still may not get all the required ships ready in time. As it is, they have four to replace due to the space battle. There are tooling requirements by the manufacturers for some of the parts needed and long lead times associated with them. Besides, they are already producing something else. It looks like something major is going to have to happen to get everyone on board.

As the Meritor ship approaches the Earth's solar system, all the planets can be clearly seen. They got a glimpse of Saturn, and are now passing Jupiter, Mars, and in the distance there is the "blue marble," Earth. They slow as they approach. They avoid the moon, in order to keep from interfering with moon space traffic and maintain station-keeping in space just on the other side of the SCCC. The ship is not visible to the naked eye but at close distance a decent array can see an anomaly in space. However, ships in the immediate area would have no reason to sweep this close to the SCCC, and the SCCC's arrays are sweeping outward into space. This explains their current position.

The Meritor ship is equipped with light transporters, just like in the hotel, but they can point them in whichever direction they want and can transport at great distances. To avoid panic, Steve wants to transport in an area that will not draw too much attention. They need to speak to Will Pickett and Geri first. They don't know who may be in Pickett's office; it is usually teaming with all kinds of people. However, Geri's office is not so busy... that will be their target.

Before they leave, the emissary gives them what looks like a Zehrea but it in fact provides for communication between the three of them and the ship. The pilots will stay on board for support. He has selected an area that should be the FLIGHT office. It appears to be empty at the moment so Steve and Deon are going in. Once they explain what is going on, they will introduce the emissary.

Dressed in their spacesuits both men stand on the pads. They fist bump for good measure and are beamed to Flight Director Powell's office. They arrive perfectly in the center of the office—damn, how they love Meritorian technology. They take their helmets off and set them on the table in the corner of the room. They each take a seat in the chairs in front of his desk and wait.

Just fifteen minutes or so later, they hear Geri Powell's voice as he comes up the hall. They both stand and turn toward the door. Geri enters, looking directly into Steve's face. He looks as if he's seen a ghost.

"What the hell! You're supposed to be... How did you get... What are you guys doing in my office?" Geri hugs them both hard and shakes their hands. He's obviously genuinely relieved that they are alive.

Steve speaks in a very measured and calming tone. "Don't be alarmed. We know you guys have been worried about us. We also know about the battle and what happened to our ships. But we're back and we have a lot of critical information to give you, Will and our government."

"You're damn right you do—and we're going to-hell-to freakin' Pickett's office right now!" Powell says.

"Geri, if you don't mind," Steve says, "we don't want to be seen just yet. Would you kindly make sure the hallway is clear before we move? We don't want to cause a panic."

Powell, eyes still wide in unbelief, looks at them both as if he's been slapped with a fifty-pound tuna.

"Well, ah... sure... that's... ah... that's probably a good idea," he stammers. "Just wait here." He bolts out the door, closing it behind him.

Director Powell is sweating profusely as he walks a short way down the hall. The hallway is clear and he blasts into Director Pickett's office.

"Will... You are not going to believe this... I have Wilory and Striker in my office! That's right—my office! They say they know about the battle in space, and they have important information for us!"

"How in the world did they get here? Well, don't just stand there—bring them in. I'm clearing my schedule!"

Powell checks the hallway once more. There are a few

people passing by and he waits outside his office door as they walk by. They clear and he opens the door, signaling to the astronauts to follow. They walk along the hallway towards the director's office. As they enter Pickett's office, he is as calm and collected as usual. However, the look on his face is serious and penetrating. He shakes their hands slowly and speaks.

"Well, gentlemen, it is good to see that you are alive and I'm glad I haven't lost one of the best crews at the SCCC. We were all very concerned. I'm sure there is a perfectly sound explanation as to why you have been out of contact for nearly three weeks—so let's hear it. By the way, how did you get here?"

"Ah... we got a ride from some of our new friends," says Steve. "Director Pickett, it's a long story so I'll just jump right in. After we had radioed in, we became bored and decided to explore the moon. As we did, we came upon an unusual cave, of which we radioed in the coordinates. We came upon a huge hole that was unnatural and we wanted to climb down a ways to at least obtain some rock samples. There was a tremor, our climbing devices failed and we fell. We thought we were goners. To our surprise, a wormhole opened up and we found ourselves transported to another civilization."

At this point, the look on Pickett's and Powell's faces went from penetrating to surprise. Steve continued, "We were captured, interrogated as spies and released. The planet is called Meritor. Their civilization is far more advanced than ours. They housed us and treated us very well. In fact, we met their Brajeh... king. There is so much more to tell you, but in the interest of time, the Meritorians are aware of the battle we fought in space. This is the same enemy that destroyed their former planet. They used the wormhole as a disguise to relocate their people to their new planet. The enemy is actually two species: the Khorathians, who are the brains and the command and control; and the Chemdi-Shakahr, who are the muscle. This is the enemy who engaged us in space and destroyed our ships. The Meritorians fought them before and will

125

do so again, but they want an ally this time. They would like to propose an alliance in order to defeat the Chemdi-Shakahr, who are now headed for Earth."

There is a pregnant pause as the two men desperately try to wrap their minds around all that they have just heard. This is a lot of information to absorb in a short period of time, even for these educated, intellectual men.

"So you are saying that the people... Mer-i-t-o-r-i-a-n-s, want to help us?" asks Pickett.

"Yes," says Steve. "In fact, with the anticipation that we will agree to an alliance, they have already dispatched battleships to our solar system to help when the Chemdi attack."

"What do they want? If they want an alliance, why didn't they send a representative as well?" asks Powell.

"That's a great question," says Deon. "They did. We just wanted to give you a short brief before we introduced you to their representative who they call the emissary."

"Well," says Pickett, "of course I think the people of Earth would be interested in an ally if their intentions are pure. The question is what will it cost us and how do we know they won't take over our planet as well? How do we know that both species are not working together? Either way, this is way above our heads and we'll obviously have to pass this up higher. We would still like to meet the emissary in an effort to learn more about what we're going to say to the President and staff."

"That's a good question—and you can meet him right now," says Steve. He taps the communication device and tells the emissary to beam to his current location. Almost in an instant, there he is, standing there in their midst. Steve and Deon are amused to see the looks on Pickett's and Powell's faces—simply priceless.

CHAPTER SEVEN
The Emissary

Corky is not one to be left out of anything, especially this particular meeting. In his spirited manner, the little dog runs over, sniffs the emissary and sits down next to him, as if to say, "This guy's all right." Everyone in the room is amazed.

"What manner of creature is this?" asks the emissary.

"That's my dog," replies Pickett. "He's a Bichon Frisé. His name is Corky. He is but one of over three hundred species of dogs on Earth."

Corky suddenly pops up from the floor like a piece of toast out of a toaster, runs over behind Mr. Pickett's desk and leaps into the porthole window—his favorite place to sit. Only this time, he begins barking, as if something is outside— not a friendly, excited bark, but more of an alert, a warning. Director Pickett turns and looked out. The same old view as always.

* * *

The Chemdi-Shakahr arrives at the wormhole moon to investigate. They enter the cave and are looking at the great hole, which they have seen many times. The Chemdi commander lures two of his troops toward the hole. Without notice, he pushes them in. As they fall, the wormhole opens and they are gone. The Chemdi commander immediately informs High Command. They are pleased and unsettled at the same time, having no idea where the ill-fated Chemdi have gone. They suggest to the commander that he send a team through with a long-range communication beacon so they can get a fix on the destination on the other side. It could very well be the new home world of the Meritorians. They prepare the beacon as ordered and are ready to follow orders.

On Meritor, the security minister observes the Chemdi ship landing on their moon and making their way to the wormhole cave entrance. He quickly alerts the security chief, who is not surprised, having anticipated that the Chemdi might have determined the location of the cave and its purpose from some of the prisoners of the Earth vessels.

Balan-Gaal sends teams to engage and arrest the two invaders and then immediately orders a redirection of the wormhole. He will direct it to a planet that Meritor has previously banned—a highly hostile planet that is environmentally harsh due to its high temperatures, and replete with deadly creatures of every kind. These creatures are viciously predatory in nature; they fly, crawl, swim and burrow under the ground in the pursuit of their prey. Most are efficient, silent hunters and ultimately show themselves to their prey when it's entirely too late. Hunters from Meritor used to test their hunting prowess by hunting the creatures on the "Banned Planet" but too many hunters were lost and the planet is now banned for Meritor citizens. If the Chemdi chooses to send any more troops through the wormhole, this is what will await them.

* * *

A middle-aged couple has set sail for a late-night cruise out of Bermuda Harbor on their Beneteau 57 sailboat. It is a gorgeous night and they want to see the stars, share a bottle of wine and spend some quality time together. They do not venture out very far —just a little before "Bowditch Seamount." They drop anchor and open a bottle of wine to begin their ten-year wedding anniversary celebration. Laughter fills the air as they enjoy the celestial canopy of stars and some great conversation—no talk of work or household stuff; just quality one-on-one relationship talk. The view is glorious. They cuddle each other and drink in the moment. The years of struggle and sacrifice building their business begins to wash away. This moment is absolutely worth it.

Unexpectedly, the winds start to pick up. Having sailed for many years, they know that this is strange; there isn't a cloud in the sky. The winds are getting stronger now and as they look into each other's faces, they decide to reef the mainsail and lower the jib. They had wanted to stay out a little longer but for safety's sake they decide to come about and get back to Bermuda.

Suddenly, about two hundred yards away, the sea looks as if it is boiling. Whitewater is being thrown twenty or more feet in the air. The water appears to be boiling and bubbling over an expanse of about four square blocks in size. Although scared, the couple feels compelled to stay and observe the phenomenon. The boiling water seems to subside and eventually calms, leaving a swirling froth of whitewater on the surface. An object appears in the midst of the foamy waters. It looks like a person. The husband immediately jumps into the dingy and heads in the direction of the body in the water. It's a man dressed strangely, like a space officer of some sort. Although he's unconscious, he seems to be alive. He pulls the man into the dingy and heads back to the sailboat.

They drag the man on board and begin to head back to Bermuda as fast as they can, radioing in to the Bermuda Rescue Coordination Centre (RCC) for medical attention. The RCC replies that they are quickly dispatching a vessel with medical personnel to meet them and recover the man.

* * *

Back on the SCCC, the director addresses the alien (The Emissary) standing before him in his office. This is the last thing he would ever have expected to experience today when he woke this morning.

"Hello. I'm Willard Pickett, director of this Space Command and Control Center. This is my flight director, Gerald Powell."

"You can call me Geri," says Powell.

The emissary does not waste any time. "To answer your question as to whether our intentions are pure, they are. It's a matter of survival. We can go to war with the Khorathians and Chemdi ourselves. The fact is, we will incur many casualties and lose many valuable resources in the process. Since they have not found our home world so far, their focus is now on Earth. It would be Frala to assist you in their defeat and gain an ally at the same time. This is a Khorathian strategy that is sound."

Steve Wilory chimes in: ""Frala" is their word for pro-active."

As a look of confusion descends over the directors' faces, the astronauts bring them up to speed on the enemies and their relationship and history. The emissary fills in the gaps. In a little less than an hour, they understand with greater clarity the events leading up to the current moment. Director Pickett is pleased and has a clear vision about what to say to his superiors.

As for the astronauts, they are to go and see the flight surgeon first, get refreshed, fed, and prepare to go to the surface where they will be debriefed by military intelligence. The director tells them that following their debriefing, they will be free to return to their families for twenty-four to forty-eight hours—but even that was tentative; they could be called back at any time.

The emissary will return to his ship until they have a clear game plan as to when he will have an audience with the President and staff. They all understand that time is of the essence. Its now beginning to make better sense—except for the fact that the director's dog has been acting strangely. Corky has developed a sudden obsession with something outside—although when the director looks out to see what the matter is, he sees nothing. Nevertheless, the little dog is emitting an odd growl and will not leave the window.

* * *

The prisoner was released as planned. The helmsman did exactly as instructed by the commander and deliberately submerged the spaceship near the sailboat of the human couple. They will take the bait: the former human prisoner. Once he's released, the gathering of Khorathian intelligence will begin. Although the ship is a Chemdi-Shakahr vessel, the ship's commander is Khorathian. They entered Earth's solar system and Earth's atmosphere undetected. The inhabitants of Earth obviously cannot yet detect the ship's signature through the modified shields. So far, the commander is pleased with the crew's performance. Here they will collect intelligence for the coming attack and invasion of Earth. They will provide recon for the Khorathians as well as resources to complete missions of subversion, sabotage, and terrorism to confuse the enemy.

The ship also has on board specialists in the biomedical adaptation of intelligence-gathering devices. They create and surgically insert intelligence apparatus into the bodies of their victims; the devices tap into the body's nervous system so they can hear, see and influence the host to do their bidding on a limited basis. This technology also doubles as a way to terminate the host when necessary. With such simple creatures as humans occupying the Earth, it will only be a matter of time before Earth is added to their collection of conquered worlds.

* * *

The couple pulls into the harbor and the patient is turned over to the Bermuda Authorities and transferred to King Edward VII Memorial Hospital. He is extremely disoriented and, though he tries to speak, cannot be readily understood. His Space Command credentials give them a clue and they call to verify his identity. When they say his name is Major Todd McNeal, there is a stunned silence at the other end of the phone. As the doctor explains how he arrived at the hospital there in Bermuda, Space Command leadership is adamant that they make him comfortable but keep him there until their people arrive to collect him.

* * *

Steve and Deon are in a shuttle headed for Space Command Headquarters on Earth. They have already received their clearance from the SCCC flight surgeon and will be debriefed on Earth before taking some much needed time off. Seeing the United States from their current altitude is a sight they have missed for some time, and they are looking forward to seeing their family and friends again.

The shuttle touches down at headquarters. Security is waiting for them as they exit the ship.

"Security?" Deon exclaims.

"Yeah—I don't like the looks of this," replies Steve.

They are quickly escorted to a boardroom where various government types are waiting. As they sit at the table with a pitcher of water and two glasses before them, the questions begin. For two hours, they are asked question after question in an effort to determine whether or not they are fit for duty, as well as whether they have been turned into spies by this new potential ally. Lie detector specialists are brought in to assess them further.

Both astronauts pass with flying colors. The Space Command team is amazed: every story, every account regarding the wormhole, the planet Meritor, the Brajeh—all of it—is told in earnest, with no detection of any form of deception in their voices or physiology. This will all be rolled up and briefed to the CIA, NSA, and other agency directors, even the President himself. They are given their final exit brief concerning what they can and cannot say to family and friends under threat of being charged with treason and imprisoned. Captain Wilory and Major Striker acknowledge that they will remain silent and are released. They walked out together, say their goodbyes and go their respective ways. They will try to enjoy the fruits of their labor for as long as their superiors allow it.

* * *

Aboard the Space Command and Control Center, Director Pickett is finishing his official statement and forwarding it to Space Command Headquarters. He is exhausted from the tempo of the day and is ready to retire to his quarters for some much needed sleep. Flight Director Powell has been running the SCCC while the director prepared his report of the astronauts' return, the Meritor emissary, and all the rest. Director Pickett is trying to wrap his mind around meeting another intelligent species for the first time. He's concerned for the crews and his staff on the SCCC, who could be in harm's way at any moment. He knows there are going to be casualties—and maybe a lot of them. All of this is almost too much to bear.

Just then, Flight Director Powell enters the office. "Will? You won't believe what I just got in."

"What's that?"

"Todd McNeal has been found... in Bermuda."

The director looks at Powell to determine whether or not he's kidding and realizes that he's dead serious.

"How the hell did he end up there? The last time we saw him, he was being taken by those monsters on the Colin Powell."

"The doctor says he's talking, but it's nothing he can understand at the moment. Space Command is sending a team to bring him to headquarters."

"Just when I thought my day could not get any stranger!" quips Pickett.

* * *

The Chemdi-Shakahr has received orders from high Command to deploy every troop they have to transport the necessary communications gear into the wormhole. Their mission is to establish a location where they can transmit a homing signal so the new planet can be located and mapped. The Chemdi Commander wastes no time. He sets the ship's autopilot for it to return to base. He commands all Chemdi—approximately one hundred in all—to exit the ship and proceed to the wormhole. With precision, they obey immediately and line up in formation.

Suddenly, the ship's engines fire. It begins to lift off the alien moon. The troops maintain discipline and don't even look at their only ride home, as it takes off before their eyes. It begins forward flight and quickly flies away.

The commander looks at them like only a true warrior could, raising his weapon in the air and pointing it forwards before letting out a war cry like no other. He then whirls about, his cape flowing around him with his movement and he charges into the cave with purpose. His troops follow. The commander leaps into the wormhole with reckless abandon, all four arms and two legs extended, and his troops follow. The wormhole opens with brilliant light and consumes them all. There is no turning back. They will complete their mission or die.

One by one they are thrown out of mid-air and fall to the ground, where they scramble around, desperately trying to get out of the way before another Chemdi warrior falls on top of them. Finally they have all arrived. Disoriented from the intergalactic trip, they slowly start to stand, looking around them. They are located on the very edge of the desert, and can see a plush jungle in the distance. There is also a fairly high mountain—the perfect spot to set up their communication gear and transmit the homing beacon. They head in the direction of the mountain.

The land is lush with green, purple and orange plants that give off an aroma that is almost intoxicating to the Chemdi-Shakahr. They feel almost as if this mission is going a little too well for them, but ignore this feeling and follow orders. It takes almost a full day to reach the mountaintop. They clear a few boulders away with their weapons. There is very little wind to endanger the security of the beacon nevertheless they secure the beacon with self-inserting stakes. They are not sure when nightfall comes on this new world, if at all. They know they have been up for quite some time and the commander gives the order to rest. Like most soldiers, they can sleep almost on command. Chemdi don't need as much rest as humans, but they still take advantage of the order. The beacon is sending a very strong signal and they should get a reply back in a couple of Earth days or so.

Once they were rested and have eaten, the commander announces that the jungle they passed on their way to the mountain would be a good place to set up camp and build shelter until the Chemdi ship comes to extract them. The commander leads the way, all one hundred following. The sun is closer to the planet and the temperature is sweltering. Their capes blow in unison as they move together toward the jungle. As they leave the mountain terrain to cross the desert, there is not a sound but the soft squish of their steps in the sand as they go. It's been about half a day and they're closing in on the jungle about one Earth mile away.

Those in the back of the formation notice that there is suddenly one less Chemdi—and then two, then four. Something very large is moving under the sand. Now that they are alerted, the Chemdi draw their weapons and stop moving, looking from left to right for whatever it is that has taken their comrades. On the right side of the formation, with lightening speed, a tentacle shoots through the ground and another Chemdi is taken. Again, more on the left side. The creature is too fast to shoot at, and if they did while it was taking one of their comrades, they would likely kill him too.

The commander orders them to move out quickly toward the jungle, and the Chemdi obey with impressive speed. The creature is incensed and shows itself. It is the same color as the sand and has the look of a crab with the horny tentacles of an octopus. A few of the Chemdi fire at it, hitting it with plasma blasts. The creature rewards the shooters with a seventy-five-foot toss in the air. It lets out a terrifying screech, and three more creatures appear from the sand.

The commander yells for them all to move to the jungle. The Chemdi are fast, but the beast covers a lot more ground in just a few steps. The plasma blasts seem to slow the creature down and the remaining Chemdi continue to close in on the jungle. As they arrive amongst the trees, the beasts are not slowing. The Chemdi spread out. Another deafening and different screech cuts through the air, immobilizing the Chemdi and the inbound creatures. The sound is coming from a charging centipede-type creature with long legs as thick as an elephant's. It has beaked mouths on the bottom of its body. It quickly closes the distance to the inbound crab-like creatures, ignoring the Chemdi altogether. It rises and pounces on two of the crab-tentacle creatures. Bright-green goo squirts out like a faucet, splattering some of the Chemdi, as it starts to devour two of the creatures at the same time. The remaining two creatures fall back and retreat back into the sand.

The commander points up toward the trees and the troops follow and start to climb. One of the trees looks a little thicker than the others. A Chemdi scales it nonetheless. As he gets toward the top, an eye opens and the "tree" screeches, eating him with a loud crunch. It then unfurls its wings and flies straight up, circles and pounces on the centipede-like creature, and begins to eat it. The commander climbs rapidly down the tree and signals to his troops to retreat further into the jungle. His troops follow, only about eighty-two now in all.

* * *

Steve pulls up to his familiar home. It's about 2:00p.m. The girls should both be in school. His wife's car is in the driveway. He had called his wife Jean as he left headquarters. Oh, how excited he is to be home. He has only just closed the car door when his wife bolts out the door and jumps into his arms. Her legs wrap tightly around him. He drops his gear on the lawn as he supports her buttocks. Her blond hair covers part of his head as she hugs and kisses him. After over twenty years of marriage, she stills gives her man a hero's welcome.

She had been so scared; she knew that the Space Command and Control Center wasn't telling her everything and she knew something was wrong. She's just glad to see her man come home. He lets her down and she grabs his gear. They head straight up to the bedroom to get reacquainted then take a long nap.

* * *

Deon arrives at his place, a swank loft apartment—everything in its place and a place for everything. It seems diminished somehow. As he puts his gear on the bedroom floor, he sees an envelope on the pillow where Ilene normally sleeps. He opens it and sits on the edge of the bed to read.

"My dearest Deon,

I have enjoyed the time we have spent together, but my heart aches when you are not here. I realized that I am a creature who needs the comfort of one who will be home more often than not. I will always remember the love you gave me, and how you always made me feel safe. I'm sorry, but the long time away is too much for me to bear. I will always love you.

Love Always,

Ilene.

Her clothes and toiletries are gone. He immediately tries to call her number, but it has been changed. He thinks to himself, "Some homecoming."

He pauses for a moment, then goes to his closet and picks out his most comfortable jeans, white linen shirt, his black gator cowboy boots and black leather motorcycle jacket. He leaves his swank condo to enter the sanctum of the garage to reunite with his longtime somewhat sinister-looking friend: his modified Harley-Davidson Softail Custom. A jet-black beast with fine metal-flake gold trim that's shot with three coats of clear, and gold accents also on the front of the raked forks and front and rear wheels, which are also painted glossy black. The handlebars are short in comparison to those of most bikes and feature small but very bright turn signals at the very ends. It has a low-profile seat that can accommodate two. The flat-black two-in-four, down-swept exhaust pipes make it look extremely angry, only to be upstaged by the three-hundred-millimeter tire in the rear. This bike screams "Bad-ass on board!" He puts on his low-profile half helmet, kicks up the kick-stand and fires it up. It starts the first time, grumbling with it's rough, idling legacy Harley sound, only with a guttural twist, courtesy of the headers. He revs it in the garage to announce to the night what's coming and rolls out slowly before heading to his favorite bar. He has spent a ton of money on this bike, which is nothing short of a rolling work of art—and as daringly unique as its rider.

It's a nice ride through the streets of his hometown. The city lights reflect off the glossy black iron horse. Its ride is smooth and deliberate. He can feel the eyes of guys and gals staring at him and his bike as he slows to a stop at the traffic lights. He gives the engine a small rev for good measure, making them all wish they were either driving it or riding on the back. The traffic light turns green and he lets the engine roar unapologetically as he speeds off. Even those with no interest in motorcycles would be hard-pressed not to be impressed by this beast of a machine.

He pulls up to the bar and parks his bike on the end next to three others. It stands out like a king in comparison to the other bikes parked there. The three owners of the other bikes look at him with barely concealed scowls.

"Hey, there, pretty boy—you got a nice iron horse there!" one says.

"Thanks," replies Deon.

He makes his way inside and sits at the bar. The three guys also come in and take a table. Deon orders a drink, looks at the television to see what's on and minds his own business. A group of ladies at a table start to take bets as to who will dare go over to speak to him first. They giggle like cackling chickens. Deon sees them, nods his head and smiles a small smile then looks back at the television. One of the girls musters up enough courage to take action and walks directly over to him.

"Hey, handsome!"

Looking as uninterested as he can, he says, "Hey."

She flashes a perfect smile and says, "My name's Christy— I'm wondering if you'd like to help me with something?"

"Depends on what it is, Christy."

"My girlfriends have a bet going to see which one of us had the nerve to come over and kiss you... I volunteered."

"Oh you did, did you? And why would you want to do something like that?"

"Because you're very handsome and you seem like a nice guy who wouldn't mind."

"I see. And without sounding like an opportunist, what's in this deal for me?" "Well, maybe we can work that out later. The bet is for one hundred dollars."

"I see. Sounds reasonable."

He immediately stands, glances at the three guys at the table, looks at the girlfriends and looks back at Christy, who is indeed a gorgeous specimen of a woman by any standards.

He brushes back her silky black hair so the three goons can clearly see, and puts both hands on her hips. She stares at him, her eyes open wide. He slowly comes close to her face, about a half inch from her lips, and looks her directly in her eyes. Her eyes close and he gives her a classic "Cary Grant" kiss, in front of everyone. Her girlfriends let out screams and cat-calls, drawing further attention to the two kissers. Deon pulls back slowly, leaving one hand on her hip for effect. He then cocks his head to the side as if to say, "Is that what you were looking for?" and retakes his seat. She is stunned. She comes closer to hug him and he, with one arm, returns the gesture.

"Would you like a seat?" he asks.

"Wow. Sure." Feeling giddy, Christy gestures to her friends to pay up, which they gladly do.

Just as they begin with the normal get-to-know-you conversation, there is a tap on Deon's shoulder. "Hey, pretty boy—you think you can just come in here and kiss on our women?" It's one of the angry bikers.

"Guys, you don't want any trouble. Besides, if she where yours, she'd be kissing you instead... I think. Want a mint? Seems like you can use one."

The biker dude's eyes glow with red-hot anger; Deon thinks he looks like a pissed-off troll. The biker rears back to throw a punch. Deon, seeing his projected punch from a mile away, redirects it from his sitting position and pulls his arm in the prevailing direction, with the result that the guy bangs his face on the edge of the bar and is knocked out cold. Everyone who has witnessed the scene cringes on hearing the loud crunch as the guy's head meets the bar. There is a general gasp as the would-be thug crumbles to the floor.

"Uh-oh, that must have hurt," says Deon. He turns to Christy, "Would you like to go someplace else?"

"Yes—like right now!" she smiles.

Deon pays his tab, grabs her hand with his leathered glove and they head for the exit. As they get to the door, one of the other biker dudes gets up from his seat and blocks their way.

"Move aside!" Deon says.

Biker Dude number two exclaims: "Where in the hell do you think your going, you black son of a..."

"Actually, out the door—and so are you." Deon replies calmly.

Now enraged, the biker rears back to throw a punch at Deon. With expert martial-art accuracy, Deon avoids the blow, countering with a swift palm strike directly into his solar plexus. Winded by the impact of this incredibly painful strike, the biker's knees buckle. He crumples like a wet paper bag and falls backwards through the door. Deon and Christy step over the downed biker and proceed to walk to his Harley hand in hand.

Deon spots the third biker coming after them. "Get on the sexy bike at the end of the row," he says to Christy.

She immediately does as she's told. Sirens can be heard in the distance and the crowd is spilling out of the bar to see what's going on.

Biker number three walks up to Deon and draws a nine-millimeter pistol at close range. "I can't let you leave after hurting my buddies like that," he says.

"If your buddies had kept their hands to themselves," Deon replies calmly, "There would not have been any problem Hoss, and you know it. Besides, I was simply defending myself."

"I don't care who you are or what you say—you are going to pay for what you did."

Before the biker even has time to take another breath, Deon has disarmed him of his weapon and is now pointing it straight at his face. The crowd that has gathered in front of the bar gasps in shock at the altercation unfolding before their eyes.

Deon takes the weapon apart, removing all the bullets from the magazine and dropping all the parts to the ground.

"Who are you?" the biker asks.

"It doesn't matter friend. And by the way, you might want to consider getting a new set of friends."

Deon climbs aboard his Harley and puts his helmet on Christy and starts the bike. Christy wraps her arms securely round his waist. He backs it out and rides off with a victorious roar. The crowd is speechless, swearing that they have never seen anything like that except on television or in the movies.

Deon and Christy arrive at his swank condo. Christy is jacked up on adrenalin after seeing such a violent spectacle. The sound of the Harley and the vibration she felt between her legs is almost too much sexual stimulation for her. As they burst through the condo door, she doesn't even see the beautiful place he has—she marches Deon immediately right to the bedroom, each of them removing clothes and leaving them strewn all the way from the front door.

She wears him out for about forty-five minutes then falls asleep. After about thirty minutes of cuddling and basking in the afterglow, Deon gently covers her gorgeous body with his 1200-thread count Egyptian cotton sheet. He steps out of the bedroom quietly, careful not to disturb her, and, standing in nothing but his underwear, orders Chinese food. He puts on the UFC and waits in his favorite chair.

Although his heart is still broken, he takes a minute to embrace the full experience of the evening—the initial heartbreak, then his night out, the beautiful Christy in his bedroom —as well as the experiences of his last few weeks. Certainly Christy's company has made the whole heartbreak episode a little better. He is sure this will speed up his emotional recovery, for he has been in this place unfortunately many times before.

Heading to the kitchen, he opens a bottle of wine and pours two glasses, taking a sip and settling back again in his favorite chair. The food comes quickly. As he begins eating, he hears the familiar shuffle of female feet across his hickory hand-scraped floors. He takes out a porcelain plate for his guest and serves her. They share great food, a few laughs, and a little discussion about how he learned to do what he did tonight at the bar. Then it's on to more "quality time" in the bedroom followed by some restful sleep. Neither stirs until morning.

* * *

The Secretary of Defense is seated on his couch in his office. He has reviewed the interviews of the "Relentless" crew and an additional report from the director of the SCCC. Although it is laid out clearly in front of him in black and white, he still cannot believe what he has read. He calls an emergency confab of his staff at six a.m. the following morning—time is of the essence and this cannot wait. He will not sleep in his own bed tonight; he will rest his eyes, wake, take a shower in the office and be ready for the early morning meeting. One thing is for certain: it is clear that the United States and the world are at great risk and the decisions they are going to make today will define their future for generations to come. They cannot afford to get this one wrong. His staff begins contacting all the major players. After informing his staff to wake over one hundred people, he adds two to the list.

* * *

As the last Meritor battle cruiser joins the other ships not far from Earth's moon, the admiral for the fleet wants to meet briefly with all commanders before the impending battle begins. They have never gone to battle with an unknown ally before. This is no different than any other battle they have fought, though. They are concerned about how to differentiate the enemy ships from Earth ships—they don't want any friendly fire incidents. The admiral is confident that this possibility will be worked out before the battle begins.

* * *

Steve slowly opens his eyes. He is laying his head on his favorite memory-foam pillow, reflecting on how he has always loved the great care his wife has taken in making their home a comfortable retreat for their family and guests. The sheet feels almost as luxurious as those on Meritor. He rolls over toward his wife and smells her fragrant hair. Her body is soft and firm—a result of her diligent time spent in the gym and occasional spa treatments. He is very grateful to have such an elegant, conscientious wife. He knows he's living the dream. He slides out of the bed so as not to disturb her and goes into the kitchen. He hears the girls in the den and shuffles into greet them.

"Daddy!" they shout.

He lavishes hugs and kisses on his little Katie and Laura as only a loving father can. They admire their dad and feel especially safe and secure when he's there. They will likely marry men just like him. He sits and talks with them about their lives and asks genuinely sincere questions while simultaneously listening for any needs they may have. He avoids answering the probing questions they ask about where he's been and why he was so late returning home. He reassures them that he was safe and will do his best to always return as promised.

After reconnecting with them, he walks into the kitchen to grab a beer. He goes outside to the patio and sits in one of the two chairs he shares with his wife in the mornings when he's home. The night sky is completely clear and he gazes at it. His forehead wrinkles as he thinks of the new enemy heading toward Earth. He does not want to alarm his family—in all honesty, if the enemy breach our forces in space, there may not be any safe place his loved ones can go. Frightened people often do stupid things. Having them head off to their cabin would not make sense, especially when the sheriff's office is about twenty miles into town. Their best bet is to stay put. He wants to share this information with his wife, but he cannot. He will simply give her as much direction and guidance as he can.

Suddenly he hears his cell phone ringing in the bedroom. He rushes to answer. Too late—the well-toned arm of his wife hands it to him from under the covers, her head covered with a pillow. He takes the call downstairs. "Captain Wilory."

"Captain Wilory, I'm with the SECDEF's office. We need you to come to an emergency meeting at the Pentagon immediately. We have people on the way to pick you up in an hour to take you to your jet," says an official voice.

"Yes, ma'am. I will be ready. Thank you."

He turns to go upstairs to give his wife the bad news, but she is already standing at the top of the stairs, her arms crossed. "Really, Steve?! You just got home! You said this job would be a walk in the park and that it would provide us more time together. This is not the retired life I had in mind. Does this have anything to do with why you were so late coming home?"

"My love," he answers, his tone calming, "you're exactly right. He makes his way back up the stairs to hold her. I cannot discuss the particulars, at least right now." He pulls her close and kisses her gently. "I love you very much and I want you to be strong for me and the girls. In fact, now may be the time to take them to the range and get them used to using a firearm. Teach them exactly like I taught you. Do you think you can do that? Besides, Katie has been asking to learn forever."

"Steve, you're scaring me. When will you be back? This is not fair! I know, I know. You would think I would be used to it by now, being a naval officer's wife. But you're retired now. They can't just do that to us anymore! We have a life!" She yells.

"Sweetheart, we don't have much time. I have to go to Washington—the Pentagon, to be exact. They're coming to pick me up in an hour. I will explain what I can when I return. Okay? How about a little sugar for big daddy before I go?" He raises his eyebrow and picks her up. She screams with a giggle and they spend quick-quality time together before his ride arrives.

* * *

The phone rings for the second time and Deon knocks it off the table. He leans over to grab it and answers. The SEC-DEF's staff informs him of the meeting and he acknowledges. He is not prepared for attending a meeting with the SECDEF, especially with his hangover—but his military training kicks in and he gets ready for his trip to the Pentagon. He hadn't expected to have to address the brass, especially as high up as the SECDEF. This is going to be interesting. He leaves a note with his number and plenty of cash for a taxi ride home for Christy. She's a sweet girl and he would definitely be open to seeing her again.

* * *

Two federal agents deliver Major McNeal to Space Command HQ, Earth, Cape Canaveral. The medical team receives the major curbside and immediately take him into the lab to begin a full physical workup. He still looks a little dazed and certainly not himself, almost pensive. They will do their best to get to the bottom of what is ailing him and what might have happened to him. The senior staff looks on with great concern bordering on suspicion.

As the doctors look at the MRI scans, they notice three strange little tumors in his body, consistent with scar tissue in the local areas. Doctor after doctor looks at the scans and cannot figure out exactly what they are. They will wait for the labs to come back, but they are leaning towards exploratory surgery. They have a few hours but expect the final decision to be made shortly. Because Space Command is a military branch, the doctors do not need the major's consent; they may do to the patient whatever medical procedure they deem necessary. The decision has been made by the director to proceed with the surgery immediately. Space Command has a state-of-the-art medical facility and will be using robotic surgery to complete the procedure.

* * *

It has been days since the Chemdi-Shakahr arrived on the alien planet. Surely no one would purposely choose such a place to settle an entire civilization. The commander knows that they have been tricked by the Meritorians; he's lost warriors and they have to survive until a ship returns for them. There may be fewer of them to be rescued if they take too long. Never the less, orders are orders. After some time, there is a call from a ship in orbit. The commander gives the captain coordinates to the extraction area. They just may live to tell of their adventure after all. He vows to get back at the Meritorians for this treachery.

* * *

Steve and Deon arrive at the airport at the same time. The opportunity to fly on a corporate jet is quite enjoyable—very few people get to fly this mode of transportation.

The takeoff is smooth and the flight attendant is a hottie. She serves them a wonderful meal...on china and they watch a movie. The time passes very quickly and before they know it, the wheels are touching down.

The ride to the Pentagon is short and swift, and after walking for what seems like forever along its never-ending halls, they finally arrive at the conference room. The joint chiefs of staff are present, together with all the secretaries. Additional staffers and selected invitees are also in the room.

All eyes are on them. Some people appear awestruck, as if the two astronauts are celebrities; some just scowl. The aide directs them to their seats and they all sit waiting for the secretary of defense (SECDEF) to enter and be seated. No one knows what the meeting is about. A military aide walks in like a stiff toy soldier and announces the secretary. All stand and he begins the meeting. "Be seated, everyone. Thank you for coming at such short notice. Nearly eleven days ago at 03:23 Zulu time, Earth Space Command vessels were attacked by a ruthless enemy called the Khorathians and Chemdi-Shakahr. This is a very capable enemy with technology more advanced than our own. Four of our ships were destroyed, as well as most of the crews on board. We understand that we still have crews stranded on an alien moon waiting for rescue. Until the President rescinds his "stand down" order we cannot recover them.

"In addition to the attack that destroyed our ships, data was gathered from one of the ship's computers and it is likely that enemy now knows Earth's exact location. It is also likely that security protocols, capabilities and other valuable data have been compromised and that they are now headed our way to attack and even invade our planet.

"Additionally, as hard as it is to believe, there is a proposal for an alliance from a leader from another world. This same enemy attacked them and their desire is to form an alliance in order that we may fight and defeat this enemy together.

"After having reviewed all the data presented to me, including the battle report video from the SCCC, statements from the crews, and recent statements from Captain Wilory and Major Striker—thank you gentlemen for coming," he adds, turning to the astronauts, "in my mind, there is only one clear conclusion. I am going to brief and recommend to the President that he first rescind his 'stand down' order so that we can recover our people. I will also recommend that we talk to the emissary sent by the leader of this other world and gladly accept their proposal of an alliance.

"Time is of the essence and war can start at anytime. I know that you all have questions, but I cannot answer them now. We will have another confab after I speak to the President and we will discuss the particulars at that time. Thank you all for coming. You are all excused. Keep a tight lid on this until further notice and don't go too far. Captain, major, please stay behind," he adds.

The room clears with the exception of Steve, Deon, the chairman of the joint chiefs of staff, his two assistants, the senior enlisted advisor to the chairman of the joint chiefs (CJCS) and the vice chairman. A total of seven people remain in the room.

The SECDEF begins to speak again but is interrupted by the CJCS. "Excuse me, sir. Sorry for interrupting, but how do we know that this emissary is not working for the enemy? How do we know this is not some ploy to beguile and compromise us from the inside?"

The SECDEF replies, "Mr. Chairman, you are right. I don't know. This is the best intel I have and I am forced to go with what I've got. Captain Wilory, you and the major spent considerable time with our guests—is there anything you might be able to add?"

"Sir, I can do better than that," Steve replies. I can have their emissary explain these and other questions for himself."

You could have heard a pin drop on the plush, burnt-orange carpet of the conference room. Every person present stares, wide-eyed, as the realization that they are about to encounter a real alien for the first time hits them like a ton of bricks.

The senior enlisted advisor replies, "Wait—what about security? None of us are armed."

"Call in the two sentries," says the SECDEF. "They are sworn to secrecy, as we all are."

The sentries enter immediately and Steve taps his Zehrea. "Emissary, please beam to my current location."

In an instant, the emissary is standing before the highest-ranking military officers of the United States of America. Most stand. Some remain seated. Some literally fall back into their chairs. All have a look of awe and wonder on their faces. No one dares say a word.

* * *

The chief flight surgeon is a board-certified brain surgeon. This procedure should be a walk in the park for him. Unfortunately, however, he is not aware that the tissue in the major's body is alien in nature and if disturbed enough will respond. At first, the tissue appears to be wrapped around certain nerve centers. As the surgeon tries to peel away the tissue, it simply re-wraps itself, only a little tighter each time. As he uses the forceps to pull back the tissue once more, a dark green substance is released, which immediately scars the ends of the forceps.

"Oh, my gosh!" the surgeon cries. "This substance is highly corrosive—it's oxidizing my scalpel! What the hell is this?"

His hands shaking a little, he quickly takes a sample of the liquid substance and a small piece of tissue to have them tested in the lab. He surmises that there is nothing more he can do until he gets the lab results back—it's just too dangerous. He leaves the closing of the patient to his assistant and exits the operating room to scrub. Once this is done, he bolts out the door and heads immediately to the director's office.

"Doctor?" the director says, looking up from the papers he is reading.

"We have a problem," blurts the surgeon. In my over forty-five years of practicing medicine, I have never seen tissue like this or tissue respond like this. We have sent a sample to the lab for analysis, but I already know what the results will be: origin unknown."

"Are you saying that the tissue in the poor major is foreign, as in alien in nature?"

"What else could it be? We know he was on the Colin Powell when the enemy took him. Suddenly he shows up here with foreign tissue in his body? Why here and why now? What would an enemy gain by releasing him back on his own planet? I think they may be using him as a human drone. In any case, he has to be quarantined until we know more about what we're dealing with."

"Thank you, doctor—and please do not repeat this to anyone else. Keep me informed," the director says.

The doctor rushes out and the director picks up the phone to make a call to the one person who may be able to shed more light on this.

* * *

The officers continue to stare in awe at the real-life alien. The emissary bows and with great poise and confidence. With patient delivery, he addresses the highest-ranking military officers in the nation. "I am most honored to be in your presence. I am the emissary of the Brajeh of the planet Meritor. I come to propose an alliance with our world in an effort to defeat the imminent attack of our enemy. You are not sure whether I am friend or foe. I ask you, esteemed war leaders of Earth, would a foe simply station warships on the other side of your moon if they were going to attack?"

Immediately, his Zehrea projects detailed and vivid images of the numerous Meritorian warships in space, just beyond Earth's moon. Everyone's eyes open wide as they stare in awe at the majestic ships before them.

The emissary continues, "If we were a foe, your inhabitants would be our servants and your planet would be burning in space—yet this is not the case. We are here as an ally, so that we may learn from each other and live in peace."

The chairman of the joint chiefs turns to the SECDEF. "Sir, I think I can speak for everyone when I say that we fully support your recommendation to form an alliance with the king of Meritor."

The secretary of defense replies, "Thank you, Jim. Your timing could not be better—we have a meeting with him in less than one hour. Let's go! Emissary, we will ask that you enter our next meeting the same way you did here. Chairman, will you kindly contact the Secret Service and tell them of our special guest?"

"Yes, sir," replies the chairman.

* * *

Dr. Thomas Edleton is the premier physician for extrater-restrial studies for the government. He is now retired, after having worked in Area 51 for nearly thirty years. He has seen the most unusual physiology of all physicians in the world—and has now been recalled out of retirement to serve once again. He is brought to NASA to examine the results of the surgery and medical scans. His conclusion is that they are alien bioelectrical data graphs; their purpose is to collect and transmit data collected by the host. This technology has never been seen before and is highly advanced. The question is who is doing the collecting?

His recommendation is to leave it in place and trace the major back to the source. The director agrees and they release Major McNeal to return to his home. A security detail will observe and surveillance will be put in place courtesy of the NSA. Communication will be passed to higher levels in government.

* * *

As the blacked-out SUVs arrive at the White House, the chief of staff greets the SECDEF and staff in the foyer. The secret service director arrives to gather information on the emissary to access whether or not he is a threat. Truth be told, as a Khorathian, if the emissary wanted to kill everyone in the room, there would be very little anyone could do about it. Understandably, the Secret Service is desperately trying to wrap their human minds around something that before today was only a myth—and it frightens them.

They are led to a conference room with almost double the usual complement of security to accommodate the senior staff security requirement. Key players will be present and a deadly incident would be disastrous. They are seated with those already at the conference table: the President, vice president, chief of staff and White House attorney. Staffers and aides line the perimeter.

The President begins. "Thank you, Mr. Secretary and all of

you for coming. I have read your brief and I am encouraged yet concerned at the same time. We do not know anything about these visitors from space. We do not know if they are the enemy or working with the current enemy that is threatening us. At the same time, after seeing the capability of their ships that destroyed ours, we could certainly use the resources they can provide to defend our planet. In essence, we do not have a choice. Is that your understanding as well, Mr. Secretary?"

"Mr. President, my staff and I have been in meetings all this morning. The crisis at hand is urgent. We have met the emissary from a planet called Meritor. He assures us that an alliance with us is the best course of action for all concerned. They have battle cruisers at station-keeping on the other side of our moon and have offered to assist us with our technology. The enemy is ruthless and their intent is to defeat us and make us slaves. Mr. President, an attack is imminent and we need to act now. My staff and I highly recommend accepting the alliance."

CHAPTER EIGHT
What's Wrong With Corky?

The SECDEF looks at Steve, pausing for effect. Then he nods his head.

"Emissary," says Steve, "your presence is requested by the President of the United States of America."

As is the emissary's custom, he immediately appears among them, standing between Steve and Deon, dressed in his usual hooded garment, his hands clothed in his sleeves.

"Hands! Let me see your hands!" the Secret Service agent in charge shouts.

The emissary slowly removes his four-fingered hands from his sleeves and opens them, his palms held upwards. "I am unarmed, people of Earth, and I mean you no harm. I am here as a friend and ally on behalf of the Brajeh of Meritor."

"Lower your weapons!!" the President yells. "I only want two Secret Service agents in this room. The rest of you, leave the room... now!"

The Secret Service agents are miffed; after all, it is their job to keep the President safe, and in their opinion, two agents are by no means sufficient. The President has spoken, though and there is nothing more they can do. They reluctantly leave the room as requested.

"I am Maurice De Lamonte, President of the United States. I must say that I cannot speak for the governments of the entire planet—I can only speak for the United States. Although we are the super-power of Earth, in the interest of time, we cannot allow this matter of an alliance to be bogged down in United Nations' procedure and formalities. However, if we, as a country, make an alliance with you, we are aware that our alliance will benefit the entire planet.

"Maurice De Lamonte, President of the United States..." the emissary replies.

Steve leans in to the emissary and instructs him to address the President simply as Mr. President. The emissary nods his head three times and starts over.

"Mr. President, your internal affairs are of no concern to the Brajeh of Meritor or its citizens. I am here simply to extend an offer of an alliance between our two worlds. It is to both of our advantages that we fight our enemies the Khorathians and the Chemdi-Shakahr. We were defeated once and it is our desire not to go to war this time without an ally. Since the Chemdi attacked your vessels and killed your people, we thought you would be agreeable to such an alliance. We would share our technology, strategies and whatever resources would assist you to defeat this enemy with us. Although we would prefer that you take whatever time you desire to consider our offer, the time of their imminent attack is upon us. We are certain of this. They may already be in your solar system. We have prepared ourselves to help if you agree to our offer, and we do so without any expectation of obligation or reciprocation."

The President is moved by the proactive stance the Meritor ruler has taken toward Earth. He makes his decision on the spot. "Mr. Emissary, as the President of the United States, we accept your offer of an alliance and will set a time to discuss the terms of this alliance in detail."

The emissary bows toward the President. "Mr. President, we gladly accept your offer and I will inform our Brajeh."

* * *

Major McNeal enters his apartment and takes a shower. He's exhausted from all the medical procedures, interviews and interrogations. His apartment has a dank smell of the garbage he forgot to take out. He does so and eats some leftover

Chinese food that was in the refrigerator. He watches a little TV, catches up on the local news and retires. As he's sleeping, he begins to dream. His dreams are of driving to nuclear plants and electrical power plants all across the country. He sees himself taking pictures and observing the security personnel and cameras. The dream is incredibly vivid. He's sweating, tossing and turning on his bed. He wakes to get a drink of water, feeling very disturbed by this dream and wondering why it occurred. Running his hands through his hair with frustration, he looks around the apartment is if it can somehow provide an answer. He knows one will not be forthcoming, at least right now. He flops down on the bed and slowly brings his feet in under the covers. He will continue to have similar dreams like this until they are fulfilled.

* * *

During a confab of key administration leaders, the President comes to the conclusion that Captain Wilory and Major Striker may be too close to the new alien race to be objective and may even be subject to being compromised. He decides to split them up and reassign them to programs that can well use their experience and expertise.

The Brajeh of Meritor has made a special request that Captain Wilory be assigned as their special ambassador, according to the emissary. It is not normal State Department protocol for foreign dignitaries to select their own ambassador. The President realizes that his fear of them being too close should not get in the way of what is important. However, since this is the first celestial appointment, and the gravity of interstellar war is at hand, he takes it under advisement and honors the request.

The discovery by Captain Wilory and Major Striker of Meritor is the most significant finding of this century. No one can deny this fact. The President honors and rewarded them with new roles due to the gravity of imminent war. Captain Wilory (Ret.) has been recalled from retirement by executive order and promoted to brigadier general. He will be the new—

and the first—United States Ambassador to Meritor.

Major Striker, promoted to Lieutenant Colonel Striker, will be assigned as the lead program manager for the weapons retrofits program of all Earth spacecraft. He will head the installation of Meritorian weapons to Earth spacecraft as well as manage the testing, training, and fielding of these weapons. He will be leaving for Area 51 in the morning to take up his new post.

The President has invited them to dinner in the private residence at the White House. He pushed it out three days so they could arrange for their significant others to arrive in Washington. Wilory's wife and their two daughters arrive around noon the next day. No waiting at airports for them— the President sends one of the government jets and a security detail, since Steve is now a U.S. Ambassador.

Deon, on the other hand, simply stays in town at a very nice hotel; he has no significant other—or at least one whom he can disclose right now—so this time he will be going solo.

They meet at the White House and have a wonderful evening with President De Lamonte and his family. He has a girl around Katie's age and a little boy aged seven. The kids spend most of their evening in the Presidential theater watching movies. Mrs. De Lamonte and Jean seem to hit it off famously. The food is amazing and the service even more so.

The President is a real science-fiction buff, so he takes every opportunity to ask questions about their time on Meritor and their experiences in the space program. He loves great stories. It is a fantastic evening. After the storytelling, the President gives his guests a tour of the presidential residence, including the Lincoln bedroom. He is incredibly well informed, not only about all of the historical data on his personal residence, but the entire White House. He is obviously a brilliant man and a true family man as well. He even invites them to stay overnight but it is too much overload for Deon; all he wants is to retreat to his hotel and reminisce quietly about the evening. Steve and Jean accept the invitation. The girls are thrilled. Steve asks if he can escort his friend home and return. The Secret Service accommodate him.

After the dinner, the two long-time friends take a break at a bar in the city for a little "man talk." They share their amazement about their current status and all of the events that have led them here. Steve shares the conversation he had with his wife and family. Deon shares his conversation with his family in North Plate. They are all brimming with pride about him. For Steve, it may mean having to relocate to Meritor. He is not sure of what it will look like, but it is truly an exciting time for both men. They reminisce about missions and times they have shared in the past, and then come full circle, back to the amazing evening they have just spent with the President and his family.

As the evening comes to an end, they stand, give each other a long "man hug" and express their thanks and gratitude for their friendship—neither of them keen to let the goodbye come to an end, as they do not know when they will see each other again.

* * *

Major McNeal wakes the next morning dripping in sweat. He did not sleep very well. After a shower, he eats a little breakfast and heads out the door, jumping into his car and heading to North Anna, North Carolina. He plans to take pictures of the power plant there. McNeal is driving within the speed limit, being careful not to get a ticket.

Two government agents are in tow. They hang back so as to not draw any attention to themselves. It's about a one-hour drive and he is ten minutes from the destination so he stops to get breakfast. He is neither excited nor depressed.

Little does he know he is a human drone for the Chemdi Shakahr and his actions will have devastating results.

* * *

The Meritor cruisers are still at station-keeping on the other side of Earth's moon. The remaining fleet has joined the armada of twenty or more ships. Having engaged with this enemy before, the Meritor captains know that the Chemdi-Shakahr is a ruthless, cruel enemy—cunning and strategically sound. They never expend any resources unless they have a clear advantage and victory is imminent. The captains are concerned about how they will communicate with the Earth fleet. The Emissary may have the final battle plan since he is currently in contact with the humans. In any case, they will engage when the battle starts. They will observe the moments of the Earth ships, and hopefully anticipate their strategy. The captains have all been briefed on the battle at the Wormhole moon. They are aware that the Earth ships, although formidable, are likely out-gunned and not as experienced as the Meritorians at fighting an enemy as seasoned as the Chemdi. In any case, they will honor the orders of their Brajeh and do so to the death.

The Bombardier Global Express comes to a stop at the Area 51 hangar. The cabin entry door opens and out comes Lieutenant Colonel Striker. His new aide, Virginia, is right behind him finishing the notes he's just communicated on the aircraft about tasks he wants to see started immediately. This role will stretch him in ways he has never been challenged before. He's nervous but focused. His team greets him and directs him to an SUV on the tarmac.

"Greetings, sir. I'm Adrian Brown, your coordinator here at Area 51. Basically, you say it—I see to it that it gets done."

"Thank you, Ms. Brown. I'm starving."

"We prepared a brunch for you, sir and all of your senior engineers, project managers and supervisors. We have also arranged a tour of the facility. There are a number of projects already in progress that we would like to show you," replies Brown.

"Great job, Adrian—and thank you for the warm welcome. I'd like to see the status of the projects you are already currently working. There will be new tech coming online and if there is anything that will be superseded by it, I want to stop work immediately on those projects. We have little time to waste and a lot of work to do."

"Yes, sir!"

Lieutenant Colonel Striker is fitting very well into his new shoes as program manager, his superior engineering skills evident immediately. His leadership of the organization is positive and deliberate; he's starting to display ability that people nearly twenty years his senior fully appreciate and respect. He will be making demands of the team very early in his relationship, so he knows he has to build a level of respect and competence early on.

The emissary did not disappoint with his promise to provide Meritorian technology to assist Earth in their fight against the Chemdi. Weapon systems are being delivered so the engineers can start providing solutions for installing them on Earth spacecraft. Since the weapons use a different energy source, provisions for that source will be made on the Earth ships as well. Striker is just the man for this job, and he will make it work. He is eager to have a ship ready to test as soon as possible—the Chemdi-Shakahr could strike at any time. He has pushed aside research and development for a time and made installing the weapons on the ships the main priority. Obviously his teams are not too happy but they understand the immediate need to get the Meritorian weapons fitted as quickly as possible, and they will try not to disappoint their new project manager.

Deon heads to his car and takes the drive home to his government-furnished home. Walking through the door, it strikes him that it is just like his last apartment: empty—no one there. He pulls off his clothes, leaving a trail of items behind him, and hops into the shower. Turning on the water, he leans against the wall and lets the water rush over him. He feels overwhelmed with his new responsibility and what it means if he fails. He thinks about the six-hundred-plus people at the facility and their families, the Space Command, and all those who have died so far in battle. He cannot let them down.

If only his dad were here...

Suddenly, out of nowhere, he starts to cry uncontrollably. He misses his dad very much. Had he been here, he would have been able to comfort and encourage him. The steadfast source of stability he had all of his life was gone at the time he needed him the most. Deon, for the first time ever, feels truly alone.

* * *

Steve used to love the comfort that he used to get while wearing his Space Command flight suit—the colorful patches, the American flag on the shoulder, the name tag with his gold wings above his name and the unzipped leg pocket he stowed his flight cap in. Even so, wearing a dress suit to work isn't so bad. He has a new office in Washington, where his main focus is on maintaining a good relationship with their new celestial ally—he strives to head off any misunderstandings before they start.

He knows that the Whitehouse, like the Pentagon staff, is concerned that the very enemy that killed our people is of the same species representing the Meritor king. The only thing that satisfies their fears for now is the fact that the Meritorian battle group is standing by on the other side of our moon, and the tech they shared with Earth is currently being installed on our ships. That said, Earth is appeased for now. He and Colonel Striker are the only Earthlings to have seen these people and experienced their ways and hospitality. He knows better than anyone, so far, the kind of people they are—and notably that they do exactly what they say they will. He hopes he can keep this alliance together and that it will last.

He is also concerned for his family's future. Will this post require him and his family to relocate to Meritor? Everyone knows that ambassadors live in the host country. He is honored that the President has appointed him based on the Brajeh's unwavering request, and he knows it's the first time this has happened to anyone in history. He does not take the position lightly; he's highly appreciative—however, the President hasn't had the conversation yet about relocating. The urgency of impending war is burying the formalities under the sand for now. He knows that sooner or later, it's coming.

* * *

The sun starts coming up in Newport News, Virginia. There is a small, motorized skiff on its way out to sea. An old fisherman from Batten Bay is headed on his way to Virginia Beach. No fishing for him today, though; he's just going to visit an old friend he heard is under the weather. He's already passed the Naval Ship Yard and is now making his turn south. He sees a majestic aircraft carrier along with one destroyer and a cruiser. It seems to be just an ordinary day like any other, and the morning is glorious. He'd wanted to get started early because he's promised the Missus he'll be home in time for dinner. Throughout their twenty-seven years of marriage, he has always tried to keep his word, especially to his beloved.

As he comes onto his final course, he hears something scrape lightly on the bottom of his boat. He doesn't pay it much attention—it's likely debris of some sort. He continues on his way. A little while later, though, he hears it again— this time more pronounced. He slows the boat engine so as to not damage the prop. He's sailed these waters many times before—knows them like the back of his hand. There should be nothing that would scrape the boat like this in this area of such deep water. As he continues, he is startled by a very loud scraping sound that this time starts to lift the boat. He quickly reverses the engine but to no avail; the boat stops abruptly, so much so that he is thrown forward and falls to the floor of the boat. He stumbles and hears the hull creaking, as if he has run aground on something. There is something pushing on the hull—he can hear it straining from the obvious pressure now being applied. He desperately struggles to grab for the radio microphone. Straightening his cap, he begins to transmit. As he concentrates on the microphone, a sudden noise rips through the air; a long shard of metal has punctured the hull of the boat and rips straight through the carotid artery in his left leg. Water rushes in as the boat tears into several pieces. It sinks in less than thirty seconds. No radio call was ever made.

* * *

A sudden flash of light radiates out for miles. The rounds shot by the alien vessel move at three times the velocity of a naval rail gun round (approximately 16,500 mph). Almost immediately the carrier is hit first, followed by the other two ships moored beside her. They blow up and sink, a millisecond between them. The spectacular explosions can be heard for miles around. Black smoke billows from all three ships, now reminiscent of what the ships looked like during the attack on Pearl Harbor. The damage is devastating. The carrier's hull is obviously broken in half, and one-half of the ship is drifting away from the other. The other two ships are already underwater, only one antenna now showing. People are screaming, running in all directions. Those who were working on or near the ships dive into the water to save others who have been blown into the water. Bodies begin to fall from the sky, littering the dock like fallen birds. The scene is chaotic and pitiful. People are pointing toward the sea where the lethal light originated.

The naval military police race out toward the location in zodiac boats to save a handful of survivors. Other MPs race out to where witnesses say the shots came from. The waters are now just as calm as before. There is no sign of anything except for a little engine oil, a cooler containing three beers and fisherman's tattered baseball cap. The authorities are perplexed. They inform Naval Intelligence. Naval Intelligence is not happy as they inform the Pentagon. The SECDEF is suspicious; the naval joint chief orders the dispatch of the first anti-submarine aircraft available and an SH-60F Seahawk anti-submarine helicopter out of Naval Air Station Patuxent River, Maryland to check out this underwater threat. The SH-60F will be on station in approximately thirty minutes.

The alien vessel is concealed under the waters and its

captain heads south. He is pleased about the carnage he and his crew just caused. He looks forward with great expectation to making more.

* * *

Colonel Striker walks out of his home and gets into his waiting car. As he drives into the facility, he takes a deep breath in anticipation of what the day ahead holds for him. He walks into the meeting and is met by numerous smiling faces. "Good Morning everyone," he starts. "Okay, okay—I give up. Why all the smiling faces?"

The chief engineer speaks excitedly, "Sir, we have been using the tools provided by our alien friends. They are amazing. We are doing the same amount of work in a couple of hours that it would normally take us weeks to accomplish. Sir, this just might work."

Deon pauses for effect then replies eagerly, "Show me."

As they walk into the work area, seven ships are already completed with the retrofits and awaiting function testing. In fact, they are moving so fast, the test crews cannot keep up. As they approach a ship that is being worked on, they can see the alien tools welding and linking all the connections simultaneously, including all the electrical components. It is breathtakingly advanced technology.

"Let's get three test flights scheduled today. If they all pan out, we will test every third ship, to check our quality. The crews can then do the 'shakedown' testing in space. Time is of the essence, people. We have an enemy that is bearing down on us as we speak. We have to do more, faster. We're going to do thirteen-hour shifts—alert all crews," Deon says.

His assistant Adrian Brown approaches in a huff. "Sir, did you see the morning news?"

"No, I did not. What's going on?"

"We've been attacked at Norfolk. They've found a homemade video of the attack. It's incredible!"

He enters his office and immediately turns on the television. Fox News is all over the story, playing the homemade video on a loop. The tech is obviously not from Earth; it's far too advanced.

"They're already here," Deon says. "Adrian, get General Wilory on the phone immediately."

* * *

Ambassador Wilory is at his desk watching the network news in amazed awe. He taps his communicator and asks the emissary to beam to his office. He does so.

"They are here," the emissary says. "A full attack will commence in seventy-two to ninety-six Earth hours—three to four days."

"What was that that destroyed our ships?" asks Steve.

"The Chemdi have landed a reconnaissance vessel in your ocean. Its primary function is to gather intelligence and create chaos and fear. Your people must not panic. It's a very difficult ship to locate but not impossible. We will assist. Advise your people to not to engage it. We will take it from here.

"We're not ready! What do we do?!"

"I suggest you inform your government."

* * *

The SECDEF and staff are in the "War Room" at the Pentagon. The staff is on hold for the SECDEF, who is taking a call from the Meritor Ambassador, General Wilory.

"Damn it!" Says the SECDEF as he slams down the phone.

You could hear a pin drop in the room; all eyes stare fixedly at the SECDEF as they wait in anticipation of what he is about to say next.

"Dan, pull back your anti-sub package. We're going to get help on this one," the SECDEF says to his naval secretary.

"Sir, can you share what kind of help?" says the secretary.

"I don't know the details yet but I'm getting this information from a highly trusted and reliable source. Pull them back!"

"Yes, sir."

The Seahawk crews are trained experts, and are on station in thirty minutes as expected. They deploy the sea buoy and quickly acquire something—although the signal is unusual, they've got a fix and a heading. They can carry up to three Mark 46 or MK-54 torpedoes; for now, though, the best they can do is to communicate what they have found. The SH-60F Seahawk helicopter usually works off of an aircraft carrier and transmits data to the ship. However, since this particular helicopter has come directly from a testing program at Pax River, it is not armed with torpedoes nor does it have a carrier to communicate to—and yet, to their surprise, there is still one showing up on their screen. The crew is perplexed. The operator clicks on the contact. It's not a ship. It's a U.S. Navy Triton UAV! They transmit the location, heading and speed of the contact and indicate that they will continue on their return flight to their assigned carrier at sea. Their job is done.

The first available anti-submarine aircraft was a P-8A Poseidon package that includes a Northup Grumman MQ-4C Triton UAV. [Unmanned aerial vehicle.] The MQ-4C Triton is a Global Hawk modified for the Broad Area Maritime Surveillance (BAMS) program and works in conjunction with the P-8A aircraft.

The U.S. Navy VP-30 Squadron was selected to provide a P-8A Poseidon and crew to locate and destroy the contact. The crew is well aware of the events at Norfolk, Virginia and is motivated to complete their mission—i.e., inflict a little payback. Flying at a maximum speed of 490 knots or 564 mph, the CFM56-7B powered, P-8A Poseidon aircraft (Modified Boeing 737-800ERX) is on station in little over thirty minutes. Although they are based in Jacksonville, Florida, they are about to go on a training mission over North Carolina. The crew has received the coordinates of the contact based on data from the Triton, acquired the target, and is ready to engage. They give the ready signal, and the captain gives the "deploy, deploy, deploy" command. Weapons are away.

Two 600-pound Mark 54 MAKO torpedoes are released, and immediately acquire the target. They will be GPS-guided by the Triton UAV. They close in on the target, going at a blistering underwater speed of 40+ knots (46 mph). Immediately after their deployment, the captain of the P-8A gets a call to cease operations and return to base (RTB). The aircraft commander states he's already engaged the target with two Mark 54s and acknowledges the order. He turns to start the flight back to Jacksonville Florida. The captain and his crew feel astoundingly satisfied that whatever it is under the ocean that killed their shipmates at Norfolk will now get what's coming to them.

* * *

The emissary contacts a Meritorian battle cruiser commander and alerts him of the Chemdi threat in the Earth Atlantic Ocean. The commander acknowledges and begins scanning the ocean as indicated by the emissary. He detects the Chemdi vessel and begins maneuvering his ship into position to destroy the threat. The Meritorian battle cruiser will be detected by Earth's Moon Base Alpha due to the fact he will need to move a little closer to effectively destroy the alien vessel under the sea. As the Meritorian ship approaches, the communication traffic swells from the moon base to the SCCC.

"Director Pickett here. Go ahead, chief."

"Chief, we're getting reports from the moon that sensors are detecting an alien ship approaching," says Chief Kelly

"Okay, Carla—I'll be right there." Corky is barking more than usual, and the director is getting a little annoyed. "Corky, enough!" The little dog turns his head slightly to the right and retorts with a short bark.

The director walks into mission control and comes up alongside Chief Kelly.

"Sir, they sound panicked. They have very little in the form of defensive weapons, and they are afraid they will be attacked like the other ships," She says.

Just as they are speaking, there is a communiqué from the new Meritorian Ambassador.

"Carla, I will take this one in my office," says Pickett.

"Greetings, Mr. Ambassador."

"Thank you, director—but you can still call me Steve. Listen, I have some urgent information for you. There is an enemy vessel in our waters, and the Meritorians are going to take care of it for us. Tell your people on the moon not to be alarmed. They are the good guys and they are helping us. Make sure they do not engage. Besides if they did, it would not be much of a fight."

"Roger, Steve. How do we know who the good and bad aliens are?"

"We're working on that as we speak. We think that we will transmit a special code that will operate like an IFF (Identification Friend or Foe). We will get the details to you as soon as we can."

"Thank you for the information, Mr. Ambassador. I will update my crews."

Steve was glad he had thought of contacting the SCCC; he might have been instrumental in avoiding a serious friendly fire incident. His phone rings.

"Steve—Deon!" booms Striker.

"Deon! Hey, good to hear from you!"

"Better hearing from you, old friend. Hey, I have some important information for you."

"Shoot."

"According to the emissary, we have three to four days before a full-on attack from the Chemdi. Whatever you are doing, you must do it faster and deploy ASAP. We don't want the enemy catching our ships on Earth."

"Wow. Is that what the Norfolk thing was all about?"

"That and more. That's all I have for now. Keep your head down and make me proud out there," says Steve.

"Thanks, buddy. Maybe we can catch up over dinner sometime. I miss Jean's cooking."

"She and the girls would love to have you over. It's been too long. We'll set it up. Talk to you later... Colonel." says Steve and hangs up.

The underwater alien vessel has spotted the P-8A Poseidon and prepares to fire. It surfaces just below the surface of the water and the two gun doors open. They target the aircraft and prepare to fire. As the alien ship fires the rounds at the P-8A aircraft, the ship is suddenly rocked by one, then two explosions. The explosions to the alien vessel change the trajectory of the firing solution and the Chemdi miss the aircraft. The commander is far from pleased. He proceeds to target the electrical power plant that powers the city and releases a volley of six rounds.

The Chemdi's attack on the P-8A results in a loud bang that is heard and felt inside the aircraft. The P-8A Poseidon is hit in the right horizontal stabilizer, also damaging the right elevator. The aircraft is shuddering and seems to be getting increasingly worse. The pilot slows and looks to make an emergency landing. They are in the flight path of Marine Corps Air Station Cherry Point, so they set a course for that airport. The commander has declared an in-flight emergency. Cherry Point emergency equipment will be standing by.

The six volleys fired from the Chemdi vessel were very accurate, disabling electrical power and the reactors themselves, with the result that the reactor's cooling system is now offline, meaning no cooling for the reactors. The explosions can be heard for miles around. Numerous people are killed and scores more wounded. Smoke billows in the sky and alarms are going off all over the facility. Secondary explosions are now heard and people are scrambling to evacuate.

Unknowingly, the intelligence for this attack was provided compliments of Major McNeal. As the major was about thirty minutes way from the blast, the agents were notified of the explosion and told to bring him in. They now have the major in custody and will bring him to Washington.

Three blinding lights are viewed in space from the SCCC, Moon Base Alpha and from most of the people in the Southern Virginia and Northeastern parts of North Carolina; the rounds are leaving plasma trails in their wake as they compress the air. The Meritor ship does not disappoint—the blasts are somewhat quiet at first, growing increasingly loud as they enter Earth's atmosphere and approach the intended target. They hit the Chemdi underwater vessel perfectly. A mushroom cloud similar to a nuclear blast emanates, flash-boiling hundreds of thousands of gallons of seawater. Dead fish and sea life float to the surface on about a nine-hundred-foot radius. The underwater Chemdi vessel is destroyed and alien debris begins to litter the ocean.

The cloaked Chemdi ships, located not far away from the SCCC, want to return fire. Their fleet commander tells them to stand down. His hope is that showing restraint in avenging the death of their fellow crewmembers in the submerged reconnaissance vessel will fool the Earthlings into thinking that the Chemdi are still far off, which will hopefully result in them working to a false timeline as they will assume they have more time to prepare than they actually do.

The President decides to hold a press conference to inform the American people of the situation. He advises them to stay in their homes and take shelter, warning them of difficult days ahead. "The need to be good citizens during this time of crisis is critical to our survival. I encourage you to be brave for your family and friends." He commits to using every resource at his disposal to defend the sovereignty of the United States and Earth, ending with his trademark words, "May God bless you all and may God bless America!"

The United States military "war machine" gears up for battle. So far, they are not sure whether there is going to be a land conflict but they are not taking any chances; all military personnel are called back from leave. The reserves and National Guard are called into service. This is as real as it gets.

CHAPTER NINE
The Battle Begins

Deon deploys as many ships as he can. Some are not finished but he dispatches them with work crews still on board. "We'll simply finish up in space." He knows that his friend Steve, Ambassador-General to everyone else, would not give him bad intelligence; he has trusted him for years with his life, and he's not about to start doubting him now.

Many of the space destroyers are the first to go, with smaller, more maneuverable ships called renegades flying as cover. The renegades are basically a seat, engine, cockpit and a number of guns—often fondly referred to as an "Galactic A-10 on steroids." Redesigned to carry a quantum cannon and one of the Meritorian laser cannons as well, it packs ten times more punch than its previous version. The Star Destroyer has its usual complement of weapons as well as a Meritorian laser cannon.

Once they are all deployed, there will be about sixty ships in all. The newly modified ships will take the lead, with the SCCC ships falling in behind. They have not had all of their ships retrofitted with the new weaponry and as such are more vulnerable. As they enter space, they will spread out in a chevron formation. They still do not know their enemy, so the strategy is simple: destroy as many ships as possible. This is the first time Earth has gone to war in space. The tactical strategy will be to detect the enemy quickly and coordinate their firepower.

The SCCC has been very busy also. Honeywell and Raytheon engineers have gathered data from the Colossus and used it to fine-tune new updates for the sensor arrays. This software keys in on the parameters that initially helped the Colossus crew to detect the alien ships. Without an enemy ship to test it on, they are basically guessing how effective the software is, so will carry out a beta test to trial it on the SCCC. The software is being downloaded and should be installed and ready in an hour.

Colonel Striker is very pleased so far with the way his team at Area 51 has executed things. He will join the fleet with the new Meritor weapon system and the IFF and will test it. Once approved, he will send all the plans and software files to the emissary to distribute to the Meritor commanders so they may replicate them for their ships also. As the ship deploys decoy targets, the crew test the Meritorian weapons system. It is nothing short of amazing and its tracking features are just incredible; it can track multiple targets, and once the target at hand is destroyed, it seeks out other targets to assist. This feature is optional—but could well prove invaluable in a fire-fight in which they are outnumbered and outgunned. The rate of fire and the velocity are significantly higher and faster than the Earth weapons. It would not surprise the SCCC leadership if crews used this as their primary weapon of choice.

* * *

The Chemdi-Shakahr commander was patient and did not fire on the Meritorian Destroyer—a wise choice because he now has sixty or more easy targets to destroy at will. He prepares his crew for battle; they ready all weapon systems and tactical arrays. Well-trained space warriors from a long line of generations of warriors, they nevertheless know that this will not be an easy fight—after all, the Earth creatures managed to destroy not one but two of their flagships, both commanded by highly skilled captains and crews. They will not underestimate the creatures of Earth again.

The Chemdi commander orders each ship to pick one ship to concentrate their firepower on. They will all fire simultaneously, with the aim of surprising the Earth fleet. They must be ready to fire in succession for this to be successful. All commanders report that they have acquired their targets and are ready. The fleet commander's ship is the key to their battle plan; rather like the player of a chess game, he can see all ships in relation to the battle space and can coordinate the battle with a simple wave of his alien hand—made possible by his special array that communicates to every single ship. If the Earth fleet realizes this and can destroy this ship, they will have a fighting chance of winning this battle.

* * *

Meritor Security, Intelligence Cell, has received and authenticated intelligence from a credible source on Khorath: the Khorathian leadership is sending another wave of ships to Earth. If this is true, the Earth will be overwhelmed after fighting the first wave. Meritor cannot allow their first ally to fall. They too will send whatever remaining ships they can without putting Meritor at risk. The Brajeh has made another special request, that an additional four Khorathian bodyguards also join the fight to assist in whatever way they can. The request has been granted and the four appropriate the fastest ship they can find. As they are about to dispatch, an additional passenger asks to join their crew. They do not make much of the matter, welcome the new passenger aboard and depart.

* * *

Director Pickett exits the door, closing it behind him to shut out Corky's incessant barking. "What in the world has gotten into to him lately?" he wonders as he makes his way to tactical to speak with the software engineers, GNC, GPO and WEPS. He wants to make sure that this array is going to serve the SCCC—not hinder or even hurt it; he's very uneasy about deploying new software updates just before going to war, preferring a tried-and-tested system. The Earth leaders, including the SECDEF, believe that if the software works as advertised, they will be able to detect enemy ships earlier and respond faster. In a situation where they do not know this enemy, this may prove to be highly valuable and even save lives.

The software is installed and the arrays boot up. The newer version looks great and has better usability—except for one thing: there is a red blotchy patch on the lower screens. The Honeywell and Raytheon engineers are talking quietly to each other; the NASA engineers are utterly perplexed.

"So, walk me through this, guys," says Pickett. What are we supposed to see if the enemy is out there, gentlemen?

"Hmm, red, sir," says the engineer.

"Red. Are you sure this is not a glitch? I have a window in my office, and I do not see any ships. According to your graph, they should be visible."

One of the youngest engineers, who looks no older than twenty-two or so—an MIT graduate with high honors—has been silent so far but speaks up now, "Gentlemen, we must consider the fact that if the software is good and if it's working, what it is showing is true. The red indications on the screen are enemy ships—in other words, they are at our front door and have likely been there for some time."

The room falls quiet as everyone contemplates this possibility. Then one of the older engineers starts to rebuff his theory, "That may be true, but in our business we confirm our findings with at least one other indication of some sort. We have none. Perhaps we can load this update on a number of ships, to verify?"

Director Pickett interrupts, "No! We have no time for this! We do have another indication: my dog Corky had been barking at the window for at least a week now. He never does that. He is sensing something that we as humans cannot! Go to red alert! Alert all ships that we are under attack! Do it and do it now!"

The engineers look at each other as if Pickett is crazy.

Then the young engineer says, "It is conclusive that animals can sense danger like earthquakes, storms and the like long before humans do. It's a proven fact. Perhaps the dog is right."

The old-guard engineers throw their hands in the air, dismissing this possibility. Little do they know they will soon see the confirmation they say they need.

*　*　*

The emissary has received the updated information that the Khorathians have sent a second wave of ships to Earth. This clearly is an indication that they believe that Earth and Meritor may defeat them. He does not share this information with Earth command yet, but alerts his commanders to assist Earth with the initial battle: once they have the Chemdi on the run, they will break off a number of Meritor battle cruisers and destroyers to surprise the inbound armada and engage before reaching Earth.

Director Pickett has ordered the Earth spaceships to maneuver towards the indicated coordinates, making an executive decision to approve the new software and ordering all ships to upload and install as they are on the way. Colonel Striker and his team are aboard one of the destroyers—a front-row seat for the battle. The captain offers to transport Deon to the SCCC or to a safer location via shuttlecraft but he declines; he is not going to put anyone in danger on his account. He will ride this out. He has a nagging premonition in his mind that he should call someone right now but the person escapes him. But of course—the emissary!

He taps on his Zehrea and the emissary answers. "Greetings, Colonel Striker."

"Emissary, it is good to hear your voice. I am currently in space, and we're about to engage the Chemdi-Shakahr."

Colonel, listen to me very carefully. The key to winning this battle is to destroy or disable the command ship; it synchronizes all of the ships and feeds them information in real time, to enable them to fight as one. With that ship in play, you will have a very difficult time defeating this enemy—it is both tough and powerful. I will send you our most recent electronic layout of their command ship. When the time comes, you will know what to do. Safe return, Colonel—and remember... the Chemdi code."

CHAPTER TEN

The Battle Is Fought

As the fleet makes its final turn to engage the invisible targets that are only visible on the screen, there is a sudden blinding light from afar off. All the commanders have a sense that this marks the beginning of a very difficult day.

In the SCCC, all of those in mission control are blinded as well.

"What the hell was that?" yells Pickett.

"Sir, it came from the direction of the red blips on the screen," the WEPS replies. "We're under attack!"

"God help us!" cries Pickett. "Battle stations! Lower the blast shields!"

The blast shields are made of a very light, extremely tough titanium material. Although not completely impervious, it will withstand multiple direct blasts. They roll down at a moderate speed until completely closed. The staff in mission control is now completely dependent on their sensor arrays. It's official—they are at war.

Colonel Striker sends a message to the fleet commander relaying the information shared by the emissary: that the key to winning the battle is destroying the alien command ship. The commander does not respond immediately.

Of the first sixteen ships hit by enemy fire, four are completely destroyed. The fleet commander still cannot see the vessels—only the target identified on the sensor screen. He says under his breath, "We are not going to last long at this rate."

"Commo officer, open a channel to all ships. This is the fleet commander. Concentrate your firepower on the targets on your screens. We will have to trust our sensor arrays until we can see our enemy! All ships fire!"

The multiple blasts from all fifty-six ships light up space like the sun. Even the alien enemy must have taken notice. The targets are hit with great accuracy, disabling some of the ships' cloaking ability. Quantum cannons are ablaze and rail gun rounds litter space with their plasma trails. Again, more ships are revealed and the Earth ship armada sends more firepower down-range.

* * *

The Meritorian commanders see the battle raging and immediately head in the same direction. They will flank the enemy ships and cover the Earth fleet from above so as to not destroy allied ships.

The Meritorian fleet commander addresses the fleet as they enter the battle. "It is my honor to go into battle with you all. Battleship commanders, make destroying the ships with regenerative weapons your priority as soon as they are identified. Division Six, destroy all the outliers and be prepared to meet the inbound Chemdi battle group as soon as we detect them on long-range sensors. We will crush this wicked enemy who killed our ancestors, our families and friends. We fight for our allies, for Meritor, and our Brajeh! Fleet command out."

The enemy ships deploy their fighters. Earth deploys its space fighters and renegades. The Chemdi and Earth fighters seemed evenly matched in their capabilities, except the Chemdi weapons are more advanced. The Meritorian fighters are better matched for the Chemdi. Earth fighters may have an additional advantage over both alien fighters in that they are each paired with two drones that match every move of the host aircraft while keeping the appropriate separation formation distance. Each drone also has a collision avoidance system that will sacrifice itself for the safety of the pilot. The weapons of the drones match and exceed those of the host aircraft. This gives one fighter the advantage of three.

The heavy renegade fighters/bombers seem better matched in terms of their weapons but are not as maneuverable as the enemy fighters. The fighting is fierce, and Earth is suffering losses four or five to one. The Meritorian fleet has started to pound the enemy ships and the losses on Earth's side decrease as the enemy's losses increase. The Meritorian fighters arrive on the scene and are very effective; they seem to be getting the better of the enemy fighters. The Earth fleet starts to believe they just might have a chance. The fleet commander acknowledges the message from the colonel and has his team in engineering do analysis on the best way to exploit the enemy vessels' weak spots.

Then it happens. One of the Chemdi battle cruisers breaks off the enemy formation and takes aim at the SCCC. They fire their regenerative weapon at the residence area of the space station. A large chunk of the station is removed and regenerates two miles away in space. The electrical power, environmental systems, all life-sustaining umbilicals are severed. Crewmembers can be seen floating in space. Furniture and all manner of household goods are now space debris.

All of the fleets witness this horror and focus their firepower on that evil ship, destroying it completely. The Meritorian battleships begin to target and destroy every ship they can identify that has regenerative weapons. The Earth ships join in as well, many crewmembers battling through their tears for their friends and loved ones.

This single act is the initial forging of Earth and Meritor into a cohesive fighting force. Although the Meritorian commanders cannot speak the English language, they project their next targets on Earth ship screens of the targeting systems on the newly installed Meritorian weapon systems. Although this was not what the system was originally designed for, Meritorian captains make it work—helping both fleets to concentrate their collective firepower on every Chemdi ship on the targeting screen. From this point in the battle, the Chemdi losses start to grow; both fleets have destroyed all regenerative ships and they are now concentrating their focus on the remaining enemy vessels. Suddenly, Meritorian ships begin exploding one after another! They are being flanked by the second wave of Chemdi ships! Earth and Meritorian losses begin to mount.

As the destroyers continue to do battle, it appears as if they are not going to be able to take out the enemy command ship. Colonel Striker knows it will only be a matter of time before they too meet the fate of those killed on the other vessels. He has to do something.

As many times as they fire on the enemy command ship, it appears to be impervious to their attacks. Thinking like an engineer, Deon calculates that the best way to destroy it is from the inside. He grabs his gear that he brought from Earth.

"Sir, what are you doing?" his engineers ask.

"I'm going on board the enemy ship. Do we have explosives on board?"

"I don't know but I'll find out!" The engineer runs out of the lab and grabs anyone he can who might be able to help. He quickly returns with one of the Special Forces personnel.

"Captain Gibson, SOCOM (Special Operations Command), Sir. You said you needed explosives?"

"Yes, I do. I plan to pay that command ship a little visit," Deon says.

"Sir, these are SOCOM assets. Besides, this is our line of work. Begging your pardon, sir—although we respect your zeal and determination, this sounds like a job for us."

"Captain, you and your team do not understand this enemy. I have received special training and I assure you that your team will not be prepared for this fight."

"Sir, that may be true, but this is our fight, and we're good to go."

"Captain, this enemy is not human. These creatures have four arms, an articulating spine, great strength, speed and agility. In fact, your greatest strengths will likely be your weakness, especially concerning your team's choice of weapons. I don't have time to explain it all to you, captain. All I know is something has got to be done to help our fleet—and I believe I can do it."

"Sir, with all due respect, I know who you are—I have seen you on TV, and we've been briefed. You seem to have some pretty high-speed gear—heck, even we don't have that stuff... yet. Truth is, I signed for this ordnance. Let me call SOCOM Command. Wait one second."

He gets SOCOM on a secure link from the ship and talks to his commander, a colonel as well, rapidly outlining the situation. The colonel all but insults Striker for wanting to beam aboard the enemy ship to set explosives, and calls into question his skill set to even execute such a maneuver. He denies the use of the explosives based on his opinion. Striker understands that the colonel is merely assessing the situation from his limited Earthly perspective. If the SOCOM commander sends Special Forces over to that ship, he will be the one who is in "over his head" on this one. Deon does not engage the SOCOM commander any longer but decides to call his friend instead.

"Steve? This is Deon. I desperately need your help." He explains the situation. The ambassador is the only human alive who understands the significance of what Striker has been taught and the importance of what his alien teacher has trained him in.

Steve puts on his political hat and goes to work. He briefs the emissary, and they both seek an audience with the President. The President is in the war bunker but has full communication with his staff, specifically the SECDEF and the joint chiefs.

"Mr. President, I will be brief in the interest of time. Colonel Striker has presented a plan that I believe will be successful. Colonel, if you please," says the emissary.

"Well, sir, the Chemdi are coordinating all of their ships

from the command ship. Its destruction could be the key to winning this battle. They will be not expecting us to attack them from the inside. If I can beam in from the emissary's ship, I can likely take the bridge and plant explosives. This will disable the ship to take the pressure off of both fleets. We then move to Engineering to do the same to finish the job. Their ships will not be able to coordinate with the command ship and will be confused. Both fleets may be able to destroy them," explains the colonel.

"Is there another enemy ship that can do the job of the command ship?" asks the SOCOM commander. "Also, how do you expect not to get shot during this process? Besides, only our SOCOM operators are properly trained on the new ordnance that we have."

"The Chemdi code, sir," says Colonel Striker.

The emissary continues, "The Chemdi have a code that has been in their culture for eons. They will not use a weapon to defeat their enemy that will give them an advantage; they will use the same or a similar weapon of their enemy. Only then, if they should die at their enemy's hand, will they consider it to be a death of honor. I understand your special warriors are exemplary in their skill and style of warfare. However, there is none on your planet that would stand a chance against the Chemdi—except for one. That is Colonel Striker. I have seen him fight with Chemdi simulation trainers and he is an expert with the Chinese long sword or Jian. He's the first of your species to defeat the simulation. The chief of security of our planet trained him himself—he is known in our galaxy as being the only one to have defeated five Chemdi at once. His name is Balan-Gaal.

"The colonel's thinking is sound in that it is so bold that even the Chemdi or their leadership will not expect it. It could work with the help that I am willing to provide. He is under your authority. Both our worlds need his help."

"Mr. Emissary, are you saying that you are willing to risk your life with the colonel in the belly of that enemy ship based on the colonel's idea?" asks the President.

"Yes, Mr. President. I am. If we do not do the unexpected, the outcome will certainly be the possible defeat of both fleets and the enslaving of the people of Earth by the Chemdi-Shakahr. Sir, time is of the essence—we are losing ships."

The SOCOM commander adds, "Sir, if you don't mind, SOCOM will provide an explosive ordnance disposal (EOD) specialist to set the required charges."

"SOCOM," replies the President, "we appreciate the support. Give Colonel Striker whatever he needs. God speed, Colonel, to you and your team."

"Sir, we could use a diversion to get close to the command ship," says the colonel.

"We'll make it happen," says SECDEF, nodding toward his joint chiefs. "Make a plan, gentlemen—and give them hell!"

The secretary of Space Command starts calling out orders to his staff.

Immediately, Colonel Striker, the SOCOM EOD specialist and the emissary beam to the emissary's ship. They level alongside the destroyer and get the needed explosives—high-tech, small devices that pack an astounding punch.

The colonel's staff is in shock, afraid for their colonel; they all think he is in way over his head on this one.

"Excuse me, colonel, but don't you think SOCOM can handle this? After all, you're a pilot and engineer—these guys train for this all their lives!" says one of his senior staff engineers.

"Dan, I know that all of you are worried," replies Deon. Yes, I am a pilot and engineer. I'm also more than that and have special training in what I'm about to do. Please don't worry. In fact, if you truly want to help, I can use your prayers."

"If you say so, sir. You've got them—from all of us," replies the senior engineer.

The Area 51 team says their farewells and good lucks. The colonel taps his Zehrea, and he and the EOD specialist disappear to the emissary's ship.

As the remaining Meritorian ships approach Earth's solar system, they begin picking up communication of the battle. They increase their speed to enter the battle to render aid. As they approach Earth, they encounter debris of all kinds—mangled parts of destroyed ships, fields of unknown liquids, human and alien remains. Anger arises paired with an unwavering tenacity to destroy this enemy with their new ally. The Meritorian commanders engage the Chemdi ships from the furthest distance possible to include the command ship. As they approach, they see Earth and Meritorian ships sustaining severe damage, some getting totally destroyed. The Meritorians receive a message from the emissary as to what their new mission is. The fleets turn their attention to other ships in an effort to give the emissary and the boarding party a chance to accomplish their mission.

Deon has on his Alocae-Cha and his "Shelah" the weapon given to him personally by Balan-Gaal. He also has his Tanto knife strapped to his side, ready for any close-up Chemdi engagements. The emissary looks at the colonel and the EOD specialist to ensure they are ready. Striker puts his hand on his Tanto knife, looks back, turns the Shelah into a Jian and gives a short nod back without saying a word. They have the exact location of the bridge on the Chemdi ship and the beam coordinates are set. The emissary gives a nod to the pilot and the team beams directly to the bridge. There is no turning back now. They are fully committed.

The emissary materializes in the midst of three Chemdi. Deon materializes in front of two more, and the SOCOM EOD specialist materializes behind Striker. The emissary kills a Chemdi instantly with a single blow and as the other two Chemdi reach for their weapons. The emissary quickly cuts off both of their bottom sets of arms and kills them both.

A Chemdi sitting at what looks like a communication panel hits the intruder alert. An alarming sound accompanied with a strange syntax is heard. Striker kills one Chemdi, evades the blade strikes of the other, blocks with the Jian and thrusts the blade into the Chemdi. He then quickly imagines the wide blade of one of Balan-Gaal's bodyguard. The blade rips through half of the Chemdi. The Chemdi falls to the floor. The Chemdi at the helm leaps from his position like a gazelle and lands in front of the EOD specialist. He pulls out two medium-sized blades with his upper arms and begins swinging them in a crisscross pattern as he approaches. The EOD specialist draws his HK MP7a1 and starts firing. The bullets hit the Chemdi, but he keeps coming. Striker throws the Jian from across the room, striking the Chemdi in the back. The EOD specialist continues to unload the rest of the twenty-clip magazine into the Chemdi, and he falls to the floor.

"Hurry," says the emissary. "More will be here in moments!"

Striker quickly removes his weapon from the dead Chemdi and nods at the EOD specialist.

The emissary says to Striker, "Very imaginative, Colonel!"

The EOD specialist quickly affixes three explosives to the bridge—one on the helm, one on what looks like a weapons control panel and one on the communications panel. They each have ten-second timers and will auto-sync when just one is activated.

"Let's go!" says Striker.

They exit the bridge into a hallway, and the door closes behind them. They head toward where they think Engineering may be. As they make their escape, the blasts shake the ship. Suddenly the hall fills with smoke, fire and angry Chemdi-Shakahr. The Chemdi are incensed that there are enemy intruders on board their ship. They search frantically for them. The emissary is not slowed by the smoke and falls Chemdi one after the other with his bladed weapon of choice. Striker is impeded by the smoke, however, and takes more time to do the same.

The captain of the command ship enters the remnant of what used to be his bridge. The blast has weakened the structure of the ship and its hull is about to breach. His yell is loud.

Due to human physiology, the Chemdi-Shakahr language is not understandable to humans—but they don't need to understand the Chemdi language to know that the Chemdi captain is pissed.

Striker and the emissary are well aware that they are rapidly running out of time. Although they are on the move and are killing Chemdi as they go, it seems that for every one they fell, another two arrive on the scene. They finally retreat to a hallway that is not yet filled with the enemy and wonder how to get to their objective. As they stand facing each other, the emissary sees two Khorathian bodyguards of the Brajeh materialize behind Striker. Looking in Striker's direction, the emissary says something very unexpected.

"Ah... It is good to see you. We can use your help! More Chemdi are about to arrive."

Striker whips around and sees three individuals stood behind him: two Khorathians and Miiya!"

"Hey! What are you doing here?" he shouts.

Ignoring his question, Miiya says, "We can make it to Engineering this way!"

The two Khorathians and Miiya clear a definitive path, and start moving smartly toward Engineering. Miiya puts her sword away and picks up one of the Chemdi's plasma weapons. As they move ahead, they can see the doors leading to Engineering up ahead. Ten or more Chemdi come pouring out of Engineering ready for battle.

Suddenly, Miiya is hit by a plasma blast and falls to the floor. She keeps firing. "Go!" she yells.

Two Khorathians stow their edge weapons, and one picks up a plasma weapon from the killed Chemdi. The other Khorathian helps Miiya to her feet and takes her weapon. They enter Engineering, and Chemdi bodies begin to fall almost in mass. Some get a few shots off, but the shots are in vain. The Khorathians quickly clear Engineering with their ultra accurate shooting skills. Deon takes advantage of this to wave in the EOD specialist. He sets the last remaining charges. As he

JOHN WILLIAMS

does, a dying Chemdi's hand touches his leg. The agitated specialist kicks the Chemdi twice for his offense. What he does not know is that the seemingly insignificant brush of the dead Chemdi security officer's hand was the actual attaching of a micro-tracking device onto the pant leg of his uniform.

The specialist signals his job is done, and the entire team beams from the Chemdi ship to the Khorathian cruiser. The medium-sized cruiser quickly clears the Chemdi command ship and moves away at incredible speed.

The Khorathian takes Miiya to the ship's infirmary and lays her gently on the examination table. Striker quickly enters the room to comfort his alien friend.

"What the hell are you doing here?" he says.

"Hell? What is hell?" she replies.

"Sorry," he says.

They both say at the same time. "Another Earth expression."

"The Brajeh sent more of his personal bodyguards to assist for he suspected that Earth would need help. As we approached Earth's Solar System, we heard the impending mission broadcasted over our secure communication net, and we knew that's where we would be most helpful." Miiya replies.

Deon caresses his friend's face. "Thank you for coming. Your help was greatly appreciated."

Miiya welcomes Deon's caress, seeming very comforted by it. It would appear she is falling for the colonel.

The Khorathian physician attends to her wounds and sedates her so that she can rest. Meritorians are not only four times stronger than humans; their bodies heal about three times as fast. She will be fine in no time.

* * *

The sudden blast of the Chemdi command ship is spectacular, bright and loud. All present in the battle space witness the demise of the ship and struggle to stay clear of the flying debris and quickly focus on the Chemdi fighters that the command ship is no longer coordinating. The Earth Star fighters and renegades are having a field day destroying the Chemdi fighters. The Meritorian fighters have launched from their cruisers and are on their way to assist. The battle has now clearly swung in the favor of Meritor and Earth.

* * *

Deon asks the pilot to beam him and the EOD specialist back to the Earth Space destroyer and he does so. Striker and the specialist are met with a heroes' welcome. Although they had their doubts, the results of the team's efforts are undeniable. The SOCOM EOD specialist is very impressed with Striker's ability. He had not expected such a capable operator from an NASA pilot. He feels that Striker was as capable—maybe even more so—than other SOCOM operatives he's previously worked with. He learned something today, and takes a private moment to apologize to Striker.

"Sir, I just want to apologize. We at SOCOM don't usually work with people we haven't worked with before or who have not been recommended by SOCOM or other SF teams. You are a pilot and engineer. I didn't think that…"

Deon holds up his hand and stops the captain. "It's okay. I realize that having to work with someone like me might be a long shot in the eyes of most everyone, especially SOCOM. I get it. Fortunately for me, the best operative I have ever met trained me himself. He fought these beasts before and gave me valuable insight and knowledge on how to kill them. There was no way you or your leadership could have known that. You did a great job up there. Thanks for the help."

* * *

The remaining Chemdi ships are still putting up a significant fight. The Meritorian cruisers and battleships step up their attack; the Earth ships are using every weapon and tactic they can to quickly destroy the remaining ships.

Two more Chemdi ships break off and head toward the SCCC. They fire multiple volleys at the SCCC, hitting it in different areas. Blasts are heard throughout the SCCC, and people are killed. Three Earth ships take up a defensive stance and fire everything they've got at the Chemdi Ships: aluminum rail gun rounds, guided missiles and quantum cannons are all a blaze. The battle is fierce, and with the help of the Meritorians' ships, the enemy ships are defeated and no Chemdi ship ever attempts another attack on the SCCC.

As the Chemdi ships are destroyed in ever-increasing numbers, they start to retreat. Earth ships stand their ground to protect Earth and the SCCC as the Meritorian ships give pursuit to retreating Chemdi ships, continuing to destroy them. Earth and Meritor have inflicted a significant scar in the hearts and minds of the Chemdi and Khorathians that day. This is one experience they will not soon forget.

* * *

Aboard the Earth destroyer, a sudden commotion can be heard in the hallway of the ship. The first to leave the ready room is Captain Gibson, the EOD specialist. The familiar sound of an HK MP7a1 echoes loudly through the hall, the sound vibrating off the metal bulkhead of the ship. Striker and the engineers look at each other and jump to their feet. Striker's Alocae-Cha is in his bag but there's no time to put it on. He grabs his wand and enters the hall. As he sees the bloody scene he exclaims to himself, "There are freaking Chemdi on the ship!" He thinks quickly and taps his Zehrea, alerting the emissary.

"Chemdi just boarded our ship! Alert all ships!"

Almost immediately a Chemdi slices across Striker's chest wounding him significantly and knocking the Zehrea off of his tactical jump suit. Striker goes into survival mode and kills the Chemdi. There appears to be at least seven of them. A group of four are moving toward him. Deon is at an advantage in the hall as it is narrow, and the Chemdi have a harder time maneuvering than he does. He sees the dead captain on the deck. He never stood a chance. He sounds the red alert and continues fighting.

Deon kills the last of the four, but not without sustaining more significant wounds. He knows he's in no physical shape to fight any longer but he continues to pursue the remaining four Chemdi nonetheless. He finds his way to the bridge were everyone is dead, including the captain. The four Chemdi are not surprised by his entrance and start to walk toward him. The lead holds up his hand indicating that he alone wants the privilege of killing Striker.

Striker is protecting his right side due to possible broken ribs from the last fight. The Chemdi approaches with a well-adorned staff reminiscent of the Japanese weapon called a Bo —basically a long pole. He attacks, overwhelming Striker easily. Striker is now on his back with the Jian in the guard position to protect himself. The Chemdi raises the weapon above his head to deliver the final blow. Suddenly, his weapon is met with what appears to be a miniature Trident and a modified Syrian Sabre. Immediately the Trident is thrust into the chest of the Chemdi, impaling the two hearts of the enemy. He falls to the deck floor. Miiya has saved Striker. She proceeds to kill the remaining Chemdi on the bridge.

The Chemdi damage the bridge, mimicking the mission Striker and team just completed on the enemy command ship. The space destroyer is severely damaged and is now falling toward Earth. They cannot control the ship and must evacuate. Striker grabs the phone in the bridge and communicates a message.

"Attention all hands. This is Colonel Deon Striker. The ship has been compromised and is falling toward Earth. All personnel—abandon ship!"

Just as he finishes, the ship's third in command pops onto the bridge and yells at him. "Hey! You are not authorized to give that order!"

"Sir, look around. You cannot control your ship; we're falling into Earth's atmosphere, and we have minutes to get your people off!"

The operations officer quickly picks up the phone and communicates the same message with the additional order to use the escape pods. Miiya secures Deon's weapons and his

Alocae-Cha. She then taps her Zehrea, and she and Striker are beamed immediately to the emissary's ship. Escape pods litter space as they exit the ship, whose bow is now beginning to glow red as it enters the Earth's atmosphere.

The emissary contacts Ambassador Wilory to assist in securing emergency medical attention for the colonel. Steve arranges an ambulance to take him to the nearest hospital, which from his location is Howard University Hospital. Miiya and Striker talk before he's beamed down.

"So you're a colonel now?" says Miiya.

"Actually, a lieutenant colonel. I was promoted after I returned from Meritor." "Congratulations. You are seriously injured. Why weren't you wearing your Alocae-Cha? You know that you cannot endure fighting more than one Chemdi for long without it."

"I know. I had no time. I was trying to save one of our team members," Striker says sadly.

"We have just met. It would be most unfortunate to lose you so suddenly." Says Miiya.

"Thank you for saving my life. I don't usually put myself in a position like that."

"Don't make it a habit. Besides, we still have a number of dates to go on."

Striker laughs—then stops quickly, in pain due to his injuries. "Right. I'd like that very much."

The pilot yells out, "We're over Washington, sir. Ready to beam him to the ambassador's location."

"When will I see you again?" Miiya asks.

"I don't know. When are you returning to Meritor?"

"I don't know."

"I get the impression that we will see each other soon." As he finishes speaking, his voice fades and he passes out.

* * *

The Meritorians destroyed four additional ships as the Chemdi retreated. The battle space around Earth is now secure. The relationship between Meritor and Earth has been a forged forever. There is now a mutual respect and honor that comes only through battle. Crews in both fleets are starting to repair the damage done to their respective ships. Earth crews are tending to the wounded and organizing transport to Earth. Meritorian medical staff are tending to their wounded and moving medical personnel to ships that have the most wounded and casualties.

The emissary and Ambassador Wilory decide to hold a gathering of Meritor and Earth Commanders to discuss and share their experiences. The emissary feels this will further solidify the relationships between the two worlds. There are also discussions in the medical arena about sharing medical practices on a trial basis. This represents the beginning of a new age in technology, medicine and socialization with the first alien civilization that Earth has ever had.

The Khorathians and Chemdi-Shakahr now know that whatever their plan, it will be tougher to achieve now that the two planets are allies. Earth and Meritor have learned many lessons. There is a lot of data to go through, and many after-action reviews to be conducted. Both worlds will walk away stronger and better prepared for the next fight. Now it is time to heal, mend, rebuild, refit and implement improvements on all that was learned.

The remaining Earth ships are patrolling the battle space in case there is another Chemdi-Shakahr attack. The repair tenders have already been deployed to a number of ships to begin battle damage assessment and repairs. A remnant of Meritor ships will remain on station, while the other Meritor ships are scheduled to return home.

The destroyer boarded by the Chemdi is now burning as it falls to Earth. Its current trajectory is headed toward the coast of Ireland. The Irish Navy has been alerted and will patrol the area. It is already breaking up as it plummets to the Earth. The largest section of the ship will splash down in minutes. The flagship of the Irish Navy arrives at the perimeter of the impact area. The helicopter patrol vessel the L.

É. Eithne is standing by, along with other vessels, to rescue survivors. Burning debris is already falling into the ocean; the largest piece of the ship can now be clearly seen as it burns on re-entry through Earth's atmosphere.

Sailors from the L. É. Eithne line the railing, watching the battered and twisted space vessel break apart as it plummets to Earth. Each piece hits the ocean with a tremendous splash, sending plumes of seawater hundreds of feet into the air. The Irish Navy was wise to wait in the perimeter—huge waves fan out as the sea claims the space destroyer to a watery grave. Slowly, the Irish Navy approaches. The helicopters dispatch to sweep the area for survivors.

CHAPTER ELEVEN

We Heal, Mend, Repair And Improve

The doctors are perplexed. The puncture wounds have been irrigated and sewn up, but one wound in particular does not seem to be healing like the others. In fact, the flesh surrounding it seems to be deteriorating, and is not responding to the usual drugs. He should be recovering normally but in fact he's getting worse and there is a strange pattern forming under his skin. The doctors are concerned and are consulting other physicians around the country, including the space station.

Ambassador Wilory had been following Striker's movements through his staff with great interest. He heard that he was rescued from the destroyer that crashed in the ocean, and successfully taken to the hospital. He is the first to visit. The nurse has just finished re-dressing Deon's wounds as Steve walks into the room. He notices the strange spider veins that have appeared around the wound inflicted by the Chemdi, which are now starting to appear on other parts of his body as well.

The doctor walks in. "Mr. Ambassador! It's a pleasure to meet you. We are doing our best for him."

"Thank you, doctor. He's my friend—we go way back. Please let me know if there is anything I can do."

"Certainly, sir. We're contacting the best doctors we can find, Mr. Ambassador." Although Steve is listening, he has another plan in mind.

As he exits the building, he calls the emissary. He will

know what to do...
And he does.

* * *

The SCCC had been put through its paces engaging in Earth's first space battle against an alien enemy. Although war is a terrible thing, fighting alongside your fellow man or woman builds the sort of team cohesion that cannot be built any other way. The team has survived a seasoned alien enemy with better weapons and proven tactics forged over many wars. Although they lost good people these last few days, they are happy to be alive and to have survived to live another day. They have become Earth's first space war veterans—although you wouldn't know it from the way they just continue doing their jobs. The controllers are talking to other ships and getting them the help they need.

Medical shuttles pepper space as they move to and fro evacuating the wounded and deceased. Large Earth shuttles also join the ballet of ships bringing medical supplies, food, equipment and parts to support the triumphant SCCC and space fleet.

Director Pickett is extremely proud of his fleet and grateful to the Meritorians for their help. As he looks at the amazing people all around the control room doing their jobs, his is impressed and almost becomes overwhelmed. He comes to himself and begins giving people direction. He wants to close off the part of the residential wing destroyed by the Chemdi-Shakahr with a force field. Teams have already started repairs on the space station and on the many damaged Earth ships that are still space-worthy. The severely damaged ships will have to return to Earth for repair. Space Command is not sure when the next battle will be so they're not taking any chances. During the battle in space, the Tactical side of the SCCC was very busy and could have probably used three more controllers. The director will make room in the control room to make that change once the residences are repaired.

He has lost track of the two guys from the Pentagon. He's

heard that they made their way back to Washington. Apparently they both left just before the battle broke out. Director Pickett was more than pleased by their departure.

On board the emissary's ship, Miiya is preparing a special Meritorian medical bag. The emissary has disclosed Colonel Striker's condition and he knows what ails him. Earth Medicine will not work in this case, and if left untreated, Colonel Striker will certainly die. He will receive a special visitor to his private room tonight; the ship's crew is monitoring the hospital room for the opportune time to send Miiya to the colonel with the treatment he needs, hopefully undetected. Time is of the essence.

The nurse takes a look at Colonel Striker one last time. Whatever it is that is making his temperature rise, doctor's orders are that she monitors him every hour. She checks his monitor and uses a laser thermometer so as to not to wake him. He hasn't been sleeping very soundly and the doctors want him to rest. She straightens his covers, adds a little water to the flowers sent buy his staff and quietly leaves the room, ensuring the door does not make a sound.

Suddenly, Miiya appears at his bedside. She goes over to the door and cracks it open just a little. The nurses are engaged in deep conversation. She closes the door without a sound and approaches Deon's bedside. He is very pale, his skin almost gray in color. His face is drawn, like that of a man who has lost too much blood. His lips are severely chapped and his breath is shallow. She begins scanning his body and confirms that he has been poisoned by the Chemdi-Shakahr's blade. The scanner reveals the poison around the entry wound in spite of the bandages. It originates from a deadly animal indigenous to the Chemdi home world. It is most potent when first applied to a weapon. The effect of the poison loses its potency over time. This is likely why Striker is still alive. She places the scanner on the bed, leans in and says to the weakened colonel, "I am here to help you, great Earth warrior. You shall not die, my friend. Besides, you still owe me that date, Deon."

The colonel is nearing delirium from the effects of the poison. Although he faintly recognizes Miiya's voice, all he can do at this point is groan.

She then pulls out an instrument that looks like a fancy miniature flashlight. She begins scanning from the very top of the colonel's head and moves the instrument down his body. It makes a little noise but not enough for anyone to hear outside the room, she thinks. She scans the door as she moves the wand over Striker's body. The process is done in about ten minutes. She completes the treatment then puts the wand back in the bag and scans the colonel again with the medical scanner. Confirmed—no poison present. For the moment, there is no visible sign that he is any better. As she puts the scanner back in the bag, she sees a shadow moving beneath the door. She hears talking and the voice is approaching. Suddenly the room door opens!

"Hey! Who are you and what the hell are you doing to the patient?"

Miiya tries to calm the woman. "Please lower your voice, I am here to help. Earth medicine will not cure him."

"You are not authorized to treat him—much less to be in his room! I'm going to get help!" As the woman whirls around to go out the door, a faint but distinctive voice speaks out.

"Virginia. For God's sake, this is not Area 51, so please keep your voice down and stop yelling at my friend." It is Striker.

The silence is deafening; you could have heard a pin drop.

Virginia, Striker's aide, had wanted to visit her boss and keep him company for a while. She really had nothing else to do until he assigned her something so she thought she would come and visit him personally. Suddenly the door opens again. Miiya, who has her hooded robe on, turns away. Virginia stands directly in front of the nurse to distract the attention away from Miiya.

"Please, there is a little too much noise in here. If you cannot keep it down, I will have to ask you both to leave!" says the nurse.

"I'm terribly sorry, nurse. That was my big mouth. It won't happen again, I promise you," Virginia says.

The nurse gets called and turns to exit the room. "Please try to remember this is a hospital," she adds for good measure, then disappears as quickly as she came.

There is a pregnant pause as Virginia turns, leans in and looks closely at Miiya.

"Virginia," Deon says, "I want you to meet Miiya. She is from the planet Meritor. She was the first Meritorian I ever met. She is a kind person and a very capable security officer. Moreover, she has become a dear friend."

Miiya is taken aback by Deon's words, clearly moved. "Please, Colonel, you flatter me. I'm simply here on orders from the emissary."

"You know the emissary? We have heard so much about him. I've seen him on TV once or twice," says Virginia.

"Yes, she does, and that is 'need to know' information," Says Striker.

"Wow. You are the first alien I have ever met. Is your ship on our planet?"

"No. Actually we're orbiting your Earth."

"So you saved my boss's life. You should stay for a while and allow us to show you our appreciation," Virginia answers warmly.

"Sir, I beg your pardon for rambling on like that. I almost forgot why I was here. They said that you were seriously ill and I just had to come."

"Virginia, thank you for coming. You are probably pulling your hair out waiting for me to assign you something to do. I know I've been out of the office for some time and I promise I'll give Adrian a call to assign you a new project in a moment. However, can you do me a big favor first? Will you briefly keep watch outside the door so I may have a moment with Miiya, please? It's sort of confidential."

"Oh, of course, sir. I will be right outside, sir." Virginia im-

JOHN WILLIAMS

mediately leaves the room, ready to use a cover story that the colonel is having private time with medical staff, should anyone approach.

Striker waits until the door is completely closed before speaking. "So what did you do to me? I could see you waving those strange instruments over my body."

"One of the things that attracted me to you most, Mighty Earth Warrior, was your obtuse boldness—however, you, my friend, are sometimes too bold for your own good. You should have been wearing your Alocae-Cha! The Chemdi might not have gotten close enough to nearly kill you."

"I know, I know—but I had already taken it off and when I was alerted that the Chemdi had breached the ship. I had no time to put it on."

"Apparently the Chemdi duplicated our mission to their command ship and decided to board at least four Earth ships in retaliation. All attacks were repelled, but at great cost. Your ship was the only one lost. The Chemdi used a very deadly poison on their weapons that killed most all of the crewmembers instantly... except you. The only thing I can surmise that saved you is the possibility that the poison that was on the weapon of your assailant had been exposed for more than four Earth hours. After four hours it loses much of its potency. You are lucky to be alive. The instruments I was using are tools we use on our own people to eradicate the poison. I wasn't sure it would not damage to your human physiology so I lessened its strength. It seems to have worked."

"I am lucky to have a faithful friend like you to save my assets—yet again," Deon smiles.

"Just doing my duty. Besides, I have already invested a great deal into you." Then she leans over and kisses him, as they had on Meritor. Deon cannot sit up without great pain. Miiya compensates for the distance.

"You must remember; whatever damage the poison has done will take time for your body to heal. I was able to remove the poison and heal some of the damage, but not all of it."

There appears to be a commotion outside the door. They can hear Virginia's voice speaking to a male, likely one of Striker's doctors. Miiya gently caresses Striker's face and kisses him on the forehead. "We will see each other again," she says. She then taps her Zehrea and is gone in an instant.

The chief medical doctor has come to re-examine Deon. He is not prepared for what he's about to see.

* * *

Two black SUVs with a Lincoln Town Car sandwiched in between them come to a screeching halt as they pull up in front of the Wilory home. All of the vehicles are armored. Agents deploy quickly from both sides of the SUVs with the accuracy of synchronized swimmers. From the bulges under their jackets, they are obviously packing some significant heat. Some guys are carrying the KRISS Super V and others the FN P90. Anyone who seeks to do the ambassador harm will certainly regret it. They proceed toward the house and fan out from the front yard, methodically sweeping to the back.

Jean, Steve's faithful wife, comes out of the house with a perplexed look on her face. She hasn't seen her husband in four weeks, since he accepted the ambassadorship of Meritor. This is his first time home and he is excited to be back. He has some news that may not please his wife but they will discuss that at the right time. He's just happy to be home.

Steve exits the car and waves to his beautiful wife.

"What's this all about, honey?" asks Jean.

"Hi, honey! I'm happy to see you too!"

Jean cocks her head to the side like a young girl, feeling bad for diving straight into practicalities instead of first greeting her husband.

"Aw, I'm sorry. It's just that I missed you and then suddenly there are men all over our house!"

They give each other a long embrace and trade a few kisses, ending in a very long smooch.

"We have much to talk about," Steve says.

They repeat their usual ritual of showering and enjoying

time in their very comfortable king-sized bed. About an hour later, there is a cautious knock on the door.

"Mr. Ambassador? Mr. Ambassador—are you all right, sir?" asks the head agent.

Jean's eyes open wide and she tries to stifle a giggle. "That is too weird! They're not staying are they?"

"Well, honey, some may just retreat to their vehicles. There is something I need to discuss with you," Steve says as he gets out of bed and wraps a soft terrycloth robe about him. He cracks open the door and says to the agent, "Thank you, Dennis. I'll be right out."

"Yes, sir. Of course, sir."

"Would you and your troop like some coffee?" Jean asks Steve.

"I think that they would like your coffee very much. Besides, I know you've been dying to show off your new espresso machine," Steve says, hugging his wife affectionately.

"Yeah—I had to wait for the secret service or whoever they are... because my husband stays away for such a long time," she replies playfully.

After Jean has dished out coffee to the agents, she and her husband retire to their usual spot outside on the deck. Steve broaches the topic at hand carefully. "You know, dear, things are changing for us."

"No kidding. I know that face and that tone of voice of yours when you've got something serious you have to say. I don't know how much time we have together, so just spit it out, Mr. Ambassador."

"Well, as you know, ambassadors are most effective when they're a representative in their host country. They want me to reside on Meritor."

The silence was deafening. Jean has been with Steve through all the military years so she knows what it means to pick up your entire life and move... multiple times. But she had never contemplated the possibility of moving to another planet. She says nothing for quite a while, just sits, nodding her head, and looking somewhat shell-shocked. Steve, wisely, says nothing, awaiting her reply.

After having seemingly embraced the stark reality of moving off the planet, she pulls herself together and she begins to fact-find in her usual charming, endearing manner. "So, how do we get there? What will be our living arrangements? How often will we be able to come back to Earth? Who will protect us—and if needed, what would be our exit plan?"

Steve looks at her, his eyes saying, you are the best woman any man could have in this world or any other.

"First, let me say that I love you very much and I appreciate your willing spirit," he replies.

"You are my husband. We said 'for better or for worse.' I'm not sure which this is but we will do this together, like we always have."

They share a long embrace. Steve continues, "The Meritorians have more advanced ships than those on Earth and have already assigned us one with crew. It will transport us to and from Earth. The embassy staff will consist of about one hundred other people, including the usual cadre of Marines, so we shall not be alone or abandoned. The Meritorians have identified a temporary residence where we will be staying."

"Why temporary, hon?"

"It's temporary until the new residence is completed. Their building us a brand-new embassy to our specifications and the design will take time."

"Wow—this will be an adventure!" Jean says.

They continue talking until the early hours of the morning, covering everything from food, clothing, getting news from home, security, and more. They are in agreement and, in one voice, they will break the news to their girls.

* * *

The room is filled with doctors specialized in hematology, pulmonary, cardiology, and circulatory care. Each and every one of them is stunned and confused at the recovery of Colonel Striker. They had not been able to identify what was causing the degradation of his health and they need to know what turned it around.

"Colonel, I am very happy for you," Dr. Thomas says. "I'm looking at your charts, blood work—everything is... to be honest, suspiciously better. Even your slightly high cholesterol has improved. Most patients would take months to see this kind of an improvement to their cholesterol, not to mention everything else that you had going on. Heck, even the healing of your wounds is accelerated. Excuse me sir, but you are holding out on us and I respectfully request... no, I demand... I respectfully demand answers, sir."

In his room of about five doctors and two nurses, you could hear a pin drop. Deon looked at them all and took pity on them—after all, if someone came into his hangars and got ten times the work done in half the time, he would not let them leave until he got answers.

"Gentlemen, you know that we now have an alliance with Meritor. The reason I recovered so well is I received medical attention from one of their medics.

"Excuse me, colonel," Dr. Thomas says angrily, "but you are my patient. No one should be treating you without my permission!"

Deon holds up his hand. "Doctor, do you have an antidote for a deadly poison that originates from the Chemdi-Shakahr home world? If not, do you have the means to get it?"

The doctor was silent. He had no reply for that. Deon continues, "You see, doctor, the blade that pierced my chest was tainted with such a poison. There is no medicine on Earth that would have saved me. The emissary sent a medical aide to see if they could help—they did and I'm alive. We are in a new age where we're going to have to consider putting aside our egos and what we think we know, and focus on the results and the opportunities to learn from them."

The doctor looks ashamed as he reflects on Deon's words. After all, he is a medical physician and Deon is right. The doctor knows that the method used to save the colonel's life could likely be used in other areas of medicine, and is keen to explore this possibility.

"I am in no official capacity to arrange a meeting with you and Meritor's Physicians," Deon continues. "However, I know someone who is. I can make a phone call and you all can sort it out—okay?"

The doctor is pleased. Little does Deon know, this one phone call will turn the medical community on its head and change Earth medicine forever.

* * *

The SCCC was badly damaged during the battle in space. Mr. Pickett is doing all he can to manage its repair and get the station back to its functional state. He hasn't been to Engineering for quite some time so he is making a visit today to see how the station has held up under the attacks of their new enemy. He walks the halls feeling very proud of his people for managing to withstand the attack of this very dangerous enemy. They survived. He does not take their success lightly.

As he walks the halls, his little dog in tow, he sees a few cracks in the floor from the explosions in the resident wing, but for the most part the lower decks seem to be intact. As he goes, he greets everyone he comes across—although his little sidekick Corky gets most of the attention. The staff of Engineering are amused at the director's quick little furry friend darting into Engineering ahead of his master—they know the director is not far behind.

"How's it going?" bellows the director.

"Well, sir," replies the chief engineer. "The reactor is at peak performance—and with any luck, should be for the next fifty years."

As the director talks to the engineering staff, Corky noses around Engineering for a bit, sniffing all over as dogs do, when suddenly, he runs to a storage area and starts digging at the doors and barking. His yapping goes on for a couple of minutes before the director yells, "Corky, be quiet!" The little dog quiets for a few seconds then starts again, this time barking

JOHN WILLIAMS

louder and digging frantically at the door with his little paws.

The director tries to carry on his conversation with the chief and his staff, growing increasingly irritated at the yapping. In the end, he can't stand it any longer and walks over to pick up his little pet. As he picks up the little Bichon and turns to walk away from the doors, they suddenly burst open with a loud noise. Pickett and his little dog go flying across the room like dolls. The staff looked in the direction of the commotion. What they see terrifies them. It's four Chemdi-Shakahr. There can only be one reason they are there: they want to blow up the reactor and destroy the station.

One staff member thinks fast and runs from the room to alert the SCCC. Mr. Pickett, now lying on the floor with a broken hip, crawls to the communication station and hits the alert alarm, to warn the SCCC. "Attention all personnel. This is Director Willard Pickett. You are ordered to evacuate the Space Command and Control Center. We've been breached by the enemy and they're going to blow the reactor! Again, evac —immediately!"

Suddenly, there is a weapon blast and the director's voice falls silent. He slides onto the floor, drawing his last breath. His faithful pet Corky remains by his side, whining pitifully and licking his master's face.

The Chemdi advance, killing everyone in sight. They shoot at the little beast but he's too fast; Corky barks at them in protest as they keep trying to shoot him. One of the Chemdi attaches a device to the door of the reactor core and activates it. Corky immediately heads for the door, barking ferociously.

At that instant, Geri Powell opens the door and enters Engineering. He immediately sees the Chemdi and glimpses his friend lying lifeless on the floor. Tears well up in his eyes. His boss, co-worker, mentor and friend is clearly dead. A shot blasts past him. "C'mon Corky, let's go boy!" and the little dog follows.

He runs up the hall, the little dog close at his heels, and yells out to crewmembers as he goes to evacuate the station.

The controllers in the SCCC coordinate the ship movements and get the ships out of the hangars. People grab what they can and race toward the ships or escape pods. Powell takes the elevator to the main level and marshals people up. "Let's go! Let's go—move it, people! This place is going to go up any second now!" Powell knows that many of the nearly fifteen thousand people are already deployed on ships in space or for medical or reclamation on Earth; he figures the remaining four to five thousand stand a good chance of getting off in time. In any case, he is not going to be satisfied until he gets everyone off.

He enters the SCCC control room and states, with all the authority he can muster, "Everybody, listen up! You have done a great job. Stop what you are doing. Get up and head to the nearest ship or escape pod. Do it... now!!"

"What about you, sir?" asks the EECOM controller.

"You are all my responsibility. I will be fine. Just get going. This place is going to go up at anytime!"

The controllers do as instructed and evacuate the control room. Powell looks out the windows to see all the ships leaving, some with construction scaffolding still attached. He feels a sense of relief that his staff have obeyed his orders and evacuated the station. He heads for the last remaining escape pod, Corky still in his arms. As he looks around mission control one last time, there is a deafening explosion and the station shudders violently. He runs to the pod and enters, hitting the "Evac" button. He hears the locks disengage and the engines fire, and the pod accelerates at very high speed. The explosions from the SCCC come in rapid succession and terrifyingly abrupt shock waves are one on top of the other. Debris pelts the exterior of the escape pod, and fiery fragments fly past. He feels the G-force as the pods begins to turn and follow the preprogrammed navigation protocol; it will begin a descent into a shallow orbit of the Earth. Not long after, it will enter the atmosphere, splashing down close to Cape Canaveral. Escape pods can be on the surface in anywhere from forty minutes to two hours from launch, depending on where they enter the atmosphere.

Looking out of the pod's windows, the flight director sees other pods and the various ships that have also escaped. His pod clears the debris quickly and starts a smooth transition into Earth's atmosphere, the ride growing bumpier as the pod's altitude decreases. SCCC Director Willard Pickett saved many lives that day with his quick thinking before he died. Powell looks at Pickett's little dog, a wave of deep sadness engulfing him at the loss of his friend and mentor. Overwhelmed with emotion, he breaks down and weeps uncontrollably.

* * *

The NASA Cape Canaveral teams pour out of the main building in droves. They can see the explosions in space from Earth, and scramble as many vessels as they can in anticipation of recovering survivors arriving in the escape pods. Grieved at the thought of how many souls may have been lost, they know they cannot think about that now. They must focus on saving the living.

CHAPTER TWELVE

The Chemdi Strike Back

Ambassador Wilory has been in discussions for a week now with the emissary, the government, and the medical community. The U.S. Surgeon General's office will host an official briefing on the medical care of Colonel Striker. Since he is a member of the military, Striker's consent is not necessary. The government has invited the finest minds and medical professionals from all over the world. The auditorium is standing room only and absolutely no photography of any kind is permitted. Security is extremely tight, with cell phones, tablets and all other devices being checked at the door for this invitation-only gathering.

This is a test case—the first public exposure of a citizen of Meritor to humans. This particular setting has been chosen because doctors are formally trained in science and should be able to behave with a certain amount of professional etiquette and decorum. This all came about following a request from one friend to another: Striker called his friend the ambassador to arrange a meeting with his doctor so that he could disclose how his life was saved and the effects the alien tech had had on his body.

Striker had been expecting a straightforward, quiet meeting—but unbeknownst to him, his request had morphed into this major symposium of the best medical minds in the world. The event is being held at the Hilton Chicago, a luxurious facility perfect for such an event.

Deon was released from the hospital nearly a month ago

now and has been invited to this symposium to share his part of this incredible story. The deputy surgeon general makes the introductory speech, welcoming the finest minds in the world, then opens with Striker's story.

Back in the green room, the special guests wait, carefully guarded by special agents. Although they are each located in different rooms for security purposes, Deon is keen to see his friend, Miiya. He exits his room.

The security guard immediately steps up to him. "Sir, we're instructed to keep you in your room until called, sir," the guard warns sternly.

"Listen, I know the 'special guest' personally—I just want to say hello before she goes on, that's all."

"Sir, that's not our orders."

The agent on duty sees the exchange between the security guard and Striker and says, "Wilson, it's all right. He's one of us. I'll vouch for the colonel."

Striker thanks the agent and gently knocks on the door adorned with two more security guards. There is no sound, no verbal permission called out; the door simply opens.

Striker walks in, and to the right just behind the door is a robed being with a hood covering its face. "Miiya? Is that you?"

"It is I, Deon. How are you?" Miiya replies. She is not quite used to the human way of affection but, like all Meritorians, she remembers everything she has experienced like it was yesterday. She remembers the hug Deon gave her on Meritor and she responds first this time, with a hug followed by a Poaghh, the Meritorian kiss. Deon is pleasantly surprised.

"Why are you here?" asks Striker.

"I was asked to show your Earth doctors the tools that I used to remove the poison and repair what damage I could in your body. In fact, Meritor is in the process of making these same tools available to Earth so that your people may benefit from them."

"Wow—that's remarkable. It will change the way the world performs medical care forever!"

"Exactly. As our new ally, we want to share our technology with you, as agreed. In return, we want to learn and trust that you will share your technology with us. Believe it or not, although some of your tools and techniques are not as advanced as ours, some of them are still very effective."

'So why didn't a Meritor physician come to this symposium?"

"On Meritor, we pride ourselves in using resources as sparingly and as efficiently as possible. Our physicians are on the home world; it would take time for them to prepare, learn your language and customs and travel here. Since I am medically trained and already possess those abilities, the emissary chose me for this task," says Miiya. "Meritorians have the ability to remember everything we learn and experience. The result is that many of us have excellent abilities across many different skills. We have observed that most humans tend to specialize in one or two skills. Not so with Meritorians. We can learn expertly whatever we apply ourselves to for a lifetime. I must also add that, as my father is the security director for the planet, he might have influenced the decision for me to present before your world physicians. Does that answer your question, Deon?"

Deon is amazed. Not only is he imagining what it would mean for Earth if humans had that ability, but he recalls what Balan-Gaal said regarding his daughter, before Deon had left the planet. Is this an attempt to keep Miiya in contact with him? "Wow, that is amazing."

There was a knock on the door. It was time for Miiya to make her presentation to the medical world. "Thank you, Deon, for visiting with me. I would like to visit with you again."

"It's a date then," Deon smiles. Although Deon knows she's not human, the fact that she is a very powerful, capable being is what makes her so attractive to him. He could only imagine what his peers would say—but nevertheless, he wants to see where this leads. If only she could be closer. He knows her home is Meritor for now, but should the opportunity present itself that she could have more time on Earth, he would definitely pursue a relationship with her. He can only hope.

She smiles at Deon with such affection, gently touching his face and give him one last Poaghh before she exits the room. The security detail escorts her to the wings of the stage and she waits to be introduced.

Miiya walks across the stage as if she is floating on air. Silence fills the room—the sort of silence that would embarrass or even startle your everyday human. But Miiya remains calm. She stops at the podium and introduces herself to the world for the first time, thus beginning her journey into Earth's history forever. Her command of the English language is now excellent.

"Greetings, physicians of Earth. My name is Miiya of the Imperial planet of Meritor. It is my pleasure to address you all today. Let me first say that, although I am not a physician, I am well trained in Meritor medicine and I am well able to thoroughly explain the tools and methods used to facilitate the recovery of Colonel Striker. I was already in this solar system and, under the circumstances, so as not to put Meritorian physicians at further risk, they chose to use my medical training to make this presentation. This was the wish of our government, and you can be assured that I have the expertise necessary to explain, in detail, the medical equipment and the process used in Colonel Striker's recovery."

Miiya's presentation is nothing less than extraordinary. She is clear, concise, and moreover, intoxicatingly charming. She even schools the entire room of world-renowned physicians on the workings of medicine at a molecular level that has yet to be discovered by humans. Within the space of fifty-five minutes, Miiya of Meritor has turned the medical community on their heads, and her presentation will keep them there for at least another decade. The presentation goes viral immediately, with over four million hits on YouTube in less than an hour. She becomes an instant celebrity—something she does not particularly want. The medical community's taste for this knowledge is insatiable. Universities and research hospitals from countries worldwide bombard the U.S. Surgeon General's office with requests for physicians to come from Meritor to teach them more.

*　*　*

Although the cooperation between Meritor and Earth was supposed to yield wonderful benefits for both worlds, it seems Earth has benefited most from the agreement. The Kingdom of Meritor does not mind this, however; their new ally is exactly what they needed. That said, they want to assist them in the rebuilding of the new Earth space station. Much like the techniques used to modify the Earth ships with new Meritorian weapons, they will use the same to construct the station in less time.

Meritor requests a presence on the space station, with space headquarters on the planet. Earth agrees. So as it stands now, Meritor is building an embassy on Meritor for Earth's ambassador, and Earth is building an embassy for the emissary of Meritor on Earth, to Meritorian specifications. Earth is also providing land and a compound for Meritor personnel who will staff the space station.

The Meritor emissary arranges the introductions between Meritor engineers and builders from Earth—a first in Earth's history, and a new relationship the likes of which there will be many more. The Meritorian technology can render Earth materials like steel, titanium and aluminum stronger and lighter, enabling Earth engineers to create unique shapes and to use these materials in new ways and in different applications. On another level, Meritorians have a molecular engine that can produce materials like translucent steel and aluminum. Indeed, the Meritorians have fast-tracked Earth by decades with their new technology.

*　*　*

The emissary has informed Ambassador Wilory that his residence is ready on planet Meritor and wants to know when he will be coming so that they can properly prepare for his arrival. His ship is on its way and the Meritor staff has been prepared. His wife is a little anxious about the move, unsure of what to expect. His girls are excited—however, his youngest daughter does not want to come at this time, preferring to remain on Earth to finish college.

The entire family is required to attend a series of briefings by the government before those who are going make their final departure. Ambassador Wilory will go on ahead to meet with Meritor dignitaries and prepare for his family's arrival.

* * *

The crowd around Miiya is making the Secret Service nervous. Apparently all are legitimate physicians seeking only to hear more about her world and their medical procedures.

Miiya's security detail has whisked her off the stage and through the backstage area to where her transportation is waiting. A group of alien dissenters who do not like the alliance between Meritor and Earth are demonstrating outside.

Colonel Striker had been hoping to meet with her for an after-hours drink, but unfortunately for him the Secret Service has beaten him to it; as he exits the green room into the hall, he finds it eerily empty and realizes she's already passed through. The Secret Service have all left. Deon bursts out of the exit doors to the street. Two black cars and four SUVs are lined up like Union Pacific freight cars. As he approaches, he sees Miiya's leg disappearing into the waiting car. She pokes her head out and waves her hand for the colonel to join her. It is almost as if she knew he would be coming. Three Secret Service agents are all talking into their wrists. The agent who is about to close Miiya's door holds up his hand at the colonel. Almost immediately, he gets the okay to permit the colonel to join. This is where their incredible evening begins. They head to the awaiting banquet held in her honor at a private location, for selected guests only.

"So, are you the belle of the ball?" Deon asks on their journey to the venue.

"Belle? What is belle of ball? I know, I know, it is an Earth expression," Miiya laughs.

As she exits the vehicle and enters the hall, a few of the Earth females gawk at her in amazement; others laugh. Earth females can be so cruel. However, Meritorians have a sensory perception that goes beyond human ability. Although she sees a couple of the women snicker at her, she can sense that it's out of jealousy and that the women are actually intimidated by her presence. She regally follows the procession along the corridor to the banquet hall and is directed to her seat at the main table. She whispers a request to the Secret Service agent.

"I would like my guest to be accommodated too, please," Miiya says.

The agent speaks quietly into his sleeve, and three people quickly arrive at the table and start shifting everything down to make room for the colonel. Striker noticed frowns and grimaces from those who had hoped to sit next to Miiya, but he clearly does not care.

A toast is offered in her honor by the U.S. Surgeon General, and distinguished guests gleefully oblige. The atmosphere is similar to that at an Academy Awards after-party. The guest of honor is the talk of the night and the press are eating it up. They seem to be already making a thing of Miiya calling the colonel her guest.

The surgeon general wants to have a brief conversation with her and she graciously accepts, turning to Deon and saying, "Colonel, may I meet with you later?"

"Sure. I..."

Miiya interrupts, "I know how to find you."

She quickly leaves with the surgeon general and his party. Deon is escorted by the Secret Service to his own hotel. He thanks the agent and walks into the lobby. "That's a first," he thinks to himself as he walks through the elevator doors —"I've just been dropped off at my hotel by the Secret Service!" He's a little tipsy, but this night has been really special. "One for the books," he thinks. He would have liked to have spent more time with Miiya. Maybe next time. He turns on the sixty-inch television and flops on the bed, too hyped up to sleep. Nothing on the TV appeals to him so he flops on his back, clicks the television off and stares at the ceiling. He thinks about his infatuation—maybe even love—for an alien named Miiya.

He voices out loud: "In fact, I don't care that she's not human; seeing her just does something to me. I can't explain it."

He slowly dozes off to sleep, still half-dressed in his Air Force dress blues.

* * *

The ship is very elegant—far from the condition of the ship that sped the former Captain Wilory and party from Meritor to Earth for the first time. This ship is definitely fit for any executive, foreign dignitary, and certainly an ambassador. It comes complete with Meritorian staff. The security detail is a little nervous, not knowing anything about the Meritorian staff on board the ship—highly unusual and against security protocol, but there is frankly nothing they can do about it. Truth be told, if a physical altercation were to occur between the Marine Corps security detail and the Meritor security detail, to be sure, the Marines would likely easily be overwhelmed by the physiology of the Meritor guards. In short, they will just have to trust them.

Ambassador Wilory is very comfortable and enjoying his trip from Earth to Meritor. They will be landing shortly at the new embassy built by the Meritorians. Earth construction would not be adequate here. As they approach the landing pad, the ambassador can see the nervousness of his Earth staff. They have never been to Meritor—or indeed any other unknown planet—before. The ship lands safely and the embassy is a sight to behold; it's absolutely stunning. The Meritorian flora and fauna is breathtaking as they walk from the pad to the building; the construction itself appears to be in a pearlescent stone-like structure that gleams in the light of the two suns. Beautiful flowers, the likes of which they have never seen before, adorn the balconies. As they approach, they realize that the waterfalls originating in the crystal-clear pools are moving upwards, in reverse. The pools are teaming with brilliantly colored, exotic-looking fish. The Meritorian staff lines the walk and receives the Earth Ambassador's party. They will be there to train and support the Earth staff. However, not all of them will stay on.

A very stately looking Meritorian gentleman appears to be the household chief of staff. He is trained in at least four Earth languages, all manners of Earth protocol and has received virtual extensive butler training from The Guild of Professional English Butlers and the International Butler Academy and Kasteel Oost, The Netherlands. In short, he's the "head butler of butlers." He will liaise with the ambassador's chief of staff.

The Meritor household chief introduces himself. "Greetings, your Excellency. I am, your Meritor chief of staff." I am here to serve you and your Earth staff at your pleasure, sir.

"Thank you, Yost," the ambassador replies.

Yost gives Steve a tour of the grounds. They are breathtakingly beautiful. The residence features a smaller version of the Meritorian gym that they trained in before, and even has a personal trainer just for him. The kitchen is more similar to an Earthly gourmet kitchen. They have really done their homework; it is utterly impressive.

The staff is lined up outside of what looks like a garage. The household chief introduces the ambassador to their equivalent of a facilities engineer, who seems giddy with excitement. Before the engineer opens the doors, he proudly says something to the chief of staff, who translates. "The engineer says that you have the only one of its kind in all of Meritor."

The door opens and it's a replica of his 71 Chevrolet Corvette, adapted to fly as the other Meritorian vehicles do. Steve stands there in awe. He feels so warmly welcomed. No ambassador of any country or planet could be more pleased. Overwhelmed, Steve suddenly feels tired from his trip and all the excitement; he politely excuses himself and makes his way to the living quarters.

As he enters his residence bedroom suite, he excuses his security detail for the moment and closes the double doors behind him. Falling to his knees on the thick, exquisite carpet, he weeps, both hands covering his face. His hopes and dreams to someday become a statesman have come true—yet in the most remarkable way. It's far more than he ever could have asked for. He gives thanks to his holy God for having done this, and he feels a great sense of humility.

* * *

Deon stirs on the bed as he sleeps, dreaming that he's heard a knock on the door. Although his body is sound asleep, it is actually his sub-conscience hearing the knock on his room door. In his dream, he's trying to find the door in this vast place but he cannot. He hears the knock again, a little louder this time. He wakes up with a start and snaps up from the bed, shuffling to the door and looking through the peephole. It's someone wearing what looks like a very beautiful scarf and shades. Heck! It's Miiya! He opens the door.

"Well, hello there. I was sort of in the galaxy and thought I would stop by."

"Wow. For someone who has been learning the English language for only a few months, your use of humor is actually very funny. Impressive. Please, come in!"

"Oh, you will find I'm full of... un-expectancies...?"

"Could you mean surprises?"

"Ah, yes... That is the word I wanted to use...surprises."

"So what brings you here? I thought you were spending quality time with the surgeon general and friends."

"Humans can be so petty and fearful. They do not know that I can sense such feelings in spite of their words. I grew weary of their senseless conversation so I left."

"So how did you get here?"

"Are you going to be unimaginative also?" she quips.

"Wow," Steve said again. "That was also pretty good. You sound almost like my ex!"

"By the way, your former mate misses you terribly. As I was scanning your location, I saw your former residence. She was there looking at your former video files," says Miiya.

"You mean our old home movies?"

"If that is what you call video files, then yes."

"Wow. I never would have thought that. She treats me like she hates me—and she was the one who cheated!"

"Cheated?"

That's when your mate mates with another."

Miiya looks as if she has been hit in the gut. The look on her face is one that Striker has never seen before. She is clearly distraught. "What—did I say something wrong?" he asks.

"No. You did not. Mating with someone who is not your mate is forbidden on Meritor. It is punishable by one of two ways: death or choosing to survive the Uallion Desert for three days with Uallion worms in your body. Death is almost always the result."

"What is the reason for the worms?"

"Uallion worms are very painful once in the body. They do not like movement beyond their own will. When moved, they secrete a toxin that causes severe hallucinations. It's a miserable experience, I am told. This punishment is to deter citizens of Meritor from mating with someone other than their mate. Our society takes mating very seriously because it is the foundation of our Cöblects and social structure. Cöblects is what you on Earth call families. Mating with others besides your mate is so rare, you hardly even hear about it. In fact it's kept quiet to avoid alarming the masses."

"Wow," Deon replies. You Meritorians take commitment to whole new level. So if you and I were to..."

"Not so fast, Earth hero—you have much to learn," Miiya says with a smile.

They stay up talking until six o'clock in the morning, kissing and hugging, but nothing too sensual. Because of the deep commitment involved in their relationships, Meritorians take their time when courting. Suddenly, Deon falls asleep in the midst of their conversation. Miiya's stamina is practically endless compared to Deon's. She sits up in the bed next to him and watches over him like a mother hen. She's more emotionally invested than he realizes; Meritorians form a deep devotion to those they consider their potential mates. At this point in their relationship, Deon has the potential to deeply hurt her feelings, and is not even aware of it. He does know that Miiya is not some date of the type you pick up in a seedy bar, but a very sophisticated female of a completely different race. He is wise enough to take things slowly, and realizes that he might just need a little help on this one.

CHAPTER THIRTEEN

Reciprocity

The ride is incredibly smooth compared to other SUVs she has been in, Jean thinks to herself as the four-vehicle detail whisks her and her youngest daughter to her husband's Washington DC office. They will be given their final briefing before boarding the ambassador's ship that will take them to Meritor to join her husband. She's very nervous because she's never traveled in space before. Space travel was her husband's gig, not hers. She knows how meticulous her husband is and she trusts him to handle all the details, in particular their family's safety. Her daughter, although excited, is also wary of the trip to an entirely different planet, but as far as she's concerned, they have each other and will join her Daddy very soon. She will delay college life until the fall. She has yet to select one but she's getting close. This is an opportunity of a lifetime and the university will be there when she get's back. She knows that there is no need to apply like other students. She knows that there are great benefits to being an Ambassador's daughter.

The briefing lasts about one hour, thirty minutes. Jean can't help but wonder why they couldn't have simply said all of that over the phone or in an e-mail. Government, she thinks to herself.

The ship awaits them and they are notified that they are ready to beam up, and their belongings with them. The process is almost instantaneous. Amazed that they did not feel anything, they now find themselves in the comfort of an alien spacecraft. It is luxurious to say the least. Jean's daughter Kate has never seen real aliens before, and feels frightened and excited all at the same time. Both women are surprised at how close to modern-day aircraft the alien ship appears; the cockpit, although very futuristic, is laid out similarly to those on Earth, only with a lot more style.

The guards looked like beings not to be trifled with; very tall, they each have what looks like a very large handle hooked to their belts—obviously a weapon of some kind. Both women are shown to their seats.

One of the remarkable skills of the Meritorians is that they are masters at research and customer service and have the ability to accurately duplicate things, down to the slightest detail. They offer Lady Wilory and Katie refreshments. The ladies order what they would usually have on Earth; Jean a sweet tea, and Katie chocolate malt. The taste of both is mouthwateringly delicious. Jean smiles at her daughter. "If this is any indication of what food will taste like on Meritor, it may not be as bad as I imagined!"

Katie nods her head, busy enjoying her malt through a bright-red straw.

As they settle in, they can see space out of their windows. They also see two other ships alongside theirs.

Katie waves over the attendant and asks, "Excuse me, what are the other ships for?"

"They are our escorts," the Meritorian attendant replies. "They will provide security for us."

Soon after, they feel a powerful sensation of acceleration. They are on their way to their new home!

* * *

Since suffering defeat at Earth, the Chemdi-Shakahr are determined to hinder their enemies in any way they can. The alliance of Meritor and Earth could mean more supply runs between both worlds. They will look for any such missions and attack them. They are aware that this is like looking for a needle in a haystack, due to the unlimited routes that can be taken between Earth and Meritor. The Chemdi still do not know where Meritor is—but they do know where Earth is. They will make their best guess.

The communications officer of a Chemdi ship on patrol notifies the captain that he is tracking a three-ship formation leaving Earth's orbit; the mother ship is rather small in size, possibly a diplomatic cruiser. The captain gets to his feet, various scenarios going through his head: He can stay cloaked and attempt to follow the ship to Meritor—if indeed that is where it is going. Or perhaps he can simply destroy the ship and its escort, demoralizing the alliance. Finally, he considers taking any potential VIP passengers and imprisoning them for a while, then demanding ransom—the release of Chemdi-Shakahr currently being held as prisoners on Earth.

He motions to his commo officer and addresses his crew in a commanding voice. "Attention all crew; we will be engaging a three-ship enemy formation. They are no match for us but stay alert. Its fighter escort can still be very deadly. We will attack and hold their passengers. We will then ransom them for our brothers being held as prisoners on Earth. We will exchange their scum for our elite Chemdi-Shakahr!"

The Chemdi let out shouts and wails of agreement in response to their captain's plan.

The Chemdi close in on the three-ship formation. The Meritor crew notices movement coming in their direction. "Sir, we have a Chemdi-Shakahr cruiser closing in on our position!" says the Meritor shuttle co-pilot.

"I see it. Transmit the coordinates to the fighters!" responds the captain.

He alerts the crew of the danger, and orders them to secure the passengers. The formation is just short of the halfway point, so any help from Earth or Meritor would not arrive in time, but the captain sends out a distress call anyway. The crew braces for the imminent attack.

The Meritorian communications officer on the nearly finished SCCC receives the distress call from the Meritorian ship. He alerts the SCCC leadership and, although they know the battle may be over before they arrive, two cruisers are dispatched immediately to get there as fast as they can.

Meanwhile, back on Meritor, Ambassador Wilory is alerted by the Meritor chief of staff about the situation—his family is in danger. The chief of staff tries to remain as calm as he can as he delivers the grave news to the ambassador who is standing behind his desk.

"Are you sure, Yost?" Steve asks, his face full of concern.

"Unfortunately, yes, sir."

"Get me Colonel Striker on the phone!"

"Phone, sir?"

"Ah—right. Contact Colonel Striker, please—right now! I need to talk to him!"

"Yes, sir. Right away."

Deon is never far from his Zehrea. He carries it like a cell phone—mainly just in case he gets a call from Miiya. He stirs from his sleep in the bed of his hotel room, hearing the Zehrea tone ringing from the inside of his dress blues jacket pocket. Miiya reaches over and answers in her language.

"To whom am I speaking?" asks Yost.

"This is Miiya, Meritor security captain and Meritor ministry of medicine, medical advisor."

"It is my honor to make your acquaintance, but unfortunately on a very somber occasion. The Meritor U.S. Ambassador requests to speak to Colonel Striker."

"Of course. He is sleeping; I will wake him." Miiya gently caresses Deon's face. He doesn't stir. She breathes a harmless mist of moisture from her lungs and wakes him. He wakes up wiping his face.

"Hey, what was that? Are you spraying me with water? What was that for?" Deon exclaims as he comes to.

"There seems to be an urgent matter from your friend," she says, handing him his Zehrea.

"Colonel Striker here."

"Deon, it's me, Steve. My wife and daughter Kate are being transported to Meritor, and I have just been informed that a

Chemdi ship has been moving toward their position to attack. I need you to save my family. There is no one else I trusted enough to call. Their last position was at the halfway point between Earth and Meritor. The SCCC has sent two destroyers but they will not make it in time. Do you think you can?"

"I'm so sorry to hear that, Steve. Sure, of course I'll try it. I need to assemble my team but even if I could be airborne in thirty minutes, even a Meritor ship cannot make it that fast. I'm afraid I will arrive just ahead of the destroyers. Unless of course..." Deon trails off.

"What do you have in mind?" asks Steve.

"Let me make a few phone calls and I'll get back to you. In short, I have commissioned a prototype that has not been tested but in theory shows great promise—and now may be the right time to test it. In the meantime, call the SECDEF and let him know I will need support. I'll call you back."

"Thank you, Deon. Consider it done!"

"Miiya, let's beam over to my facility at Area 51. I need to have the team beamed over as well. Also, can any of your Khorathian friends help?" Deon asks.

"I will ask them but they are under direct orders of the Brajeh. I will contact my father."

"Great! Let's go!"

As they use the ship in orbit to beam from Chicago to Groom Lake, Nevada, Deon wakes his team and explains the situation. They have been working on a prototype ship that redirects the quantum energy and routes them through the engine exhaust giving them a quantum after-burner effect. This has never been tested in flight but the engineering is sound and should provide a significant boost in energy, thereby increasing their speed—but by how much, no one yet knows. The colonel has been working on this since first arriving at Area 51. Since his first trip from Meritor to Earth, he has had in a mind a ship that could fly faster between the two worlds. This is an opportunity to find out whether his idea really was achievable. He explains the scenario to his team.

They're afraid; they have no data yet and want to do more testing. They do not want to put their hero at risk.

The ship is new and is large enough to carry a small team. The oversized engines give it a fast and angry look. It is armed with quantum cannons and missiles, as well as the latest sensor arrays, communication gear and anti-electronic warfare package available. It's the most advanced ship in the Earth fleet so far and the DoD will be watching its performance with great interest. It could be just the ship to save his friend's family. It will likely fly as fast as a Meritorian ship, without the quantum afterburners, so if they do not work, they will still get to the VIP ship—but the question is whether this will be before or after the engagement...

The SOCOM operators have been briefed and are also beamed to Area 51—eight of them in all. All the pieces are in play, with the exception of the Khorathians. Miiya is prepared to battle alongside the colonel, as before. They board the ship and receive final instructions from the engineers. As yet, there is no reply from the Brajeh concerning Khorathian assistance. So be it—they will proceed anyway.

They take off and fly toward the last reported coordinates. They will update their navigational data as they get in range of the three-ship formation. As they clear Earth's atmosphere, they have set in the navigation and engage the quantum system. All crewmembers are in the standard five-point harnesses—the colonel had insisted on seats designed by the German Recaro GmbH & Co. KG, the best restraint systems used in race cars, aircraft etc. The only thing missing on the ship now is a racing stripe. The ship accelerates at mind-blowing speed. The pilot throttles back so as not to injure the crew. As they continue to accelerate, he pushes the power to seventy-five percent of the burners' capacity. So far, so good—at the current heading and speed, they just might be there in a little over forty minutes. Striker commands they push it to eighty percent, bringing their new arrival time to just under twenty minutes.

The Chemdi-Shakahr ship is cloaked and still tracking the VIP formation. They will be in transport-beam range in just under thirty minutes, and are preparing a boarding party. Chemdi love to board alien ships because they usually have the advantage and they're experts at it. Their doctrine is to board with the knowledge that they will lose some fighters, but these are a distraction to enable the core team to achieve the main objective. This mission will be no different.

Striker and his team are suited up, Striker wearing his Alocae-Cha. The JSOC (Joint Special Operations Command) team has a version developed by the collective manufacturers of Earth. Striker has both and prefers the Meritor version as well as his Shelah, given to him by none other than Balan-Gaal himself.

"Sir, we're in range to beam you all to the ship," the captain says. "However, we have to cut the quantum burners and de-cloak."

"Do it," replies Striker.

They drop their speed and are de-cloaked. The ship's metaphasic shields will enable them to beam to the other ship without the need to drop the shields. The team is fully armed and prepares to beam aboard. Striker gathers the team into a huddle. He knows what's at stake and he says a simple prayer. "Dear God, we're attempting to kill the wicked and save the innocent. Give us the strength and wisdom to do our very best. May no harm come to them in the process. Give us victory this day as we go. In the name of Jesus, we pray. Amen."

The whole team says "Amen." Miiya, not quite sure whom Striker was praying to, nevertheless got the gist that it was clearly a deity whom he respected and one he thought could help. Without a beat, she also said, "Amen."

The Chemdi begin to materialize in the midst of the VIP cruiser. The Meritor sentries and two Khorathians go into action, their weapons drawn. Perhaps this is why the Brajeh did not answer.

Colonel Striker's crew has completed a mission similar to

this before—the difference being that they are trying to protect versus destroy.

The captain of Striker's ship cries out, "Sir, the enemy is boarding in multiple locations and decks!"

"We don't have enough operators to match. We'll board on the same deck as the package," Deon says, alluding to Mrs. Wilory and daughter Kate, "and split up. Half of us will take the rear and sweep forward. The rest of you will take the forward part of the ship and sweep aft. Let's move!"

The team boards the VIP ship as instructed and goes to work. Striker's skill at defeating the Chemdi is impressive; he is killing them with the same efficiency as his instructor Balan-Gaal. The first wave of Chemdi drop like flies. They are no match for the rapid, ultra-accurate firepower of the Khorathians. The security detail moves Mrs. Wilory and Katie to the rear of the ship for better protection—or so they think; Chemdi have a nasty habit of boarding a ship in multiple locations and on multiple decks. The fight continues. The JSOC teams have been given the latest plasma and laser weapons, which are highly effective. The Chemdi get a few choice shots off, killing two of the Special Forces operators. JSOC operators return fire killing four Chemdi. JSOC operators now carry transporter tags; when an operator is down, they affix these tags and the wounded are immediately beamed to the mother ship. The two downed operators are therefore no longer on board.

The Meritor security detail moves the package toward the rear of the ship and descends to the next deck down. Miiya takes the lead and follows Meritor security. Arriving at the next level, they come face to face with a group of Chemdi who were waiting for them. The Meritor guards fire and kill four. The Chemdi pull back as if to retreat, but the Khorathians finish the job. As they continue down the corridor, more Chemdi, who had obviously been hiding in the storage rooms, start to flank them, splitting the Earth team up.

Suddenly, a Chemdi shoots the Meritor guards who are

on either side of Mrs. Wilory. Another Chemdi grabs her and beams to their ship. The fighting becomes fierce; Miiya is cutting down their numbers very quickly and the JSOC operators gather their composure and go into battle.

As Colonel Striker approaches the lower deck, he hears the screams of Steve's daughter. Making his way through the few Chemdi, he heads in that direction. The team is clearing the quarters as they go. Deon approaches and sees the downed Meritor security guards; as he turns the corner, he is met with the most disheartening sight he has ever seen. Miiya and the team are at a standstill. In the center of the corridor, he sees little Katie in the clutches of a Chemdi. His lower arms are tightly wrapped around her and he has a huge blade in his upper left hand, which he is pushing against her neck!

The Chemdi is making a guttural sound in their native language, repeating over and over, obviously meaning, "Stay back!" The team is holding fire, for fear of hitting the terrified, sobbing teenage girl.

"Katie," Deon yells, "it's going to be okay, baby! It's going to be okay!"

She barely gets out the words through her tears. "Please… They took my mom." And with that, the Chemdi beams her off the ship. It happens so fast.

Deon lets out the most pitiful scream, as if he himself were her father. "Katie!" Overwhelmed with anger and frustration, Striker begins to beat and kick the ship bulkhead with his Shelah. His team looks on sadly, overcome with disappointment and shame at having failed their mission. Their inability to save the two women is like a punch to the stomach.

* * *

Yost walks into the ambassador's office a little slower than usual and closes the double doors behind him. The ambassador's back is to the door as he stands looking out of the window into the courtyard below. It won't be long now before he sees his beloved wife and daughter.

"Mr. Ambassador," Yost says, "I must apologize, but I have

terrible news, sir."

"What is it, Yost?"

"Sir, it's about your family. Their ship was ambushed and I'm sad to say that they were taken by the Chemdi."

The ambassador crumbles to his knees as if he has been kicked in the gut, covering his head with his arms and weeping uncontrollably, his forehead pressed into the floor. The faithful Meritor chief of staff puts his hand upon the ambassador's back to comfort him. There is a soft knock on the double doors as they are slowly opened. His Earth staff rush in to see what the commotion is all about. Yost fills them in and they immediately rush to Steve's side, dropping to their knees as they comfort their ambassador, weeping with him, their grief and sorrow raw and deep.

* * *

Colonel Striker and his team run toward the bridge to see if they can pursue the ship. He helps up a Meritorian guard as he enters. "Captain, can we pursue the ship?!"

"My apologies, colonel—we cannot. The ship cloaked almost immediately and there is no way to track it long-range. It could literally be anywhere," replies the captain, his voice somber.

Striker and his team reluctantly return to their ship. They will head back to Earth. He knows he must contact his best friend immediately and apologize for his failure to save his family. There are no words to describe the level of anguish and frustration Striker and his team is feeling. In truth, they were up against a stacked deck; the Chemdi-Shakahr board ships like this routinely—it is part of their military doctrine. They are literally experts at it, and even the best of military forces would have a hard time defeating them. Additionally, the fact that they boarded the ship at multiple locations made it very tough to figure out which area to best concentrate their manpower. Their efforts were overly ambitious at best. Nonetheless, they will conduct an "after-action review" to determine what they could have done differently.

228

Although the colonel is the first human to engage and kill a Chemdi-Shakahr in battle, he is keenly aware that this is a young man's game and that he does not have many years left of leading missions.

The SECDEF has heard the news of the ambassador's wife and daughter being taken by the Chemdi-Shakahr. He is not pleased and wants answers, starting with the SOCOM team. They are contacted in-flight and informed that they are to divert to Andrews Air Force Base, Prince Georges County, Maryland where a convoy will be awaiting to take them to the Pentagon for debriefing.

The Department of Defense has already decided that from now on, VIPs will be required to travel with a heavy escort. Meritorians are welcome to join but Earth citizens will no longer use a small ship detail to travel to Meritor.

Ambassador Wilory has had his moment to grieve and has now switched over to tactical mode. This is usually when he is at his very best, especially when the lives of the most important people in his life are at stake. "Yost, I request to see Balan-Gaal! If anyone can devise a plan to get my family back, it is him," Steve says.

"I will summon him at once, Mr. Ambassador," replies Yost.

It does not take long for Balan-Gaal to arrive, surrounded as usual by his formidable security detail.

"Mr. Ambassador, congratulations—and I am deeply sorry about your family. I am at your service. How may I help you?"

"As you know, my family is in the clutches of the Chemdi." Steve's chin trembles as he asks the most difficult question: "Are they still alive?"

"Mr. Ambassador, I cannot say for sure, but my assessment of how the Chemdi boarded the ship would lead me to think that yes, they are still alive. You see, if they wanted to kill everyone, they simply would have done so. Also, their boarding party was three times the size of normal boarding parties we've seen in the past, which means they wanted something specific and were prepared to lose however many Chemdi they needed in order to accomplish their mission. Your friend Colonel Striker was fighting a losing battle from the beginning."

"Striker? Deon was on that mission?" exclaims the ambassador.

"Yes, sir, along with my daughter Miiya. He lost men and returned to his ship. They could not pursue because the Chemdi ship cloaked and disappeared.

"What is my family's fate, security chief?"

Balan-Gaal pauses for a moment, aware of the pain the ambassador is feeling. He knows all too well what it is like to have your family killed by the Chemdi. "This will be a very hard answer for you to hear: they may use them for research. Seeing how they were so determined, they may also use them as bait for a prisoner exchange. As for my last opinion, I am not at liberty to discuss at this time. I am aware that Earth has taken a number of Chemdi prisoners from the war and Meritor has also captured two. They may try to get them back. It takes a long time to develop a Chemdi warrior and they value them with high regard. I recommend patience. If they want to ransom them, they will likely contact us. However, if and when they do, we need to respond at a moment's notice."

"Thank you, Balan-Gaal. I will inform my government on Earth!" Steve replies.

"You are welcome, Mr. Ambassador. In the interim, I have assigned additional security from my personal guard as a precaution. They will keep you safe. Now, if you will excuse me." Balan-Gaal departs as quickly as he arrived, as is his custom.

Steve can tell that there may be more to this than meets the eye but he's not on Earth and has no other alternative but to trust his hosts.

* * *

It is dark and dank, and there is a strange smell of decay in the room. The smell is not necessarily human. They are lying on what seems to be a very large padded operating table that is slightly tilted downwards. They are completely naked. Their arms and legs are spread, similar to the famous Leonardo da Vinci's Vitruvian Man drawing.

Two Chemdi-Shakahr enter the room along with a Khorathian. The Chemdi stand guard. One of the creatures begins scanning Jean's body very carefully using a wand of some sort, careful not to touch her at all. He seems to be very interested in and concentrating on Jean's abdomen and womb area. His movements are slow and deliberate. Jean just lies there and does not say a word.

He then begins scanning Katie. She is not as calm as her mother. "Don't you touch me, you freak! Where are my clothes?" Katie screams, tears rolling down her face.

The Khorathian begins probing Kate's body. He uses an overhead apparatus to insert one needle after another in her chest, legs and abdomen. Katie's screams can be heard all over the facility. Her mother is crying also, as she desperately tries to console her daughter. The experience is heart-wrenching. The needles produce just a little blood as they are removed. Finally, Katie passes out and the screaming stops. The examination is not life-threatening but is painful.

A light mist that is sprayed on their faces and they immediately sleep. This is likely one of many examinations that will be performed on the two women.

CHAPTER FOURTEEN

A New Era Begins

Balan-Gaal is heading the investigation to ascertain where the ambassador's family may have been taken. Meritor is monitoring all Chemdi and Khorathian transmissions. Since there are Khorathians on Meritor, deciphering their messages is simple. The language of the Chemdi is very difficult, although some Meritor scholars are trained in most of their language; however, there are many dialects used only by military commanders, which makes the task much more difficult. There has been a breakthrough in the intelligence gathering, though—they may have an inclination as to their location.

Balan-Gaal is busy devising a plan that could be ready to go at a moment's notice. He intends to go himself, with his awesome bodyguards and an additional team. If his family is there, they will recover them or die trying.

* * *

The SECDEF and his aides are in the conference room along with Striker and his team, including Miiya. The SECDEF aide begins the questioning. "So, Colonel Striker, tell us about the intel that you received before dispatching for the recovery mission," says the aide.

"I received information from the Meritorians that there was an enemy ship bearing down on the VIP ship's position and that we had very little time to intercept."

The questioning continues for the next two hours. The panel concludes that there was nothing the team could have done to prevent the snatching of the ambassador's family. He then thanks them for their service and their duty to try to recover them. The SECDEF makes a request to the colonel that he needs to train other teams in what he knows about defeating the Chemdi-Shakahr in battle. In fact, he and Miiya will temporarily be assigned to Marine Corps Base Quantico, Marine Corps Training and Education Command, Quantico, Virginia, to instruct Special Forces personnel from around the world in weapons and tactics to defeat the Chemdi. They can expect to be there for approximately three to four months. Striker and Miiya accepts. They request a Meritor simulator to train with for the duration of their stay. Knowing how the government works, they will like the simulator so much they may simply keep it.

* * *

Meritorian Intelligence is buzzing with activity. They have received a message from Khorathian High Command. The Chemdi-Shakahr is willing to surrender the two human females in exchange for all the Chemdi fighters that Meritor and Earth have captured. They assure Earth that the prisoners will not be harmed. The message includes a video feed with time/date stamp encryption authenticating that they are truly alive. They have three Meritor days to deliver the prisoners, at specific coordinates. If they do not, the ambassador's wife and daughter will be killed.

The message is communicated to Earth through the Meritorian ambassador. Washington is not pleased. The United States Government is committed to getting Jean Wilory and her daughter released and gives orders to prepare a ship to transport all of the captured Chemdi fighters, as requested. They will coordinate the exchange with Meritor. They want as many "eyes on" as possible in case something goes wrong.

Ambassador Wilory looks haggard. He has not been getting much sleep and the sleep he does occasionally achieve is fraught with nightmares about his family and what they are going through. He's literally a tortured man. His staff has been rallying around him twenty-four/seven; he has a propensity not to eat so they ensure that they fix his favorite foods to try to encourage him to eat and keep up his strength. Finally the Earth chief of staff threatens him with an IV drip if he doesn't start eating something. That does the trick.

Steve is desperate to know what conditions his wife and daughter are being kept in. Surely someone must know. He summonses Yost, who glides into the room in his usual way. "How may I be of service, Mr. Ambassador?"

"I am struggling to get to sleep. I cannot help but wonder what they're doing to my wife and daughter. Can you help?"

"During the war, a number of Meritorians were captured. Toward the end of the war, to be captured was to be killed. Earlier on, they would hold their prisoners for the opportunity to exchange them. While they held prisoners, they would do experiments on them to access our weaknesses. That is all I know, Mr. Ambassador."

The ambassador fights back his tears. He hopes against hope that they are in good health and that their experience as Chemdi prisoners isn't too hard for them. He will continue to pray for their safety and prompt return.

* * *

Back on Earth, the Chemdi prisoners have been loaded on a ship and are now preparing to join the space battle group led by the star battleship Maximus, joined by two star cruisers and a couple of destroyers already orbiting Earth. The five-ship formation is waiting for the tender to make the trip to the predetermined coordinates given by the Chemdi-Shakahr. All agree that it feels like a trap, but they're going anyway. Meritor cruisers will rendezvous with them as well. If the Chemdi try something stupid, they are going to have a deadly fight on their hands.

The Meritorian armada takes off and heads into deep space to meet with the Earth fleet. Balan-Gaal, on board the flagship, does not trust the Chemdi one iota; he and the fleet are prepared to act. In his mind, this is not the way to impress the people of Earth that Meritor is more than capable of protecting Earth statesmen and their families. The Brajeh is embarrassed about the whole incident and has demanded that the security chief resolve this—and fast.

Balan-Gaal is no fool and he suspects that a traitor is behind this event. He has a plan and it is already in motion. Not long after his fleet departs, a second battle group is dispatched, with orders to remain out of detection range.

* * *

Colonel Striker and Miiya are quickly becoming well respected in the Joint Special Operations Command (JSOC) community. Operators from all over the world—the United Kingdom's MI-6 and SAS, Israeli Commandos, Philippine and South Korean special forces, The Russian Spetsnaz, the United States Navy Seals, Marine Corps Force Recon, Air Force Combat Air Controllers, CIA, FBI, NSA, German KSK & KSM, the Swedish Särskilda Skyddsgruppen and others are all getting a chance to play with the Meritor simulator. A hundred or so people are present to observe this technology—assorted officers from various branches and countries, and even unnamed branches. Some are in uniform, others in plain clothes.

The Chemdi simulator is the exact model Striker first used when he went to Meritor. As the operators are taught various techniques, they are put into the sim with Chemdi to see what they have learned. One New Zealand operator, a self-proclaimed thirteenth-degree black belt, thinks he's going to show the class what he can do. His weapon of choice is a pair of Chinese "Ring" Daggers. Miiya starts the simulation and everyone waits anxiously for the demonstration. The Chemdi appears with one single blade about two feet long. The operator is very impressive with his fancy footwork and spinning daggers. The Chemdi circles him like a Lion about to pounce on its prey, its long cape dragging on the floor. As the operator performs his fancy technique, he misses the Chemdi's telltale lifting of his shoulders, indicating he's about to strike. The Chemdi initiates a strike with its lower-left arm. The operator blocks it with his daggers. The Chemdi then comes over the top with the upper-right hand, knocking the operator out cold. He falls to the ground on his back. The Ring Daggers literally fly across the room. His classmate runs over to see if he is all right and helps him up from the floor. The man is dazed and his pride is hurt but he survives the day. Some of the class members snicker; others remain completely silent. All are focusing intently.

Striker begins, "Well, boys and girls... This is why you do not futz around with a Chemdi. In this setting, our colleague was simply knocked unconscious. In a real fight, he would be dead. Chemdi-Shakahr has two more arms and hands than you do. They also have about seven times more stamina. This is the reason I am wearing this body-enhancement suit. My version is called an Alocae-Cha. It's lightweight and gives me the ability to fight with almost as much stamina as they do. Without it, the Chemdi will have the advantage. The U.S. Government has contracted manufacturers to come up with a body-enhancement suit of their own. Once we're finished here today, you will be fitted and issued one.

It's Chemdi tradition to defeat you with the same type of weapon that you're using on them. This is why we use edged weapons; it gives us a fighting chance to defeat them. With guns, we face the chances of being shot increases four times in one.

We're going to be teaching you basic and advanced fighting skills on how to defeat a Chemdi-Shakahr. Your first priority is to assess the best approach to initiate your attack. Your focus should be to engage the enemy, kill him, and be prepared for the next. You will also notice that they keep a wide stance, so you are not going to outmaneuver them easily. They have articulating spines, which mean they can turn almost completely around without moving their feet. As our colleague has learned, leave the fancy theatrics for martial-art tournaments. In a real fight, techniques like that will just get you killed. By the way, we have slowed the movement of the Chemdi simulation about forty percent to assist us with your training. The Chemdi's real response time is a lot faster."

He nods to Miiya and she re-sets the simulator.

"Together, Miiya and I will fight four Chemdi initially, and can ultimately fight up to as many as ten to demonstrate what we are about to teach you. We will see how it goes. The speed is set to the normal setting, so what you are about to see is the actual speed and power of the Chemdi in a real fight. Let's begin."

Miiya starts the simulator. She turns her Shelah into her usual weapon of choice, the modified Syrian Sabre, with two opposing blades, one over the other, and takes her usual stance. Striker takes his real Chinese long sword and takes his stance. The simulation starts and four Chemdi appear. Adorned in their dark purple floor-length capes with the signature gold piping, their stares are cold from those four deep-red eyes—a terrifying look that chills to the bone. Their disposition alone almost makes a person want to give up before they start.

One Chemdi steps forward and proceeds toward Colonel Striker as if he's going in for the immediate kill. Striker ducks, spins in the opposing direction and thrusts the blade through the Chemdi, puncturing both hearts. Miiya produces an additional short blade, blocking the Chemdi with her sword and stabbing them twice in the hearts with lightning speed and accuracy. Two down.

One of the two remaining Chemdi kicks Striker squarely in the chest and he goes flying across the floor. The Chemdi whirls about using his cape as a distraction and approaches quickly to stab him on the ground with his spear. The spear goes into the floor as Striker rolls to the right. He leaves his Jian on the floor and quickly grabs the spear. He tucks in his knees and lifts his legs, using the spear as a launching point to put his legs around the Chemdi's neck. He extends his legs, wrapping them around the Chemdi's neck and uses his short blade to stab the Chemdi through the top of its skull. The Chemdi collapses on the floor. He rides the Chemdi down to the floor, does a forward roll and recovers his Jian.

Miiya is still fighting the last Chemdi. The Chemdi lifts its battle ax over its head to kill Miiya. As the raised ax reaches the top of its swing, Miiya thrusts her sword under the Chemdi's chin into its brain. The mighty Chemdi falls to the floor. Two more appear.

Striker and Miiya are now positioned back to back. The Chemdi do not attack immediately; they are adapting and learning the fighting behavior of their enemy. This time, the Chemdi has a blade in each of its four hands. Striker taunts the beast but he does not go for it. He looks as if he's waiting for something. Miiya holds her stance also. Striker's beast engages with both lower arms but Striker counters every attack with his Jian. As the beast continues, Striker blocks both blade attacks and the Chemdi lifts his upper shoulders to attack with the upper arms. Striker wisely reads the attack and backs off enough to cut off both of the beast's upper arms. He lets out a curdling howl. Miiya's Chemdi sees the fate of his colleague and attacks her with all four arms. Miiya spins away from the attack with great poise and severs the beast's left leg. He falls like a tree trunk to the ground. Both Striker and Miiya kill their respective distracted beasts.

The two more appear, this time with different weapons in all four hands: a mace, a short blade, a trident and a spear. They are on the attack. Striker and Miiya's strategy is different this time. They are trying to stay away from their enemy until the opportune moment, flipping and jumping out of the way of the attacking Chemdi. The most deadly of the weapons is the mace. They crisscross, to confuse the Chemdi and cause them to get into each other's way, but the beasts do not fall for it this time—again they're adapting to the humans' fighting style.

Striker's Chemdi knocks his Jian out of his hand with the mace and Striker evades. The beast is solely focused on Striker and suddenly, out of nowhere, a modified double-bladed Syrian sword pierces its skull and it falls to the ground. Striker quickly grabs his Jian and renders Miiya the same courtesy, throwing his Jian with great speed and accuracy so it pierces through the center of the side of the Chemdi's head causing him to fall to the ground also. The engagement is complete.

A roar of cheers, whistles and catcalls erupts from the class. Striker, now dripping with sweat, walks in front of the group and holds up his hand. "These are some of the techniques you will also learn. Any questions?" The class is very impressed and continue to cheer and clap. The questions come one after another. The operators are eager to learn all that they can from the skilled instructors. The class and officers have never seen anything like it. They are convinced that they are in the right place and the training they will receive will be very useful if they ever have to engage the Chemdi-Shakahr.

The day's training complete, Colonel Striker and Miiya meet up for some quiet time. Miiya is keeping abreast of what is happening back on Meritor and sharing it with Deon. Both feel deeply disappointed that they failed to save Mrs. Wilory and her daughter; they both hold themselves responsible.

"You know," Deon says, "we have heard all of the analysis and reasons why our team was against incredible odds, and by all intents and purposes we were doomed to fail even before we left Earth. Even so, I still feel we could have saved them and if I had only spread our team out like the Chemdi did, we would have prevented Steve's family from being taken."

Miiya looks at him and caresses his face with her soft yet powerful four-fingered hand. "Deon, we had no way of knowing that the Chemdi would beam multiple teams to the vessel on different decks. We did not train for that. Yet, in spite of that, we still found them and killed many of the enemy. We were only seconds too late. We applied "frala" and adapted better than even they expected. Sometimes things simply do not turn out like we would hope. My father knows this all too well. He taught you the skills that you have shared with your people these last few days. He is a warrior of warriors. So you too must embrace this reality, just as he did when his family and chief of security were killed by the Chemdi. He carries this burden even until this day.

She looks deeply into his eyes, as if she can see the dark spot of guilt on his soul, and embraces him with a love that transcends time and space. Striker returns her embrace, feeling safe and completely nurtured in her arms, like he's never felt before. As she squeezes him tightly, he ponders how this special relationship will all play out. Oh, how he wishes for more moments like these.

Their embrace reluctantly ends and Deon's mind snaps back to his dear friend and how he must be feeling right now. "Have you heard anything from the emissary or your father?"

"No. I usually get a steady flow of information. This time I have heard nothing. This is very strange for me. They are keeping this very quiet whatever they are planning. The last time such a thing happened, we were making plans to leave our planet. They did not want to expose our plans to the Khorathians or the Chemdi. They must suspect that there may be a traitor among us."

"Are you saying someone from Meritor fed the mission coordinates and travel plans of the ambassador's family?" Deon asks. "That would certainly explain how they located their position and why they boarded the ship the way they did. This whole plot could be an inside job—and if that is the case, the ambassador himself may be in trouble!"

"If that is true, then the best place for him to be is on Meritor. My father is the very best at what he does. Your friend is in good hands."

The first set of Meritorian ships arrives at the coordinates before the Earth armada. The ships are majestic to behold and the Earth commanders feel a great sense of comfort as they join the group. There is too much firepower here to start a fight, so hopefully the Chemdi will have come to the same conclusion.

The second set of ships to leave Meritor arrives at their

coordinates. There are no other ships present yet. Their orders are that, should they confirm enemy contact bearing down on their position, they are to join the rest of the fleet immediately. They radio in to the fleet.

The communications officer alerts the captain. "Sir the fleet wants to know our position."

"Send it."

The fleet acknowledges his position and his orders are to remain there. If they receive contact from the enemy, they are to immediately rejoin the first fleet.

Suddenly a long-range contact begins closing in on their position. They call in the contact and confirm that it is bearing in. The captain gives the order to rejoin the fleet at maximum speed and they disappear.

* * *

The security detail marches into the Meritor Command Center with great vigor. They are obviously going to arrest someone. The Meritorian officers all watch as the security detail moves its way into their work area. They surround the workstation of a Khorathian—one of three chief tactical officers at their Warfare Command Center. They are arresting him for treason; he is suspected of sending and receiving suspicious communications. Balan-Gaal had ordered that he be given false data to transmit to one of the ships at the rendezvous point. All of the data is encrypted, so even the controllers do not know what they are sending—only the tactical officers have both the codes and the encryption keys. There are usually three on duty. Based on the location of the ship, the Meritorians knew which officer it was. His treason was further confirmed when a Chemdi-Shakahr ship started to close in on that very ship's position. No doubt, he will have an appointment to experience the pain of Uallion worms in the Meritor desert.

Balan-Gaal requests the commander of the fleet to signal the Chemdi. His communications officer is signaling on all frequencies. Balan-Gaal is known for never going into a situation without a distinct advantage and this situation is no different. He anticipates that the Chemdi may try to keep the hostages once they have their prisoners, as an act of humiliation for defeating them at Earth. Balan-Gaal had Meritor engineers build a scanner that will detect human tissue to a very detailed degree. Normal Meritorian ship scanners are not designed to do this. The results will be displayed on devices worn by Balan-Gaal and his four elite guards.

The Chemdi reply and de-cloak before the Armada. Their battle group is about ten or more ships, matching the Earth and Meritor ships. A single Chemdi ship moves slowly in the middle, about halfway between the two groups, and stops. The two enemies will beam their citizens to their respective ships simultaneously.

"Scan that ship for humans!" commands Balan-Gaal.

"There are two human life forms on the ship, commander!" the communications officer replies. He looks at his loyal and trusted bodyguards. "If things go wrong today, it will be up to us to make them right. We will recover the ambassador's family—even if we die during our mission!"

They all stand a little straighter with a new fire in their eyes. Saluting their commander with a simultaneous thump of their fists to their chests and a loud shout, they all hold out their weapons of choice.

Whatever the Chemdi-Shakahr are planning, it is already doomed to fail because five of the most deadly fighters in the galaxy will be coming down on them like the worse meteor shower they have ever seen. Failure is simply not an option for them.

* * *

Ambassador Wilory is slowly pacing back and forth in his office. The fact that he knows nothing about the prisoner exchange disturbs him. His chief of staff and Yost approach his office at a faster than normal stride, a look of cautious hope on their faces.

"Mr. Ambassador! We have news that the fleet has engaged

the Chemdi at the predetermined coordinates. It should not be long now, sir," says his chief.

"I hope you're right. I just want my family back."

A crowd of embassy staff approach, led by Lillian, a maid of African descent who is known for singing Christian praise music throughout the day. She has a unique, beautiful voice, and a cheerful and humble disposition, despite the fact that she is light years away from her home on Earth. It is said that she has become the resident encourager and spiritual advisor of the staff. She approaches with a bubbly smile on her face, as if the ambassador's family is already in the Embassy. "Mr. Ambassador," she says, "if we might, sir, we would like to pray for the successful rescue of your family. Would that be okay?"

The ambassador doesn't skip a beat. "Absolutely!"

Steve Wilory recalls in that moment the few prayers he has prayed over his sailors at Christmas and Thanksgiving dinners at sea. He also recalls witnessing a Seal team commander once who often prayed over his troops before sending them off on a mission from the carrier.

"Come on, everyone," Lillian says enthusiastically. "Gather round!" What a sight to behold; Meritorians and humans of Earth all holding hands to pray for the safe return of the ambassador's family.

Lillian begins to pray. She is eloquent and natural in her prayer to God, almost as if she is talking her Earthly father. She starts by thanking Him for all He has done, and for their safe arrival at Meritor. She laces the prayer with Bible scriptures and examples of victories won by the Israelites as they fought their enemies and prevailed during their time. She prays for the protection of the ambassador's family by his mighty heavenly angels, and asks that no harm come to them or the many troops deployed by Meritor and Earth. She closes by thanking God in advance for hearing her prayer as they join hands and remind Him that He said, "Where two or more are gathered in His name that we would be in their midst." She ended by saying, "In Jesus's name, and all those gathered here said, Amen!"

There isn't a dry human eye in the room—each and every person present feels that something very special has just happened, as if He has actually heard them. The Meritorians look perplexed but honor this human tradition by joining them willingly and without hesitation.

The ambassador looks peaceful and calm for the first time in days. He thanks his staff sincerely for their concern and support. They smile and nod their heads in reply; some even curtsy.

The staff disperses as fast as they gathered, but not before offering to get the famished-looking ambassador something to eat—he has not eaten properly for a few days.

* * *

The Chemdi receive the Meritor armada's signal and reply: they will begin the transfer process. The Earth prisoner ship has begun the process and all the prisoners are beamed to the designated location. The Chemdi-Shakahr confirm that all are received and accounted for, indicating that they will transport the human prisoners now. The Meritor ship scans that the Chemdi transporters are energizing. Both Earth and Meritorian crews wait, filled with anxiety and anticipation. The beam materializes on the Meritor flagship. There appear to be two forms in the beam.

"Captain," the transport officer says, "there is something wrong! The forms coming though the beam are not human!"

Almost immediately, the communications officer responds, "Captain, one of the Chemdi ships is leaving; the remaining ships are powering weapons!"

The captain of the Maximus wastes no time; he fires the quantum cannon at the Chemdi's flagship engine nacelles, disabling their ability to fire their primary weapons. One of the Meritor destroyers also fires at the Chemdi prisoner ship's engine nacelles to keep the ship from leaving the area.

Balan-Gaal acts fast, signaling to the captain of the flagship who orders the crew to beam Balan-Gaal and his team over to the Chemdi vessel as close to the Earth hostages as possible.

They materialize in what looks like a holding-cell area. The materializing process is slow due to the thickness of the armor in that part of the ship—if they are to get the humans off the ship, they will have to move to an area with less armor. They surprise about seven Chemdi in the holding cell area. The sentries take them all out with amazing speed. Balan-Gaal doesn't draw his weapons once. Mrs. Wilory and her daughter are behind a force field. The sentry with the two-foot-wide blade thrusts it into the ship's wall, severing the controls. Immediately the field drops and the two women are free. Looking exhausted, and clearly terrified, they take tentative steps towards their liberators. The Meritorian female provides them with suits, to cover their nakedness—the first clothes they have worn in quite some time. Balan-Gaal affixes two Zehrea on the women. The moment they get to an area that they can beam them out of, they will ensure the women leave first.

"Plot me an exit!" Balan-Gaal says into his communicator.

The ship's crew gives him two choices. He selects one and they head out, moving as a team, the ladies in the middle.

They can hear the heavy steps of Chemdi approaching. As they come into view, they see that there are about twenty or more. The lead team member switches with the female sentry, raises her weapon and fires. A flat beam encompasses the entire hallway from one side to the other, ripping the Chemdi in half. Not one of them survive. The team continues on rapidly through ship, trying to locate a less-armored area.

They have about ten meters to go when three Chemdi appear in the hallway in front of them, each carrying a large weapon. They fire, and a particle diffuser ray spews from the emitter. A sentry blocks the ray with his shield, simultaneously throwing what looks like two knife-edged, laser-infused boomerangs. The ray destroys a third of the shield as one blade severs the head of a Chemdi at the throat and the other zips through its face, cutting off the top of its head.

The other sentry throws his spear at the third Chemdi; as it enters its body, approximately twenty staggered blades immediately expand out of the shaft, slicing through the Chemdi's body and killing it instantly. The sentry recovers his spear and assumes a defensive stance.

The location of the extraction point lies at an intersection of four corridors deep within the ship—a highly vulnerable position for Balan-Gaal and his sentries. He calls for the extraction of the women. Each sentry takes a hallway, as does Balan-Gaal. The female sentry stands with the women in the center to protect them. The beam materializes and they transfer to the ship. The four brave Meritorians see hoards of Chemdi coming at them from all four hallways. They brace for the fight of their lives.

The star battleship Maximus and her battle group is taking fire from the variety of Chemdi Ships but the Earth ships are giving better than they are getting. The quantum cannons of the Maximus fire with reckless abandon, disabling every ship they hit. The targeting systems are ultra-accurate, enabling the cannons to rapid-fire at will, literally taking ships out in a matter of minutes. The Chemdi are in complete disarray, some even abandoning ship. The star destroyers fire self-guided missiles, finishing the job of destroying some of the Chemdi ships. Earth has lost one destroyer so far.

The Meritor fleet has given the Chemdi fleets a good beating. The Chemdi are now rescuing their stranded crewmembers and retreating. The captains of both Earth and Meritorian fleets extend professional courtesy, by not targeting the Chemdi rescue tenders, but working together to distract the Chemdi and give Balan-Gaal and his team as much time as he needs to rescue the ambassador's family.

A wave of Chemdi warriors fill the corridors of the ship. Balan-Gaal transforms into a Meritorian killing machine. His cape whirls and swirls as he moves with poise and accuracy. His sword and trident flash blindingly as he falls one Chemdi after another. The elite guards are carbon copies of their liege, mimicking him in delivering death and carnage to the Chemdi. Balan-Gaal gives the order to evacuate back to the ship but his guards refuse, insisting that he go first. Balan-Gaal has trained them well and knows that they will not obey that order. To save their lives he obliges them, killing two more Chemdi and beaming out first. As he does, the three remaining guards fight back to back.

The Chemdi are so close in proximity to the guards, the ship's crew can only beam one out at a time. One more goes, and now there are two. As they attempt to go together, one of the elite guards is dealt a fatal blow and killed by the Chemdi. They swarm the body. Balan-Gaal will not leave his elite guard behind. He orders the captain to fire a round close to the fight so he may recover the body. The captain knows the security chief and he will not be denied. The captain himself goes over to the firing station and fires a round, hitting the hull of the Chemdi ship to disperse the Chemdi. The crew beams Balan-Gaal in close proximity; he now stands a few feet from the fallen guard in the smoke-filled corridor. As he recovers his warrior, he spots a Chemdi commander standing in the distance, shrouded in smoke. He recognizes him. They stare at each other for a moment, then the Chemdi commander raises his weapon and lowers it across his body in salute to the security chief. Holding the body of his fallen guard, Balan-Gaal nods his head. A split second later, he is beamed back to the ship.

The last two Chemdi ships retreat. The Meritorian and Earth fleets have learned to work together more effectively. The Chemdi-Shakahr has learned that they will have to adopt new ways of defeating the Meritorian and Earth fleets.

Jean and Kate Wilory hug and weep uncontrollably as the reality sets in that they are safe and their horrific ordeal is over. The captain sets course to Meritor at maximum speed to reunite the two women with the ambassador. Both are in shock, becoming hysterical when the Meritorian medical staff make attempts to treat them—so much so that the Meritor physician resorts to a wireless scanning-type device to induce sleep by triggering brainwaves that mimic REM sleep. It is vital that he treat the patients' wounds but wants to do so without causing them any more emotional trauma. They will be met on Meritor by another Meritorian medical staff, specifically trained to practice on humans. They will pick up the remaining medical treatment, and follow it through to recovery.

The physician notices that Jean is pregnant and initiates the protocols required for pregnant humans: prenatal care, supplements and other requirements, in accordance with Earth biological data. Unaware that the Earth Meritor ambassador does not know his wife is pregnant, the physician forwards both patients' data to the medical team on Meritor, to enable them to make the necessary preparations. The patients' vital signs are sent live, and they will monitor the two women until they arrive at the embassy infirmary.

News of the recovery of the ambassador's family is sent to Meritor and Earth. It is met with jubilation on both planets —cheers and whistles ring out on Earth; well-wishers bring flowers, cards and gifts to the Wilory home. Their street is a sea of media vans and reporters. On Meritor, the scene is much the same: elation and joy spread like a wave, and celebrations are already being planned for when the women make a full recovery.

Yost and the chief of staff wake the ambassador from his sleep—which requires very little effort; he hasn't slept soundly since his family's abduction.

"Mr. Ambassador! Mr. Ambassador! Wake up! They have recovered your family. They're alive and on their way to Meritor!" says his chief.

Steve wakes, sits bolt upright and yells, "What? They recovered them? When? Are they okay?" He can't stop smiling.

"Sir, we do not yet have all the details but we have been told that they are sleeping. They should be here in approximately three Earth hours. You should rest too sir, for at least another hour or two."

"I can't possibly sleep now!" Steve cries happily. "I need to make sure everything is ready for their arrival!"

"Sir, we have taken care of everything. You only need to wake and greet your family. They will be going to the infirmary for a period of time for observation," Yost says gently.

"Is that far from here?"

"No, sir—it's here in the embassy, on the first floor."

"Very well. Wake me in an hour! Thank you."

As soon as the two staff members have left the room, Steve breaks down and weeps. He is so relieved and happy that his wife and daughter are safe and will be with him within just hours. This is more than he expected and he is so very grateful.

* * *

The star ship retrofits are more than halfway completed in Area 51. The weapons, sensor array, and engine upgrades will bring Earth into a new age of space warfare thanks, in large part, to the Meritorian Government. Their sharing of their technology has given Earth an advantage that would likely have taken them a couple of decades to discover and implement on their own. Ships are being dispatched to the SCCC once they have completed their "shakedown" flights and all discrepancies repaired. The once battered space fleet has been replenished and there are more ships in space than the SCCC can handle. Colonel Striker's Assistant PM is handling the project while Striker is on assignment at Langley. Although she has been doing a great job, she will be very glad to give the PM role back over to her boss. She's very proud to work for someone so capable in so many skill sets. If she is truly honest with herself, she has to admit that she's got a little crush on him. She would never say it out loud or dare to tell him—in fact, she would rather be drawn and quartered than share her feelings for him and would commit bloody murder on anyone who would slightly revealed it.

* * *

Lying in bed, Steve Wilory can't sleep; his mind is buzzing with thoughts of being reunited with his family. He gets up and sits on the edge of his bed. He keeps telling himself that there is certainly something he can do before they arrive. He puts on his favorite terry cloth bathrobe and heads downstairs to look at the infirmary where they will be staying for a few days. It is very sterile, probably too sterile. It may even remind them of the examination room they may have been held in while in captivity—if what Balan-Gaal and Yost had told him about the Chemdi's conducting research on their prisoners was correct. This will not do. He wonders to himself why they can't be cared for in their own rooms where they would be more comfortable. Not quite sure what time it is, he doesn't care at this point—he heads off to his chief of staff's private quarters. As he's wandering through the hallways, Yost appears like a ghost from Christmas past.

"Good Morning, sir. Is there anything I might do for you?"

"Actually, there is. I was wondering; why do my wife and daughter have to stay in the infirmary—can't they receive the same care in the comfort of their own rooms, surrounded by their personal belongings?"

"Well, sir, you're the ambassador; I suppose if that is what you prefer, we can certainly do it. I will begin the preparations immediately, Mr. Ambassador."

"Thank you. Thank you very much." Steve is ecstatic. This is so much better. There must be more, he says to himself. Flowers! They both love flowers!

He heads for his office and finds a knife, then strides to the back doors and flings them open—only to be met by two Meritorian guards. They salute him and stand by his side as if they anticipate he will need their assistance. He remembers spotting flowers close to the house when he first arrived at Meritor. That will be the next stop. The nighttime sun is still up so he can see the flowerbeds pretty well. Jean likes daisies. There are no daisies on Meritor, but he remembers having seen yellow flowers. He spots them and pulls out the knife to cut them. The guard immediately grabs his arm before he has the chance, raising his other hand and holding up one of his four fingers.

Not sure what he has done wrong, Steve says, "Okay, okay. I know I'm not on Earth, heck maybe this flower is poisonous —I'll ask my staff." He heads sheepishly back towards the main building—but not without recovering his pride by giving the guards an order. "Carry on!" he calls over his shoulder.

Suddenly, a blinding flash lights up the sky. A ship is landing on the grounds. It must be his family! He stands back, feeling the wind whirling around him from the engines. The shuttle lands and the doors open. First comes the security detail, then the Meritor medical staff, and finally...

* * *

As the newly upgraded fleets of Earth ships are deployed and new ones come on line, Space Command wants to take the opportunity to get in lots of training for its captains. Ships were lost during Earth's first space battle and new captains are being promoted and are coming on line. The enemy is still out there and they want to pass on what the veteran captains have learned.

Some three hundred captains—both young and older— fill the room. Space Command is showing live video footage of what ships' commanders did right and not so well. They discuss weapons and tactics. The Mavericks were very effective in the fight to defend Earth; it is agreed that focus needs to be placed on how Space Command can use them more efficiently. They even discuss the latest engagement: the "Wilory rescue."

Lastly, the coordination between the Earth and Meritor fleets is vital for concentrating all the firepower where it's needed most at any given time. This makes the two worlds a force to be reckoned with. This information is crucial to the many battles they yet have to fight with the Chemdi-Shakahr; Space Command's and Meritor's use of this is will determine the success of both planets.

* * *

The medical staff escorts the floating gurneys of both

women into the embassy. The Meritor chief medical officer leads Jean Wilory's gurney personally; he seems to be making quite a fuss over her. The ambassador notices this and his concern increases.

Once inside the infirmary, the nursing staff attends to the needs of both women as the chief medical officer greets the ambassador.

"Mr. Ambassador, I am the chief medical officer and have been caring for your wife and daughter since they were beamed to the ship. Both women are doing fine but we are concerned about the baby."

You could have knocked Steve Wilory over with a feather. He stutters and stammers, clearly overwhelmed by the statement. "B-b-baby? What baby?"

"Sir, you must understand that..." the medical officer tries to explain but is instantly cut off by Steve.

"My daughter has no business being pregnant! What the hell? She is in for it when she gets up! She knows better than that—and what are we going to do with a newborn on Meritor? If Jean kept this from me, she's going be in for it too!"

The chief medical officer interrupts him. "Sir, it is your wife who is pregnant!"

Steve looks as if Mike Tyson has hit him in the gut. He is stunned into silence. The wise medical chief wisely walks away, to allow the news to sink in. He busies himself with monitoring the women.

Steve, realizing that his wife has just been through this horrific ordeal with their unborn baby in her womb, is deeply ashamed of himself for the anger he had felt just now. Only a few days ago he had been weeping at the thought of his wife and daughter being killed by the Chemdi, and they are now here and alive in the very same building. He feels a sudden, overwhelming rush of relief and gratitude. Having come to his senses, he enters the infirmary. Jean is moving agitatedly in her bed. The affect of the sedative is wearing off. He walks up to her ever so gently, and looks at her with penitent eyes and a pierced heart.

"Hey, you. You gave us all quite a scare."

She tries to sit up to hug her husband but the doctor wags a finger at her.

"No, no, honey—the doctor is right. Please rest. You're resting for two now."

Jean looks at her husband almost with contempt. "What do you mean by that?"

Although Steve is already the father of three grown girls, he can't help but feel that giddy "first-time father" feeling; he beams down at his wife, a boyish, silly grin on his face. "My love, you're pregnant!"

Jean laughs as if he has told her a really bad joke. Steve holds his position and fixes her with a stare, as is his usual way when he is really serious about something.

She knows that look all too well and the reality begins to sink in. "Oh, my God! You are serious!"

"Yes. We're going to have the first human baby born on Meritor!

"What if I don't want to have the baby here, Steve? What about prenatal care—vitamins, doctor's visits? What about…"

Steve stops her from speaking by gently touching her lips with his fingers. "My love, it's going to be okay. They have better care and technology here than we do on Earth. The chief medical officer has specialized training on humans, including pregnancy. Hey—can we just be happy right now and enjoy this moment?"

Jean looks at the joy on her husband's face and relinquishes. This is indeed a happy moment, and one that should be fully appreciated. Just as they kiss once more, the air is filled with a familiar voice Steve has longed to hear for the last few days. He turns from his wife.

"Daddy?" says Kate.

"I'm here, my love! I'm so glad you are alive and safe!"

"Daddy, they hurt me," she says through her tears.

"I will see that they pay dearly for what they did to you and your mom, my love. I promise."

Kate continues to cry, her whole body shaking as she collapses into her father's arms. She feels truly safe for the first time in days. She will never forget the awful experience of being held prisoner by the Chemdi—however, this very experience will clearly define who she will later become.

CHAPTER FIFTEEN
The Chemdi Return To Earth

As the relationship between Earth and Meritor continues, both planets benefit. Meritor is enjoying a relationship with an ally whom they trust. Earth is benefiting from galactic security, new technology and great advances in medicine. The Meritor embassy is still inaccessible to the public at large due to fear-mongering by a radical few. Earth does not want to take the chance of jeopardizing the Meritor ambassador's safety. The abduction of Jean and Kate Wilory by the Chemdi caused enough serious damage to the relationship between Planet Meritor and Earth. Officials from both sides have since been repairing the relationship through formal and informal gatherings of world leaders, which have proved very effective. The Meritor Government is fully committed to the relationship and will do whatever necessary to repair it.

Meritor space commanders and captains also held a summit at which they all met face to face for the first time. Language translators provided by the Meritorians facilitated communication between the crews. They traded war stories and even laughter. They all felt a great sense of accomplishment at having defeated the Chemdi together; an event like this promotes team cohesion—critical for future battles.

Now that Colonel Striker and Miiya have completed the training of hundreds of Earth special operators, Colonel Striker is being reassigned to Area 51 and Miiya is being recalled to Meritor. They have enjoyed each other's company and will miss the time they have spent together. They decide to celebrate their success with a trip across the country from Hamilton, Virginia to Groom Lake, Nevada. Striker has more than thirty days' leave that he's never used, and following all his exploits, Space Command has no problem granting him his leave request. Since Miiya basically works for her father, her return date is at her own discretion.

Striker has been flying space cruisers for quite some time and during that time has been very frugal with his money, investing it wisely; his original plan was to save in order to be able to build his dream home for his retirement. However, during the time he has spent with Miiya, his heart has been so moved that he wants to do something very special for her. He recalls her saying that she would love to see the United States —so he decides to change his "dream house" plans and to purchase a Ford F-250 Lariat and a gorgeous Airstream thirty-foot trailer. He wants to gift her with a trip to see some of the most beautiful parts of his country; they will tour some of the nation's famous national parks as Colonel Striker makes his way back to Groom Lake, Nevada. He feels this is a worthy investment since neither of them is sure how long it will be until they see each other again.

Besides, Miiya doesn't want to go places where she will draw unwanted attention—many Americans aren't yet sure how they feel about aliens living in the country. So, to avoid any altercations, they will make stops at the Gauley River National Recreation Area, West Virginia, Big South Fork National River and Recreation Area, Kentucky, Ozark National Scenic Riverways in Missouri, Tallgrass Prairie National Preserve, Kansas, Medano Creek, Great Sand Dunes National Park and Preserve in Colorado, Zion National Park, Utah and ending at the Great Basin National Park in Nevada, then head to their final destination at Groom lake. It will be a trip of a lifetime, and they aim to create memories together that they will never forget.

After understanding the sacrifice Striker has made in curtailing his retirement plans and using those resources to make this trip possible, Miiya's love for Striker grows even further; she feels ready to explore it with him at a deeper level.

* * *

Once the chief medical officer was satisfied that Jean and Kate Wilory were stable, he permitted them to be cared for in their own quarters, to enable their mental and emotional recovery to continue in their own surroundings amongst the things they love.

Kate sleeps a lot. It may be her way of processing all that she's been through. She's not ready to talk about the experiences she has suffered.

Jean is still reeling from the news that she's pregnant and a little concerned with the inevitability that she will be giving birth to their baby on Meritor. Two caregivers have been assigned to attend to her every need until the child is three years old, and are coordinating with Jean and Steve about arrangements for the nursery—colors, fabrics, basinet or crib, toys and the like. Steve knows that, seeing how the Meritorians achieved a precise replication of the interior of a southern American-style home, creating a beautiful, traditional nursery will be a walk in the park for them. The entire embassy staff is excited about the prospect of having a baby in the embassy. For many, it will be a welcome distraction.

"Steve, honey—does this mean that our baby will become a citizen of Meritor?" "No, sweetheart. The embassy is technically on Earth soil—American soil to be exact," replies Steve.

"I see. And what about prenatal vitamins?"

"They have all the necessary data and more to replicate whatever drugs or formulas you will need to provide care for our baby, my love. They have already proven that they will do an outstanding job. Also, remember; their technology far exceeds Earth medical technology." They continue to discuss every detail Jean can think of, until finally she is satisfied that all will be well. Steve then takes her for a walk through the beautiful gardens of the embassy in a levitating wheelchair. Jean does not quite feel herself yet, but she's trying to be strong for her husband and unborn baby. They walk along one of the many paths that network the gardens, soaking up the beauty and fragrance of the magnificent flora and fauna planted by the Meritor staff. They will return to explore another one tomorrow.

* * *

When Kate wakes, her face looks like steel. It's no longer the face of the sweet, bubbly teen the Wilory family once knew. No; this Kate has had a dose of frank reality and speaks only when she feels the conversation is becoming too superficial. She verbally jerks the conversation into reality with subtle quips and cutting sarcasm.

In her mind, she's no longer Daddy's little girl. Although no man took her virginity, she feels violated just the same and is bent on exacting revenge. She will find a way to get back at the filthy beasts that did those painful things to her and her mother. She is a ninety-five-pound human being of quiet rage looking for the day she gets to unleash that rage on the Khorathians and Chemdi-Shakahr.

She's going to be methodical like her father: first things first. She has made a list of all of the things she will need to make her goals possible. She will need the kind of martial arts and weapons training that her Uncle Deon has—but she knows that if she asks him, he will most likely see through her plan and decline her request. She will need to find another source. She embraces that she may need to be away from her family for a time. She is confident that an opportunity will present itself, so she will be patient and wait. In the meantime, she will try to pick up as much training as she can along the way.

* * *

The last of the day's Sun rays gleam off of the roof of the Jetstream thirty-foot trailer as the sun goes down in a clearing near the Gauley River in the Gauley River National Recreation Area. The landscape is breathtaking, set against the sound of the gurgling river water as it gently flows downstream. Deon has officially taken off his "Colonel Striker hat" and is just plain Deon, a camper from North Plate, Indiana who's with a very hot alien female named Miiya. They build a little campfire and Deon is about to grill some chicken that has been marinating in the camper fridge since they left Virginia—and it smells delicious. Miiya is busy bombarding Deon with all kinds of questions about the area, starting with the possible dangers. He assures her that they are minimal and that whatever they encounter, they are more than able to handle.

She moves the conversation on to their relationship. They discuss their desire to continue moving forward and what it could mean for them, either on Earth or Meritor. They are aware that the road ahead will be filled with many challenges but they are willing to give it a try.

They finish their meal and Deon extinguishes the fire before they retire to the luxurious bedroom of their Airstream where the Meritor love ritual finally begins.

* * *

Due to the recent events, Balan-Gaal, Meritor chief of security, needs to assign bodyguards to the ambassador's family. Although they are on Meritor, enemies still abound. He is looking for candidates but he knows that there is only one person who will fit the position perfectly, and that is his own daughter, Miiya. Steve is already acquainted with her and there is no one on Meritor with her live-combat experience and skill. She will be notified and will take up her post as soon as she arrives on Meritor.

* * *

On the Khorathian home world, the High Command is determining a strategy that will strike panic into the hearts of the people of Earth. The Meritorians have already experienced their wrath; however, Earth has had only a taste. Their plan is to bypass the great war plan for now and simply cause fear, chaos and destruction on Earth, thereby distracting the leadership, causing them to redirect key intelligence resources. When the chaos reaches its peak, the Chemdi will be ready to strike.

At that point, they will direct the Chemdi-Shakahr to send saboteurs and suicide teams to launch indiscriminant attacks around the world. These attacks must be very public. They should cause as many mass casualties, especially to women and children, as possible. They want to shut down whole cities with the fear of what their new enemy will do next. Their challenge will be to get Chemdi warriors on Earth undetected. They have a plan that requires them to steal an Earth ship. They will patiently wait for the right opportunity —they need vessels that are not tactical in nature and that routinely fly past Earth's moon.

* * *

Ensconced in the womb of the new Airstream camper trailer, amidst vases of freshly cut wildflowers and a collection of lightly scented candles, Deon and Miiya kneel on the bed facing each other, their fingers intertwined. As they hold each other's gazes, the fire in their souls burning strong, Miiya speaks softly in her native language. It sounds beautiful to Deon's ears even though he cannot understand a word. She touches his chest very lightly, stroking him in a downward motion. Deon begins to hum—her touch feels so soothing. Miiya begins to hum in harmony with Deon—a sensual song that only they understand. As she continues, a hormone is released from her fingers and penetrates rapidly into Deon's skin; a romantic elixir that is a combination of a powerful hallucinogen and the equivalent of a male enhancement drug. Deon immediately becomes extremely aroused and his heart begins beating more rapidly.

Miiya exposes the upper part of her sexy alien body to Deon for the first time. She is exotically intoxicating. Again, the body of a Meritorian female largely resembles that of a human female, to include breasts. Deon's heart is beating faster now. He hears her breath deepen for the first time. It has a raw, passionate, guttural sound that even Earth women know. Her chest touches his, and Deon's heart reaches a dangerously critical level. Miiya retreats from her lover and stands before him as a newlywed would before her husband on their first night. She now uses the same powerful body that has killed many Chemdi-Shakahr on the command ship in Earth's first battle and again in the first rescue attempt and final rescue of Jean and Kate Wilory, to dance the most sensual dance he's ever seen. The master bedroom is not very large, but she skillfully uses its space to her advantage, and the priceless spectacle is wondrous!

She loses the final article of clothing from her sexy body, which Deon thinks to himself she has to be one of the sexiest creatures he as every seen. She signals to Deon that he is the only mate she will ever have by showing him the one thing that is never discussed or disclosed to anyone except in privacy of two monogamous Meritorians: her third eye. Deon is not ignorant as to the significance of this, and he beholds this gesture as the treasure that it truly is.

She rejoins him on the bed and they hug and kiss over and over, relishing in this time they have waited so long for. Everything about the moment is perfect. Miiya begins stroking his chest again, once more releasing the alien hormone onto his skin. Deon's arousal grows urgent; his heart races and the sensation intensifies rapidly.

Then suddenly it happens, Deon's face goes from smiling from sheer ecstasy to being contorted in pain. Miiya looks at his face and senses something's wrong. Deon is now grabbing at his chest. He tries to speak to her but can't get a word out. He feels as if there is a starship crushing his chest. He can't believe this is happening, No, not to me! he thinks.

Miiya quickly realizes that perhaps the second dose of the hormones to his body may have been too much; Deon's heart is in cardiac arrest. "I'm having a heart attack!" he croaks in disbelief before collapsing on the soft bed. Miiya leaps from the bed and starts rummaging frantically through the closet for her bag, before moving on to an overhead cupboard. She knows that they are miles away from any first responders and that any potential help would not arrive in time—but she believes there may one thing in her bag that can save his life. All she has to do is find it!

* * *

The Chemdi have dispatched a ship to monitor Earth ship movements to and from the moon. It is a very long flight from the Chemdi home world and they arrive on the station in view of Earth's moon. They are hoping the shuttles and ships that service Moon Base Alpha may be the easiest to contact without making direct contact with an Earth or Meritor destroyer —they are looking for an opportunity to board and hijack one as a means to get the special ops Chemdi onto the Earth. The Earth pilots fly a very disciplined and accurate pattern; they seem to stay well within the airspace that is protected by their space fleet. The Chemdi will stay cloaked and wait patiently for their opportunity to board and hijack one.

* * *

Adrian Brown is running the facility at Area 51 with precision and poise. She is ahead of schedule and the retrofits have all been completed. The special maintenance team is now focusing on battle damage assessment and repair for the space fleet. The government wants to include as many upgrades to the ships as possible as the repair process continues. The team is well equipped and ready to do the job. One ship after another returns to Earth and is parked in its respective bay where it is shored up and secured for inspection, disassembly and repair. The Meritorian technology will speed the process but this will only apply to the retrofits—that is, sensor arrays and weapons; the rest of the work will have to be done the old-fashioned way. It will take about two to three months in total to complete these repairs and upgrades. The Space Command will be careful as to how many ships are pulled out of service so as to not leave Earth exposed.

Adrian had expected to hear from her boss by now, seeing that his assignment at Langley is over and he is returning to Groom Lake to work. He did call to say that he would be taking about thirty days' vacation before his return but that he would like her to give him an update every week. Her secret crush on him is growing by the day, ever since she did her homework on him before he arrived—it's not every day you meet someone like Striker. In any case, she is grateful to work for such an accomplished engineer. She will reach out to him later this week.

* * *

Balan-Gaal has assigned a temporary team to the Meritor ambassador and his family. The three bodyguards seem very capable. As they practice together, Kate asks them if she might join in their daily ritual, which takes place each morning and evening on the outside portico. They welcome her and she starts to make this a part of her own daily routine. The exercises look like your typical martial arts "Kata." She is very determined and practices with tenacity and determination to perfect what she is learning. The security lead is very impressed and enjoys her presence.

One morning, her dad sees his little Katie with the security team. He is pleased to see that she is making an effort to get into the swing of things with physical exercise. Little does he know that, on the inside, she is no longer "his little Katie." This Katie will be a force to be reckoned with when her time comes, and he will not believe it at the time it's revealed. She will be a force for good against evil, although driven primarily by emotion. He waves and smiles at his daughter and she waves back innocently. The ambassador is very happy to finally have his family in the embassy on Meritor.

* * *

Two fairly new pilots are on their tenth mission fresh out of flight school. They usually fly an intermediate-sized cargo vessel but all are in maintenance today, so instead, they will be flying one of the captain's launches, to deliver a few supplies to Moon Base Alpha and back. It was literally the only ship available and the flight director felt it would be a nice treat for the rookie pilots to fly it today. The pilots are ecstatic

—the captain's launch is usually for use by the captain of the ship only, for traveling to the Earth's surface or another ship. The SCCC is assigned with two of such vessels.

The pilots run through the checklists, start the engines and begin their journey to Moon Base Alpha. The ship is fast and a joy to fly. The interior is reminiscent of a high-end luxury car, fancy seats, burled walnut wood trim, etc. They will be travelling at 45.4 Mach or 30,000 mph. They will make the 238,900-mile trip to the moon in 7.9 hours. When they finally arrive, they deliver their cargo and prepare to stay the night. They eat, drink and enjoy the company of their friends and colleagues before sleeping in a comfortable bed. They will be well rested for their trip back to the SCCC (Space Command & Control Center) tomorrow.

* * *

Deon Striker lies unconscious, flat on his back, sweat running from his chest. Miiya finally finds her bag and rummages through the items she carries with her at all times since being dispatched to Earth— her Alocae-Cha, her medical scanner and other personal items. She pulls out the medical scanner, the same one that saved the colonel's life the first time, and scans Deon's body carefully to locate the female Meritorian hormones she has used on him, which she believes have caused the cardiac arrest. She programs the scanner to remove the hormones, returning his body to its normal chemical state. Once this is done, she prepares to perform CPR, in the hope of reviving the colonel.

She learned CPR at the Langley training facility as a prerequisite to training the world's Special Forces teams. She begins. At first Striker does not respond, but after a while his heart begins beating normally on its own and he starts to breathe again. His eyes open slowly. Dazed, he smiles his usual crooked smile that she loves so much.

"Hey," he says.

Once again, Striker has cheated death.

* * *

The pilots' sleep was peaceful but they wake with a slight headache from the numerous bottles of wine consumed the previous night. They are nevertheless well fed, rested and prepared to return home—not bad for an eight-hour trip. After eating breakfast and saying their goodbyes, they head directly to the docks where the ship has been inspected, fueled and prepared for flight. Again, they run through their checklists and embark for the SCCC. The captain pushes the throttle, enjoying the rush of power that all pilots love. Well aware that he may not get a chance to fly this ship again, at least for quite some time, he wants to make the most of this flight and really see what this baby can do. He pushes the throttle a little further, and the pilots are pleasantly pushed back into their seats. They smile at the feel of profound acceleration as they head toward the other side of the moon out of radar range, steering momentarily beyond their normal planned flight path—the captain wants to attempt a few maneuvers similar to those of a fighter aircraft. As he completes one maneuver after another, the pilots are exhilarated, laughter ringing out throughout the vessel.

"Dude, that was awesome!" the copilot exclaims. "Let's do just one more!"

"No can do," says the pilot. I think we've had our fun and we're already beyond our flight pattern. Let's head back."

"Yeah, I guess you're right. New heading..."

Suddenly they hear strange noises in the back of the aircraft and the copilot turns to check it out. But it's too late. To their surprise, four Chemdi-Shakahr emerge from the back of the ship. One immediately rushes forward. As the captain is keying his mic to make a distress call, a Chemdi's upper arms quickly grab both their heads and break their necks. No call is ever made. The Chemdi have achieved their goal: they have successfully stolen an Earth ship and now have their personal transportation to Earth.

CHAPTER SIXTEEN

The SMAR Team Is Born

The Chemdi know that their window of opportunity is small so they must move quickly. Four more Chemdi are beamed on board the captain's launch. The bodies of the dead pilots are removed and the Chemdi study the consoles. They quickly learn how to do basic maneuvers then head toward Earth. The integrated flight director indicates the flight path, so flying toward their destination will be easy. Not drawing undue attention may be the hard part.

* * *

Deon runs his hands through his hair and asks: "What happened?"

Miiya holds her hands up to her face. "You experienced cardiac arrest. I'm sorry—it was my fault."

Deon softly grabs her wrists in an effort to get her to look at him. "What do you mean, it was your fault?"

When I was stroking your body, a chemical was released from my fingers onto your skin. It contains a very high dose of my hormones, which are released before the mating process. I did not know that your human physiology could not withstand the high dosage. I almost killed you, Deon. I ask your forgiveness. I am not worthy to be your mate."

Just as Deon is about to reply, his phone rings. It's Adrian Brown, his second in command at Groom Lake. He holds up his finger, as if to say: "One second."

"Colonel Striker," he says, unable to hide the stress in his voice.

"Hi, boss! Am I interrupting?"

"Ah, no—not at all. What's up? Is everything okay?"

"Well, I know that you're on vacation and all, but as you get closer to Groom Lake, I was hoping that once you're back, we could have a sit down and chat for a bit before you come back to work. Nothing formal—just a friendly drink or something."

"Can't it wait until I get in the office?" Deon said, keeping his tone soft so as to not embarrass or offend.

"Sure! Silly me—I know you're on the trip of a lifetime. I apologize for intruding. I just wanted to get re-acquainted with you before you arrive—you know, catch up and stuff," she said nervously.

Deon senses that she perhaps might want to get a little more personal than what is normally required on the job. He lets her down easy. "You know, Adrian, I understand that I've been away for quite some time and you have been left to run things in my absence virtually on your own. I want you to know that I truly appreciate it. You probably—rightly—feel that you did not quite sign on for all of this, and if it were me, I would probably feel the same way. Let me make it up to you; how about we do something special for the team the first day I'm back? Let's buy sandwiches or do a barbeque for the team and cater a lunch for the senior staff. After lunch, I'll excuse the staff, and you and I can visit for a while. How about that?"

Adrian is pleased. It is clear that he has not forgotten her and that he definitely appreciates her efforts in his absence.

"I don't know what to say," she replies with a smile.

"So it's a date then. I'm looking forward to it! See you then." He hangs up and contemplates for a while. He is starting to realize that he has neglected his team while running all over space and then Langley. But to be honest, it was not his fault. In any case, he is a talented leader and he will spend time with his team upon his return.

Deon turns to Miiya. "I apologize for the interruption. Where were we? Ah yes...you said that you felt that you were not worthy to be my mate. Actually, it is I who feels unworthy of you; you deserve to mate with a Meritorian who can give you all of the things you need and desire. Maybe we should reconsider our relationship."

Miiya, although very emotional on many different levels, knows deep down that Striker may be right. She says: "You may be right. I would like to meditate on your words for a while."

She assumes a laying position on the very soft bed and rests her hands on her chest, almost as if she was lying in a casket. She ponders his words with great care, and meditates for the next hour. Deon slides back into the 1200-threadcount satin sheets of the luxurious bed and falls asleep. They will continue their journey in the morning.

* * *

The Chemdi continue their trip toward Earth, heading for a lighted land mass. They need to land in a remote area in order to remain undetected. Anyone they encounter before they begin their mission must die.

The ship touches down in a country suburb just outside London, United Kingdom, and drops off a Chemdi team consisting of two. Green fields and forest cover the landscape and keep the Chemdi concealed for now. It will not be long before all hell breaks loose. In the cover of darkness, the Chemdi start walking toward the town to find a hiding place, looking back briefly at the departing ship as it lifts off and proceeds to drop off the remaining teams.

The Chemdi-Shakahr approach the city, their gold-piping-decorated capes swirling around them in the wind like garrison flags. In their hands they carry edged and laser weapons. Once they start their attack, civilians and uniformed Bobbies won't have a chance. They find their way to the London Underground, which for the time being is deserted. They jump down on the tracks and walk until they find an alcove, then leap up over the power cables and start to plant their five-inch nails into the wall using nothing but their powerful hands. In this position, now they just need to wait for the right moment to redeem the honor of their warriors lost in their first defeat in space against Earth and Meritor.

* * *

A controller alerts the SCCC flight director that one of the SCCC ships is way off course. It's the captain's launch.

"Where the heck are those two bobble heads going?" says the director.

"Sir, it looks like they just left the United Kingdom and they're on their way to France," answers the controller.

"See if you can reach them on the radio!" Powell says.

"Sir, we tried—there's no reply."

"Pull up the ship's remote camera."

On viewing the spectacle, it becomes clear that Chemdi have taken control of the ship and have infiltrated Earth.

"The ship has been commandeered by alien hostiles. Shut it down remotely!" Powell commands.

The controllers send a "shut down" signal to the ship and the director alerts the Pentagon of the breach. The signal is relayed to satellites so it may not reach the ship immediately.

The ship is very fast and they drop two more Chemdi in France; they immediately dispatch and find a place to hide until the right moment. The ship continues its journey of death. Two more Chemdi are dropped in Dubai. They too easily find a place to hide in the city and settle in patiently to wait. The last team of two will be dropped in one of the most populated cities in on the planet, Tokyo, Japan. They will soon find a place in which to take cover.

As they continue their journey to Japan, two F-35H's approach and suddenly the ship shuts down. The F-35s stay with the ship until it impacts the water In the Sea of Japan, not far from the shore. The Chemdi swim to shore and hide along the Japanese harbor, biding their time.

* * *

The sunrise is beautiful in the Gauley River National Recreation Area. Miiya is already up and is busily securing the gear in the trailer and the pickup so they can leave after breakfast. Deon stirs in the back of the trailer. He opens the blinds to see the sunrise. He's had a fairly good night's sleep, but spent much of the night going over in his head what happened last night. He is full of questions, but pushes them aside for now and focuses on their trip. He does not want to spoil it for Miiya.

Heaving himself out of bed, he greets Miiya from behind with a warm hug around the waist. She strokes his hands and puts her cheek next to his.

"How about some breakfast?" asks Deon.

"Sure."

Miiya has grown fond of bacon and eggs. Deon cooks some for them both and they share a beautiful morning together. This was the whole purpose for this trip. They exit the trailer and get into the pickup, as excited as two college kids leaving campus for Spring Break. Next stop: Big South Fork National River and Recreation Area, Kentucky. The drive from West Virginia to Kentucky is three hundred and seventy-two miles—though it won't seem that long as they so enjoy each other's company and the time flies. Striker reiterates again, "Hey, don't worry about last night. I'm fine, there was no way you could know that would happen. Thanks to you and Meritorian technology, I feel great. Okay?"

She looks at him and simply nods: "okay."

* * *

With all of the Chemdi in place, the Chemdi ground commander sends a message to all of his warriors, now strategically located throughout the world, to start their attack at first light.

In London, one of the train operators notices something strange-looking in the tunnel and calls it in at five thirty a.m. At approximately six thirty a.m., the London Police service respond with two officers, who arrive at the Piccadilly Circus Underground station with their usual British swagger and a touch of caution. As they enter the station, they spot something unusual: two figures clinging to the side of the tunnel wall.

One of the Bobbies calls out, "You there! Had a little too much to drink, have ya? You're not authorized to be here. Come down now!"

One of the figures appears to shift its weight.

The other officer gets out his flashlight and sidearm, a 9-mm Beretta.

The lead officer repeats his order. "I said come down now and there won't be any trouble!"

The Chemdi wait for them to approach just a little closer.

The officer is not amused by his defiance. "Okay, that's quite enough! Either you come down now or we'll get you down!"

The Chemdi leap from the wall like two hungry cougars and attack the officers, ripping their limbs from their bodies and tossing them directly on the tracks. Almost immediately, they desert the grotesque spectacle and disappear further down the track. There is a faint light and the squeal of wheels on the tracks as a train arrives. The Chemdi will continue to Oxford Circus station where early morning commuters will be waiting for the next train. Their plan is to brutally attack them.

* * *

The Pentagon has received and acknowledged the report from the flight director at the SCCC and has put all security forces on high alert—the highest, level A. They know the countries that the shuttle made stops in. Troops will be deployed into city streets around the world to deter any alien attacks. Analysts are working double shifts to scan CRT cameras for any suspicious activity, and drones are also being deployed over major cities to assist. USAF AWACS aircraft are being dispatched to detect any unauthorized entry into US and foreign airspace. No asset in the U.S. inventory is exempt. United Kingdom, Germany and Asian forces are following suit. The Chemdi's attack plan may not turn out to be as successful as they anticipated.

* * *

The Chemdi in France are hiding in Paris at the Luxembourg Gardens, the Sixth Administrative District. They wait until daylight to attack.

The Chemdi in Dubai are in Jumeirah Beach Park planning their attack of the Beach Plaza Center.

The British Joint Intelligence Organization alerts the London Police service that it has identified two unidentified personnel making their way up to Oxford Circus station through the tunnels. They appear to be alien combatants. The SAS, who has been specially trained at Langley, has been alerted and are on their way. The police are doing their best to clear the Underground but there are too many people already gathered. As the Chemdi approach the station platform, a woman sees them and lets out a bloodcurdling scream. The Bobbies immediately head her way but they are too late—a Chemdi's blade has already silenced her. The crowd witnesses the dastardly act and pandemonium takes over as they try to get away, pushing and shoving amidst yells and screams of terror. The two Chemdi morph into a lethal mix of eight arms and blades. They begin cutting people down as fast as they can get to them. Within seconds, more than twenty people are dead. The Chemdi continue to kill with reckless abandon— now forty, now fifty men, women and children.

Suddenly, the screams and shrieks of these British citizens are mixed with the courageous, fuming battle cries of SAS commandos. They are indiscriminately shoving people out of the way to gain access to the Chemdi. Some are using guns; others their blades of choice. The British public watch in awe as their heroes do battle with the wicked, sinister-looking Chemdi-Shakahr.

The Chemdi use their capes as a distraction, whirling about to thwart their enemies as they fight. A number of the British commandos are fooled and pay the awful price for their failure; others are not, and one Chemdi falls to his demise.

The last Chemdi momentarily defers his attention from the commandos and kills two more civilians who are standing too close to the action. He lets out a roar and continues his fight with the commando attacking high, only to be rebuffed by the commando's 1895 pattern half basket infantry officer's sword, a family heirloom. The Chemdi attacks low; the commando manages to sever one of his lower arms. Angered, the Chemdi flails in desperation, realizing his death is imminent. The commando pierces his Spartan sword into one of the Chemdi's hearts, spins and pierces the second. The Chemdi collapses to the train platform on its knees then falls to the ground. The SAS commandos have prevailed; the last Chemdi is dead. The platform erupts in cheers and whistles. Their long-established confidence in their troops is confirmed. The London Police service quickly cordon off the bloody area for investigation. Scotland Yard is already on the scene and has alerted domestic and international authorities.

French authorities have been getting reports of a spaceship sighting in the Sixth District area and are investigating. All of Paris is on full alert, with surveillance camera analysts working overtime to scan the area for anything suspicious. One analyst sees two shadowy figures in the brush, now moving toward a crowd of people. He alerts his superiors.

"Hey! Everyone! I've got something! There two alien figures approaching a crowd in Jardin du Luxembourg Park!"

The administrator directs all police and security forces to that location. He knows that there will be casualties but he will try to save as many as he can.

The assistant to the Secretary of Homeland Security bursts into the secretary's office. "Sir, there has been a hostile alien attack in London! It's confirmed: two alien hostiles have killed about forty people! The video is already on YouTube!"

The secretary is furious. "How in the hell did they get on our planet undetected in the first place? Where was Space

Command or the DoD?"

"Sir, we're trying to answer those questions as we speak. In the meantime, what are your orders? Where do we go from here?"

Deploy the response teams. Although we are not trained to fight such beasts, we can at least monitor and contain them until the cavalry arrives. Hey, and get that video off of You-Tube!

"Will do, sir. I'm on it," replies the assistant.

* * *

Former Flight Director, now SCCC Director Pickett is answering difficult questions from the Department of Defense. They want to know how the aliens got past them and entered the planet. The DoD believes there must be a support ship close by and want the SCCC to find it and destroy it.

Although they are very short with the new director, he knows that they are right—in fact it was the captain's launch that they had been using. The former crew had gone to the moon. That's it! The support ship must be near the moon! Immediately the director assigns and orders destroyers to patrol space surrounding the moon. They are not sure what they will find but are ready for a fight if it comes to it. The new arrays installed during the retrofit are working perfectly; if there are any enemy ships out there, they will find them and they will feel the sting of Space Command's quantum cannons.

Back in Dubai, the Dubai security forces have received the alert from Interpol of the hostile alien attacks in London and have deployed their Special Forces teams. They know that the rogue ship has made a stop in Dubai and their forces should be on alert. There have been reports of strange noises and even the sighting of a spaceship in the Jumeirah area. They are patrolling the Jumeirah Road area for strange activity. They won't be disappointed.

The two Chemdi begin their attack, moving from the Jumeirah Beach Club toward the Century Plaza, attacking and killing people indiscriminately as they go. They are indiscriminate about who they kill—women, children or men: a woman and her children having lunch are all cut down. People who witness the dastardly deed try to rush to their aid, but are also cut down. Their attacks are swift and accurate. They pass the zoo and head directly to the Plaza. The Dubai police have been notified and Special Forces are also on the way. So far, about fifty people are dead in their wake and there will certainly be more.

Three police cruisers arrive and block the street. They don't bother to identify themselves, but simply exit their vehicles and open fire with fully automatic weapons. The Chemdi respond with their laser weapons, blowing up all three vehicles and killing all twelve men. They move on like it's simply another day at the Chemdi office. People are screaming, in full panic mode. The Century Plaza management has been notified and is trying to evacuate the Plaza. This is exactly what the Chemdi wanted; the people will be running into their path instead of the Chemdi having to chase them—perfect. As the hoards exit the building, they are so panicked they do not see the Chemdi right away. The sea of people behind them are pushing and shoving people out the door. By the time they do, it's too late. The Chemdi are killing people with their edged weapons as fast as they can. Piles of dead Dubai citizens begin to block the exit doors, their blood staining the concrete walkway, the pandemonium is dire.

A number of Dubai security force trucks pull up to the Plaza entrance—the Special Forces. Mortified, saddened and angered at what they see, they prepare to resolve the situation. One very tall bearded gentleman, then two, now four start charging the Chemdi, Arabian sabers in hand—they are about to put their Langley training into practice. The Dubai SF team engages the Chemdi immediately. The lead SF operative cuts off a Chemdi's upper arms, then one of the lower arms with great strength and accuracy. As it turns, obviously in great pain, he ducks the blade of the Chemdi and quickly stabs him in both hearts. It pauses and drops to the ground. Two other operatives follow suit, killing the second. The Chemdi attacks in Dubai are over.

* * *

The two Chemdi have found a hiding place in Tokyo, in a port near Koto-Ku. They were the only team that deployed with a signal amplifier—this will enable them to beam down Chemdi, twelve at a time, from long range. They have found a suitable place in a nearly empty warehouse to set this up this equipment without being detected. They begin to assemble the apparatus to bring more Chemdi to the scene. Their equipment is nearly completed and they signal the Chemdi ship to prepare for transport. The ship signals back and transports of twelve Chemdi to the designated location. The process does not take long and the twelve arrive in full battle gear, ready to do what they have come for. The ground commander signals again for another group to be beamed down.

Star destroyers are fast for their incredible size, and even more so with the upgraded engines. The three-ship formation about thirty minutes from the moon has yet to find any sign of an enemy ship with its sensor arrays. They continue to scan the entire area before calling in their findings. The crews are fully briefed on their mission and are eager to do their best.

The captain of the task force gives the first officer operational command and retires to his office where he gets comfortable with a cup of tea and a good book. No sooner does he sit down in his easy chair than his FO summonses him to the bridge. They have a confirmed contact of an enemy ship just outside of sensor range. The captain calls the crew to general quarters; sleeping crewmembers are woken, off-duty members come back to duty, and the entire ship prepares for battle.

The three-ship formation goes to a tactical formation and they move as one to engage the enemy target. The enemy ship is currently cloaked and is moving away from the moon —but unfortunately for the Chemdi, it's too late. The star destroyers target the coordinates as communicated by the fleet commander and each ship fires its compliment of six quantum cannons, making them a total of eighteen in all. The blasts are loud and unapologetic. The blinding light of the blasts can be clearly seen by the inhabitants of Moon Base Alpha. The cannons hit their targets; the first two blasts disable their shields, and the remaining sixteen blasts decimate the Chemdi ship. What remains is a debris field of what used to be a Chemdi ship with a crew of three hundred. The crews of the Earth ships cheer. Little do they know they have saved numerous lives in Koto-Ku, Japan.

* * *

A warehouse foreman is making his way to go and check a shipment that is to be loaded tomorrow. He figures he will save time by cutting through the empty warehouse. As he enters, he hears a strange noise and slows his pace. Looking to his right, he sees fourteen Chemdi and a glowing orb on the floor. The door slams shut behind him, alerting the Chemdi, who quickly turn and shoot their laser weapons in the direction of the noise, literally blasting the door, the doorframe and about four feet to each side of what used to be the door. The Chemdi commander rebukes them for drawing too much attention. They must quickly make a plan and start their mission, so as not to lose the element of surprise.

The foreman makes it to his office. He's so shaken he pulls a flask out of his desk and gulps down a few mouthfuls as he calls the National Police Agency (NPA), all the while checking nervously via the window of his office to see if he's being followed.

After speaking to the foreman, the chief of police takes no chances and contacts The Japanese Special Forces—the Tokushu Sakusen Gun, or the TSG. They were also one of the many teams invited to participate in the training held at Langley, VA—he recalls they are a spirited bunch with a great love for their country. They are eager to use their skills to defeat this enemy now on Japanese soil.

The Chemdi have no choice; they know they may be met with resistance soon so they begin their reign of destruction where they are. They exit the warehouse in full view of the public. One of the fourteen uses a large laser weapon, firing multiple times at a docked cargo ship. Massive explosions occur on the ship and it begins to sink right there in the harbor. The Chemdi fan out and begin killing anyone in view. They are looking for a way to make it to the city. In all of the commotion and smoke, they jump onto a barge that is moving out to the Tokyo Bay. A few passersby see them and start to alert the police. The tug captain sees the commotion but cannot see the people trying to warn him that he has stowaways aboard his barge. He continues his voyage as usual, the barge moving slowly up the bay as it approaches the bridge. Once it draws alongside the bridge, the Chemdi use it to exit the barge and head for the city.

The Chemdi ground commander spots three large apartment buildings up ahead, and decides that one group will target the residents in those buildings—even the best Earth soldiers would have a hard time finding and destroying them in such a place. Four Chemdi break off and head that way. The remaining Chemdi head for the city. They know the authorities are not far behind, and they have all heard of the "Long-Blade Warrior" and they hope they do not run into him—the human who was bold enough to board and destroy their former command ship. They are talking about no other than Colonel Striker. Little do they know that Striker has already imparted his experience and skills to many others, and that the Chemdi will eventually meet them. They take refuge under a smaller bridge to hide until nightfall when they will make a stealthy entrance into the city.

The TSG arrive at the dock where the Chemdi sank the cargo ship and killed about thirty people. Witnesses are pointing up the bay to where they saw them stow away on a barge. The TSG commandeer a boat, load their gear and go upstream after them; they will pursue them and will not return until the Chemdi are dead.

Following the direction of the barge, they see fresh scrape

marks on a bridge where they might have gotten off. They pull over the boat and pursue, gathering in a clearing and scanning the area. They see three tall apartment buildings a little way away, and upon closer examination, the captain sees some commotion in the distance. They head in that direction.

* * *

Within minutes, Jardin du Luxembourg Park, France is turned into a blood bath. Chemdi are killing innocent people in droves—so efficient, they are making sport of it. The French Police arrive on the scene; the French Commando Marines are also on their way, approaching from the east, and the French Special Forces will arrive in three minutes or so from the south. The local police have been issued with FAMAS assault rifles. They begin firing at the Chemdi immediately, trying their best not to hit civilians but more focused on killing the Chemdi. One of the Chemdi draws his laser weapon and kills the two officers approaching on foot; other officers keep shooting from behind the cover of their vehicles. The Chemdi evade and pursue other civilians out of the line of fire. The French Commando Marines approach as ordered, one setting up immediately in a sniper position and starting to fire at the Chemdi using a 50 cal. sniper rifle.

French Special Forces have also arrived on the scene now and are engaging. The sniper takes out one of the Chemdi; Special Forces finish off the other. The Chemdi have left a hundred and two people dead in their wake.

The Department of Defense is receiving reports in from France, Dubai and the UK. The stories of the heroism of the SF teams will be recorded, studied and discussed for years to come. They have only one remaining area of concern and that is Japan; no communications have been received as to whether or not they have engaged the Chemdi there yet. U.S. Air Force air commandos have been dispatched out of Kadena Air Force Base and are on their way to assist.

The Japan TSG commander sees people running out of one of the apartment buildings; they are covered in blood and he is not sure whether it's their own or someone else's. He sends in a four-man fire team and a medic. As the team enters the building, they see people pointing up the stairwell. The team heads up. There is no one in the hallway on the first floor, so they continue on upwards. Floor two, same. They hear screams and yelling as they approach the third-floor stairwell door. They access that level and begin clearing the hall: to the right stands a tall, caped figure holding a man up in the air by his neck, his legs flailing about helplessly in the air; four more figures are positioned just up ahead. The SF operator yells in Japanese to let the man go. The Chemdi immediately reacts by breaking the man's neck. He falls to the floor like a bag of dirty laundry.

The SF operators open fire. The six hundred rounds per minute of their Heckler & Koch HK417s and the six hundred and twenty-five rounds per minute of the FN SCAR rifle riddle the body of the Chemdi, puncturing his two hearts instantly. He drops to the floor. The three remaining Chemdi turn and fire their laser weapons at the five-man team, instantly killing two of them. The remaining TSG team members take cover and radio in for additional help.

The ground commander of the TSG is just getting off of a call with SF High Command and tells them his current location. They are vectoring in U.S. Air Force Commandos his way via V-22 Ospreys. The commander tells one man to stay behind to receive the Air Force; the rest are going to join the team inside, third floor. They immediately dispatch to the building. As they enter, they see their team moving forward in cautious pursuit of the Chemdi. The team now stands at twelve in number. They remember what they have learned: Chemdi will fight with whatever their enemy is fighting with. So, to save the team, the commander orders them to stow their guns and use their edged weapons.

They run to catch up with the Chemdi. Screaming can be heard coming from an apartment over to the left; the TSG team approaches and kicks in the door. An elderly man has fallen foul to the Chemdi's blade while trying to protect his wife of forty years. The noise of the breaking door causes the Chemdi to turn around. The lead operator taunts the Chemdi, knowing that they love a good challenge, especially from "weak" humans. The Chemdi takes the bait; he pushes the now widow to the floor and joins the operators in the hallway. Her husband dies never knowing that he had succeeded in saving his beloved wife.

The Japanese lead makes the first move. The Chemdi appear to be toying with him. The others join the fight. The Chemdi is good but he's outnumbered—obviously a straggler that got caught. One of the operators cuts its thigh, and from that point, the situation quickly goes downhill for the Chemdi; it is dead about five seconds later. They immediately take off and start scanning the floor for the rest of the Chemdi, having no idea how many more there are. As they go, terrified screams and yells can be heard all over. The Japanese quickly kill the last two Chemdi. They then clear the rest of the floor and radio in that they will be exiting the building.

The Chemdi dispatched to go into the city slowly climb into the back of a parked cargo truck that is heading toward Shinkiba. The truck takes off and they stay quiet, keeping low. Along the journey, they see a building with a large gathering of people in front of it; they jump off the truck and hide themselves in the foliage in a large clearing across from the building. The club, known as "Ageha", is a popular dance club; more than a hundred people are lined up waiting to get inside for a night of Techno Music and dancing. The ten remaining Chemdi make this their next target. The ground commander will dispatch five outside to attack those waiting and take the rest inside. They cover their four arms with their cloaks and their countenance with their hoods, approaching stealthily and quickly.

* * *

As Miiya and Deon make their way to their third stop of the trip, they're discussing the hot news topic of the day: the

Chemdi attacks in the UK and France. They have announced possible attacks in Dubai but there are no real details yet.

"Wow," says Deon. "I didn't know our training would be so relevant or that the SF teams would have to use it so soon."

"The Chemdi are ruthless and smart," Miiya replies. "They pick their targets well and execute even better. This does not make sense."

"What do you mean?"

Remember, these creatures travel space and have advanced weaponry at their disposal—why would they do suicide missions like this? I think there is something else at play. I think this is merely a diversion to draw Earth's attention from something more significant."

"That's very clever thinking, Miiya—but what could it be?"

"Deon, I do not know. I can only tell you what I would do if I did."

* * *

The Chemdi commander of one of their mobile outpost ships is moving at lightning speed, preparing to drop out of it just above the Earth's atmosphere. He is to avoid the structures detected in an area along the coast to the east; his mission is to land undetected and establish a new Chemdi base. His ship hits the Earth's atmosphere and he slows to keep from leaving any visible trail. The ship is a flying Chemdi base that encompasses every convenience Chemdi will need, including transport, fighters, reconnaissance ships, and communications.

They can exist here for the equivalent of two Earth years before they will have to be resupplied. This ship has the potential to cause Earth a significant amount of damage. The ship lands and its long stabilizer legs plunge into the Earth as easily as a doctor's needle in the rump of a patient. They will anchor the ship securely for the next two years or more. It contains its own cloaking device, so aircraft, satellites, and the like will not be able to visibly detect it. The Chemdi aim to establish small strongholds all over the world; these will further their mission to expend Earth's resources and distract the Earth people from the Chemdi's plans to invade them.

* * *

Warehouses and buildings are plentiful in the area. Japanese Government cameras are scanning carefully for the intruders. One of the cameras captures a Chemdi crossing the road and alerts the crisis team. They respond quickly, diverting the U.S. Air Force V-22s from the TSG landing site, vectoring them to the reported area. A patrol boat will light the clearing they're to land in.

The Chemdi approach and start their bloody attack. People run in all directions, screaming and crying, trying desperately to get away; most end up fleeing one Chemdi only to be killed by another. The Chemdi go through the crowd at an alarming speed.

The V-22s make their approach over Yumenoshima Stadium and can see the lights of the patrol boat. The pilots are experts and land the aircraft perfectly in the clearing, the aft of the aircraft facing the building. The boat lights up the building, revealing the horror of the commotion before them— flashing Chemdi blades, dead bodies littering the ground, and blood, so much blood. One of the snipers picks a Chemdi off in the street as the team dispatches to the gory scene. The lead USAF SF operator uses his automatic shotgun with extreme accuracy, taking down two, then three Chemdi. The remaining two begin to use their laser weapons and kill three SF operators. The USAF ground commander is wise and orders them to put their guns away. He pulls out two Chinese war swords with twenty-three-inch blades. The Chemdi waste no time and engage him—but this Air Force commando learned at Langley and has since further perfected his skills. The Chemdi goes down in less than thirty seconds. The USAF SF operators quickly enter the club to try to stop the remaining five inside.

The Chemdi inside the club are so focused on killing the innocent, they do not even notice the commandos entering the building. The lead commando simply thrusts his sword into the back of a Chemdi and kills him without resistance. Four more to go.

The commotion draws the attention of the remaining Chemdi, who turn in unison, focused intently on the commandos. The commandos, well versed in the Chemdi's modus operandi, immediately switch to their edged weapons. The ensuing fight is bloody, resulting in serious injuries and the death of one of the commandos, but finally, the U.S. Air Force prevail. The Ageha club will never be the same again.

* * *

The SECDEF wants all the intelligence he can get on all the Chemdi engagements. The leaders of the UK, France, Dubai and Japan are all lobbying for a combined force to combat incursions such as these from this day forward. This effort will be void of any possible political wrangling or divisiveness. This force will focus on one thing only: to hunt down and kill Chemdi on our planet, wherever they may be hiding. The media frenzy has made it easy for such a proposal and the President of the United States has already approached Congress with a declaration. Other countries are also requesting funds from their governments to help with this effort.

Japan will be hosting a high-level summit to effectively discuss this initiative, inviting key countries to participate. All countries will be on one accord in this effort to defeat further alien attacks.

The Chemdi's plans have backfired in that, instead of making the people of Earth fearful, their attacks have polarized and unified the Earth citizens to work toward a common goal—to defeat their new alien enemy.

* * *

The sunrise is glorious and the smell of fried trout, freshly caught in the river, fills the air as Deon makes breakfast. Miiya is dozing inside the Jetstream trailer, halfway between sleep and waking, but is acutely aware of her surroundings—a Meritorian trait. Deon plans to fry a few eggs once the fish is done and toast some bread in the trailer to complete the morning feast. His mind is still whirring in the wake of the news of the Chemdi attacks. He's immensely proud of all the operators worldwide who completed successful engagements with the Chemdi.

Just as he carries his mouthwatering creation into Miiya, his cell phone rings. Seeing the number, he contemplates not answering—it's a Florida number and there are only a few people in Florida who have his number. This is not one of them. He shudders for a moment then answers.

The operator asks, "Lieutenant Colonel Striker? Yes, sir, please hold for General Steele, USSOCOM commander." [USSOCOM: United States, Special Operations Command.]

"Dang!" Striker says quietly. "It's the commander of USSOCOM! There goes my vacation!"

Miiya glides out of the master bedroom and sees the expression on his face as he slowly shakes his head. She raises the palms of her four-fingered hands to silently ask, "Who is it?"

Deon covers the mouthpiece and whispers, "It the USSOCOM commander!"

"Good morning Colonel," the commander's voice comes over the line. "I'm General Dwight Steele, USSOCOM commander. First, let me say that your destruction of that enemy mother ship was masterful. Not bad for an Air Force jet jockey who's never been in SOCOM or on a SOCOM mission before. I, together with many others, am truly impressed. When we were first approached with your proposal, we were genuinely concerned as to whether or not you could pull it off. To our utter surprise and great satisfaction, you did. This is the reason why I'm calling. In this past week, we have seen these aliens breach our skies and attack us on Earth without warning. It was only due to the training that you and your alien colleague provided that we were able stop them at all. The United States and the world at large are grateful.

"However, just because they are grateful doesn't mean

they aren't afraid of what else may be awaiting them in the form of alien attacks. The President wants a solution—and he wants one now. That said, we want to build an international team that will hunt and destroy this enemy. In fact, we want you to build it and kill this enemy anywhere they show up. Furthermore, we want you to stay ahead of them, anticipate them and focus on gathering the intelligence you need in order to be proactive against their attacks. I need someone with your experience and knowhow to be in charge, colonel. By the way, this position requires a minimum rank of a full-bird colonel. You will fill the position as a lieutenant colonel and pin on your bird insignia in about a year. Your base will be in a secret location with everything you need at your disposal. What do you say, colonel—can I count on you?"

Deon is ecstatic, his head buzzing with thoughts as he realizes he's going to become a full-bird colonel before the age of forty. He pulls himself together for a moment and asks a few specific questions.

"General, I am grateful for the opportunity. However, what exactly do you feel I can bring to the table? Certainly there are other men in line for this promotion, Special Forces guys even—and probably more worthy of it than I."

"Colonel, you have education, experience, achievements and humility, all of which confirm to me now more than ever that I've picked the right man for the job. I don't need a political hack at the helm who's looking for the next promotion; nor do I need someone who doesn't know this enemy the way you do. Your unique experience and successes are what have brought us to this decision.

You should also know that there was pushback about this appointment from others who were in line for promotion, just as you mentioned, so you will need to achieve eyebrow-raising success right out the gate in order to send a message. Do I make myself clear, colonel?"

"Sir, it sounds like a big job that's fraught with the opportunity to fail on more than one level. That said, I would not have time to manage the politics."

"There won't be any—and your assessment is very astute," the general continued. "This is why I have handpicked some of your staff; they are loyal, highly experienced, and will do everything in their power to ensure that you will not fail."

"Sir there is one more thing," Deon says. "I would like to add two people to your list: Miiya, the alien who assisted me, and Miss Adrian Brown, my assistant at Groom Lake."

"As you wish, colonel. So does that mean you accept?"

"Yes, sir, it does," Deon replies firmly.

"One last thing: this position puts you on an international stage right now—be mindful of this when you engage your enemy abroad, and make sure to coordinate with the locals beforehand. You may need their support another day. Got it?"

"Yes, sir. Will do."

"Congratulations, colonel! I'll be in touch. Steele out."

Deon hangs up and turns to Miiya. She looks serious, the look of worry is clear on her face.

"What was that all about, colonel?"

Meritorians have excellent hearing, probably exceeding that of most Earth dogs.

"I know you heard the whole conversation," Deon says. "USSOCOM wants me to head a special team here on Earth and I will need your help. I have a sense there is a lot about the Chemdi that I still do not know, and I need your help to learn what those things are."

"I am willing to help. However, the final decision is not mine. I must return to my planet."

"Will you go back for a long time?"

"No. I want to see my father. Much has happened since we last spoke. Although his words are not many, I know that he would like to see me. I too need to see him."

"I believe that a formal request for your help will be made to your embassy by our government. The process should go pretty smoothly since we have worked together before. I say it may take a couple of months."

"That is acceptable. I'm sorry to cut short our time to-gether. I know that you wanted to show me more of your planet and I truly wanted to see it," says Miiya gently.

"No worries. I have cherished the time that we have had together. We will do it another time. I trust that things will work out like they should."

"Things are changing. I will need further guidance from Meritor. I will first go to the embassy, then on to my planet. Do you still have your Zehrea?"

"Of course. I am never without it," Deon smiles.

"I will call you when I return."

They finish their breakfast and Miiya begins to gather her things. They share a compassionate embrace and numerous kisses and Poaghh. They stare into each other's eyes, knowing that it may be some time before they see each other again... if at all. Miiya touches her Zehrea, speaks a few Meritorian words, and in seconds is gone.

As Striker packs up the camp and stows all the gear, he thinks about the last few weeks with Miiya and how very in-toxicating—not to mention nearly fatal—their time together has been. Deep inside, he knows that, if he had a choice, he would do it all over again, even if it meant that he would never see her again.

He starts the engine of the Ford F-250 and queues up his "Deep Space Cruise" playlist on his iPad. First song up: "Ja-maica Funk" by Tom Browne. It puts an immediate smile on his face and he turns it up. It reminds him of the days he flew missions on the "Relentless." He pulls the Airstream out of the picture-perfect clearing onto the highway and heads for Groom Lake as planned, to close out his affairs and address the team. He can't wait to tell Adrian his little surprise. "She's going to flip!" He thinks to himself, smiling.

* * *

Back on Meritor, Steve is receiving communications traffic about current events on Earth. Through the assistance and cooperation of the Meritorian Government, a secure link has been established between both worlds via their outstanding technology. The system is something like a highly technologically advanced combination of an e-mail browser and Skype all rolled into one. The ambassador has seen the Chemdi attacks in four different countries, as well as the aftermaths. People on Earth are frightened, and Earth's governments resiliently resolve to prepare for the worst and respond with swift and decisive action. He is not aware of the fact that his good friend Deon Striker has been promoted and will be running an International Chemdi Crisis Response Team.

He walks to his bedroom to have tea with his wife, who is now about four months pregnant. As he enters the room, he smiles at his wife, who is surrounded by staff, all flitting around and making a great fuss over her. Jean looks radiant. She is doing her best to put the vivid images of her and her daughter's abduction by the Chemdi behind her; she still has the occasional nightmare about her experience, but they have reduced significantly with the Meritor doctors' help.

"Good morning, my love!" Steve calls cheerily.

"Good morning, dear. I was starting to worry that you would spend a good portion of your morning in your office and miss our walk through the gardens today."

"Oh, no—what, miss out on one of the best parts of my day? I wouldn't miss it for the world."

Jean smiles and gives a little chuckle. She knows he is just saying this to please her but she loves him for it all the same. "So, how are things back on Earth?" she asks.

"Actually not so good. I didn't want to ruin your day with this but there have been coordinated Chemdi attacks in four different countries—the UK, France, Dubai and Japan. Scores of people have been killed including women and children."

"My goodness! How did they get to Earth without being detected?" Jean asks.

"They stole a ship from Moon Base Alpha."

"That's awful. They're such evil creatures! I feel so terrible for the parents who have lost their children," Jean says sadly.

"Yeah, well, that's not the whole story. I hear there is something in the works in the form of a response. No details yet."

"Well, they should kill them all!" Jean cries. Just then, her heart-monitor machine starts to bleep. The doctor rushes in.

"What's going on? Why is her heart rate up? Everyone out and right now!" says the physician.

"We were talking about the events at home and she…" says Steve.

The doctor interrupts him. "She may be your wife, but she is my patient. Her heart rate affects the unborn child she is carrying. You must not discuss things that will cause her alarm, Mr. Ambassador."

"My apologies, doctor. Sorry, honey."

"Oh, he's just so fussy," smiles Jean. "I feel absolutely fine. Don't forget our stroll in the garden, honey!"

"I won't," Steve calls over his shoulder as he exits the room. "I'll be back in an hour or so." Then he turns and rushes back in, plants a kiss on her lips, and leaves before the doctor can rebuke him again.

***

The U.S. Government swings into immediate action. Congress holds an emergency session to approve funding for the new SOCOM organization. The USSOCOM commander puts his staff on twelve-hour shifts to complete all the work that has to be done. They need to start recruiting the very best of the best for this new team. All of the members of the teams who defeated the Chemdi will be the first recruited; pilots and support personnel with be pulled from current staff, and they will continue the process until all slots are filled.

The commander has commissioned DARPA to come up with an aircraft and associated support equipment that will get teams around the world at a moment's notice—to serve both as transportation and a Combat Support Team Command Post. No resource will be left untapped for this team. They also approach the NSA for their very best assets in intelligence gathering, which will be conducted using the latest in electronic technology. Every aspect will be monitored, from weather, to communication, to defense satellites around the world. They will also write code for their own applications native to the mission. Technicians, electronics techs and skill sets of all kinds will be brought in to support the team. Their base will be at an undisclosed subterranean location with the capacity for storing multiple aircraft. It will be fully equipped with all the material they need: research and development, training facilities, and sleeping quarters. They could independently sustain themselves indefinitely if needed. Their only slight vulnerability would be the opening of the facility for the arrival and departure of their support aircraft—but sensor arrays will detect anything within a hundred miles of the facility. They will utilize satellites, aircraft, ships, Galaxy Hawks (Latest generation of drones), and all matter of drones to detect possible enemy movements. It's as top notch as you can get.

* * *

Deon leaves the Great Sand Dunes National Park and Preserve in Colorado, setting off on the fourteen-hour ride to Groom Lake, Nevada—though he realizes his thirty-foot-long trailer may make the trip a little longer. He's got an early start and will likely drive direct.

As he drives, he thinks about his next assignment and what that will look like. He does not have any information yet from Commander Steele as to when and where he will be reporting; he will touch base with him tomorrow. For now, he contentedly guides his pickup and trailer down the road, his head now full of thoughts of Miiya: the sound of her voice, the smell of her silver-bluish hair, the soft, gentle touch of her four-fingered hands. He sighs as he thinks about the possible happy times ahead for him and Miiya.

The shrill ring of his cell phone ruins the moment. "Hello,

Colonel Striker?" It's Adrian.

"Adrian! How are you?"

"I'm fine, sir. I just wanted to call to get an update as to when you will be arriving."

"I'm so glad you did. In fact I should be there in about five hours. Do you think we can meet up?"

"Wow. That's too early sir. I thought you had at least a week or so left?

"Yes, Well things have changed again and I have much to discuss with you. There's no time like the present."

"Sure. Where would you like to meet?" asks Adrian.

"How about that roadside diner just outside of town?

"It's a date. See you there!" Adrian replies, a lilt in her voice.

* * *

Miiya has been at the Meritor Embassy for about a week now and has completed her debriefing with the Meritor superiors on Earth. She is cleared to leave and return to Meritor. Although she had much to disclose, including her camping trip, she kept the intimate relationship between her and Striker to herself.

A Meritor cruiser is orbiting the Earth, ready to receive her at any time. She taps her Zehrea and is immediately beamed on board. The ship's crew welcome her warmly, all of them excited about having the daughter of Balan-Gaal on board. They have heard of her exploits but don't mention any of them—protocol demands it. They have the coordinates locked in and three Meritor warships are ready to join the armada to escort the ship back to Meritor.

* * *

Balan-Gaal paces the floor of his office. He has prepared everything for his daughter's arrival. It's been quite some time since he has seen her. He is bursting with pride about his daughter's many exploits he has heard about, and for how she has fought bravely next to the humans, resulting in great victories. He has also recently heard that, as a result of her and Striker's training, countless lives have been saved across Earth. He couldn't be more proud of his daughter.

As much as he is proud, he misses his little girl's company and hugs—even though he knows she's not little anymore, she always will be a little girl to him. He feels that he must not show weakness, though, due to his position and the teams of people he commands. At the same time, she is the only family he has left on Meritor.

He looks around. His staff has carefully prepared all of her favorite foods, and her favorite flowers spill from vases placed throughout the home. He has organized for live music and has also invited a few of her closest friends to make her feel welcome and at home. It reminds him of the many gala events he and his former mate used to host in their home when she was alive. She would be proud if she could see all the arrangements he made. To think that he used to complain about all the fuss she used to make over every detail. He feels ashamed that he never truly enjoyed such moments with her while she was alive.

* * *

Deon spots the lights of the diner glimmering faintly in the distance—a welcome sight. It's a clear night, and the stars dotting the Nevada sky seem close enough to reach out and touch. He drives carefully—cows roaming the roads are commonplace here, and most of them are black or brown, making them pretty hard to see. Hitting a cow with an F-250 towing an eleven-thousand-pound trailer would not be pretty. Adrian calls again just as he pulls up at the diner—he can see her through the window.

Soon he is walking through the door. Before he can make the turn to walk down the aisle, Adrian has jumped from her seat and is hugging him, her arms thrown around the neck.

"Whoa, there! Hey!" says Deon.

"I'm sorry," Adrian says shyly. "It's been a long seven months and I am so happy you're back."

"I see. Let's have a seat and talk for a bit." Deon says gently.

They sit in a booth out of earshot of the other clients. The waitress immediately pours them some coffee, takes their order and puts it in to the cook. Service here is pretty fast. Deon can see the stress Adrian's been under and wonders whether it was the right thing to have thrown her in the deep end of the pool at Groom Lake. However, he is a pretty good judge of character and Adrian's work ethic is outstanding—if he had to pick someone all over again to take his place, he would still have selected Adrian Brown.

"Hey, first let me say that without even visiting the site and looking at the operation, I already know that you have been doing a great job," Deon starts. "I did not receive one phone call from Space Command or the Pentagon about any problems at Groom Lake. In fact, I reached out to make a few calls to see how the retrofits were coming and I got answers like, 'They're going great—in fact, some spacecraft came out ahead of schedule with zero defects.' And it's due to your leadership that I was able to totally focus on training the teams at Langley. Thank you very much for your hard and excellent work."

Adrian began to tear up at Striker's words. The maintenance industry can be a pretty thankless job; people are rarely given the credit they deserve for the highly technical work they do on a daily basis. The aerospace industry is one that demands perfection from human beings every day, and most of the time people deliver.

"Well, thank you very much, colonel. Its not every day you hear words like that, especially from high up. I appreciate it."

"You are most welcome—but I'm not finished. I'm not here to resume my job," Striker says.

"Are you saying you're leaving for good?" Adrian asks, shocked.

"In fact, not only am I leaving for good, but I want you to continue to work for me as my assistant in a new role I have been asked to fill."

Adrian looks like a deer caught in the headlights. She doesn't know what to say. Striker can see her trying to reconcile her expectations about what she had thought would happen at Groom Lake once Striker arrived. She did not expect the current state—a job offer. After a few seconds, she switches to question-and-answer mode.

"Ah... okay. So what is the new role and where will we be working?"

"I'm sure you've been watching the Chemdi attacks around the world?"

"Yes—those creatures are ruthless and terrifying."

"I have been tasked to command a new team that will be responsible for gathering intelligence, hunting and destroying this enemy on Earth. The location is yet to be disclosed but the base will be in a secret location."

Deon can see the wheels turning in her head— she's the type of person who would not normally volunteer for a position like this, but if asked would take it on with everything she's got and excel at it. This is precisely why Striker has selected her.

"Well, I will have to break my lease early. And..." Adrian begins.

Striker interrupts her. "Not to worry about all of that. I'll take care of it. What do you say? Will you take the position?"

"Yes, of course," Adrian smiles.

Thus, Adrian Brown becomes the first among likely hundreds of people to be recruited for this unique team.

* * *

The Meritor cruiser makes its way to Meritor, with heavy battle cruisers in tow. Miiya looks regal, as she sits comfortably in its luxurious cabin. Another Meritorian female approaches to chat with her to pass the time.

"Is it true that you worked with the people of Earth?"

"Yes, I did," Miiya replies.

"What are they like?"

"People of Earth are very much like Meritorians: they

are passionate and they love their families; although they are more physically frail than we are, they are very brave and display maybe even more of a fighting spirit than we. They have many qualities that I admire."

"Is that what the astronaut is like?"

"Astronaut?" Miiya replied.

"Yes. It is said that the one who destroyed the Chemdi Command ship, and the one that you saved from poison, appears to be fond of you."

"The astronaut is truly a unique individual and I have grown fond of him as well," Miiya says with a smile.

A senior crewmember places a hand on the female's shoulder and says, "Let our guest rest. She has been through much and needs to relax before arriving at Meritor."

The inquisitive crewmember apologizes for disturbing her, and Miiya graciously accepts. She leans back in her seat and almost immediately falls asleep.

* * *

Balan-Gaal is so excited to see his daughter that his staff notices a change in his behavior the likes of which they have not seen in a long time. Sitting in his home office, he sings to himself as he goes over the final touches of the celebration.

Just then, a communiqué comes through from the Meritor Earth ambassador. It is a request for Miiya's assistance—the ambassador wants Miiya to help the Earth Special Forces to track and hunt Chemdi on Earth. She will be temporarily attached to the embassy and assigned as needed. Balan-Gaal knows that this is right thing to do but he's going to be a little selfish and will ask to temporarily assign her to the Meritor ambassador's security detail. He wants to spend a little time with his daughter before she returns to Earth—he is not sure how long she will be there once she goes back, and he senses that it may be a very long time. So he decides to devise a plan to keep her with him a little longer. He replies to the request and asks for additional time in order for her to give some advanced training to the ambassador's security detail. He is certain that they will agree without question, especially since she is the one of the operators who rescued the ambassador's wife and daughter from their Chemdi abductors. The other reason is that there is no one on Meritor, with the exception of her father, with her combat experience.

The reply comes through quickly: "Permission granted."

Balan-Gaal could not be more delighted.

* * *

After sharing a few drinks and a good catch-up chat with Deon, Adrian takes a chance and asks him about Miiya. "Sir, this is truly none of my business and you don't have to answer, but I must ask: are you and the alien female a couple?" She now looks like a child who has just had her new puppy stolen.

"Adrian, since we're being honest, may I ask you a question? Are you interested in having a relationship with me?"

Adrian looks as if she's been smacked across the face with a two-by-four. "Ah... wow... that was direct... No... Yes... hmm, sort of. Now answer mine!"

"Miiya and I are interested in each other. Where it leads is anyone's guess. Regardless, we are strict professionals and whatever our relationship, it will not affect our performance. As for office relationships, I do not do office romances with subordinates. It makes the atmosphere weird and affects the team in a negative way. Besides I need you to be objective. Our having a relationship would mess up everything. Wouldn't you agree?"

She replied almost immediately. "Absolutely—just messes everything up."

"So we're good then? We both understand what we're doing... going forward?"

"You are my boss—that's it," Adrian answers with a smile.

"Well, it's getting late. I need to get up early tomorrow. Thanks for your time," Deon says.

"No worries, sir. We're golden."

Deon shakes her hand in a professional manner... takes another look at her face and gives her a platonic hug. He pays their bill and exits the diner. As he heads towards his vehicle, he sees her looking at him through the window and he waves before climbing into his truck. Adrian is a very attractive woman and would be probably be an awesome girlfriend and more. But he knows that in her role, he cannot have any emotional ties with her. After all, there is always the possibility that one mission can be his last. He will need someone who will stay focused and help the next Commander with clarity if that were to happen. He will need her to serve the next guy/gal like she currently serves him.

Striker heads for Groom Lake, about a thirty-minute drive down the road. He parks his trailer in the RV parking area and unhitches it. He will clean it out tomorrow.

He walks into his apartment. The maid's had very little to clean up but it looks and smells great. He showers and climbs into his luxurious bed. Sleep comes quickly and he will not move until morning or until he gets an important call.

* * *

The space cruiser draws closer to Meritor and the crew prepares to make their final approach to orbit around the planet. Miiya sees her planet come into view—it is but a spec in space at the moment, yet her heart begins beating a little faster. She was unaware of how much she had missed her native home.

She starts thinking about her father and her favorite places. She recalls the first time she showed her special place to her beloved Major Striker for the first time. Feeling her cheeks flushing, she looks around, a little embarrassed. No one's noticed. She remembers the picnic they had alongside the stream and the sounds of the birds singing. She remembers the smell of the meadow and the conversation and laughter they shared that day. What an incredible moment, she thinks to herself.

The ship begins to buffet as it starts to enter the atmosphere. It will not be long now. The City comes into view—the spectacle is breathtaking. She is finally home. As the ship approaches the landing pad, she sees a crowd gathered, waiting. She can see some of her former colleagues and of course the four towering bodyguards adorned in their "Elite" robes—her father's security detail. And standing amidst them, there he is, waiting for her. She feels herself growing overwhelmed by a feeling of pure, immense joy.

* * *

DARPA has ordered the retention of a few of the dead Chemdi so that they can carry out analyses on their enemy's anatomy. The physiological branch wants to determine their strengths weaknesses. The technical branch wants their weapons in order to reverse-engineer them.

Although the result of the Chemdi's encounter on Earth was deadly, it has yielded a treasure trove of incredible resources that will benefit Earth's ability to research their new enemy. They waste no time, working around the clock to gain as much information as they can. They are not going to be selfish; they have invited the best minds from around the world to come and assist, including medical staff from Meritor, to speed up the process. Again, the attacks of the Chemdi have polarized the leaders of Earth instead of causing the fear that the Chemdi hoped for. Earth, for the first time, is unifying the efforts and resources of foreign countries to fight this common enemy as one.

* * *

General Steele and his staff have been very busy. They have already started the recruitment process, securing the resources necessary to support the new SOCOM team. So far, they are looking into outfitting the fastest jets possible to carry the combat teams to anywhere in the world at a moment's notice. The final product will not be available for some time so they need an interim solution now. They are looking into using exactly what the Chemdi used—the captain's launches. He's made a request to Space Command to send every launch they have to DARPA so they can begin the process of retrofitting them to their needs. Space Command was not happy. Perhaps there is another solution. Meritor's manufacturing process is very capable and can speed things up quite a bit. They will look into this pronto.

* * *

The ship lands securely on the landing pad and the doors open. Security deploys and Miiya follows shortly thereafter. An honor guard lines the walkway to the VIP terminal.

This is too much, Miiya thinks to herself. Friends call out, smiling and laughing, each one greeting her as she slowly makes her way forward. At the end of the walk stands her very proud father, Balan-Gaal. They embrace and Poaghh. His personal bodyguards take it from here and they all head to a waiting transport vehicle. Her friends will join her at the house. As she gazes around at the familiar city, she can't remember it ever having looked so beautiful.

"My daughter," her father says, "it seems that it's been many templos since I last saw you. I have heard much of your exploits and the assistance you have given Earth. Please, share these with me."

"Father, I have helped the people of Earth; however, I was simply a member of a team. We did those things as one Kholect." [Meritorian for personnel unit.]

"How did the major fare with the training he received?"

"Father, he has embraced your training and has mastered it. In fact, in some ways he has adapted it into his own style and truly excels in it. He is also a Colonel now."

Balan-Gaal is not surprised. He had seen something in Striker that was highly intelligent, coupled with his well-trained and skilled physical form; he knew that Striker had the raw makings of a great warrior, even as an Earthling. As Miiya shares the events of the attack on the Chemdi command ship, Balan-Gaal listens with great attention, impressed at the cunning and bravery of Striker and his team.

Then she shares the failure to recover the Earth Ambassador's wife and daughter from the Chemdi and how it made her feel.

"Under the conditions you were facing," Her father says, "it was a very dangerous and uncertain mission from the outset. What made the matter worse is that you could not anticipate that the Chemdi would board on multiple levels of the ship. We have not encountered this particular technique being used in battle before; it was brilliant on their part and made the recovery completely unpredictable—and extremely difficult at best. The fact that you got to the hostages at all is impressive. Planning an operation like that is not futile; however, one must be completely cognizant that the outcome can be as random as the stars in space."

Miiya feels so much better after her father's assessment—after all, he has fought and defeated many Chemdi before and is the father of the techniques now used by both the Meritor and Earth security teams.

"We will have more time to discuss such matters, my daughter. I want this visit to be one of peace and rest. You have certainly earned it."

At that instant, the transport pulls up in front of their home. The servants receive Miiya with warmth and love—after all, most of them helped raise her. She greets them all as the family they are. The friends who had been waiting at the spaceport finally get a chance to greet and embrace her.

The banquet is simply exquisite, loaded with of all of her favorite Meritorian food and drinks. Meritorian musicians play her favorite songs, the music fills the house. More guests seem to be arriving all the time. Her father is delighted to see her interacting with her friends as she did before she left for her interstellar journey. He feels that she needed this and is grateful to his staff for making Miiya's homecoming a resounding success.

* * *

It's currently a cold 22.9 degrees Fahrenheit in McMurdo Station, Antarctica, located at 77 degrees, 51 minutes S., 166 degrees, forty minutes W.—and with the wind chill, it actually feels more like eleven degrees. The aircrew of the 109th Airlift Wing of the New York Air National Guard have just finished their morning breakfast and completed their mission briefing. They head out to do their preflight inspection of their LC-130. The aircraft is specially fitted for landings on snow; they will be taking off for their flight to New Zealand today.

The flight engineer steps out into the cold air on his long-cord, ready to communicate with the captain. He monitors the four engines as they are started. Once they are all running, the engineer re-enters the aircraft and closes the door. The aircraft taxis to the end of the runway and the crew is given permission to take off. The captain lines up on the runway and begins the takeoff roll, lifting off and beginning their climb to a cruise altitude of FL350 (35,000 feet).

As they continue their climb, the navigator spots a strange two-ship formation about five thousand feet below them. He can't make out what type of aircraft they are, but can see that they are moving fast like fighters. He knows there are no fighter aircraft bases in this area, and what is particularly unusual is that they are flying towards Antarctica instead of away from it. A second or two later, a moisture cloud covers the formation, as if they have broken through the sound barrier, and they disappear. The captain tells the navigator to file a report. He makes a note will do so when they arrive to their destination.

* * *

All of the guests have now gone home. Miiya and her father sit together in contented silence on the porch out back, where they used to sit when she was younger. As a little Meritorian female, she would ask her father about the stars, planets and any other question that came to mind. Tonight, their moment is pregnant with silence. She has seen much and has no words. She has cheated death numerous times and is completely sober about her mortality.

"Miiya, you have seen much, my daughter," her father says. "You have escaped death, my little one. It's okay to be sad and to feel what you feel. Even a good warrior needs a quiet place to rest."

Miiya gets up from her chair and sits on her father's lap like she did when she was a little girl. Throwing her arms around his neck, she begins to weep, letting go of all her fears and pain. In her father's arms, she finally feels it is okay to be vulnerable. She doesn't have to be strong or brave for herself or her team right now. Her father has always been there for her, and this time it is exactly what she needs. Balan-Gaal holds her for a long time.

* * *

Colonel Striker has slept for about eleven hours, replenishing his body after the long drive from Colorado to Groom Lake. He walks into the kitchen, switches on the coffee machine and starts to cook breakfast, turning on the television to catch up on the day's news. As he looks around his apartment and savors the familiar surroundings, he suddenly realizes that he will never come back here again. The movers will surely come sometime this week to move him to his new assignment, wherever that is. The phone rings, breaking into the middle of his thoughts.

"Good afternoon, colonel," says General Steele. "I know you said that you wanted me to take care of the political end but I need your help. Congress has already started the process of appropriating the funds your team will need. However, they would like a chance to talk to you and ask a few questions. They want to meet with you tomorrow. A jet will arrive at Groom Lake to pick you up in about three hours' time."

"Very well, sir. I will be there."

"Great. I'm looking forward to finally meeting you, colonel. We'll have a little dinner and I will catch you up."

"Thank you, sir," Deon replies.

"We'll see you tonight. Out here."

Good thing I always have a dress uniform hanging in the

closet, Deon thinks to himself. He finishes his breakfast and prepares to leave, mentally going over in his head the questions he may be asked. The day passes quickly and before he knows it, it is time to board the plane for Washington, D.C.

After the aircraft lands, the general's aide is waiting for Striker at the bottom of the stairs as the Global Express aircraft door opens. Striker is quickly whisked away in a black SUV and is now headed downtown. The general is already waiting at the restaurant as the aide escorts Deon to his table. The general stands and greets the colonel. He is a tall man, and at a glance appears years younger than he actually is; a closer look, however, reveals deep lines that are no doubt a result of years of planning warfare and prosecuting various conflicts.

"Come, have a seat, colonel," says Steele.

The waitress stands by, waiting for Striker to sit down.

"It's an honor to finally meet the man responsible for destroying that enemy command ship and saving countless lives. I admire your courage—you made a believer out of not only me, but all of us at USSOCOM. I'd be lying if I were to tell you that some of our staff had their doubts. Yet you proved yourself to be a doer, and that is exactly what we need. What would you like to eat, colonel?"

Deon studies the menu quickly and replies, "I think I'll have the New York Strip."

"Excellent choice. Now, let's get down to business. The team will be called the Strategic Mobile Alien Response Team or S.M.A.R. Team. It will be based in a subterranean location that will remain undisclosed to all but you and your staff. Pack your bags, colonel—you're headed to Arizona, not far from where you are now." "Arizona? That's great!"

"Not so fast, colonel; you and your team won't have much time for getting to know the locals. In fact, no one can know what you do or whom you work for. We will designate where you go for R&R [repair and reclamation/recreation] and how you will get there. Secrecy will be at the core of everything you are and do. If one of the Chemdi hear of your location, or can identify any of your team, it will compromise the entire mission."

"Roger, sir. I'm tracking."

"Now, about this congressional hearing; it's simply a meet-and-greet. You can relax. They already see you as the hero you are. Reply precisely to their exact questions, be professional and you should do fine."

"I'll do my best, sir."

"I have another meeting. I have to go. We will send a car to your hotel in the morning. Enjoy yourself and stay as long as you like—the tab's on me," Steele says.

The general and his aide make a brisk path to the front door and get in the black SUVs waiting outside. He is gone.

* * *

Miiya sleeps peacefully, just like she did when she was little. She awakes refreshed and goes downstairs to see her father already eating on the patio. She joins him at the table.

"I have temporarily assigned you to train up the ambassador's personal bodyguards," her father says. "You are well experienced now for such a task. Teach them everything you know. You have the most recent exposure with the Chemdi. The ambassador should have the very best security we have to offer."

"Yes, father. How long will the assignment be?"

"Until it is completed."

Miiya has always put duty before herself and knows that whatever her father's answer, she will comply. As she stands up, to go and get ready to leave for the embassy, he asks one more question.

"Ah, Miiya—tell me, how is Colonel Striker?"

"Daddy, he is an outstanding human. I have learned much from him. He's as intelligent as he is courageous. I think he has finally found his life path. He has been put in charge of a team that hunts and kills Chemdi on Earth."

"The Meritor Ambassador has requested that you be assigned to assist a special Earth team," her father says. "Is this the team you are speaking of?"

"Yes, Daddy."

"Mmm, it seems you and Colonel Striker frequently find a way to work together. Miiya thinks to herself: "Is my father trying to tell me that it is permissible to join with a human?"

Balan-Gaal continues: "Your life path is yours, my daughter, and you do not need my permission to follow it. In any case, you have my blessing. I liked him from the beginning; he is a rather charismatic Earthling who has the tendency to grow on you."

Miiya hugged her father, relieved that her relationship with the human wasn't going to be a disappointment to him.

Shortly after, she arrives at the Earth Embassy and is enthusiastically greeted by Ambassador Steve Wilory.

"Miiya! What an honor and pleasure to see you again! You are most welcome in our home. I cannot say another word without first thanking you for trying to save my wife and daughter. I read the report—your sacrifice and bravery are second only to your father's."

"Thank you, Mr. Ambassador. I am grateful that your family was recovered successfully. How are they?"

"I'm glad that you asked. They're upstairs in the living quarters. I will take you to them."

The housekeeping staff are initially startled by Miiya's presence when she and the ambassador entered the living quarters, as they head for the ambassador's master suite. The human housekeepers have never seen a Meritorian female security officer before. Mrs. Wilory is sitting up in bed reading a book. When she looks up and sees Miiya, her face lights up like the sunrise and she hugs her and shouts out in joy—so much so that Katie comes running down the hall to find out what all the commotion is about. When she sees Miiya, she joins her mother in all the excitement, both of them laughing and crying at the same time as they remember with gratitude the kindly face of this would-be rescuer.

They talk about her reasons for being there and how

happy they are that she is joining the security detail, even if it is on a temporary basis. Miiya thinks to herself that it is going to be very hard to leave this temporary assignment when the time comes for her to depart.

* * *

The Chemdi Commander of the Earth base on Antarctica is not happy that his flight crew may have been spotted—this mission is all about the element of surprise. If needed, they may have to destroy the base across the little continent to ensure this does not happen again—but of course this could have the opposite effect and get them noticed in spectacular fashion.

The commander is patient. His orders are clear: "Build up the base and personnel until instructed to attack. His crews will train and acclimatize themselves to Earth's atmosphere. There are currently three hundred-plus Chemdi on this base. The Chemdi are beaming them down slowly to build them up to around one thousand. The ultimate goal is to take remote areas and hold them. They will accumulate bases all over the world and cause the people of Earth to expend their resources in order to fight the Chemdi, to the point that the Earth beings become overwhelmed. They will then seek to establish a larger continent and occupy.

The Antarctica base is manufacturing the resources such as Chemdi food generators, communications stations and all items needed for a small base to sustain itself. Chemdi station commanders will then be directed to attack Earth towns and cities by high command, and some targets at their own discretion.

* * *

The Congressional hearing goes as planned. The Congressional leaders are impressed with Air Force Lieutenant Colonel Striker. He has returned to Arizona and is now touring the SMAR Team facility. He is not concerned so much about creature comforts as he is the gear his team will need to engage and defeat the enemy. He wants to see what DARPA is up too and wants to have input as to the gear they are developing for his team. He has tactical vehicle field support representatives (FSRs) he wants to bring to DARPA with him to give their recommendations also—after all, they are going to be responsible to keep the new high-speed gear operational.

As the new and first commander of SMAR, He will need these and many more skill sets if he is ever to defeat this cunning and intelligent enemy. He calls a meeting so the team can officially meet him and each other. As he looks upon all of their faces, he knows that this may be a one-way trip for some, and perhaps the last place that a few will leave for retirement. He is humbled and focused on leading this energetic, talented team of powerful people. They will become the unstoppable force to stop the Chemdi in their tracks on land, sea and air in the near future.

Colonel Striker communicates his vision, their mission, and his expectations. The SMAR Team will be a force that their enemies will soon come to know and fear.

The End

Look out for the next book in the series:
Wormhole Moon II - Paradigm Shift

Reader's Discussion Guide

1)   Knowing Captain Tumang's history, how did it make you feel when he died in battle?
2)   Who were your favorite character(s) and why?
3)   Did you feel that the way the astronauts fell into the wormhole was believable?
4)   Did you like the international aspect of the book?
5)   Who were your least favorite character(s) and why?
6)   In what direction would you like to see the relationship between Miiya and Striker go?
7)   Was there anything about the book that inspired you—e.g., a specific character(s), events, location, interaction, technology?
8)   What did you like most and least about Meritor?
9)   What did you learn from the book?
10)   Would you like to see the book made into a movie—if so, why?
11)   What were the most emotional moments for you in the book?
12)   Have you shared the book with your friends—if so, how many? If not, why?
13)   Are you looking forward to Wormhole Moon II? If so why?

Message from the author

Thank you for reading my book. It was truly an experience to write it and I am excited about completing the next book in the series: Wormhole Moon II. Please feel free to ask questions or comment at the resources below.

With Gratefulness,

–John Williams

Connect With Me!
Email:
John.williams.author@gmail.com

Amazon:
www.amazon.com/author/john_williams

Twitter:
@JWilliams_Auth

LinkedIn:
http://www.linkedin.com/in/johnwilliamsauthor/

Pinterest
https://www.pinterest.com/jwilliamsflask/
Goodreads
http://bit.ly/JohnWilliamsGoodreads

ABOUT THE AUTHOR

John Williams

 John Williams is a an 27+ year aviation professional, screen-play writer, musician, EZine Articles Expert Writer, Trip-Advisor Senior Writer, Quora writer and published author of 14 books. You can find John's books at: www.amazon.com/author/john_williams. Thank you for reading my books. I hope you enjoy them as well. Thank you. -John

Made in the USA
Middletown, DE
22 June 2023

32509650R00187